ROME

BEN KANE – Kenya-born, Irish by blood and a UK resident – has a passion for history that has taken him to more than sixty countries and all seven continents. He has walked hundreds of miles in Roman military gear, including Hadrian's Wall, and is known to lead archaeological tours in Italy and Germany. Eleven of his nineteen novels have been *Sunday Times* Top Ten bestsellers. Published in fifteen countries, he has sold more than 1.5 million books worldwide. He lives in Somerset, UK, where he writes full-time.

Also by Ben Kane

The Forgotten Legion Chronicles
The Forgotten Legion
The Silver Eagle
The Road to Rome

Hannibal
Enemy of Rome
Fields of Blood
Clouds of War

Eagles of Rome
Eagles at War
Hunting the Eagles
Eagles in the Storm

Clash of Empires
Clash of Empires
The Falling Sword

Spartacus
The Gladiator
Rebellion

Lionheart
Lionheart
Crusader
King

Standalone Novels
Napoleon's Spy
Stormcrow

Short Story Collections
Sands of the Arena

ROME

BEN KANE

ORION

First published in Great Britain in 2025 by Orion Fiction,
an imprint of The Orion Publishing Group Ltd.
Carmelite House, 50 Victoria Embankment
London EC4Y 0DZ

An Hachette UK Company

The authorised representative in the EEA is Hachette Ireland,
8 Castlecourt Centre, Dublin 15, D15 XTP3,
Ireland (email: info@hbgi.ie)

1 3 5 7 9 10 8 6 4 2

All the characters in this book are fictitious, and any resemblance
to actual persons, living or dead, is purely coincidental.

A CIP catalogue record for this book is
available from the British Library.

ISBN (Hardback) 9781 3987 1465 6
ISBN (Export Trade Paperback) 9781 3987 1466 3
ISBN (Ebook) 9781 3987 1468 7
ISBN (Audio) 9781 3987 1469 4

Typeset by Input Data Services Ltd, Bridgwater, Somerset

Printed in Great Britain by Clays Ltd, Elcograf, S.p.A.

FSC www.fsc.org MIX Paper | Supporting responsible forestry FSC® C104740

www.orionbooks.co.uk

Always.

PROLOGUE

Constantinopolis; 23rd day of Mensis Ianuarius, AD *393*

Five-year-old Galla Placidia stared through the open window, unable to take her eyes from the dark clouds rushing in from the coast towards the palace. 'A storm is coming,' she said. 'Father won't like it. We will get rained on.'

Elpidia, her nurse, short, stout, appeared behind her and pushed the window to. 'It does look threatening, but the bad weather should hold off. God will look after your father the emperor, and your half-brother Honorius, whose big day it is. Come, you must ready yourself as well.'

With a last glance through the glass at the lowering clouds, Galla obeyed. As was her habit, she walked along one of the blue lines that broke up the multicoloured marble floor. 'Where is Mother?'

'She is abed,' replied Elpidia, indicating that Galla should sit on the ebony-legged stool by her dressing table.

'Is she ill?' Galla was used to this.

'She is pregnant; that is not the same thing.'

'Will she be coming to the parade?'

'She would like to, but the surgeon has advised against it.'

'Why?'

'It is best for the baby.'

'I would like a sister.' Galla thought for a moment. 'Arcadius is mean – he didn't allow Mother and me into the city until Father arrived – and Honorius is not interested in playing with me.' Reaching Constantinopolis with her mother just over a year before, excited about meeting her two 'new' brothers, Galla had been baffled by Arcadius' hostility and Honorius' indifference.

'Hmm.' Elpidia, a slave, had her opinion, but knew her place.

'Father was so angry with Arcadius,' said Galla, remembering. 'He told me I would have my own property from then on.'

'It's a lovely house.' The size of a villa, it lay in a grand quarter close to the imperial palace.

'I'm glad you like it too.' Galla stuck out her chin. 'Honorius and Arcadius aren't allowed to visit.'

Honorius, eight, and Arcadius, fifteen, were the children of the first wife of the emperor Theodosius the Great. Galla Placidia had been born to his second wife, making the three children half-siblings.

'Eucherius and Maria can come as often as they like,' said Galla. These were the children of the general Stilicho and his wife Serena, the latter of whom Galla knew well. Serena was kind and thoughtful. Five-year-old Eucherius was fun too, and playful Maria, a year younger, was even more talkative than Galla.

'It *would* be nice if your mother had a girl.' Elpidia combed Galla's hair with deft strokes. 'What would you call her?'

'Justa. Or Grata.'

'Those are your mother's aunts?'

'Yes. Mother's mother was also called Justina, and her half-brother was the Imperator Gratian – my half-uncle.' Galla enjoyed listing off her relatives. She wasn't completely sure what being emperor meant, except that her father, whom she adored, could do whatever he wanted.

'We need to get you into this.' Elpidia was holding up a glistening golden robe.

Galla clapped. 'It's beautiful!'

'There is a gold filigree headdress as well,' said Elpidia. 'You will look stunning.'

'What does stunning mean?'

'It means everyone will be staring at you, admiring you.'

Galla smiled; she liked the sound of that.

*

'Let *me* stand there, Arcadius!' Honorius, his expression annoyed, elbowed his older brother, shoving past to the front of the large gilded chariot. The driver bowed and moved a little to the side. Honorius made no acknowledgement.

'I am the oldest son.' Arcadius had Honorius' long face, and with it, protuberant eyes, and sounded as petulant as a child half his age. Despite his size, he didn't jostle against Honorius.

'Who cares? It is I who shall be invested as emperor today.' Honorius, also in golden robes and wearing a magnificent gold-leafed wreath, was smaller and far more stubborn.

'Of the west only.' Arcadius' tone was snide. 'I am to be emperor of the east.'

Honorius ignored him.

Standing behind her half-brothers, Galla sighed and wondered if she would ever be empress of anywhere. She wished too that Elpidia was in the chariot. She was not allowed, however. She had kissed Galla's forehead, told her to wave to the crowds, so, and to enjoy the procession.

When Galla asked worriedly about Honorius and Arcadius, Elpidia had said they would be busy and would pay no attention to her. 'Boys don't care much about girls,' she declared, adding with a sniff, 'Not much changes later on.' Galla wasn't certain what that meant, but was glad of her nurse's counsel. With her mother often ailing, it was Elpidia who fussed over her when she fell, Elpidia who watched as she ate her meals, Elpidia who bathed her and was there at bedtime. Elpidia was her world.

An officer in shining armour appeared at the side of the chariot, bowed and announced that the procession was about to start.

Honorius squared his shoulders. Arcadius moved until he was just behind his brother. Galla was content. She could see their father in his own chariot, and could move freely about the back of the vehicle, thereby seeing both sides of the street.

Trumpets blared. The soldiers assembled in the palace courtyard cheered. The driver snapped the reins, and the four black horses moved forward in unison. Out of the palace they went, and into the city. A wall of sound was their greeting: shouts, applause, blessings being called down on Honorius. Galla could not believe her eyes. To left and right were the biggest crowds she had ever seen, thousands of people. More people than she could have believed existed. There were men, women, children. They were old, young, rich, poor, sick, hale and every shade in between. Bearded, smooth-cheeked, unshaven, with plaited hair, braids or bald. They waved, smiled, blew kisses, threw flowers.

Galla, a little overwhelmed, forgot to acknowledge the acclaim until Arcadius, turning for some reason, chided her. 'We have to give the rabble something,' he said with a curl of his lip. 'Even if it's only a wave.'

Galla did as she was told, wondering why he was so unpleasant. He didn't seem to like anyone except their father, and that, she had heard Elpidia muttering once, was because he knew which way the wind blew. Honorius wasn't much better.

Happiness filled Galla as she began to wave. The crowd's reaction was instantaneous. A woman thought she was waving at her and screamed in joy. A boy gaped, tugged on his father's sleeve and pointed. Galla thought she heard him cry, 'She saw me!' Galla smiled at an old crone, who bared her toothless gums in delight. And so it went, all the way to the massive ornate Golden Gate, where the procession exited the city.

Elpidia had told Galla that the paved road they followed, the Via Egnatia, led to the seventh coastal suburb, the Hebdomon. There, amid the royal palaces, churches and vast open spaces, Honorius would be crowned emperor. Crowds lined both sides of the road, almost as deep as within the city. Units of immaculately turned-out soldiers stood at regular intervals, raising their standards and shouting Honorius' name as the chariot drew near. Small boys dared one another to run alongside it, waving frantically. Her brothers ignored them, but Galla waved and smiled. How wonderful it would be, she thought, to lead a procession like this one day, alone, with the people's acclaim aimed just at her.

The seven-mile journey passed in the blink of an eye, and although the banks of black cloud remained overhead, the rain they threatened did not fall. Elpidia had been right, Galla decided. God had blessed this day for her half-brother.

Climbing down from the chariot, Honorius was surrounded by soldiers, and as their approving father watched, he was thrown into the air with a loud shout of proclamation. He landed and was hurled aloft again. As if by magic, the clouds split, and dazzling sunlight lanced down, lighting up the entire forum.

Laughing, Theodosius came running from his chariot and jumped into the children's one. 'It is a sign from heaven!' he cried, embracing Arcadius and Galla. 'God Himself favours our house!' To Galla, he whispered, 'You should be recognised also. This very day I will name you *nobilissima puella*, "most noble girl".'

Wrapped up in Theodosius' hug, encompassed by his love, Galla was the happiest she could ever remember being. One day, she thought, her father might name her *augusta*. She could be an empress, as her half-brothers were emperors.

Theodosius went next to Honorius, now wrapped in a purple military cloak, and embraced him. As the emperor placed a diadem on his son's head to fresh cheering by the soldiers, Arcadius leaned towards Galla.

'You will never be honoured in this way,' he muttered. 'You are only a girl. You will never rule, unless you have a husband, and even then, he will be far more important. Women are good for nothing except bearing children.'

Galla did not know how to respond. Her eyes filled with tears.

Arcadius turned away, satisfied.

I don't care what he says, thought Galla defiantly. I *am* worth something.

CHAPTER I

Near Florentia, Etruria, Italia; Mensis Maius, AD *406*

The sun beat down from a cloudless sky, a burning globe in the vast blue. An eagle soared high on the thermals. The rolling countryside was covered in latifundia; all had seen better days. Laneways and entrance roads were overgrown, thick with brambles and nettles. Buildings were ramshackle, in poor repair, abandoned. Still, though, as they had done for close to a millennium, vines covered the south-facing slopes, and in the fields wheat grew, and barley, emmer and spelt. The young crops rippled in the faint breeze. Skylarks sang above, but the landscape was empty of people, and there was no activity around the houses or farm buildings. A lone unseen dog barked its unhappiness.

From the north came an ancient road, the Via Aurelia, and over its ruts and broken paving slabs marched an army, tens of thousands strong. Cavalry led the column, foot soldiers followed. Officers barked out commands. Messengers rode from unit to unit, relaying orders. A pack of strays loped alongside, watchful for dropped food scraps and well-aimed kicks from less appreciative soldiers.

Trees were scant by the roadside, nor would there be a halt for hours. Vadomar, riding near the front of the column, was tired and hot, and sick of the journey, which was in its seventh day. The constant grumble among his comrades was that they would much rather head towards Roma and a week of leave than seek out and destroy their enemies.

Invaders did not just appear at the frontier and ask for permission to enter the empire, however, and their quarry, Radagaisus, was no different. He and two other tribal leaders had unexpectedly crossed the Alpes the previous autumn with many tens of thousands of warriors at their backs. The vast barbarian host had split into three, and any resistance in northern Italia was soon overcome.

In the subsequent months, one of the three armies had been defeated by Huns allied to the empire, and another had returned whence it came, but Radagaisus and a sizeable force yet rampaged up and down the land. Florentia, the focus of their current assault, had been under siege for half a month. It was towards that town that the Roman army marched. Unlike many of his comrades, Vadomar was itching to reach it, to fight after what had been a long and boring winter.

In the main, the empire's slow response had been thanks to the out-of-nowhere appearance of Radagaisus and his host. It had not helped either that the Goths were so numerous. Gathering a force large enough to defeat them took time. Stilicho, most senior commander of the imperial army and Vadomar's leader, had finally done so at Ticinum, to the north. His soldiers originated from all over, but in particular the garrisons along the Rhenus. At least two thirds were not Roman. Vadomar was Gothic, for example. There were Huns also, and Alani.

It was amusing, thought Vadomar, how so many barbarians were marching to save Florentia, and Roma, Radagaisus' stated objective.

A lanky individual, Vadomar sat his horse with an easy grace, his feet not far from the ground. He was a *bucellarius*, one of Stilicho's personal retainers, named for the *bucellatum* hard biscuit eaten on campaign. He had been in the Roman military for ten years, working his way up the ranks to his current position, and had hopes of further promotion. The *magister militum*, Stilicho, would not live for ever, went his reasoning, and his son, Eucherius, showed no inclination towards the military life. Vadomar dreamed of one day taking orders directly from the emperor Honorius, like Stilicho himself.

'How much further?' asked Dog, who was riding alongside Vadomar. Fond of howling in battle or when drunk, he was lean, scarred and sardonic.

'What did the last milestone say?' This was Eriulf, large, noisy and opinionated.

'Fifteen miles,' said Vadomar, pulling out his leather Pannonian cap. He wiped his forehead and sweaty ears, then replaced the cap inside his neck-slung helmet. 'Not that Stilicho will take us right to Florentia. He would be asking for an ambush by Radagaisus.'

'Five miles out, he'll stop us,' said Eriulf. 'That would be my guess.'

Dog squinted at the sun. 'Sounds reasonable. It will be late afternoon, early evening before we halt.'

'A good night's sleep and we'll crush the enemy tomorrow,' said Eriulf.

'Might not be so simple. If the scouts are correct, Radagaisus' host is larger than ours.' Dog was ever the pessimist.

'Shame on you!' cried Vadomar.

'Thirty thousand against forty thousand is no odds at all,' added Eriulf.

'Scouts could be wrong.'

'Wouldn't be the first time.'

A stranger might have mistaken the arguing and bickering as serious, but it was their modus operandi. The trio were comrades of old, who had fought side by side on numerous occasions, and got pissed together even more. Dog was the gloomy one, yet fiercely loyal to his friends. Eriulf liked the sound of his own voice, although he often claimed Vadomar was worse. And Vadomar, as his friends never tired of telling him, was the one who liked to do things a certain way. He didn't always take the constant ribbing well either, which of course meant they commented at every opportunity.

There was nothing wrong with his habits, he decided. Just because a man folded his blanket like so, went over his gear and practised the same fighting moves every morning, it didn't make him a mindless fool. Counting everything made sense too. His horse's steps from one point to another, the number of birds in the sky, how many scales there were in a section of his armour, it mattered. Why, he didn't know, but it did. If the distraction also stopped him from worrying, well, that was good. It was odd that Dog and Eriulf didn't copy him.

'Once we have sorted out Radagaisus, there's still Alaric to think about.'

This was the Visigothic war leader who had been a thorn in the side of both the eastern and western empires for years. Currently, he and the tens of thousands of warriors who followed him were somewhere between Dalmatia and Pannonia, east and north-east of Italia.

'He's been quiet for a year or two, thank God.' Like most, Eriulf was a Christian. And like most, he wasn't above calling on the old deities in times of need as well. Vadomar often accused him of being a hypocrite; Eriulf's response was to shrug and say it made sense to hedge one's bets.

'But Alaric has no land for his people, and as everyone from Roma to Constantinopolis knows, he will not be happy until that is achieved,' said Dog.

Since their entry into the eastern empire a decade before, Alaric and his host had wandered thousands of miles in search of a new homeland. Neither emperor, east nor west, wanted them, but their sheer numbers made complete removal or annihilation an impossibility. Stilicho had defeated Alaric more than once, hence his current residence on the empire's fringes.

'I don't see why they can't have Illyricum.' Vadomar was repeating something he'd heard Stilicho say. 'Kills two birds with one stone, giving Alaric what he wants and ending the argument between Ravenna and Constantinopolis over its ownership.'

Dog snorted. 'The Illyrians might have something to say about that arrangement.'

'Aye, well, you can't please everyone.' This was also something Stilicho said, and Vadomar knew it to be true. Life wasn't black and white, it was grey, and the best settlements came about when both sides compromised, each receiving a little less than it would have preferred and giving away a little more than planned. Illyricum was a sparsely populated region, he had seen it for himself, and the inlets along its long coastline offered ample locations for settlements.

Eriulf cast a look over his shoulder. 'Stilicho's on the move.'

Their conversation ceased. Preceded by two staff officers, Stilicho was riding up the side of the column. Vadomar knew why the officers looked nervous: the magister militum was fond of taking off on a whim, never bringing enough men with him as protection.

'Come along with you, Magister?' he called out in Gothic.

Bearded, with short hair and a priestlike fringe, Stilicho threw him a smile of recognition. 'Vadomar, isn't it?'

'Yes, Magister.'

'Bored?'

'A little, Magister.' It was true.

A chuckle. 'You think I'm risk-taking, eh?'

'Not at all, Magister.'

'You and I both know that's not your real reason. Follow then, you and your two comrades. It will keep this pair happy.' Stilicho gave the staff officers a look.

Eriulf was delighted to have been chosen; Dog complained under his breath, but was silenced when Vadomar told him he would have reacted in the same way if Stilicho had denied the request.

They rode past two legions raised in Italia. A few men greeted Stilicho's passing, and the senior officers saluted, but that was the height of it. The neutral, even vaguely hostile attitude was normal, but Vadomar's anger stirred nonetheless. In their arrogance, Roman soldiers resented their supreme commander for being a *semibarbarus*, half a barbarian. They followed orders, fought for him, but he was not held in high esteem, and they did not love him in the way the Visigothic and other tribal soldiers did. The same was true of the civilian population, the politicians in the Senate and, Vadomar suspected, everyone in the imperial court, including the emperor Honorius. Romans looked down on barbarians. They always had and always would, despite the fact that nowadays, barbarians constituted two thirds of the army. They were the best soldiers too.

The back-to-front proportions were indicative of a far larger problem. Every unit in the army was below strength; many existed only on official lists. Unlike the hallowed days of antiquity, citizens no longer wanted to join up. In an effort to change the situation, Stilicho had recently offered large financial incentives to new recruits. He had even decreed slaves could be manumitted if they served in the legions.

Hearing a muffled insult from the ranks, Dog spat his opinion of Roman soldiers.

Even Eriulf, usually the most jovial, scowled at the cool reception.

It didn't matter as long as they fought for Stilicho, Vadomar decided. That was what counted.

The *foederati* cavalry, Visigoths and Alamans, were next along. Fierce fighters, they cheered to see Stilicho, who smiled and waved and kept going. At the front of the column were several hundred Visigothic scouts. There was more yelling and beating of spears off oval shields, and their commander saluted with a grin.

'What news?' demanded Stilicho.

'I was just about to send word, Magister.'

'Here I am.'

'Radagaisus is breaking off the siege, Domine.' Seeing Stilicho's frown, the officer continued, 'I think his men saw mine.'

'They were to stay hidden!'

'I know, Magister. Sorry, Magister.'

Vadomar wasn't surprised by Stilicho's anger. Trapping Radagaisus' host against the walls of Florentia would have ensured a swift victory. Chasing it into the countryside offered a far less certain outcome, and potentially months of pursuit.

'They won't go south,' said Stilicho. 'The flat terrain would make them easy prey. No, it'll be east or north-east. What's the name of the small town in the hills above Florentia?'

'Faesulae, Magister,' replied a staff officer.

'Ten solidi says that's where Radagaisus goes.' There was a wolfish glint in Stilicho's eyes. 'He's given us a God-sent opportunity. Vadomar, do you fancy some action?'

Stilicho threw caution to the wind, and sent all the foederati cavalry and most of his bucellarii to the attack. If it hadn't been for his staff officers' insistence, Vadomar overheard, the magister militum would also have taken part. More than nine thousand horsemen, a veritable army, they rode for Florentia at a fast pace. The Via Quinctia was empty, any farms close by ransacked or burned, barns emptied. The surviving locals were in hiding from the Goths, who as Vadomar often commented to his comrades, passed through the countryside like a plague of locusts.

Not long after midday, with the temperature close to summer's heights, they neared Florentia. The bucellarii, who had taken the lead, came to a gradual halt about half a mile from the town, which was situated on flat ground between a set of low hills to one side and the Apenninus mountains to the other. A boiling mass of humanity could be made out: men running hither and thither, riders moving away to the east, and fewer in number, groups forming lines that faced Stilicho's cavalry.

'They know we're coming,' said Eriulf.

'And panic has set in,' added Dog, grinning happily.

Vadomar looked to their commander, a morose man who was devoted to Stilicho. 'Domine?'

The commander shrugged. 'There's only one thing to do.'

The *barritus* started up, the war cry of the Visigoths and their ancestors since time immemorial. Men hummed, and held their shields up to their mouths as the volume increased. The sound rebounded off the shields, escalating to a loud thundering, thousands of voices united in one purpose. It stood the hair on Vadomar's neck.

It was a long way for the sound to carry to Radagaisus' warriors, but faces turned in their direction. Fingers pointed. Men began to run. Horses reared in alarm.

Voices were indiscernible amid the din. Vadomar's commander drew his spatha. Sunlight flashed off its long blade, and when he aimed its point at their enemies, everyone knew what to do.

Vadomar urged his mount into the gallop.

Cavalry charges were second nature. Unsheathe his sword, hold it ready against his right thigh. Tilt his shield so it protected him from the air hissing past, and soon, from enemy spears. Lean forward in the four-horned saddle, moulding himself to the horse, exulting in its immense power. Sense the wind whistle by. Hear the barritus being whipped away, away into the sky. Swallow, move his tongue, try to produce moisture in his dry mouth. Take deep comfort from the presence on either side of his comrades, and behind them, of countless brothers-in-arms.

The charge had no particular formation; there was no need. Facing thousands of galloping horsemen was a bowel-loosening prospect. The majority of Radagaisus' Goths had broken long before they arrived. Some braver souls, chieftains perhaps, had rallied men, inadequate shield walls from behind which a few spears were lobbed. The veteran bucellarii and foederati paid no heed, focusing on their targets.

The first warrior Vadomar picked didn't see death coming. He heard it, though, must have felt the earth shake as the hooves drew close, because he went from a run to a frantic sprint. Shield already discarded, he dropped his spear and ran like an athlete in the games. Vadomar's angled slash opened him from shoulder to opposite hip. Blood sprayed. There was a fleeting impression of the screaming man dropping, and then he was past, on to the next warrior, who had turned to fight. His spear jabbed at Vadomar's horse, a clever move. Bring down the mount and the rider would follow.

Vadomar yanked the reins. His horse swerved, and the spear, missing its target, ripped open the fabric over his calf. From the flare of pain that followed, plenty of skin went with it. Angry, he cut down hard and split the warrior's skull. There was a moment to glance at his leg – the bleeding was slight, which meant the injury was too, or so he hoped – then he sought fresh prey.

From the corner of his eye, a dark shape flighted in. Vadomar threw himself down on his horse's neck. A spear shot overhead. Next, a metallic *spang*. A bellow of pain.

'Are you hurt?' Vadomar shouted.

'What does it sound like, fool?' A litany of savage oaths left Eriulf's lips.

Vadomar risked a glance, and was relieved to see Eriulf still in the saddle. Apart from a deep gouge along the top of his helmet, he seemed free of injury. 'Head hurt?'

'Like I've been on the wine after payday!'

'Moaning as usual!' Dog came riding between the pair of them and reined in. 'Good sport, eh?'

Eriulf growled agreement, but Vadomar's bloodlust was thinning. There was no glory in killing panicked men, no bravery in hacking down warriors without shields or spears. Show him an enemy who wanted to fight, that was a different prospect, but there was scarcely a Goth to be found with the heart to do so. Courage leaches away fast when one's comrades flee, thought Vadomar. Of the small groups who had been standing their ground at the outset of the charge, there was now no evidence.

This did not mean it was time to rest on their laurels, as a Roman general of old might have done. The battle was not yet won; most of Radagaisus' host was unharmed, even if it was fleeing up into the green, tree-clad hills above Florentia. There was plunder to be had too. Vadomar dismounted and stripped a bloodied silver torc from around the neck of a richly dressed warrior. He laughed, and raised the corpse's purse. 'This is full!'

'Typical you find it, not me,' said Dog sourly, his gaze more on the fallen than the fleeing.

'Keep after them! You can look for coin later.' This was their commander, with his habit of appearing when they didn't want him to. 'There will be plenty of spoil for all.'

He wasn't wrong, Vadomar decided. The ground was carpeted with dead and injured. Radagaisus' warriors had taken severe casualties, and, from the shouts and ring of arms carrying from the hillside, would suffer many more before the day was done.

Vadomar had only recently heard of Faesulae, and reaching the hilltop, he wasn't surprised. Sited on a part-tree-covered ridge three miles from Florentia, it did not merit the title of town. It was small and run-down, a village at best. There was a wall, true, but like so much to do with the empire, it had seen better days. Radagaisus' warriors could not all fit inside, so they had taken up defensive positions around the settlement.

With their backs to the wall, literally, courage had returned. As Vadomar said to Eriulf, it helped knowing thousands of their fellows had been slain, injured or taken captive. Goths were by nature fearless, and never more so than in desperate situations. Many foes would have surrendered after the rout from Florentia, but it appeared Radagaisus' warriors had not totally lost their nerve.

Proof came with the first charge by the legions, which had arrived some hours after the bucellarii and foederati. Full-throated, thundering and accompanied by volleys of stones from the slingers, it was nonetheless a dismal failure. Radagaisus himself was in the front line of defence, a tall figure wearing, of all things, a Roman officer's helmet. Whether it was his presence, or the knowledge they had nothing to lose, the Goths threw back the legionaries with fearful casualties.

It was no surprise to Vadomar when Stilicho decided against a second attack. Instead he ordered the construction of a defensive ditch around Faesulae. The spoil formed a rampart the same height as a man. Old-fashioned, just as in the empire's heyday, it would, when finished, entrap the enemy host.

Realising this, Radagaisus' warriors made several attempts to escape. Stilicho anticipated this, sending in the bucellarii and foederati by turns. Cavalry against infantry was never a contest on open ground, in particular when the foot soldiers advanced in a chaotic, mentally half-beaten mob. Vadomar and his comrades wreaked bloody slaughter. Then it was the turn of the foederati. Vadomar, Eriulf, Dog, et al. The foederati again.

With the air rent by screams and wails and pleas for mercy, Radagaisus' men could take no more. They fled in utter terror towards Faesulae, discarding weapons and shields, trampling those who fell underfoot and packing the settlement to bursting point.

That should have been that. The Goths would surrender by sunrise, Vadomar and his comrades agreed over their evening cooking fire. A persistent stubbornness ran through their enemies' veins, however. The next morning, Stilicho's request for Radagaisus to surrender was met with derision, the messenger lucky to escape with his life.

The struggle became a siege, a war of attrition. Stilicho was content. As he told his men, from this point onward, hunger and disease would do it all. They merely had to wait, and throw back the occasional escape attempt. It was a well-won, deserved victory, and the emperor would be proud of them. So many prisoners had been taken, he went on, that every soldier in the army would be given one as a slave.

Drunk on looted wine, Vadomar cheered and hooted with the rest. He disregarded Stilicho's faults. Tonight, he was the greatest general of the age, a man who time and again defeated the empire's enemies.

Stick with him, Vadomar reasoned, and he would go far.

CHAPTER II

Circus Maximus, Roma; Mensis Sextilis, AD *406*

The hot air reverberated to the sound of the crowd. Waves of noise – cheering, chanting – echoed through the stairwells. The stairs were empty now, people having come long before. Tens of thousands had queued to enter the largest structure in Roma. Entrance was not an end to the ordeal either; a fight through the throng to secure the best seats followed.

Wise to this, eighteen-year-old Galla Placidia had arrived as the pompa circensis, the opening procession, ended. A slender figure in a shawl and dark blue dress, hair made up in the latest style, pearls round her neck and in her ears, Galla looked every part the member of the imperial family she was. Accompanying her were her nurse, Elpidia, and a dark-skinned Aethiopian. The latter was Darme, her major domus cum bodyguard.

'Hurry,' admonished Galla. 'Or we will miss the start of the first race.' With twelve chariots, this was one of the most important of the day.

'Yes, Nobilissima Femina.' Darme shot Elpidia a look, for it was she who was slowest.

Elpidia huffed, but picked up her pace.

At the slaves' entrance to the *pulvinar*, the emperor's loge, stood a pair of bored sentries. Comfortable in the cool shadow, their lassitude was understandable. Honorius had not visited Roma for two years, which meant no slaves were required to attend to him here. In turn that signified an easy duty at this door.

Recognising Galla, however, the more senior made a deep bow. His companion quickly did the same. 'Nobilissima Femina,' they chorused.

'Am I in time?'

'Your timing is impeccable, Nobilissima Femina.' The lead sentry stepped aside, and with a grand flourish indicated she should pass.

No acknowledgement from Galla. Elpidia also ignored them, haughty even though she was a slave. Darme came last; coin chinked as a purse exchanged hands. Keeper of the household finances and as shrewd as a moneylender, Darme had long since acknowledged to Galla that this was a small price to pay for the best view in the house. The pulvinar was positioned halfway along the length of the eastern side of the hippodrome, a grand structure in temple form standing high above the ordinary citizens' seats.

Galla paused in the entrance, awed by the sight meeting her. It was always the same, no matter how many times she came here. Built of stone on three levels, with arches supporting the structure at ground level and pillars above, the hippodrome was an immense three and a half stadia in length, and two thirds of a stadion wide. The seating – which was at full capacity today, more than a hundred and fifty thousand people – ran in three tiers along both of the longer sides, and around the semicircle of one end. Opposite were the *carceres*, starting gates, and a grand superstructure above.

Down the centre of the circuit, running at a slight angle to the seating on either side, was the *spina*. This massive double-walled barrier enclosed deep pools of water; at each end was a turning point, the *metae*, three gilded bronze cones. The top of the spina was ornamented with statues of various gods, Galla had never bothered to find out which, and two incredibly tall carved obelisks from Aegyptus. There was also a structure bearing seven stone eggs; one was removed as each lap finished. Galla preferred the seven bronze dolphins near the carceres, which dropped into a pool one after another as each race progressed. The track itself was covered with fine, high-quality sand; disturbed by the pompa circensis, it was being raked into smoothness by teams of slaves.

Galla chose a seat halfway between the front and back of the loge, Elpidia quickly placing a thick cushion on the marble. In an ideal world, Galla thought, she would have been here with Stilicho and Serena's son, Eucherius, whom she loved. There had been much talk of their betrothal in the past. She felt a pang of sadness. She did not understand why the arrangement seemed to have been forgotten, why Eucherius did not visit her as he once had. It had to be his parents, she decided.

'The final chariots are entering the carceres,' said Elpidia.

Galla's attention came back to the present. She craned her neck. The starting gates were more than a stadion and a half away to the right. 'Can you see any Blues?' she asked. The starting stalls were randomly allotted, and the result was important to the outcome of each race.

'A Blue team is going into Stall Two, Nobilissima Femina,' said Darme. 'I can't see the driver well enough to recognise him, though.'

'Stall One could be a Green!' said Elpidia, annoyed. It and Stall Two were the closest to the metae at that end. Although the angled position of the carceres ensured every stall was the same distance from the turning point, the first and second afforded the best chance of establishing an early lead.

'Correct,' said Galla, pitching her voice so they could hear. 'There he goes now. It must be Diocles.'

Name taken from a centuries-old star of the hippodrome, Diocles was the lead driver for the Greens, and for that faction's supporters he was the best charioteer in Roma. He had been a Blue until the previous year, when, to Galla's disgust, he had changed teams, presumably for a vast sum.

'It is!' she said. 'With Diocles in One, we all know who'll be in Two.'

The air rang with voices and shouts and excited cries. Requests of God mingled with the names of chariot drivers, of teams and individual horses. There were arguments over whose faction was best, and predictions about who would win which race. Like Galla, Elpidia and Darme, most spectators were keenly watching the gates to the carceres being closed, and the presiding magistrate, seated on a platform above. The sense of anticipation was palpable throughout the hippodrome. When the magistrate's white flag dropped, waiting *moratores*, helpers, would throw open the locks, allowing the gates to spring outward and the race to start.

The chariots represented four *factiones*: the Blues, Greens, Whites and Reds. The first two teams had long been the most dominant, and as the colour of her dress announced, Galla favoured the Blues. Naturally, so did Elpidia and Darme. In this first race, three chariots from each team would take part. The role of two in every three was to act as pace-setters for the star drivers, to block their opponents and, if necessary, to sacrifice their own chance of victory so their faction came home first.

'God is good. Polyneices *is* racing for the Blues,' said Galla. 'Listen.'

Sure enough, from the seating to their right, where the Blues supporters congregated in the greatest numbers, came the raucous chant, 'POLY-NEI-CES! POLY-NEI-CES!' Lengths of blue cloth rose and fell, waved to and fro in the air.

Polyneices had recently been poached from the Reds, with whom he'd notched up hundreds of victories. Like Diocles, his racing name was the same as a famous driver from centuries before. Galla had never seen him race, though.

From the Greens' seats came the response, thousands of flapping strips of green cloth and an animal roar. 'DIO-CLES!'

Galla was nervous. It wasn't surprising. Polyneices was talented, but he hadn't bedded in with the Blues. He was not long back from injury. His team of four horses changed from one week to the next, and he'd been well beaten by Diocles on the most recent occasion they had been pitted against one another. It wasn't just his average form that had her on edge. Acting on her instruction, Darme had wagered a sizeable sum on Polyneices.

It was her tendency, so respectable and upstanding at first appearance, to place large amounts via Darme on dashing, risk-taking drivers. Polyneices had a good chance in this contest, yet it was by no means certain. Galla wondered if she had wagered more coin than she could afford. She suspected Darme felt the same way. The bet had been placed, however, and there was nothing to be done about it.

Conversations died away. Expectations rose. People saw the white flag being lifted, and the quiet spread. Soon an expectant hush fell over the entire hippodrome and its hundred and fifty thousand spectators. It was, as the saying went, as quiet as the grave.

Galla was literally on the edge of her seat.

The flag came down, and a heartbeat later, the starting stall gates opened. Out shot the chariots. A great cry rose to the heavens.

'Diocles started faster,' groaned Galla.

'Only a little,' said Elpidia.

Already the chariots, following their lanes, had reached the metae and disappeared from sight. All the noise came now from the far side of the spina, and the spectators who could see the twelve hurtling down the long straight.

Galla could picture it. A few chariots whose drivers had decided to take an early lead, Diocles and Polyneices neck and neck, a small gap perhaps, then four or five chariots jockeying for position and the rest at the back, trying to keep up. In between and outside, the *hortatores*, horsemen who relayed information, keeping the support charioteers up to date with the main drivers' intentions and needs.

An enormous cheer. A name. 'CORAX!'

'He's in the lead. A Red,' said Elpidia. The supporters of that faction sat in the section close to the second turning point, and Corax was the best of their three men.

'It is early yet,' Galla quietly replied. It was something Eucherius had been fond of saying.

She was right. Few races were won by the initial leaders; it was too difficult, not to mention strenuous on the horses.

Her attention was caught by movement between the gilded bronze cones of the metae to her left. Astonished, she realised it was a small child, a boy; he was standing right above the track. A slave, she decided, so fascinated by the race that he had deserted his post, probably at one of the water pools. Now he had a bird's-eye view of the chariots taking the turn, better than perhaps anyone in the hippodrome, but he was young enough to have no common sense. A fall amid the chariots would be lethal, not to say bloody. Land in front of Polyneices, Galla worried, and *he* might crash. Guilt-ridden at thinking of her favourite driver first, she offered up a prayer to keep the child from harm.

Loud applause. Cheers.

Around the metae came the first chariot, a Red, but not as close to the spina as its driver might have wished.

The Reds' supporters were not going to give up hope that their team might hold on to the lead. 'CORAX!'

Booing and jeering from the audience around the pulvinar, followers of the Blues and Greens.

Two more chariots appeared, side by side, a Green tight against the stonework and a White a good deal wider. Taking the turn too fast, the White driver had been unable to stop himself from swinging out. The error cost him dear, as they hit the straight and the Green surged ahead.

Through the dust cloud thrown up by the first chariots emerged a trio of hortatores, then two more chariots, one each for the Blues and Greens. The excited shouts that met their appearance died down as the audience realised that neither was Polyneices or Diocles. They resurged with a vengeance an instant later as the star drivers took the turn together. Diocles was on the inside, close enough to touch the stone, a demonstration of extreme skill. No less difficult, Polyneices was as close to Diocles as Diocles was to the metae.

Galla could hardly look. The slightest error and either driver would crash, bringing them both to ruin.

It didn't happen. The pair took off down the straight, keeping pace with one another, but neither at full tilt. They were reserving their horses' strength.

The shouts soon reached deafening volume again. 'DIO-CLES!' 'POLY-NEI-CES!'

Galla was holding herself back from joining in, but her lips were also repeating the Blues' driver's name.

A mighty crash, cries of alarm from the far side of the spina.

The boy atop the metae slipped out of sight, gone to see what had happened.

A chariot rounded the bend, a Red, much wider than was advantageous.

'He had to avoid the crash,' said Darme.

Galla felt a trace of panic. Let it be a Green, White or Red, she prayed.

Her hopes came to fruition. The two chariots following were Blue and Red, but loud consternation erupted from the audience on the far side of the spina.

Galla had done the calculation. 'A Red and a White must have collided.'

'Let none of the horses have been injured, Nobilissima Femina,' said Elpidia.

Galla hated this aspect of racing too, and was glad not to witness whatever was going on. Too often she had seen horses down kicking, trapped in the traces, or getting up, and unable to stand on one leg. Even if the moratores managed to lead them out before the chariots returned, their end was the same as the horses that were unable to walk: a blade across the throat.

She hoped none of the drivers had been injured either.

God heard her, or so it felt. Incredibly, when the dust cleared a little, they saw eight horses being led out of the main entrance, close to the metae. Behind walked one driver, acknowledging shouts from the crowd; a party of stretcher bearers carried the other. He was also waving; as Darme said, it meant his injuries weren't too severe.

Teams of moratores hurried to clear the wreckage away before the other chariots returned. They succeeded, just. To Galla's amazement and the full-throated approval of the Reds supporters, Corax still held the lead when the ten remaining chariots came around the turn for a second time. And the third time.

'Men will have made money on that,' said Darme quietly, a pleased look in his eye.

Galla chuckled. 'You're one of them.'

He didn't deny it. Darme was shrewd, and was known to visit the various factions' stables.

Galla's attention went back to the race. Even when the chariots were out of sight, she sat listening to the noise rising opposite, interpreting what happened until the competitors rounded the turn to their left again. The fourth lap ended, and Corax had fallen back to the middle of the field. Another crash soon after, between the Blue and Green in second and third place; it did not force them to retire, but it sent Diocles and Polyneices into the lead at last. Coming around the turn midway through the fifth lap, Diocles moved into the lead over his rival, the length of a chariot and team. The Greens supporters went wild.

'GREENS! GREENS!' 'DIO-CLES!' 'CRINI-TUS!' 'A-JAX!' The last two were Diocles' lead horses.

Glancing back, Galla noticed Elpidia chewing a fingernail, her habit when stressed. Next she heard Darme muttering. It was so quiet she had to slide a little towards him to hear the words. Eyes closed, he didn't notice. She listened with a mixture of horror and a guilty wish for his words to come true.

'Restrict Diocles' horses' ability to run, their strength, their spirit, their acceleration, their speed. Deny them victory, tangle their feet, obstruct them. May they fall down, along with Diocles. Bind up his hands, snatch the win from him, deny him sight, so he cannot see his rivals. Lay hold of him, lift him up out of his chariot, pull him out of his chariot and onto the ground, so that he falls and is dragged all around the track, especially through the turns, and is gravely injured, along with his horses. Do it quickly.' Finished, he opened his eyes. His head turned.

Galla put on a blank face. A devout Christian, she could not be seen to approve of appeals to a pagan deity.

Just before the chariots came around the metae to their left for the sixth time, Galla saw a hortator in a blue tunic swinging wide of the turn, keeping clear of what was racing up behind. 'He's been talking to Polyneices,' she murmured to herself. 'It's now or never, that's what he will have told him.'

Diocles came into sight first, tight around the metae. Amid the billowing dust, it was momentarily hard to see if there was anyone chasing him, but Galla's heart leaped as first heads, then the necks and bodies of horses pulling a chariot, a Blue chariot, emerged from the dense brown swirl. The crowd went wild, Green and Blue supporters screaming their desire to win. Polyneices had opted for a risky tactic, cutting in close to the metae, then angling out a little to overtake. That was if his horses had enough strength left, she thought, her nerves jangling.

Down the straight they hurtled, first Diocles, then Polyneices, now only half a length behind. Corax, who had led for so long, was beaten back into fourth, then fifth position. The cheering and shouting reached new levels, a vast, rippling wave of noise in which no words could be determined. Everyone was on their feet, women, men, children. Even the nobles had risen from their marble seats at the front. Galla spied one portly toga-wearing senator actually jumping up and down. Arms waved, strips of blue cloth and green fluttered in the air.

At the metae, the two chariots were neck-and-neck, but Diocles had kept his position on the inside. They slowed to take the turn, and Galla saw him lash out with his whip, striking Polyneices' left lead horse on the head. It was cunning, because the slightest check or deceleration would give his team the chance to pull ahead again.

'No!' Galla was outraged, although the tactic was permitted.

Around the metae the pair went, and out of sight.

A baying howl rose from the seating on the far side of the spina as the spectators there were rewarded with the beginning of the final lap. Galla sat, and turned to Elpidia. 'Did you *see* Diocles use his whip?'

'I did, Nobilissima Femina.'

'It should be banned! Damage to the eye is the most common type of injury. It can end a horse's career!'

Their attention returned to the race. It was possible to estimate the position of the chariots by the moving increase in noise. Spectators opposite them who were near the metae were on their feet. Arms pointed. Hands were cupped to mouths, shouts rose. There were even people throwing things. A curse on them, thought Galla, uncaring if it was a sin to wish such a thing. Shards of pottery and pieces of broken glass were most common, but she had even heard of *tribuli* being hurled onto the track. Dreadful four-pronged iron weapons used by the legions, they always landed with one prong sticking up.

If any of the missiles landed near enough, they did not harm Diocles' or Polyneices' team. Around the turn they came, side by side in a great cloud of dust, chariots and men so coated they were at first hard to differentiate.

The Blues supporters to their right got in first. 'POLY-NEI-CES!'

'They're right!' Galla positively squealed. 'He's in the lead!'

She was aware of Elpidia rushing forward. It didn't matter. In the excitement, no one would notice the breach of protocol. Her heart leaped. Polyneices *was* ahead of Diocles – even the dust could not disguise that one of his horses was black – and his lead was increasing. The finish line was right below the pulvinar. He was so close to victory. She let out a little cry of excitement, willing the Blue charioteer on.

'POLY-NEI-CES! POLY-NEI-CES! POLY-NEI-CES!'

He crossed the line two lengths ahead of Diocles, whose horses were fading fast.

Galla turned, her face alight with joy. 'He won!'

Elpidia beamed. 'He did, Nobilissima Femina, and convincingly.'

At once Galla's gaze went to Darme. 'How much will my winnings be?'

He did a quick mental calculation. 'Somewhere in the order of three hundred solidi, Nobilissima Femina.' This number of gold coins was a fortune.

Galla clapped her hands together, her worries about Eucherius forgotten.

It was an auspicious start to the day's races.

CHAPTER III

Mogontiacum, west bank of the River Rhenus, Germania Prima; late Mensis December, AD *406*

Even with the scarf wrapped around his face, it hurt to breathe in. This was the coldest temperature Vadomar had ever experienced. He was wearing clothing enough for two: a pair of undertunics and the same number of long-sleeved tunics under his *subarmalis,* and two pairs each of woollen trousers and socks. His cloak was a bear pelt, leather-trimmed, and he was warm enough. Just.

It's your own fault, he thought, being out in weather like this. He had to be, though. Duty called. In the day, with the trees obscuring, it was hard to judge the number of men on the far bank. Counting fires in the darkness might be more fruitful.

It was a still, black night, and there were no clouds. Starlight glittered off the frosted grass, which crunched beneath his boots, announcing his presence to one and all. Although that should not matter on this, the Roman side of the Rhenus, Vadomar's hand did not stray far from his sword hilt. It paid to be careful. He had made light of the sentries' warnings of demons, Huns, Alani and Suebi, however. He told them he'd never seen a demon yet. Weren't the barbarians supposed to be on the eastern bank, he had demanded, unless they knew something he did not? The sentries had huffed and scowled, and muttered behind their hands, but they had opened the gate. He was the soldier with the official letter from

Stilicho, and had the right to do what he wanted, more or less. If he wanted to wander around in the darkness like a witless fool, that was his issue.

Vadomar wasn't surprised by their low morale and cynicism. The garrisons along the Rhenus were perilously depleted, in the main because Stilicho had ordered large segments of them to Italia earlier in the year. The threat from Radagaisus then had been real, and urgent; Stilicho, short of soldiers, had had little choice. Radagaisus was food for the worms now, though, and his warriors dead, enslaved or forced to join Stilicho's army. And here in Germania Prima, where the forts were bare of men, a fresh threat to the empire loomed.

The alders and ash trees lining the bank were bare of leaves, but their branches restricted views of the Rhenus and its western side. Searching, Vadomar found a gap, a muddied narrow track down to the water's edge used by deer and other wild creatures. Close in, the water moved slowly, and there was an oily sheen to its surface. He knew this meant it was close to freezing. Let that never happen, he prayed, knowing the gods rarely listened to mere mortals, and that he was powerless to do much else.

He took heart at the river's width. The sentries had told him it was four hundred paces. Waterways of this magnitude did not ice over, he told himself, but the knifing pain in his lungs as he breathed in fed doubt rather than certainty. Pinpricks of light winked amid the trees opposite, the fires of the gathered tribesmen. The light came and went as men walked in front of the flames or stood to savour the heat. Vadomar began to count left to right. He stopped at sixty-nine.

If six to eight men shared a tent, and each group had a fire, he estimated that between four hundred and five hundred and fifty warriors were encamped on this short length of riverbank. If the reports from patrol vessels and other forts were correct, and he had no reason not to believe them, the same density of barbarians continued for many miles along the eastern side. According to one story he'd been told, of a spy sent over the Rhenus a week since, the camps stretched inland as well. Bar a few hangers-on, wives and whores, they were composed of men of fighting age.

To come up with an accurate figure was impossible, but it seemed probable the host ran into tens of thousands. It was also conceivable, thought Vadomar grimly, that over a hundred thousand warriors were on the far bank of the Rhenus. There was dreadful purpose in their patience, their willingness to wait for the right time to cross. Rumours about their origin were rife. They were the same warriors who had entered Italia with Radagaisus but left during the summer; now they intended to test Roma again. They were organised bands under charismatic leaders who, hearing tales of Alaric's success in both eastern and western empires, had decided to try their own luck.

It didn't matter, thought Vadomar, treading a wary path along the water's edge, picking out yet more fires. They were an army. Disunited, most likely, but an army nonetheless, and their number dwarfed the Roman forces on the western bank. Even at full complement, the Rhenus fort garrisons would have been outnumbered by a massive margin. Unsurprisingly, Mogontiacum's commander, a doleful, thin man by the name of Saturninus, had reported to Vadomar that desertions were a daily occurrence, and getting worse. 'No surprise really,' he'd said, wiping a drop from the end of his reddened nose. 'Our situation is hopeless.'

'Why haven't you fled?' Vadomar had asked, curious. He'd received a haughty stare in reply.

'I am a soldier of Roma. I took the *sacramentum*. It might mean nothing to some . . .'

There had been a clear implication that Vadomar, a barbarian like those waiting on the eastern bank, would not honour the sacred military oath. It rankled.

'Visigoth I may be, but I am also a soldier of Roma. And you are not alone in having taken the sacramentum,' Vadomar had snapped.

A surprised Saturninus apologised, and they had drunk warmed wine and honey together, toasting the emperor, the empire, and victory over the invaders. Hollow words, they felt like – Vadomar had seen the same awareness in Saturninus' eyes – but it felt better than to speak the truth and despair.

It was hard not to despair here, though, alone in the bitterly cold black night, the only indication of life the fires on the opposite bank. Vadomar fought the feeling. It was possible the estimates of the barbarian host's size were wrong, he told himself. The spy who had crossed over the previous week had been terrified out of his wits by a close encounter with a warrior suspicious of his accent. A mission supposed to have lasted several days had been little more than a night and a day, scarcely enough to come up with a reliable assessment. It was true the enemy fires continued for miles along the eastern bank, but it was the oldest trick in the book to have fires by which few, or indeed no men sat.

It was ironic, because Saturninus was utilising the tactic himself, as well as other ruses such as units leaving camp under the cover of darkness only to return to the acclaim of the fort's trumpeters the following morning. He had also ordered the construction of fortlets at regular intervals along the western side, each equipped with shooting platforms and replica *ballistae*. Soldiers occupied them during the daytime, and left at night.

Shadow-boxing, army fitness instructors called it. Whether it was working on the barbarians, no one knew, but Vadomar had it in his head now that the enemy chieftains might well be delaying their crossing to maximise the intimidatory effect of their seemingly vast numbers. Stilicho had ordered him to find out the most accurate information possible before returning to Italia. Maybe he was being foolish, thought Vadomar, but crossing the Rhenus to see with his own eyes the barbarian host was not just advisable, but essential.

What Saturninus would make of his decision was another matter.

The following morning, he went to the commandant's office bright and early. The reaction he got was not unexpected.

'Are you insane? A safer bet would be to try to swim across the Rhenus wearing your armour.'

Surprised by Saturninus' vehemence, Vadomar said, 'You forget I am Visigothic.'

'And your intonation and pronunciation are those of a man who's lived in Italia all his life! I am not fluent in your tongue by any means, but I understand a decent amount. I have also taken enough prisoners to know you sound nothing like the warriors on the far bank. My man who went across, the one who was nearly undone because of his accent, only joined the imperial army two years ago.'

'There won't be much need to speak,' Vadomar muttered.

'And if there is?'

Saturninus was right, Vadomar admitted to himself, but he had made up his mind. Stubbornness took hold. 'I'm going whether you like it or not.'

'Have you a wife? Children?'

'No.'

A snort. 'I thought as much.'

'Do you?'

'A wife and two sons.'

'When the barbarians cross, you will die in the fighting, leaving your family behind. What's the difference?'

'I will be doing my duty, and I will not be throwing my life away!'

'Stilicho charged me with finding out as much as I can about the enemy's numbers. Going over the river is the only way I can see of doing that. Rely on what I have been told, and I would fail in my duty. I will not be seeking death intentionally, but if death finds me over there, well, the gods will have decreed it so.'

Saturninus held Vadomar's gaze for a long moment, then he sighed. 'You are a brave man, and an honourable one. It is a shame you are a pagan.'

'And I say it is a pity you worship the Christ god!'

The commandant belly-laughed. 'Not many dare say that out loud nowadays.'

'Are they the same men who will not join the legions?'

Saturninus shook his head in wonder. 'I would there were more soldiers of your kind.'

'Men probably say the same about you.'

'Maybe.' Saturninus smiled, and poured more wine. 'You'll be needing a boat and crew.'

'Thank you.' Vadomar raised his cup. 'May the Rhenus never freeze over.'

'That I can drink to!'

*

There was a bridge over the Rhenus, but to use it risked being seen. It was agreed that Vadomar would be rowed over in the middle of the night, then make his way into the enemy encampment and lie low until daybreak.

This was how he found himself being transported across the water the same night, in a boat originally used for ferrying goods over the river. It was no longer being used, for obvious reasons. It was a crying shame, said the soldier charged with seeing Vadomar safely to the opposite bank. Fresh mutton was almost impossible to come by now, not to mention furs. Whether the soldier considered it ironic to be complaining about a lack of supplies when he and his comrades faced an imminent invasion by tens of thousands of tribesmen, Vadomar didn't ask.

They didn't talk further. The soldier had three companions; together they expertly poled the craft towards the far bank. Mid river, the current was strong; knowing this, the crew were aiming to come ashore some distance downstream. It was again a cloudless, freezing night; they would be visible to anyone paying attention. Vadomar's hope was that, already confident thanks to their overwhelming numbers, the Goths would be asleep, wrapped up in furs and blankets. In the event, he was correct. There seemed to be no sentries, and no shouts or challenges were made.

Edging through the reeds, the boat's prow came to a bumping halt against the bank. Vadomar was ready to jump.

'Christ be with you,' one of the crew whispered.

Vadomar nodded, grateful for the sentiment even if he didn't believe it, and leaped, arms outspread to help him balance. A loud crunch marked his landing on the frozen ground, easily enough to alert anyone nearby. He crouched down, ears pricked, but all he heard was the poles' soft plash as the men turned the craft and made for home. He waited for two hundred heartbeats, when he was satisfied no one had witnessed his arrival.

Standing, grateful for the weighty folds of his bear pelt cloak, he moved his belt to make his sword sit just so. He scarf-lapped his face and pulled down his fur hat – so used to wearing his Pannonian cap that until Saturninus commented, he hadn't even considered taking it off – and then, picking up his shield, began to walk. It didn't matter where he went. Saturninus' spy had reported that the enemy encampment did not appear to be organised in any way. Explore, get a feel for it, that would be his best option, Vadomar had decided, and count the tents.

They had left crossing as late as possible; dawn would not be far off, when men began to stir, to empty bladders and rekindle fires. Everyone was still abed, however, so he trod lightly. To his good fortune, there had been no snow for days, which meant the ground between the Gothic tents was well trodden, beaten down by countless men's passage. It was difficult to be completely silent, but by moving with great care, Vadomar made little sound. If anyone awake or stirring from sleep heard him, they would not be alarmed.

So he hoped and prayed, even as an acid feeling took hold in his belly. Talking with Saturninus, the risks had not seemed quite so perilous, but now that he was here, alone among thousands of men who regarded him as the enemy, his life hung by the thinnest of threads. He did not consider the option of turning back. His reappearance over the bridge would tell its own story, and Saturninus would soon hear. Vadomar was not prepared to endure the resulting shame. Death was preferable to dishonour.

He trudged inland, away from the river-hugging alders and ash, counting tents all the while. There were stumps everywhere, the trees felled to make space and provide firewood. Oaks and beeches began to dominate. Still the tents continued, and Vadomar's count rose into the hundreds. Reaching the end of the cleared ground at full light, he entered the treeline. Not far within, he chanced on a grove in which the bodies of strangled men hung from trees, and the constituent parts of a dismembered horse lay scattered about.

Vadomar stopped dead. He had only ever heard of a sacred space like this; too few pagans remained in Italia to keep the old traditions alive. His father had told him about them, though, hair-raising tales of human sacrifice as well as animal, scores of bare-chested warriors deep-chanting the barritus, robed priests standing before red-stained stone altars, wickedly sharp knives in hand. Part of him wanted to explore the grove, maybe even pray there, but he did not dare. The wishes and pleas voiced during the ceremonies practised there would not favour him – they would have asked for his death, as well as those of Saturninus and every Roman soldier along the Rhenus. To enter risked angering the gods. On trembling legs, silently telling the gods he meant no disrespect, he retreated.

A short while later, composed once more, he walked out of the forest like a man who had been to answer a call of nature. The few warriors who were up paid no heed to him until, for no reason he could discern, one emerging from a tent called out. Vadomar did not catch the words, nor did he stop. Stiff-backed, he walked on. A hurled curse carried through the crisp air, and he readied himself for a confrontation. He counted to one hundred, though, and no one had come after him. Two hundred, the same. Relief filled him.

Unsure which way to go next – it would likely make no difference – he saw a raven flying high above the trees to the north. Content to follow a bird sacred to the thunder god Donar, he headed in that direction. He was challenged by nobody, and was therefore able to stay silent. Things did not go well, however, when it came to his estimate of the warriors' numbers.

It wasn't just Goths who had come.

Vadomar knew enough of tribal tongues to recognise the Asding and Siling Vandal dialects. There were Alani too, and Suebi. Any of the latter who were bare-headed were discernible by their characteristic hair knot. Reaching a total of five hundred tents, not wanting to lose count, he began again at one. Still the tents continued, off to the forests in the east and north, the direction he was walking. A thousand, he reached, and kept going. They seemed limitless.

At length, he stopped. To go on was futile. The truth was undeniable. More than one hundred thousand warriors *had* assembled, making an exact figure of their number irrelevant. There was no knowing when they would cross the Rhenus, but the outcome was certain.

He had done enough. It was time to return to Italia. What Stilicho would do with the information, Vadomar had no idea. The entire imperial army was incapable of defeating this horde. Make peace with Alaric, though, and the scales started to balance out somewhat. The number of warriors following Alaric varied; men came and went as they pleased, but most opinions placed their strength between sixty and eighty thousand. Add the total to the forces Stilicho could raise, thought Vadomar, his hopes rising, and the emperor would have an army capable of throwing these invaders back over the Rhenus.

First, though, he had to reach the safety of Mogontiacum. It was about midday, judging by the watery sun's position. The boat was not due to return for him until the middle of the coming night, many hours away. Vadomar decided to make for the bridge, which was blocked off on this bank and manned day and night by Saturninus' soldiers. If it was too dangerous, he would find a place to wait for nightfall, but with a little luck, he might get over the barricade unscathed. Imagining the warm wine and honey Saturninus would offer upon his return, his spirits rose.

Nearing the bridge, he slowed down. Suspicions would be aroused if he made a beeline for it. As he soon realised, it also appeared strange to walk with no purpose at all. Move too slowly past a tent, and the men around the nearby fire got more of an opportunity to look at him, to call out a greeting or a question. There had already been one offer to buy his bearskin cloak; Vadomar had snarled a 'no' and continued walking. Fortunately, the interested party had not come after him.

In order to see the bridge, he had been keeping close to the encampment's edge, and roughly parallel with the line of the river. What he did not know was how much open ground there was between the last tents and the bridge. He cursed his lack of foresight; Saturninus could have supplied the information. If it was a short distance, he could just run for it, shouting out in Latin so the sentries did not throw spears or *plumbatae*. By the time any warriors realised, he would be beyond their reach. If it was not, then he would have to come up with another plan.

Vadomar began to pray. His pleas of the gods were silent. Urgent. Fervent.

And all for nothing, he thought bitterly, as the gaps between the tents grew large enough to see the bridge. Of course there were no tents near it; only a fool slept within reach of his enemies. It was about four hundred paces, a quarter of a mile.

To have a reasonable chance of reaching safety, he would need to cover at least half the distance without pursuit. Less than that, and a well-thrown spear might hit him in the back, or fast-running warriors catch up in order to take him prisoner. For a prisoner they would want to interrogate, to learn what he'd been doing in their midst. An image of the strangled men hanging in the grove came to mind; so did being drowned in a bog, pressed down into suffocation by warriors using wicker hurdles.

He took a casual look around. Five figures ringed a fire; from what he could hear, they were grumbling about the lack of decent food and dry firewood. Watched by several others, two pairs of warriors sparred with spear and shield, practice for battle. Another emerged from a tent, head-rubbing in the rueful manner of someone who had consumed too much beer the night before. Men chopped wood, tightened guy ropes, sharpened blades. No one paid attention to Vadomar, but if he lingered longer, that would change. A decision had to be made. A faint smile creased his lips. As his father had often said, it was time to shit or get off the pot.

He took a path between two tents, nothing out of the ordinary. Reached the start of the open ground. It seemed a long way to the fortification at the bridge's end, where sunlight winked off helmets. He hesitated. Maybe he should hide up until the middle of the night, when the boat would come.

A bandy-legged figure appeared to his left.

Vadomar decided to go back into the camp, avoid causing suspicion.

'Hey!'

He started, couldn't help it. Gruffly he demanded, 'What?'

'Your shield – where did you get it?'

This was *not* a question he had expected. Unable to use his own shield because of the imperial insignia on it, he had accepted Saturninus' offer of equipment taken from Gothic prisoners. The shield was unremarkable, bronze-bossed, painted red with a dark yellow line all around the edge.

His heart sank.

'Cat got your tongue?'

Put on the spot, Vadomar struggled for a quick, truthful-sounding answer. Adopting a deep voice so his accent would be harder to determine, he replied, 'I made it myself. What's it to you?'

'You're a liar!' This was delivered in a shout.

Even then, Vadomar hoped to retrieve the situation. To run now meant a foot race with this warrior, and at least two others looking in his direction. 'Piss off and stop annoying me,' he snarled.

'Know how I'm certain it's not yours?' Bandy Legs was twisting around, talking to anyone who'd heard his challenge. 'Because of the notches in the rim. My friend had a shield like that. Funny thing is, he was taken prisoner—'

Vadomar hurled the shield. He was lucky; it hit Bandy Legs in the face, edge-on. He went down like an ox hit by a butcher's hammer, and Vadomar took off, running as if every demon of the underworld was in pursuit.

Angry cries filled the air. 'Spy!' 'Thief!' 'After him!' Feet pounded. Ice chips flew as a hastily thrown spear thwacked into the hard-packed snow to his right.

Vadomar didn't look back. Spear discarded, he ran as fast as he dared. Go too hard, and he risked slipping, which might be all the warriors chasing him needed.

Another spear hissed by. It struck the icy ground at an oblique angle, skittering away. He estimated he'd covered about a quarter of the distance. He was beyond the spear range of anyone at the tent line, but that didn't mean much if ten warriors were running after him. He risked a glance over his shoulder, and wished he hadn't. Six figures, four with spears.

Two had already thrown, he reasoned.

With that, one slowed. Back went his right arm, and he loosed.

Fighting nausea, Vadomar did the only thing he could think of: jink. To the right, three steps. To the left, four steps. Right again. Left again. All the while, his skin crawled, anticipating the spear. Used as he was to wearing armour, this was a new and terrifying experience. The steel point might lodge in his spine and paralyse his legs – he'd seen it often enough. Slipping between ribs to puncture his lungs was another possibility. He would soon be blowing pink froth if that happened.

The spear missed, passing within six inches of his right ear. It thumped into the ground in front. Slowing, Vadomar ripped it free. He might have need of it. A moment later, a fourth spear drove through the bottom edge of his cloak and caught. Unbalanced by its dragging presence, he staggered. Lips peeled back with effort, he managed to undo the large fibula at his neck. Freed, the heavy cloak and its attached spear dropped away. Vadomar had no time to rue the loss of the valuable pelt. Less encumbered, he increased his speed.

Two more spears, he thought.

At least ten-score paces separated him from the bridge. There were faces visible, watching the spectacle unfold. The soldiers would be suspicious of anyone running towards them, even if he was being pursued. It might be a trick, a ruse before the start of an attack.

'Do not shoot! I am a Roman soldier!' Vadomar shouted in Gothic, and then Latin.

No response, just another spear from behind. This one came in over his head, another near-miss. Vadomar began to jink again, shouting once more that he was a Roman soldier. If they heard, the sentries at the bridge ignored him. The shape of a *carroballista*, a portable catapult, appeared atop the fortifications. An instant later came the familiar *clank, clank* of a ratchet.

Vadomar wanted to vomit. The catapult's bolts were as thick as a finger and the length of a man's forearm, and could punch through a shield and into its wielder. He had no shield, no armour. Again he roared, 'Do not shoot! I am a Roman soldier! A servant of the empire!'

Thunk went the horsehair strings.

Vadomar had never before imagined being slain by his own. Then the bolt shot past, so quick he only heard it. Shock flooded his veins. It hadn't been aimed at him.

It hadn't been aimed at him!

New strength flowed into his legs; he put down his head and sprinted.

Another *twang*, and a third. Two catapults were shooting, maybe three.

If the last warrior threw his spear, he missed. Vadomar neared the bridge and was relieved to be beckoned forward. Swiftly he negotiated his way down into the newly dug ditch spanning the road. Its bottom was laced with hundreds of tribuli. Gingerly placing his feet, he clambered up the slope to the bottom of the rampart.

'I am a soldier of the empire,' he said again in Gothic, then Latin.

'So you claim. What in God's name are you doing on the barbarians' side of the river?' The speaker was an officer in a richly decorated metal-crested helm, and the point of the spear he was holding was aimed at Vadomar's face.

'I was sent by Stilicho from Italia. Your commander, Saturninus, knows me.'

'You're the one they rowed over last night?'

'The same.' Vadomar took a look whence he'd come. The warriors had given up their pursuit, unwilling to come within range of the carroballistae.

'We weren't expecting you here.'

'My plans changed,' said Vadomar. 'I saw enough.'

The officer sensed his meaning; his face darkened. 'I can imagine. Now, are you going to stay there all day, or climb over to the civilised side?'

CHAPTER IV

Roma; first day of Mensis Ianuarius, AD 407

It was mid morning, and Galla had slept in after the festivities of the night before. The party had not been large, not a party at all, unless three people constituted that. Two of Galla's friends had attended, Metella and Euphemia, both young widows with no family to spend the evening with. There had been lots of talk and laughter, an exchange of simple presents of honey and dates. Give something sweet at the beginning of the year, so the tradition went, and every day following would be equally sweet. It was nonsense to expect such a thing, Galla had known for a long time, but she liked the sentiment. She had felt a twinge of guilt, whispered that the custom was pagan, but as one of her friends retorted, Christian priests did it, so surely God did not disapprove.

Thoughts of God brought her back to her daily ritual. She kneeled by her bed and closed her eyes. She prayed for Eucherius and his parents, Stilicho and Serena. She prayed to see more of Eucherius, that their betrothal might become reality. Although Galla bore him little love, she prayed next for her half-brother, the emperor Honorius. She asked for him to rule with strength and wisdom, protecting the realm from its enemies. She prayed that the borders of the empire stayed secure. Rumours had reached the city from Germania Prima of an immense horde of barbarians camped on the eastern bank of the Rhenus. Galla prayed Honorius would take guidance from men such as Stilicho, rather than the nay-saying, barbarian-hating nobles of the Senate, and the narrow-minded courtiers at Ravenna who sought only to feather their own nests.

She also asked to be kept safe from Honorius. From an uncertain start in Constantinopolis, they had grown to become friends, but puberty had changed him. More than once, his lewd comments and inappropriate touching had sent her running to the safety of Elpidia's arms. When he had moved to live at Ravenna some years prior, Galla remained in Roma. Remembering the distance to his palace on the east coast of Italia – more than two hundred miles – she calmed. He was to visit the capital soon, it was true, but God watched over her. She would avoid her half-brother at all costs.

She prayed for Elpidia. Galla's parents had died before she was six, allowing her nurse to take the place of both. Solid, reassuring, a font of advice and not shy of reproval, Elpidia was dearly beloved. Slave or not, she was the foundation of Galla's existence, her guide through life.

May she stay healthy and of sound mind.

May she come to no harm, from any quarter.

May she continue to help me choose a path through life.

Prayers for her friends, then the members of her household followed. Reflecting her reduced circumstances, the latter was a short list. The Aethiopian major domus, Darme. The arthritic house slave, Fritigern. Iovina and the other girl who worked in the kitchen, whose name continually escaped Galla. Even though priests said animals did not have souls, she included Felicula, whom she adored. If it was sinful to pray for a cat, she decided, let God punish her in heaven.

Lastly, she prayed for herself. For Eucherius to visit her again, for them to marry and have a brood of healthy children. For their son to become Honorius' heir, which might lead to Eucherius and Galla becoming emperor and empress respectively. She prayed hard for that outcome, even as Arcadius' caustic remark lingered in her mind.

A loud hammering came from the *atrium*. Someone was at the front door, thought Galla with a start, and wanted to be heard. She checked her hair in her silver mirror. It would be unseemly to hurry out and see who was outside, but as mistress of the household, she wanted to. Visitors were scarce. She stood ready to open her bedroom door.

Another set of loud bangs.

She heard Fritigern shuffling and muttering curses, and smiled.

'Hurry up!' Darme, the most important slave, regarded opening the door as beneath his dignity.

Fritigern was less than impressed. 'I'm going as fast as I can!'

Hinges creaked. Fritigern spoke. A deep voice answered. The slave responded with unusual alacrity. 'Darme!'

The major domus was there in an instant. He uttered something welcoming. Footsteps, several pairs, rang out. The portal closed with a heavy bang, and bolts shot home.

Knowing Darme was on his way, Galla retreated, sat by her table again.

A gentle knock. 'Nobilissima Femina? You have a visitor.'

'Enter.'

Darme obeyed, bowing.

Galla laid down the mirror with an appearance of surprise. 'Who is it?'

'The magister militum, Nobilissima Femina.'

Astonished, she nearly asked was he sure, but Darme had seen Stilicho many times. 'Take him to the office. Offer wine and food, and say I will be there at once.'

'Nobilissima Femina.' Darme slipped back into the corridor.

Galla looked at herself in the mirror, her mind racing, wondering why Stilicho had come. Maybe God had answered her prayer immediately. Perhaps he was here to talk again of Eucherius, and marriage. She could not imagine why else the most powerful man in the empire would just call in. Joy fluttered in her heart.

Stilicho's two bodyguards, hulking men in polished scale armour, filled the space inside the front door. Fritigern and Elpidia tutted, but did their best not to stare. Galla pretended the soldiers didn't even exist. Nearing the office, one of the rooms that gave onto the atrium, she converted her confident stride, assumed for the bodyguards, to a graceful walk.

'Magister Stilicho, what a surprise!'

He rose and bowed. 'Nobilissima Femina.' His voice was gravelly.

'There's no need for ceremony. It wasn't so long ago you played hide-and-seek with me in your gardens.'

A big smile on the careworn face. 'I remember it well, Nobilissima Femina. It seems like yesterday. Look at you now, a woman grown, and beautiful.' He bowed again.

Galla's heart warmed. How was it he could be so pleasant, she wondered, while his wife Serena was a manipulative shrew? She knew this from long experience. After the death of her parents, five-year-old Galla had gone to live with Stilicho, Serena and Eucherius. Serena's early warmth towards her had soon diminished. Raising her – or rather, Galla corrected herself, having Elpidia and other slaves raise her – had been done with one purpose in mind: to marry her to Eucherius. Niece to Theodosius, wife to a general, Serena had known she would never take the throne herself. If Galla hadn't realised it as a child, she did now. Serena had succeeded in marrying her daughter, Maria, to the emperor. Having her son married to Honorius' half-sister would strengthen her position further. It made no sense, thought Galla, for the intended betrothal to have fallen by the wayside. Serena would not have made the weighty decision on her own; the final say would have been Stilicho's. Of humble origins, a half-barbarian, he also had huge social aspirations.

Her eyes went to his face, and she realised he was waiting for a response. 'You are kind,' she murmured. 'How is your lady wife?'

'Well. She sends her fondest wishes.'

'As I do to her,' Galla replied warmly, thinking, shrew. 'Would you care for wine?' Darme was already moving forward, silver cup and jug in hand. 'It is well watered down, just as you like it.'

'I will, thank you.' He waited until Galla had a cup, then raised his towards her. 'To your good health, Nobilissima Femina.'

'And to yours, Magister Militum. Long may you protect the empire.'

He liked that. He drank deep, and smacked his lips in appreciation. 'A good vintage.'

'I have Darme to thank. He has a discerning palate.'

Stilicho drank again, finishing the contents, and when Darme refilled his cup, he dipped his chin in acknowledgement.

'Are you hungry?' Galla asked.

'No, thank you.'

A short silence followed. Stilicho studied the stippled design around the rim of his silver cup. Darme could have been a statue.

Despite her nerves, Galla was no lover of tiptoeing around what needed to be said, and took the initiative. 'We have established you are not hungry. I also suspect you did not come here to compliment me, nor to comment on the quality of my wine.'

A raised eyebrow. 'You are forthright, Nobilissima Femina, for one so young.'

'I find it wastes time to act otherwise.'

A genuinely amused laugh.

She stared. Silence, Elpidia often said, was a powerful weapon.

'Your beauty cannot be denied, Nobilissima Femina, and your wine is excellent, but I cannot deny they were not my reasons for coming to your door today.'

It was Galla's turn to raise an eyebrow.

A glance towards the atrium, where his bodyguards stood. Voice lowered, Stilicho said, 'I think it is true to say you are fond of Eucherius. Am I correct?'

Galla's heart leaped, but she imagined Elpidia warning her to be cautious. 'Why do you ask?'

'He cares for you, Nobilissima Femina.'

Galla did not look at him, furious with her cheeks' traitorous colour. Anger, for the wasted years – she had been old enough to wed since her thirteenth birthday – surfaced. 'If he does, why then have I not seen him this year and more?'

She fixed a stony gaze on Stilicho, who had the grace to colour a little himself. Behind him, she noticed Darme's supportive glare, which felt good. He had served the family for decades, and cared deeply for her.

Galla took a different tack. 'It is such a pity Maria is barren.' After several years of marriage, it was common knowledge. She had never been pregnant.

Silence followed the statement.

Galla imagined a world in which she had married Eucherius. With Honorius and Maria childless, their son would have been next in line to the throne. Her eyes went to Stilicho.

Rather than rebuke her, he seemed sad. 'Maria is not well, Nobilissima Femina.'

'I am sorry,' said Galla, feeling remorseful.

'She has been ill for a month.'

'What do the surgeons say?'

'You know how it is. One says this, another says that. The third disagrees with both.' A sigh.

'Is it serious?'

'They are agreed on her condition at least.'

A little to-and-fro followed, about her symptoms, treatment and outlook. Stilicho seemed relieved to talk about it.

Galla felt genuine sympathy. Maria didn't have much between her ears, but she was a sweet thing, without a bad word to say of others. She couldn't help but feel a little pleasure, though. Maria's illness might be of advantage to her. Stilicho's visit made more sense now, but before giving anything away, she needed to test the waters. 'I am surprised you come talking of marriage. You have another daughter.'

'Thermantia is but a child, Nobilissima Femina! Honorius . . .' Stilicho's face worked.

Galla kept her own expression impassive. Maria must have told Serena something, she decided. There could be no other explanation for Stilicho's reaction, but to admit she knew of Honorius' depravities might result in some uncomfortable questions. Her half-brother's unwanted attentions were not something Galla wanted anyone to know about, so she pretended not to have noticed Stilicho's reaction.

'It is true, Thermantia is very young. I am not, however,' said Galla, thinking Elpidia would be proud of her scorpion-sting comment.

In turn, Stilicho acted as if he hadn't heard. 'It is in my mind, and Serena's, Nobilissima Femina, that a marriage between you and Eucherius would be not just welcome, but a joyous occasion.' A broad smile revealed that he expected full and immediate assent.

Galla's spirits soared. She wanted to agree, yet she held back, did not reciprocate his smile. She wondered what Elpidia would advise. The answer was instant. Be hard. Speak the truth, what gossipmongers say each and every day. 'It would benefit your family, clearly, to have not only a daughter married to the emperor, but a son wedded to his sister, a sister who could provide an heir.'

'That is impertinent!'

His force made Galla inwardly quail. More than twice her age, he was a battle-hardened general, and had also been her father figure. It was a pivotal moment, she knew it. Thinking of Elpidia, she marshalled her courage. 'How dare you speak to me so!'

A glower, quickly concealed. 'My apologies, Nobilissima Femina.'

Galla gave no indication of her delight. She let silence rule. Let him speak again first, she thought. Control, influence the conversation as much as possible.

'Will you at least consider the offer, Nobilissima Femina?'

She let the question hang. Listened to the low murmur of Fritigern complaining about something to Darme, the cries of a cart-pushing vegetable seller on the street outside.

Elpidia appeared in the doorway.

Galla would have ignored her, but reading the words 'I need to tell you something' on her lips, said to Stilicho, 'Your pardon, Magister Militum.' Ignoring his disapproving frown, she beckoned. 'What is it?'

Elpidia bowed, and when she was close enough, whispered, 'His bodyguards are worried. A messenger came in late yesterday evening with fresh news from Germania Prima. The host of barbarians seems set to cross the Rhenus – and has probably done so already. The garrisons along the river have no chance of stopping it.' Their eyes met, and Elpidia continued, 'Stilicho's position is weakening. He may need you more than you do him.'

'Very well.' Galla waved a dismissive hand, and playing her part, Elpidia bowed for a second time and left.

Stilicho's smile was a little laboured this time. 'Again I ask, Nobilissima Femina, if you will marry Eucherius.'

'Is there aught else you would tell me first?'

'I do not understand, Nobilissima Femina.'

Quietly, Galla said, 'I find it interesting how you come seeking my hand for Eucherius *now*.'

'Now, Nobilissima Femina?'

'A few days after the barbarian hordes invaded Germania Prima. It's probable they are already many miles inside the empire. Only God knows where they will stop. All of Gallia, Viennensis, even Hispania might be at risk.'

His gaze went after Elpidia; realising she must have heard his men talking, his expression darkened.

Galla kept on the offensive. 'Is it true?'

A sigh. 'Yes, Nobilissima Femina. In order to defeat Radagaisus and the rest, I had to deplete the Rhenus garrisons. The soldiers who remain cannot defeat one hundred thousand warriors.'

'How do you propose to stop them then?' Galla felt the ground beneath her shift. She knew nothing of armies and war.

He read her uncertainty. 'That is not your concern, Nobilissima Femina. I have several ideas of how to respond, and they are in train. Roma will prevail.' He managed to sound reassuring, confident and patronising in one sentence.

They stared at one another, and it was Galla who looked away first.

'If you do not marry Eucherius, you risk never finding a husband, Nobilissima Femina. In the absence of your parents, it is Honorius who should seek one for you, and he shows no interest in doing so.'

Stilicho was right, thought Galla, and she loved Eucherius. She wanted to be his wife. Nor was the world about to end. Despite the new barbarian threat, and the rumours of usurpers in Britannia, Stilicho remained the most powerful military leader in the empire, and his track record was impressive. She firmed her chin. 'I accept your offer. I will write to the emperor asking permission for the match.'

'As will I. He will not say no to both of us, surely!' Stilicho was all expansiveness and geniality now, like a man with a load taken from his shoulders. He gestured at Darme, who poured more wine. 'A toast to your betrothal, Nobilissima Femina.'

'Proposed betrothal,' Galla corrected. As they drank, she prayed that this time it would come true.

CHAPTER V

Diocese of Viennensis; Mensis Martius, AD *407*

It was a warm spring day, and birds were singing in the tree-girt deep river valley. Vadomar, Dog and Eriulf rode at the front of a small column travelling along the Via Agrippa, a road that had seen better days. Mileposts were rare; those surviving were damaged or the inscribed writing moss- and lichen-covered. Grass and blue-flowered speedwell grew between the worn-down paving stones. Snaking tree roots underneath meant that in places the surface was wildly uneven. The road's edges were crumbling, and the potholes . . . well, the trio had a daily competition running over who spotted the largest one.

Eriulf had won the previous day with a crater that would have fitted a hay cart, oxen and all. Dog had immediately claimed to have seen one that could have taken one of the great cargo ships that carried grain from Africa to Roma. The ensuing argument – Eriulf and Vadomar ridiculing, Dog protesting and cursing them both for not believing his story – had lasted for a couple of hours, and taken their minds from the journey.

This morning, though, there was little conversation beyond the necessary. Valentia was miles behind them, and it was still a long way to Lugdunum, their destination. The dioceses of Viennensis and Gallia were largely independent, but like Roma, they were powerless to put down major unrest or prevent barbarian incursions. Peasant rebels, *bacaudae*, also roamed freely through the countryside. Ambush by these had been a constant threat since crossing the Alpes. An encounter with them was potentially disastrous, because they moved about in bands of up to a thousand or more.

Should they meet any, therefore, Vadomar and his forty comrades planned to retreat. Their mission, ordered by Stilicho himself, was all-important. Find the usurper Constantinus, who had been a humble soldier in Britannia, and determine his long-term intent. Since his recent – and fortuitous to Stilicho – defeat of the Rhenus-crossing barbarians, he ruled more or less supreme in Gallia and Viennensis. Hispania seemed a possible place to attack next; and most significantly, so did Italia, the centre of imperial power.

It was Dog who first bored of endless study of their surroundings. 'Seems to me Stilicho has it arse-about-face. He should be concentrating on sorting out shit here, not Illyricum, which belongs to Arcadius! Why isn't he gathering an army to invade Viennensis and Gallia?'

Vadomar and Eriulf growled agreement.

They all knew the answer, though. Stilicho's Achilles heel was his long-held ambition to invade the province of Illyricum, either to annex it or to force the eastern emperor, Arcadius, to recognise his leadership. To this end, he had been massing soldiers at Aquileia and Ravenna for months. Alaric, now his ally, was in nearby Epirus with his army, ready to lend assistance.

It was, thought Vadomar dourly, as if Stilicho was unaware of the usurper Constantinus' recent crossing from Britannia with most of the island's imperial garrison. Unaware of how, weary of the marauding bacaudae, the populations of Viennensis and Gallia welcomed Constantinus with open arms. Vadomar checked no one behind could hear, then said, 'I would follow Stilicho to the underworld, but his aspirations to the purple have completely turned his head. He has lost all sense of priority.'

'Aye. When you have foes at your back, why pick a fight with someone else?' grumbled Eriulf.

'Especially when the someone else is your own emperor's brother,' replied Vadomar with a shake of his head. Honorius and

Arcadius were full-blooded siblings. They were not that close, but there was no great enmity between them. Although Honorius had not yet ordered Stilicho to give up on his plan, it seemed improbable he would approve of a large-scale campaign against his brother, who had promised military aid.

Dog read his mind. 'It wasn't long ago that Arcadius agreed to send soldiers west, to bolster our forces. Has Stilicho forgotten that?'

'It seems so. If the rumours that Serena also disagrees with his plan to annex Illyricum are true, he's paying no heed to her either,' said Vadomar. 'Foolish the man who doesn't listen to his wife.'

'Meanwhile, Britannia is lost to the empire, probably never to be taken back.' Waving his arm to encompass the Rhodanus valley, Eriulf said, 'And Viennensis and Gallia are following hot on its heels.'

'Even if Constantinus decides to take Hispania next, it will only be a matter of time before he invades Italia.' Dog spat into the long grass at the roadside.

'Only a matter of time before more tribes cross the Rhenus too.' Eriulf was uncharacteristically gloomy.

On and on he and Dog went, predicting the movement into Italia of fresh barbarian hordes, the sacking of Roma and Ravenna, the deposition and murder of Honorius and the eventual fall of the entire western empire.

Vadomar could take no more. 'Will the pair of you stop?'

Startled looks.

'If bacaudae attack us, will you give in without a fight?' he demanded.

'No!' 'Of course not.' Indignant answers, both.

'Do you think our comrades behind us will?'

More denials.

'Well then! Most of the army is like us!' said Vadomar. 'We're not yellow-livered, soft-handed Romans, used to nothing worse than spanking a child or beating a lazy slave. Is that what *you* are?' He grinned at their snarled protests. 'We are Visigoths! Visigoths, and we have the beating of anyone on a good day!'

Dog howled. Eriulf began singing the barritus.

Vadomar joined in, shoving away the nagging doubt that one day they would find themselves on a battlefield with no prospect except a valiant death. He did not greatly fear such an end. If it came, he would not shy away, but face it like a man, shoulder to shoulder with his friends and comrades. He had tasted enough of life, however, to know there was more to it than a glorious battle-death. He wanted a wife. Children. A farm to work into his old age. A warm hearth to sit by on winter nights while ghosts howled down the wind. Grandchildren, perhaps.

A wry smile twisted his lips. Before children, he needed to find a woman, and there wasn't much chance of that when he never spent more than a few nights in any one place. His eyes roaming from left to right, on the lookout for trouble, he let himself imagine meeting a woman the sight of whom took his breath away, imagined courting her, wedding her. Bedding her. It was a pleasant fantasy, and helped to pass the time.

'We need to water the horses. Here will do.' Dog pointed. They had reached a turn, and a rare undamaged milestone. Some distance to the left through the oaks and beeches lining the road the remains of a bridge could be made out.

Vadomar peered at the still legible inscription on the milestone. As the rest of the troop clattered by, he slipped down from his horse.

'What does it say?' asked Eriulf, reining in.

The cursive text tested Vadomar's Latin. The first two lines read *IMP. CAESAR L. DOMIT. AURELIANU. P. F.* Slowly, he said, 'The Imperator Caesar Lucius Domitius Aurelianus, pious and fortunate.'

'Never heard of him.' Dog had also stopped.

'Well, you should have,' retorted Eriulf.

'Eh?' Dog cocked his head. 'Since when have you been interested in take-it-all long-dead emperors?'

'Aurelianus' money is still used. You will have seen examples,' said Eriulf. '"Concordia militum", the writing says, the concord of the soldiers. The legions must have loved him.'

Dog snorted. 'I don't care what's written on coins. What matters is how pure the silver is, and how much wine I can buy.'

'According to Stilicho, Aurelianus was a fine military leader. He saved the empire from total collapse.' Vadomar went back to the inscription. 'Invincible, august, high priest, greatest conqueror of the Germans, Goths—'

'Much good it did him!' cried Dog.

It did feel ironic, thought Vadomar. 'He also conquered the Carpi, not sure where they lived, and the Parthians, they're in the east. He was reinvested with the powers of a tribune seven times, a consul ten times, and he was the father of his country. Proconsul also, he was the restorer of universal peace.'

'Peace, my sweaty ball sack!' said Dog. 'Look at the state of the empire.'

'He's got a point,' said Eriulf.

'It was more than a century ago, you fools,' said Vadomar, admiring Aurelianus' achievements, but aware that, as Visigoths, he and his kind would have been among those on the losing side, not the victorious.

'Enough history,' said Dog. 'My horse needs a drink. So do I.'

Vadomar checked the road was clear to the north and south, and nodded at the four men who had stayed back to keep watch. Declaring that the first to finish watering their mounts would come and replace them, he followed his friends to the river.

While a younger warrior took his horse, Vadomar went to look at the narrow bridge. Most of it was in decent enough repair; only a section in the middle had collapsed. Chopped oak trunks had been laid across the gap, allowing people on foot to cross, but the spaces between the timbers would be lethal for a horse. An image of bacaudae attacking, forcing them up against the river, popped into Vadomar's mind, and he imagined having to lead his mount over the precarious arrangement, all the while being harried by volleys of arrows and charging rebels. He shoved away the dark thought, and ordered four riders to relieve the men watching the road.

The grass was long, and still dew-covered, so the men congregated in the sunshine by the bridge's end. There was good-natured banter, sharing of wineskins, the usual camaraderie of men long used to living and fighting together. Vadomar found Eriulf crouched on his haunches, chewing on a piece of bucellatum. Dog was whetting his knife, a frequent habit.

The pair were arguing over the attributes of a comely whore they had both lain with in Valentia. It was not the first time, and Vadomar rolled his eyes. Thanking the warrior who had brought his horse back up from the water's edge, he rooted around in the leather bag tied behind his saddle. He left the cheese, opting for bucellatum only. It was hard, and not especially tasty, but it filled the stomach.

He leaned against the stonework, chewing, content. Invisible skylarks sang in the clear sky above. Bees hummed, moving over the early wild flowers growing between the paving stones and at the road's edge. A red squirrel danced along the branch of a nearby beech tree. It was so peaceful, thought Vadomar, a wonderful location. If there was enough ground for a little farm, a man might put down roots in a place like this.

'What kind of reception d'you think Constantinus will give us?' asked Eriulf.

Reality crashed home. 'I don't know,' said Vadomar, telling the truth. 'We are official messengers from Stilicho, so he won't execute us. Hopefully.'

'Listen to the man!' cackled Dog. 'Hopefully?'

'Eriulf asked my opinion. I told him. Scared?'

'Piss off!'

Vadomar chuckled. 'I never tire of getting a rise out of you. It's so easy.'

Dog's retaliation was swift. 'What about you, checking your kit? Belt buckled. Knife sitting so. Sword hanging just right. Armour not rucked up too much above the belt. Helmet fitted correctly, strap fastened. Belt buckle again. Knife. Sword.'

The last of Vadomar's bucellatum flew, hitting Dog in the face. He roared in surprise rather than anger and lobbed it back, but Vadomar ducked and the biscuit went over him, falling into the river.

'Waste of good food,' said Eriulf. 'I would have had that.'

'You eat too much already,' Dog jibed.

'And you drink too much.'

'Not possible.'

They all laughed.

A piercing whistle cut the air.

Everyone's attention went to the junction with the Via Agrippa. One of the four sentries was urgently waving. Another was galloping towards the bridge.

'The fun's over,' cried Vadomar. 'Helmets! Onto your horses!'

Everyone was in the saddle by the time the sentry arrived.

'Tell me,' ordered Vadomar, hoping for the best, expecting the worst.

'Three men, riding for their lives, and behind, a large group of horsemen.'

'How many?'

'Fifty. More. It's hard to say.'

'Bacaudae,' said Dog. 'Has to be.'

'Chasing who, though?' asked Eriulf.

Vadomar considered hiding among the trees, to let the hunt reach its own conclusion. He decided against this approach, in part because if bacaudae were in pursuit, more would come after. They always did, and emerging onto the road, he and his comrades might be caught between two groups of bandits. It was far too risky to try crossing the patched-up bridge, and he had no idea if there was a road north on the other side either. One reasonable option remained.

Vadomar issued orders to move out along the road, and to halt a short distance before the junction. They would bunch up, narrow-fronted and deep, close to the trees on their right, which would afford concealment until the last moment.

'Bacaudae chasing, but who's fleeing?' asked Eriulf.

'Some random unfortunates,' said Dog.

'We'll give the rebels the shock of their miserable lives,' said Vadomar.

'What if it's the other way around? Some of Constantinus' cavalry, maybe, pursuing bandits?' This was Eriulf.

'Then we don't interfere. If we happen upon them down the road later, I will make formal overtures, say we come from Stilicho. They won't harm an embassy, all being well.'

'At the least, we will get to see Constantinus' camp before they torture us to death,' Dog observed drily.

'Exactly,' said Vadomar.

A familiar calm settled over the group. They had been here innumerable times. Nearing the road, the front riders halted, forming a line five wide. The rest copied the move. Vadomar cut his horse out and went to the front, Dog and Eriulf following. He could hear hooves on the road, and yipping war cries.

One of the sentries who'd stayed put came to report. 'They're close now. The three in front look like Roman cavalry. The riders behind are a complete rabble.'

'Bacaudae,' said Eriulf with a fearful scowl.

'Chasing some of Constantinus' men. If we come to their aid, it might serve us well.' Vadomar ordered the sentries to follow his lead, and gave the instruction to ready spears. Quickly he ran over his kit in a mental list. Checked that his belt sat just so. Gripped sword hilt and dagger. Prepared to bring his own spear down to face forward.

More whoops and jeers, the words inaudible above thunderous hoofbeats.

'Ready?' cried Vadomar, confident that no one on the road could hear.

His men bayed their eagerness. A youngish horse, one with less experience, skittered to the side, out of formation. Eriulf barked a rebuke; the rider managed to bring it under control.

The spring foliage on the beeches and oaks was dense; Vadomar had no sight of the horsemen charging in from their right. He listened, trying to gauge how close they were, his eyes always on the road straight in front.

His wait wasn't long. One moment there was nothing to see; the next, two, then three riders were in sight. Vadomar noted their ridged helmets and scale mail. They *were* Roman cavalrymen. Bent low over their galloping horses' necks, with an occasional fearful glance over their shoulders, they were also in desperate straits. None noticed Vadomar and his group.

The first of the bacaudae appeared, wild men with spears on shaggy ponies, half a dozen of them. They weren't looking anywhere but at their quarry. Vadomar raised his spear and waited. It was still too soon. A mob of horsemen materialised, riding close together, shouting, brandishing spears and bows. This was the main body of bacaudae.

'Now!' Vadomar squeezed with his knees, and his horse went from standing start to the gallop in two paces. He came out onto the road like a streak of lightning, spear shaft tight in his armpit, his target already picked. The group smashed into the unsuspecting bacaudae, snapping apart their formation like kindling. Vadomar left his spear in a skewered, dying bandit, and drew his sword. He slashed a man's shoulder; his victim fell screaming to the road and was trampled amid the maelstrom of hooves. Feeling no remorse, for the mob of bacaudae were swarming after just three men, Vadomar stabbed another ruffian in the back and rode on.

The battle, such as it was, did not last long.

Complete panic had taken the bandits, which had been his great hope. Men who are terrified act like hens with a fox in the coop, flapping, insensible, directionless. Convinced they were being attacked by a much larger force and outclassed by professional soldiers, the bacaudae screamed. Bled. Fell from their horses. Died. Those who could overtook the three cavalrymen. Others dismounted and ran off into the trees. A few tried to fight. They were soon cut down.

Perhaps unsurprisingly, the men who'd been pursued did not stop to see who had attacked their attackers. It took Vadomar more than a mile of galloping at full tilt to get near enough to shout in Latin that he was not an enemy, that they could halt. Even then, he sensed they might have paid no heed, but the fact that he was on his own, with no one behind him, seemed to change their minds.

There was time to wonder if he'd been foolish when the three riders drew to a sawing halt, wheeled as one and came at him with levelled spears.

'HOLD! I am also a Roman soldier!' he cried, his flesh crawling with the anticipation of sharp steel.

They were scared, the cavalrymen, and their faces were perspiration-slicked. Their horses were in worse shape, nostrils flared, the corners of their mouths foam-flecked, sides dark with sweat. But they stood steady enough, and the spear tips aimed at Vadomar did not waver.

'I do not recognise your shield design. What unit are you with?' demanded one, a man with flushed features and red hair.

'I serve Magister Militum Stilicho.'

'Stilicho?' An exchange of surprised, not entirely friendly looks. 'You are not with Constantinus' army?'

Quickly, Vadomar explained. 'So you see,' he finished, 'it is to all of our good fortune that we met.'

'We owe you our lives, it is plain, and you have our heartfelt thanks,' said the ruddy-faced man, his companions echoing his gratitude. 'But I cannot vouch for the emperor.'

'Our embassy was sent by Stilicho in peace, with every good will,' Vadomar explained again.

'You and I know those are empty words. If Stilicho had Constantinus under his blade, I wager he would act but one way.'

'But he does not, nor will he have the opportunity to,' said Vadomar, 'and in such cases, potential enemies can deal with one another in civilised fashion.'

CHAPTER VI

Roma

Galla, who was aware of the dangerous situation in Viennensis but not of recent developments, perched on a stool in her bedroom. Elpidia, standing behind, fussed over her hair.

'I should have left,' Galla muttered.

Elpidia took a silver hairpin from her mouth. 'What's that? I didn't hear.'

'I said I ought to have left Roma, not been here when Honorius arrived.'

'You could still go to the latifundium. There's nothing stopping you.' Honorius was due to arrive within the next few days.

Galla thought about it. She rarely went to her small estate some way to the south, but it was pleasant if she needed respite from the city, or, as in this case, to avoid her half-brother. She had stayed there during Honorius' previous visit, when he had celebrated a triumph. I was but a girl then, she thought, remembering her intense fear. I was a woman, but barely so. I am nineteen now.

'I do not need to run and hide just because the lecher is coming to Roma,' she said.

'If you are in the city, he will expect you to watch his *adventus*.' This grand ceremony would be attended by vast numbers of the populace, greeting the emperor upon his entrance into the old capital. 'Don't be surprised if he wants to meet you privately as well.'

Galla firmed her chin. 'I won't be.'

Elpidia took a step to the side so she could look down at her. 'Are you able for it?'

Instantly their roles were reversed. Galla felt as if she were the daughter and Elpidia her mother, but she knew her old nurse had her well-being, her safety in mind. It was fortunate there was no one present to make judgement on a relationship that would be deemed deeply inappropriate.

She met Elpidia's gaze. 'I am.'

'You must not be alone with him.'

'I agree.'

Satisfied, Elpidia again took up position behind Galla, and like that, their usual roles resumed. Elpidia fussed and primped, Galla held up a silver mirror so she could comment.

Galla was pleased by her new-found determination, and also excited to witness the magnificent spectacle of the adventus. Some of her most vivid memories were of a similar procession she had taken part in as a child of five, on the occasion of Honorius' coronation at Constantinopolis by their father, the emperor Theodosius. Vaguely aware of Elpidia's fingers inserting hairpins, making the finishing touches, she fondly remembered the eastern imperial palace with its immense rooms, mosaic ceilings and marble floors, and outside its gilded bronze doors, green forested slopes spilling down to the sparkling blue sea.

That day had been about Honorius, however, and the procession from the palace out of the city. Galla and Arcadius had been clad in the same golden garments as Honorius. She had loved her filigreed gold headdress, the like of which she did not now possess. Standing all three together in an ornate parade chariot, they had travelled through the packed streets of the eastern capital, her ears ringing with the people's cheers and acclaim.

She had loved the feeling of euphoria, could feel it still. Despite her half-brother's cruel words, she wanted to be empress one day. I have every right, she thought. How it could be achieved was another thing. Her mind circled back to Eucherius. Since Stilicho's visit early in the new year, and their talk of betrothal, she had been hoping for a response from Honorius to her letter. For an invitation to dine at Stilicho's house, where a formal proposal of marriage would be made.

No letter blessing the union had come from Ravenna. Given the poor relationship Galla had with Honorius, it was perhaps unsurprising. There had been no communication from Stilicho either. No invitation. Nothing at all. While Serena's silence was possibly due to recent illness, and his due to the barbarians and usurpers in Gallia, and his reported obsession with annexing the province of Illyricum, it was hard not to be disheartened. Galla wondered if she could bring herself to ask her half-brother in person.

As was her habit, Elpidia read her mind. 'You could entreat Honorius to intercede on your behalf with Stilicho and Serena. They cannot refuse the Imperator.'

Stilicho was currently in Ravenna, supervising the repair of its defences, but a letter from the emperor could still be sent to him there, thought Galla. It was tempting, but then old, dark memories stirred. 'Can you imagine what Honorius might want in return?'

Elpidia made a face. 'If you are never with him in private, he cannot harm you.'

'Suppose he orders me to attend him in his rooms?'

Rage twisted Elpidia's face. 'I would—'

'We both know what would happen if you laid a hand on the Imperator,' said Galla gently. 'I will not have you throw away your life.'

'And I will not let that monster ravish you!' Despite the privacy of Galla's bedroom, despite the small number of loyal house slaves, Elpidia whispered.

'It will not go that far.' Galla did not feel as confident as she sounded. Yet, she decided, if there was one good thing to come of Honorius' impending visit, it would be Stilicho and Serena's agreement to her marrying Eucherius. The risk of achieving that made appealing to the emperor worth it.

Feeling no guilt, Galla prayed for Maria to remain childless so that her and Eucherius' son might sit upon the imperial throne one day. It was not sinning to wish for this outcome, she decided, because any children she was blessed with would be brought up in the bosom of the Church, serving God with faith and devotion.

*

The morning of the adventus dawned clear and sunny, auguring well for Honorius' arrival. Galla longed to witness the procession approach the city gates; she had even suggested to Elpidia that the pair of them, in hooded cloaks, make their way beyond the walls. Incognito amid the masses, and close up, they could admire the massed ranks of marching legionaries in polished armour, the proud-faced cavalrymen on their high-stepping mounts, and the *candidati*, the emperor's hand-picked bodyguard, resplendent in red tunics and purple cloaks. It would be an incredible sight, she said. Honorius would never notice them.

Elpidia's acerbic retort was that two unaccompanied women, one young and attractive, would draw unwanted attention nonetheless. 'You do not know the streets. Men who do not recognise you as a nobilissima femina are different creatures altogether to the ones you encounter.'

Galla, half expecting this response, regretfully gave up on the idea. She busied herself instead with selecting the dress and jewellery to wear for the high points of the adventus. These would be Honorius' arrival in the Forum Romanum, his speech inside the Curia – the Senate House – and the end of his journey, an entrance into the Circus Maximus. Gladiator fights and beast hunts were to take place, as well as her favourite sport, chariot racing. Galla wanted to gauge her brother's current popularity by the audience's reaction, but she also had a sizeable sum wagered on a Blue team in the first race.

They reached the Curia in good time, Darme's frequent loud announcements – 'Make way for the nobilissima femina!' – and commanding manner clearing a path through the dense crowds. The Aethiopian was in his element, head carried arrogantly high, staff held up in potential threat. Every now and again, however, his step faltered. He was growing old, Galla thought sadly. Thinking of what Elpidia had said, she whispered that employing a bodyguard might be a good idea and got back a firm nod of agreement.

Darme stalked to an ideal spot on the top step, a little to one side of the Curia's great bronze-gilded doors. A magical space cleared around Galla and the two slaves, no one crass enough to intrude by standing too close. Deferential nods and bows were offered if she caught anyone's eye. A slave hurried inside and soon returned, telling Darme that the nobilissima femina would be welcome when the emperor was to make his speech. Galla was pleased. She was held in enough esteem to allow the rule prohibiting women from entering the Curia to be ignored.

Her attention returned to the Forum Romanum. Four great arches commemorated the empire's military triumphs, under Titus, Septimius Severus, Constantinus the Great and her half-brother Honorius, this last a recent addition. The numerous colonnaded temples to the old gods – the most venerable to Castor and Pollux, the newest to the emperor Maxentius' son Romulus – were no longer used, at least publicly, yet their grandeur remained. The *basilicae*, home to lawyers, scribes and moneylenders, were as busy as ever. High above the crowds on plinths were statues of the greatest emperors, paintwork touched up for today's event, standing or sitting astride imperious, nostril-flaring horses.

The Rostra, from which public, electoral and legal announcements were made, was empty but for a couple of daring street urchins who had clambered up its front, unseen by the sentries positioned by the steps to its rear. They capered about, laughing and pointing at whoever caught their attention. Their irreverence made Galla smile.

Many senators were already inside the Curia, but it was the habit of more important ones, faction leaders or those from the oldest families, to arrive as close as possible to the start of proceedings. Galla had met some as a younger girl, although her quiet private life since meant she had had little to do with those who helped to run the imperial government. The courteous greetings and bows she received, therefore, were most welcome. As Elpidia whispered in her ear, she was not without power.

Daughter of an emperor, half-sister to the current ruler, Galla knew herself to be of the highest social rank. She had to be addressed as 'Nobilissima Femina' and bowed to. She could demand an audience with any noble or senator in the land, and they would listen to her, but whether they would act on it was another thing altogether.

The very nature of her power was ethereal, which was endlessly frustrating. She could not hold office, save as a Vestal Virgin. She could not issue a public decree or pass a law. She had no right to address the Senate. In reality, she had little power to do anything tangible. Everything she did had to be behind the scenes, negotiated, persuaded, cajoled. A man's life was much simpler. If he wanted something done, he did it, and if he was the emperor, his power was close to all-encompassing. Not for the first time, Galla wished to have been born male. It was a futile wish, and she set it aside. She imagined instead that Honorius would not only agree that she and Eucherius should wed, but would also refrain from unwanted physical advances towards her. Stilicho might be busy with Ravenna's defences and plans to annex Illyricum, but he would have to listen to the emperor, and Serena, recovered from illness, would do so too.

It was a long wait and there was no shade, making Galla grateful for the milder spring weather. If the adventus had been taking place later in the year, she would have been burned to a crisp. Elpidia, and later, Serena, had taught her how to approach such events. Eat little beforehand, to avoid feeling overfull, and ensure it was lighter food, olives or sheep's cheese. Hunger kept the mind sharp. Drink almost nothing, to remove the need to empty one's bladder. A straight spine and forward-facing chin prevented backaches. Galla kept her expression impassive, unless it was necessary to return a greeting.

The entire time, her mind turned over possibilities, noted things to remember. That senator had been friendly with her father. This one had a reputation for dalliances with young men of a certain persuasion. Another was loyal to Honorius, and therefore not to be trusted. Two older men who arrived together were long-standing allies, and led a large faction that held deep animosity towards non-Romans such as Stilicho.

'Do you hear it?' Elpidia whispered in her ear.

Galla listened. A swelling sound, made by thousands of people simultaneously giving voice, was coming from the far end of the forum. 'The procession must be drawing near.'

Elpidia shifted from foot to foot in a rare display of excitement.

Everyone loves a good procession, thought Galla. She did too, even if the person it was being held in honour of was her lecherous half-brother. It was impossible not to be stirred by the anticipation rippling through the crowd. Heads were craning, people were on tiptoe, trying to see. Street urchins in ragged clothing had clambered up every statue in sight to get a better view. One bold ragamuffin, a girl of perhaps ten, was perched in front of Constantinus the Great, himself seated upon a magnificent stallion. Under normal circumstances, the girl would have been pulled down by officials and given a hiding, but no one was telling her off. Instead, members of the crowd were encouraging her loud commentary about what she could see.

By the time the front of the procession entered the forum, the noise was deafening. People probably didn't even know why they were cheering, thought Galla, but humans were like sheep and followed what everyone else did. She was no different. Even though Honorius was a vile human being, it was easy to be caught up in the emotion of the moment. She was aware too that as the emperor's half-sister, *she* was worthy of such acclaim. As the imperial chariot came into sight, flanked by cavalrymen, she imagined herself in it, not a little child as she had been in Constantinopolis, but an empress, standing beside her husband, the emperor Eucherius. It felt wonderful. Her blood fizzed.

Something made her glance at Elpidia, who gave her the most knowing of looks. Passions stirred, Galla felt a flush rise to her cheeks. Then, confidence growing, she asked God for His assistance in persuading her half-brother to help. Honorius might do so out of filial love, she told herself, and he would not expect anything of her in return. She knew it for a fantasy, but if her prayer was answered, not a hopeless one.

The soldiers and cavalry, every bit as impressive as Galla had imagined, reached the front of the Curia, and continued around to the other side of the forum. The imperial chariot came to a halt, Honorius acknowledging the now hysterical applause of the crowd with languid waves of a hand. He dismounted, and bounded up the steps, clad in a tunic with purple stripes, tall, bearded, more handsome than Galla had remembered. To her annoyance, his good looks made it harder to hate him, to remember what he had tried to make her do.

To her relief, he did not notice her, eager as he was to enter the Curia and receive the senators' adulation. He went inside, and the slave from earlier approached, bowing deeply. Galla glanced at Elpidia, who gave her an encouraging nod. All would be well, she thought. She had decided to talk to Honorius at the Circus Maximus. With tens of thousands of people also present, he could not do a thing. He might try to engineer a meeting afterwards, say they needed to talk it over more, but she would cross that bridge when she came to it.

Galla made sure to be in the pulvinar before Honorius. It was customary for the emperor to arrive last, and she wanted to get off on a good footing. Time dragged, no doubt because in the Curia, politicians loved the sound of their own voices. Preoccupied, she watched the crowds, and in particular, the chariots making practice exits from the carceres, the rival drivers gesturing and engaging in ribaldry with each other.

A rhythmic pounding began, tens of thousands of pairs of sandalled feet thumping off stone. Through the thunder, voices chanted, repeating the same word over and over.

'IM-PE-RA-TOR!'

Galla moved forward for a better view. Honorius wasn't celebrating a triumph, the usual reason for taking a procession in from the street and all around the track, but nor was he going to miss a chance for more adulation. First came the sons of the greatest noble houses on horseback, chests puffed-out proud, followed on foot by the boys who would join the legions. There were chariots pulled by teams of two and four horses from the four factions – these received loud applause – jockeys and athletes who would provide entertainment in between races, and a group of purple-clad dancers, moving to the sound of flutes and lyres. A troupe of men dressed as satyrs, with long hair and shaggy goatskin trousers, came after, silent, watchful. Then slaves carrying incense-burning censers, decorative amphorae and statues of temple gods. Finally, in his magnificent chariot, Honorius, straight-backed, face turned towards the stands so everyone might admire him.

Galla felt none of the audience's reverence and adulation for her half-brother. She reined in her dislike. Intuit the slightest inkling of her real feelings, and Honorius would never grant her request, still less offer any help.

He vanished around the turning post, and the audience on the far side went wild. Full circuit completed, the emperor exited whence he had come, and the crowd settled again. In previous times, a sacrifice of bulls would have followed, but the Church disapproved of such bloody rituals. Julian had been the last ruler to allow the practice. All that remained before the chariot racing commenced was for Honorius to make his way up to the pulvinar, which would not take long.

Fighting her fear, Galla stared up at the sky and thought of the farm, the rows of vines and the rich smell of the ripe grapes. She imagined the harvest, her favourite period of the year, and the times she had watched the *vilicus*, a gruff but jovial type, order the slaves to wash their feet before treading the grapes, roaring that the master did not want to drink their toe cheese, now or ever. A giggle escaped her at the comedic memory.

'He is coming.' Elpidia was beside her. 'Be calm.' Quickly she returned to the back of the pulvinar.

Two *candidati* and an officer, resplendent in scale armour, appeared at the top of the staircase. The officer did not acknowledge Darme and Elpidia, but to Galla he gave a deep, respectful bow. 'Nobilissima Femina. I will tell the emperor you are here.'

Galla inclined her head, not trusting her voice.

The soldiers stood guard by the entrance to the stairs, while the officer vanished below. The subsequent wait was short, perhaps a hundred beats of Galla's racing heart, but it felt like a year. The officer re-emerged, immediately stepping to one side and bowing his head. His men did the same, and Honorius walked into the pulvinar. His gaze went first to the crowds on his left, who cheered and screamed, and then moved right, where Galla stood with Darme and Elpidia behind.

His lips curved upward. 'Sister!'

Galla bent her neck. 'Imperator.'

'Come, there's no need for such formality.' He was in front of her already, a slender finger lifting her chin so her eyes came up to meet his. 'How wonderful to see you! I left you a girl, and return to find you a full-grown woman.' His gaze travelled down her body.

Galla's skin crawled, but she kept her composure. 'You are right, brother. It is past time I had a husband.'

Curious, his attention came back to her face. 'One thing has not changed. You speak your mind, as ever.'

'That is best, or somebody will try to do it for me.' The words were tart, but Galla was powerless to stop them.

Rather than reply, Honorius glided away to the front of the pulvinar, which brought him into view of the masses below. An animal roar greeted him, and the shouts of 'Imperator!' grew even more rapid, like the beat of a Bacchanalian dancing tune. Again the imperial hand waved languidly, a part-turn of the wrist revealing Honorius' palm. The audience loved it. Women were screaming hysterically. Innumerable coloured ribbons of the four teams, red, white, blue, green, waved up and down.

For a moment, Galla forgot Eucherius. Forgot her designs on becoming empress. Jealousy consumed her that this depraved lecher, this opinionless puppet of Stilicho, who had never shown a particular talent for anything except sexual excess, should be acclaimed so. There but for the grace of God she would be. Although she would have to marry a suitable nobleman in order to achieve this rank, and he, the emperor, would have all the power, she, his empress wife, could pull the strings. And pull them she would.

It was as if Honorius sensed her disapproval. He turned towards her, smiling, still waving.

Galla beamed convincingly, and half bowed. 'The citizens of Roma are happy to see their emperor – as am I, dear brother.'

He was visibly pleased. 'Sister, I have missed you.'

'I feel the same way,' she replied, lying through her teeth, pretending not to notice the way he sized her up, in the manner of a butcher inspecting a carcass.

'Come sit with me.' Honorius tapped the soft, richly designed cushion beside him, a cousin to the one his rear end was parked upon.

'I will.' Galla's tone was light and playful.

The first race went by in a blur, a surprise win by a White charioteer. Like Galla, Honorius loved racing, but his attention strayed often, and not onto the spectators. She felt his gaze heavy upon her. If he had tried to talk to her, it would have been easier to ignore, but he did not. Determined not to engage, she kept her eyes fixed on the track below. As the first race ended and the second got under way, Honorius took the initiative. His right knee inched closer to her left one. To avoid contact, Galla would have needed to shift her cushion, and to do that would have been too pointed. So she took a coughing fit, and, seemingly unable to stop, made an apologetic gesture to Honorius and retreated to Elpidia, who rubbed her back and murmured soothing words.

'Are you well, sister?' His face was concerned.

She smiled, and eased her coughing. 'Yes. I don't know what happened. Some dust, maybe.'

Honorius waved, and a slave came forward with a glass of wine. Galla took it and swallowed a little. It was delicious, an earthy red that bettered anything Darme had ever provided. She took another mouthful, then, ignoring Elpidia's warning look, a third. She needed the courage the wine would give her. Returning to Honorius' side, she sat a little further away. The tactic worked.

Honorius' favoured driver, a Green, triumphed in the next race, which pleased him. Galla played interested and asked question after question about his horses in Ravenna, and also his hens, of which he was inordinately fond. Honorius blossomed, expounding at length about his brood mares, and the foals they were to throw this year, and how his hens had the run of his palace gardens, requiring a team of ten slaves to look after their every need. Like all those who are vain, and used to fawning, he was oblivious to the fact that the conversation was completely one-sided.

It was late in the afternoon before Galla judged her time had come. Honorius paused to quaff wine, which he had been doing with gusto, and she spoke. 'Brother?'

He smiled, teeth red-stained. 'Yes, sister?'

'I would have your blessing.'

He cocked his head. 'Indeed. Why?'

'I wish to marry.'

He set down his cup on the edge of the pulvinar and turned to regard her properly. 'I sense you have a husband in mind.'

'I do. Eucherius.'

'Eucherius, Stilicho's son.'

'He loves me.' She wasn't sure, but it seemed worth saying. Honorius arched an eyebrow, and she blurted, 'I love him too.'

'You do?'

'Yes.' A pulse beat in her throat. 'Stilicho and Serena also approve of the match.'

'I have had no indication of that.'

'Stilicho has been preoccupied at Ravenna, and with plans for Illyricum, which is perhaps why he has not communicated with you. As for Serena, she has been quite ill. I assure you, though, they both wish the match to be made.'

Honorius' eyes moved, down to the track and a race being won by a Red team. He said nothing for a long time, and Galla let him ponder. Push too hard, she thought, and his arrogant petulance would have him turn her down flat. The race finished, the Red supporters delirious with the rare victory. Honorius seemed amused, and ordered that a purse of silver be sent to the charioteer.

Another race started. Still he said nothing about Galla's proposal.

Tension gnawed her belly. If this was a waiting game, Honorius was winning. She would have liked to consult with Elpidia, which was easier said than done. I am a woman, she thought. I can make my own decisions. She beckoned, and a slave refilled her cup. She drank down half of it, and prepared to ask.

'You love Eucherius, eh?' It was said with no discernible inflection.

Her attention shot to Honorius. 'Yes,' she said softly.

'Very well, sister.'

'You agree?'

A nod. 'If it will make you happy.'

'It will!' Emboldened, she said, 'If Stilicho writes asking for your blessing, you will give it?'

'I will.'

He did care for her after all, thought Galla. Spontaneously, overjoyed, she leaned over and kissed his cheek.

His heavy-lidded gaze rested on her face. 'Let us talk more later.'

Dread settled in her middle, like an overheavy meal. 'Later?'

'We shall dine in my quarters tonight.'

Dread became nausea. Galla could picture the scene: candlelight flickering off the fresh-painted wall murals, a table laden with succulent delicacies, a slave plucking a lyre, Honorius playing the welcoming host until he sprang the inevitable trap and took her to his bed.

'Sister?' The word was packed with unspoken meaning.

'Of course, brother, I would like nothing more.'

CHAPTER VII

Diocese of Viennensis

A world away from Galla's attempts to influence her half-brother the emperor, Vadomar and his comrades rode from the ambush site to Constantinus' camp. It was a strange situation. They were in control, forty to three, but as they neared their destination, the balance of power shifted. Realising they were not going to be harmed, the trio of cavalrymen, rough-looking veterans in well-used scale shirts and battered helmets, sat up straighter on their horses. They began to chatter in a tribal argot Vadomar did not understand.

'What d'you reckon they're saying?' Eriulf spoke in Gothic.

'Probably deciding whether to cut our balls off before or after they amputate our hands,' said Dog. 'I don't like this.'

'Got a better idea?' Vadomar retorted. 'Stilicho ordered us to find Constantinus. We've done that, and saved the lives of three of his men to boot. It should be enough to grant us a hearing.'

Dog subsided, although he continued to mutter imprecations under his breath. Eriulf prayed quietly, a mark of his unease. Vadomar glanced around at the rest. They seemed nervous, the high spirits of a short time earlier vanished into the ether. 'Stay calm, brothers,' he said. 'We are an imperial embassy! Constantinus *will* respect our status.'

No one argued, no one looked content, but chins firmed and he got a few nods. He took most heart from his quick head count, which revealed there had been no desertions, even though it would have been a simple thing to do.

Leaving the trees behind, entering an area of open farmland, he immediately noticed the encampment that had to be Constantinus' base. It was large and rectangular with rounded corners and surrounded by a deep V-shaped ditch, the spoil from which had been used to form an earthen rampart the height of a tall man. Sentries were visible atop it, and there were units of cavalry charging and wheeling amid the flattened wheat in front.

'Impressive, eh?' One of the cavalrymen was watching Vadomar.

'It is. Old-fashioned, but well built.'

'Constantinus knows his stuff. Ordinary soldiers do.'

'So the rumour is true?' Until now, Vadomar had refused to believe it.

'It's no rumour! He was a plain foot slogger!' The cavalryman was amused. 'Elected him to lead us, we did.'

'His name helped,' said one of his companions.

Vadomar nodded. Constantinus the Great, first of his name, was regarded as one of the greatest emperors ever to have taken the purple. Other rumours, less charitable, were that the usurper from Britannia had been elected *only* because of his name.

A horse came galloping in from the training ground, angling so it reached them before the gate. The rider's *contus* spear and pointed helmet with tubular crest and mail neck guard marked him out as a *catafractarius*, but what drew Vadomar's attention more were the things bouncing off the horse's chest. He stared. Attached to the *antilena*, the harness that ran forward from the girth on each side, were the flayed faces of men, complete with hair. Men the rider must have slain in battle. 'He's an Alan,' Vadomar said, revolted, and unable to keep the disappointment from his voice. The Alan catafractarii were stationed in Gallia.

'They joined us a while ago.' One of his three captives was jubilant.

'Know who should be emperor, don't they?' added another.

The catafractarius, a sallow-skinned man with high cheekbones, seemed to know one of the cavalrymen. 'Who are this lot?' he demanded in heavily accented Latin.

'Visigoths sent by Stilicho. Want to talk to the boss.'

An appraising look. 'Stilicho's men, eh?'

'Correct,' Vadomar snapped. 'And we're loyal, unlike you scum.'

'Sheep-humper! Corpse-raper!'

'Coward! Oath-breaker!'

Spittle flew amid a litany of oaths in the Alan's own tongue. He rode alongside them, glancing at his fellows as if considering calling them over.

'Leave it,' advised the lead cavalryman. 'Constantinus wouldn't appreciate you killing the messenger before he'd delivered his message, would he?'

More curses, but the Alan reined in and watched them go.

Vadomar put him from his mind. It would be Constantinus who decided their fate, not a traitorous Alan.

Challenged by the sentries, they were forced to wait until word was sent to the *principia*, the camp's headquarters. Vadomar was irritated, but it made sense. Before long, the shink of mail and tramp of double-time marching feet announced the arrival of a large unit of mailed foot soldiers. Vadomar and his comrades were permitted to enter; half the soldiers formed up in front of them, half behind. An order rang out from an officer. At a slow walk, they made their way along the Via Principalis, which led to the front of the principia.

Word was spreading. Men were gathering on each side of the avenue, chattering, pointing. Soon there were jeers and insults. A bearded soldier picked up a stone, but when he cocked his arm, the lead cavalryman yelled, 'Throw that, you filth, and I'll have you on sentry duty for six months!' The soldier obeyed, but he did not drop the stone. As Vadomar and his comrades passed, he spat at them. So did several others, ignoring the cavalryman's angry retorts.

'They want to fight,' muttered Vadomar, checking belt, sword, dagger.

'We might be able to cut our way out,' said Eriulf in an undertone.

And if we do, thought Vadomar, the catafractarii will be waiting outside the walls. He had never witnessed a heavy cavalry charge, but the stories of their ability to smash enemy formations apart were legendary. In grim mood, he rode on.

They reached the principia without further incident. Unlike the rest of the camp, made up of tents, the headquarters had been thrown up in wood. Constantinus intended on staying here for a while, thought Vadomar. It was a shrewd move. Control of this area, with its links to Italia and the roads to Hispania, was vital. More of Constantinus' forces were even further south, anticipating a strike by Stilicho along the coast from Italia. If he'd had to bet, Vadomar would have wagered money on him having soldiers in the north as well, to prevent further incursions over the Rhenus. Constantinus, he decided, did not just have an auspicious name, he was a tactician also.

'I'll take you in,' said the lead cavalryman. 'Only you.'

Eriulf and Dog weren't happy as Vadomar clambered down from his horse, but didn't protest. 'Wait,' Vadomar said to the rest.

'Don't have much choice, do we?' a voice called out from near the back.

They all laughed, in the manner, thought Vadomar, of condemned men awaiting the executioner's arrival outside their cell door. 'I'll be back soon, with good news,' he said in as bluff a tone as he could manage.

'It had better be good,' warned Dog.

'It will be.' Promising Donar, the thunder god, an ox if the meeting with Constantinus offered a favourable outcome, Vadomar lifted his chin and walked proudly towards the gates.

'Who's this?' demanded the officer in charge of the dozen sentries, bearded men in mail shirts and trews. He spoke in Latin. Like the army in Italia and throughout the western empire, it appeared to be the lingua franca for the various tribes and races in Constantinus' host.

'A messenger from Magister Militum Stilicho.'

A surprised look. 'Really?'

'Stilicho himself sent me to speak with Constantinus.'

'*Imperator* Constantinus.' There was a hard emphasis on the first word.

This was no time for pedantry or court politics. Vadomar inclined his head. 'I am here to speak with Imperator Constantinus.'

The officer seemed about to ask more questions, but the cavalryman was having none of it. 'Who's more important, you or the emperor?' he barked. Cowed, the officer allowed them to enter.

The courtyard beyond was like any principia built by Stilicho's soldiers. A covered walkway around the four sides. Messengers' horses tied up in a line over there. Clerks with bundles of paperwork hurrying to and fro. Twos and threes of officers walking from one office to another, talking, gesticulating. Ordinary soldiers sweeping up dirt. Two slaves carrying a long, heavy desk. An officer in burnished mail watching them.

'Where is he?' asked Vadomar.

'In his office, like as not,' said the cavalryman. 'Likes to work, does Constantinus. He's often there from dawn to long past sunset.'

It was easy to spot where the self-proclaimed emperor would be. Two huge sentries flanked a doorway close to the great hall. They glared as Vadomar and the cavalryman approached; both laid hands to their sword hilts.

'Name and rank!' the older said.

The cavalryman obeyed with no trace of resentment.

'Who's this barbarian?'

Vadomar stiffened. To be spoken of in this fashion by someone from Britannia, a mist-wreathed isle of painted savages, was a huge insult. But this was not the time or place, he told himself. He smiled at the sentry, who seemed disappointed by his calm, and said, 'I am Vadomar, bucellarius to Magister Militum Stilicho. I have a letter for Imperator Constantinus.' Reaching into his leather satchel, he held out the wax-sealed wooden tablet.

A calloused hand grasped it. Suspicious eyes studied the imprint in the wax.

Would you even recognise an official stamp? Vadomar wanted to ask.

'Where did you find him?' demanded the sentry.

'He saved me and two comrades from bacaudae,' came the tart reply. 'He's all right. Why don't you get on and give the emperor the message, eh?' *Tap, tap, tap* went the cavalryman's boot off the floor.

The unfriendly sentry scowled, but his fellow's chin jerk was enough to make him knock on the door and go in.

Vadomar gave the second sentry a beatific smile. Small victories, he thought.

Unfriendly emerged, his face blank.

'Send him in!' a throaty voice ordered.

'Your weapons,' said Unfriendly.

Vadomar was already unbuckling his belt, from which hung his sword and dagger. 'Take care of those,' he said, with a surreptitious wipe of his sweaty palms on his trousers.

A grunt was his only reply.

The cavalryman went in first, spoke a few words. Wary of being discourteous, Vadomar waited.

'Come on!' Constantinus' voice was impatient.

A beckoning hand from the cavalryman, who was exiting.

Vadomar threw up another plea to Donar and entered. The door closed behind him, accentuating the smell of incense coming from a small clay burner.

Constantinus was sitting behind a desk piled high with parchments and wooden message tablets like the one in his pudgy hands. A jowly man with thick black eyebrows, he wore the simple clothing of a soldier. Vadomar would not have given him a second glance in the camp outside. Now, though, in the largest office in the principia, protected by bodyguards, wearing two large gold rings and an imperious expression that would have given Stilicho a run for his money, Constantinus looked the part.

Vadomar bowed as he imagined a man should before Honorius. 'Imperator,' he said diplomatically.

'I understand you saved the lives of three of my men.'

'Yes, Imperator.'

'For that you have my gratitude.'

Pleased, Vadomar bowed again.

'Well?'

Nonplussed, Vadomar glanced at the tablet in Constantinus' hands, and then at the emperor himself. 'Imperator?'

'Have you nothing else with you?'

'I don't understand, Imperator.'

A flicker of disappointment in the deep-set eyes, then, 'Who are you?'

Vadomar repeated his name and rank.

'To send you on this mission, Stilicho trusts you,' said Constantinus.

'He does, Imperator,' said Vadomar proudly.

'Do you know what the letter says?'

'If you agree not to invade Italia, Imperator, you can keep Viennensis, Gallia and Hispania—'

'An easy thing to say when the first two are already under my control!' Constantinus smiled at Vadomar's surprise. 'You didn't know? The forces in Hispania offered their support in recent days. Two imperial dioceses acknowledge me as emperor.'

Vadomar dipped his chin. It wasn't surprising. With Viennensis and Gallia under Constantinus' control, Hispania was isolated. 'Magister Militum Stilicho offers to make representations to Honorius for you to be elevated to the rank of *augustus*, Imperator.' As Stilicho had told Vadomar, this was the glittering prize, the elevation to co-emperor, the official recognition Constantinus would want. He had asked if Vadomar had nothing else with him because he'd hoped to be sent purple imperial robes.

'Honorius has not agreed yet?'

'I do not believe so, Imperator.'

'Why would he, safe in Ravenna, and my army hundreds of miles away in Viennensis?' Constantinus fixed Vadomar with his gaze. 'They tell me Honorius is weak-willed. He would rather dally with young girls, it seems, or watch his hens peck in the dirt, than rule his empire. To all intents and purposes, Stilicho rules. What do you say?'

'I have never been to Ravenna, Imperator, or met Honorius.'

'An evasive answer. People talk. Rumours spread, especially about those who rule. How long have you served Stilicho?'

'Ten years, Imperator.'

'You will have heard something then!'

I am loyal to Stilicho, thought Vadomar, not Honorius. It wasn't as if what he was about to utter were state secrets either. 'Stilicho has a lot of influence with Honorius, Imperator, and it is widely accepted the emperor has little interest in imperial policy.'

'I knew it!' A pudgy fist smacked into a palm. 'Stilicho might not be able to offer me the purple, but he is the man to beat, not Honorius.'

And instead of preparing to defeat you, thought Vadomar with some frustration, he is obsessed with invading Illyricum. Uncomfortable with Constantinus' piercing gaze, he kept his attention fixed on the usurper's stand-mounted shining scale armour, the finest he had ever seen.

'You have brought a vague promise to intervene on my behalf with Honorius, nothing more. Am I not right?'

Vadomar shifted his feet. 'It is not for me to have an opinion on the motives of the Magister Militum, Imperator.'

A snort. 'My gut tells me Stilicho gave you another task. If I had to guess, it would be to calculate the size of my army, gauge its effectiveness. Its ability to invade Italia. He wants to know how serious a threat I pose, which is natural. You are both messenger and spy.'

Constantinus was shrewd, thought Vadomar. And *he* was a bad liar, so he kept his lips stitched.

'A shout, and my bodyguards would swarm in here and cut your throat. That is the usual treatment for spies.'

Vadomar stuck out his chin. 'Envoys are not to be blamed for their mission, Imperator, but you will do what you must.'

They stared at one another, Vadomar refusing to look away despite his fear, Constantinus narrow-eyed and appraising.

'If I defeated Stilicho, would you serve me?'

The answer was instinctive. 'I would probably die in that battle, Imperator.'

A long look, then, 'Suppose you survived, however . . . would you take the sacramentum and be my man?'

'To be offered the chance, Imperator, would mean that you are merciful to those you vanquish. I would take the oath.'

'I will remember,' Constantinus declared. He made an expansive gesture. 'Stay in the camp overnight. Walk its avenues and count my soldiers. My reply to Stilicho will be brought to you in the morning, when you can leave.'

*

The cavalryman whom Vadomar had saved was called Edobichus. A Frank, he had joined Constantinus' army shortly after its arrival on the northern shores of Gallia. He was delighted by his emperor's reaction to Vadomar. 'See?' he'd barked. 'See?' Vadomar's offhand response that Constantinus had dallied with the idea of killing him met with short shrift. 'He's not like that, I tell you! A soldier's soldier is the Imperator. He knows a good man from a bad one.'

Edobichus had insisted on finding space for the entire group amid the cavalry tents and horse lines. It was the least he could do, he insisted. His announcement about who the Visigoths were elicited a surprised and delighted roar. Offers of help to erect tents rang out; wine was produced and shared around, and a requisition order was sent to the quartermaster for large quantities of meat. Mention of meat made Vadomar remember the oath he'd made before meeting Constantinus. He hoped the thunder god would wait until he had an opportunity to find and sacrifice an ox. He didn't have long to contemplate this. Tonight, Edobichus told him, they would feast and drink in friendship, and not think about the future.

Vadomar was content. Constantinus didn't believe Stilicho's offer any more than Stilicho would believe Constantinus' response, but it didn't matter. His mission was a gaming-board play, and the usurper's countermove meant he and his fellows survived. In a soldier's life, fraught with danger, it was a good result. It was satisfying, too, how Edobichus agreed to walk around the camp with him. Despite Constantinus' declaration that he was safe, Vadomar might have encountered hostility on his own. Instead he was given a tour worthy of an honoured guest.

The soldiery from Britannia were a mixture of qualities. There were units in good shape, with well-cared-for equipment and weapons; others appeared to have suffered losses through desertion or casualties, and for one reason or another had let their kit go to rack and ruin. There were wild tribesmen from the far reaches of that island, with only a few Romanised officers to lead them, and a heavily armoured cavalry unit who called themselves Sarmatians. From the pale-skinned look of them, Vadomar judged it had been generations since anyone from Sarmatia, a region north of the immeasurably far-off Pontus Euxinus, had joined their ranks.

Stroll coming to an end, half soused from the strong wine Edobichus was plying him with, Vadomar did not see the Alani horse lines until they were amid them. As bad luck would have it, the high-cheekboned cavalryman who had insulted him earlier was grooming his stallion just a short distance away. His lip curled, and he called out to his companions. 'Look! Here's the prick who called us oath-breakers!'

Self-restraint lowered, Vadomar would have stood to challenge the Alan, but Edobichus took his elbow in a grip of iron and dragged him away. 'Not worth it,' he said quietly. 'We'll both end up with a knife between the ribs.'

'Not if we stick him first!' Vadomar was outraged, belligerent.

Edobichus would have none of it, guiding him on a zigzag route through the camp, checking over his shoulder in case the Alani were following. They weren't, and although Vadomar professed not to give a shit, he was relieved. As the wine-fuelled rage subsided, he recognised it had been a lucky escape. Constantinus' rules meant nothing when there was no one in authority around. Two pissed soldiers against a mob of enraged Alani was no contest either.

Edobichus was a kindred spirit, and seemingly as fond of drinking as Vadomar was. The barely watered-down wine continued to flow. Hunks of freshly butchered beef were cooked over the fire and eaten, steaming and half raw. There was fresh bread from the ovens in the camp walls, cheese from local farms, and more wine. They played drinking contests, laughing uproariously when anyone made a mistake, and throwing back their own 'punishments' with gusto. Men walked over the dying-down fire, the leather of their boots smoking. Eriulf sang an old Visigothic war song, which was received with rapturous applause. Edobichus' response, a Frankish battle chant, went down equally well among the Visigoths.

Vadomar didn't remember passing out.

He awoke suddenly, on his back, a hand across his mouth. His eyes shot open. A man crouched over him, his face familiar. The dagger in his other hand didn't augur well.

'This will teach you to insult an Alan.' The hissed Latin was sibilant.

Vadomar lunged for the hand holding the dagger. A titanic struggle ensued, their two arms grappling in an uneven contest. Seeking to free his mouth, Vadomar savagely twisted his head to one side. The Alan lost his grip; fingernails raked Vadomar's cheek.

'Help!' roared Vadomar.

The Alan's hand clamped over his face again. He leaned forward, his dagger inching towards Vadomar's neck.

Still drunk, disadvantaged, Vadomar watched it edge closer. His strength was fading. Donar had forgotten him. Death awaited. This was not the end he had envisaged, murdered by an ebbing fire in the usurper Constantinus' camp. He struggled, writhed, trying to dislodge the Alan. And failed. Lips peeled into a wordless snarl, his enemy pressed harder, and the blade came within a finger's length of one of Vadomar's eyeballs.

'Oath-breaker,' Vadomar taunted.

Rage distorted the Alan's features.

In that tiny slice of time, hoping he had distracted his opponent, Vadomar twisted his hips, a wrestling move, and with his right hand grabbed at the tunic over his attacker's left shoulder. Pull it hard enough, he hoped, and the Alan might be dislodged.

It didn't work.

'Ready to die?' asked the Alan, smiling.

Vadomar closed his eyes.

A *thunk*, a solid sound. A surprised grunt. No momentary burst of agony as the dagger ran deep into his eyeball, no oblivion as it entered his brain. A sudden lightness as the Alan fell off him to one side. Astonished, Vadomar opened his eyes.

'Are you going to lie there all night?' Edobichus stooped, offering a hand. From his other dangled a thick log the length of a man's forearm.

Vadomar got to his feet, the movement setting his head to spinning. He staggered, then righted himself. The Alan sprawled at his feet. Vadomar kicked him, but there was no response. 'Good. You killed him.'

'I hope not,' said Edobichus. 'He deserves a worse death.'

The Alan was not dead. Revived by the contents of a water bucket, he was tied up. Everyone was awake now, Eriulf, Dog, their comrades and Edobichus' entire unit. Torches were lit and the area searched, but the Alan appeared to have acted alone. It was as well, Edobichus swore, or there would have been more deaths than one.

Vadomar's calm had returned. He was entirely convinced Donar was his friend. There could be no other reason for Edobichus, as drunk as he'd been, to have woken in time to save his life. An ox would have to be found, and soon. 'Shall we take him to Constantinus, let the Imperator deliver justice?' he asked. That seemed appropriate.

'You jest, my friend!' said Edobichus, chuckling, his eyes moving around the gathered cavalrymen. 'Does anyone agree?'

A baying shout of disapproval rose.

'I've never flayed a man's face before.' Edobichus regarded Vadomar. 'Think it's difficult when he's still alive?'

A keening cry left the Alan's lips. 'No, please!'

Edobichus drew his knife. 'Hold him!'

A veteran of many battles, survivor of half a dozen campaigns, Vadomar thought he had witnessed every variation of blood-letting, of suffering, of torture, of death.

Until that torchlit, scream-filled night.

CHAPTER VIII

Roma

'You must plead illness: a sore stomach, a headache, anything!'

Galla had rarely seen Elpidia so passionate. They had been talking about her visit to Honorius since their departure from the Circus Maximus, first in low tones so no one could hear, and since their return home hours before, at levels varying from quiet to almost screaming. Darkness blanketed the city; the night watch had gone past the house calling out that all was well. Fritigern moved about downstairs, talking to Darme as he lit the oil lamps. From the kitchen came a rich smell of frying onions and the clatter of crockery.

'I *have* to go,' said Galla, forcing the words out.

'Honorius has only one intention, do you not see?'

'If I stay at home, snubbing him, he will refuse to approve the betrothal.'

'And if the price is rape?' grated Elpidia.

They stared at one another.

'Honorius would not do such a terrible thing – he is my half-brother.' Galla's protest sounded weak, sounded like a lie, and she knew it. She wanted to believe it was true, though.

'Do you really think that, child?'

The term saw her temper flare. She was the mistress, Elpidia the slave. 'How dare you speak to me in that manner?' echoed in her head. To say it would put Elpidia in her place. It would also change their relationship for ever, and not in a good way. Instead Galla said firmly, 'I am a woman, not a child!'

'A woman would know better, would see what Honorius intends.' Elpidia sniffed. 'Have you forgotten what he did?'

'No.' Unpleasant, unsettling images sprang afresh into Galla's mind.

'Leopards do not change their spots.' Elpidia took Galla's hand in both of hers. 'Why would your half-brother be any different?'

Galla's eyes filled with sudden tears. 'He is not right – I do not know quite how to describe it, but he is different. Strange. Malign, even.' I must marry Eucherius, and I can see no other way to make it happen!'

Again, gentle pressure from Elpidia's hands, until Galla looked at her. 'Men will say anything to entice a woman, but afterwards . . .'

Galla coloured; she knew what Elpidia meant. She wondered if her half-brother really was evil. As a small boy, he had been selfish, but not ruthless or completely uncaring. The change had come after his voice broke, with Galla forever uncertain about its origins. That he had changed was unarguable. The dark memories haunted her dreams: Honorius twisting an arm behind her back, hissing in her ear that he would do whatever he wanted to her and she would *like* it.

She set her jaw. He would not ravish her. She would get what she wanted. 'I am going whether you like it or not.' She locked eyes with Elpidia, and the nurse broke away first.

'I am coming too.'

To refuse would be stubborn and also potentially stupid, thought Galla, relenting. 'Very well.'

Not long after, the arrival of half a dozen candidati and an ornate *lectica* borne by eight slaves presented Galla with another quandary. Her plan had been to travel in the litter she'd used earlier. It afforded a safe mode of transport home. To walk the streets long after nightfall, even if Darme accompanied them, was an invitation to robbery, physical and sexual violence. In the end, it seemed wise neither to spurn the lectica nor to leave herself without a way to leave Honorius' palace. Darme spoke to the litter owner, a wiry Syrian whose whipcord arm muscles were the badge of his job, and coin changed hands. The Syrian would trail the lectica at a discreet distance, and wait until it was clear if Galla needed him to take her home. When Darme asked about the danger of *latrones*, street criminals, the Syrian indicated his dagger and his slaves' stout cudgels. This was not enough for Darme, who told Galla that he would go with the Syrian. Knowing his actions were a mark of his care for her, she did not protest.

Eight men moved a lot quicker than four; mistress and slave were borne along at a fine pace. In the near-total blackness within the lectica, Galla sat thinking of the various paths the evening might take. The best but least likely was that Honorius' assent to her betrothal would remain, and that he would make no move on her. Then there was the chance he *would* make advances, and not take no for an answer. Elpidia's presence would not stop him either, if he was intent on taking her virginity. She almost convinced herself this would not come to pass.

A third eventuality was for Galla to somehow give the impression she *might* be interested in physical relations and gain Honorius' approval for the engagement. The difficulty would be to keep those relations in his mind, rather than them becoming a dreadful reality. Her stomach roiled at the idea of flirting with her half-brother, or using words that led him on, but her determination did not waver. The silence from Eucherius' parents since Stilicho's visit at the beginning of the year spoke loud and clear. Unless the emperor intervened, they had no intention of going ahead with the betrothal.

'Are you ready?' Elpidia asked as the lectica came to a halt.

Galla steadied her nerves, checked the rose-water perfume at her wrists. 'I am.'

The officer leading the candidati hammered on the door, which opened at once. They alighted, and in the light cast by the wall-mounted torches, smiled at one another. In the atrium, they were met by a major domus who somehow fawned and made clear his disapproval at the same time. Galla took an instant dislike to him, while Elpidia muttered something uncomplimentary under her breath.

The atrium was as magnificent as she remembered, its mosaic floor laying out the four seasons of the year. The *lararium*, in previous times occupied by a statue of the household god, held a small black and red Grecian urn. The major domus led them towards the colonnaded garden, glowing by the light of innumerable large lampstands. More lamps hung from the branches of the lemon and nut trees, and stood at the bases of the painted statues, leering satyrs and dimple-cheeked cherubs.

At the garden's far end, reached by a covered walkway, was a spacious dining room. The usual three reclining couches formed a U shape, with a low table standing on lion's-paw legs, its surface covered with expensive beeswax candles. Behind the couches ran a water-filled channel, fed by some unseen means, which delivered platters of food from the kitchen.

The major domus offered Galla a seat on the couch to the right of the central one, a position of high esteem. Honorius would recline to her left.

Hope blossomed in Galla's heart. The couches were large; there was room for nine guests. 'Who else is to join us?'

A little titter. 'Nobody, Nobilissima Femina. You alone are dining with the Imperator.'

Galla's eyes shot to Elpidia, whose lips framed the word 'calm'.

'Nobilissima Femina?' The major domus was indicating the couch.

She lay down, and Elpidia moved to stand behind her. The major domus seemed about to say something, but Elpidia's steely expression did its work, and he vanished towards the kitchen. Galla breathed in, breathed out, tried not to let the fear take hold.

'He will touch you over my dead body,' whispered Elpidia.

Galla twisted around. 'If he intends to ravish me, he will, and if you try to prevent him, you will die. That would be stupid!'

Steel glinted in Elpidia's hand. 'I'd like to see him attack you with this in his chest.'

'Elpidia!'

Both of them shocked by the force of her reaction, they stared at one another.

Galla found her voice first. 'You will not harm the Imperator!' she hissed.

No reply.

'Do you hear me?' Her nurse had gone too far.

'Yes, Nobilissima Femina.'

It felt terrible to humiliate Elpidia, but Galla could not have her death – Elpidia's likely punishment – on her conscience. Glad that the chalk powder she had used to whiten her face would conceal her rising flush, she settled back on the couch and imagined holding a dinner party here with Eucherius.

The comforting thought lasted a dozen heartbeats.

'Sister!' Honorius arrived, the major domus hovering in the background. He was elegantly dressed in a loose embroidered purple tunic, belted at the waist, and a gold band across the top of his head held back his wavy hair. The look was informal and oozed limitless wealth. He stood over Galla, who went to get up. 'No, please, stay where you are,' he said, gazing down his long nose. 'You are a vision of beauty.'

Uncomfortable with him looming over her *and* with the compliment, she managed, 'Gratitude. You look handsome tonight.'

He positively preened. 'Do you think so? I could not decide what to wear for so long!'

'What you chose looks perfect.' For a moment, she thought he was going to lie down beside her, but he merely stooped to kiss her cheek before taking the principal couch. Slaves moved in at once, bringing iced fruit juice and wine. Honorius raised his fluted glass. 'To you, sister.'

Galla copied the gesture. 'And to you, brother. May you reign long!'

They talked of their childhood first, and of their father, Theodosius. Galla, six when he died, had fewer memories of him. 'He was tall, with hair like yours, and he smiled a lot.'

'When he was with us, yes,' said Honorius. 'He had a different side when it came to official duty. He used to leave the door of his office open, and more than once, I saw him in a terrible rage.'

'What did he do?'

'Roared and shouted. Threw things at his secretary, anyone who was in the room. Then he would see me watching and his face would change, and he would call me over to ruffle my hair.'

Galla wondered if their father's two-sided nature had anything to do with Honorius' depravities, and quickly decided that possessing a fierce temper had nothing to do with wanting to have intimate relations with one's sibling. Besides, she thought, supping wine, imagining wedded bliss with Eucherius, and babies, her memories about Honorius might be wrong. There had been some kind of terrible misunderstanding, in which she had mistaken his intention. It was easier to believe that falsehood than truly come to terms with what she was doing here.

Food began to float down the channel from the kitchen on little wooden boats and was placed on the table by waiting slaves. There was light aromatic bread, sliced and still warm from the oven, fat green olives glistening in oil, sheep and goats' cheese, a rich yellow cheese with holes from Helvetica. Galla steered well clear of the old-fashioned delicacy of dormice, rolled in honey, covered in poppy seeds and roasted whole. Larger plates were carried direct to the table. Open-shelled oysters in great stacks. Stuffed mullet, and dolphin steaks, which Honorius assured her were delicious. There was a patina made of bream and dentex, and another with pine nuts and honey, which she preferred. Every type of bird was on offer: boiled partridge, francolin and turtle doves in a rich wine-and-raisin-flavoured sauce, oven-roasted wood pigeons, chickens, geese, and even a flamingo.

It was easy for Galla to keep the conversation flowing because Honorius liked the sound of his own voice. All she had to do was ask an occasional question, then listen in apparent fascination to his long-winded answer, nodding often to show she was paying attention. He would not have noticed, so absorbed in his own importance was he. It soon became clear he was tiring of Stilicho.

'He's been telling me what to do for ever. I've had enough,' he said, scowling. 'He tells me to send the army here. There. Somewhere else. Appoint this war leader to that position, and that to another. Make a treaty with Alaric, whose mob of barbarians has plagued the empire for years. Pay him an outlandish amount of silver. Ha! As if the fur-wearing savage hasn't become wealthy enough off the backs of our citizens.'

Galla was tempted to say Alaric was only asking for what had been previously promised, but as she had so many times since her arrival, she chose silence as the prudent option. Honorius was not interested in her view – he had not asked for it once during the entire conversation. She hoped he possessed some ability under the bluster and complaints. He had plenty of charisma when he was in the mood, but it was not enough to lead an empire, or to fight off the threats within and without its borders. Stilicho had faults, it was true, but he was a decent military leader. He put capable men in important positions, something Galla wasn't sure Honorius would do; his favourites appeared to change with the wind. Stilicho would also make a good father-in-law.

During the meal there had been frequent mention of various courtiers in Ravenna, most of whom she had never heard of, which made her think they were sycophants and hangers-on, the type attracted to the rich and powerful like wasps to a pot of open honey. They would not be successful generals in the making, nor prudent financial officials, nor trustworthy ambassadors and envoys.

I would make a better empress than Honorius is emperor, Galla thought, her emotions stirring. She felt no remorse at imagining Honorius dead, of natural causes, and herself and Eucherius ruling the empire through their son.

'Some garden-style piglet?' Honorius was offering a plate. 'It is stuffed with minced pork, chicken, dates and a host of other ingredients I cannot remember. Try some – it's delicious.'

'I cannot fit another mouthful,' Galla said; she could see slaves at the kitchen door, platters in hand.

'Don't you like it?' He was pouting.

'The food is delicious, and most wonderfully presented,' she said, smiling, 'but a hundred people could have dined here this evening and not finished the food.'

'I wanted to impress you.'

'You have, brother.'

He beamed, good temper restored. A finger-click saw the table cleared, their glasses renewed with a wine, he said, rivalling the nectar of the old gods. He giggled. 'Will I be punished for speaking like that?'

Galla, tasting the wine, which *was* extraordinarily good, shook her head. 'It is only a figure of speech.'

'The papa might disagree.' Honorius put a finger to his lips. 'But I won't tell him if you don't.' He was referring to the head of the Church, a notoriously cranky individual with a sharp eye for irreligious behaviour.

Her half-brother was drunk, Galla decided. 'My lips are sealed.'

'Let me see.'

Too late, she realised the inference he could have – had – taken.

Honorius stood with difficulty. Swaying, he bent over her, had to put a hand out to the back of the couch to stop himself from falling on top of her. 'Look at you,' he said, breath hot and wine-heavy. 'You are beautiful.'

'That is kind, but you look unsteady, brother. Take care. It might be better to sit down again.' She meant on his couch, yet he took it as an invitation, and flopped down beside her. Suddenly, his lower back was nestled in against her belly and upper thighs, and his left arm, supporting him, went behind her and was warm against her bottom. Galla felt intense discomfort, but telling herself he was drunk and amiable, and therefore easy to manage, she said nothing. Inwardly, she also knew fear had mastered her.

'I have missed you so much,' he said.

'And I you.' The lie came easily.

'Why do you not come to live in Ravenna? You should be with family, not here, with only slaves for company.' His glassy stare went to Elpidia, did not notice her stony expression, and came back to Galla.

I am scared of you, and what you would do to me, she wanted to say. She flailed for a response which would not be taken the wrong way. Nothing came. A frown creased Honorius' brow. Galla felt a trace of panic. Asked God for help. Was pathetically grateful for the sudden inspiration.

'Can you not guess, brother?' She gave him a mischievous look.

He tilted his head, curious. 'I have no idea.'

'There is no Circus Maximus in Ravenna.'

Another pout. 'The hippodrome in Ravenna is excellent. I supervised its construction myself.'

'It is not the same as the Circus Maximus.'

'Since when do you love chariot racing so much?'

She gave him a knowing smile. 'It has been years. I favour the Blues, as Father did.'

'And you go often?'

'Every time the races are held. I visit the Greens' stables too. I know their trainers, the finest horses and all the best charioteers.'

'That is unladylike behaviour,' he said sourly.

'Come now! I take care never to be alone with any of them, and Elpidia here watches over me.'

'She is a slave,' he said, sneering.

Galla could see Elpidia's face; Honorius could not, and it was just as well. She gave Elpidia a slight shake of the head, an indication not to look so annoyed. The major domus or the attending slaves might notice. To her relief, it worked.

'If you came to Ravenna, I would ensure races were held more often than in Roma. How would you like that?'

'I would love it,' she said, thinking, I could not live anywhere near you, and adding, 'But I would have to ask Eucherius.'

He leaned towards her, gaze intent. 'Galla.'

'Brother?' Every fibre of her being wanted to get away from him.

'You are lovely. Dare I say it, an old goddess sent to earth.'

Elpidia coughed, an unremarkable sound to anyone but Galla, who knew it for distress, not at his blasphemy, but her desire to intervene.

Galla smiled, looked at him, then away. His face was so close. He wanted to kiss her, it was plain. Panic swelled in her chest. A kiss was revolting enough, but what might follow soon after was far worse.

Mixed with the wine on his breath, there was fish and honey. 'Look at me, Galla.'

She did, and he moved in, lips parted.

At the last instant, she averted her head. The kiss landed on her cheek.

'What's wrong?'

'I . . . Nothing.'

'Why did you turn away? Are you not attracted to me?' His hand touched one of her breasts, and squeezed. Not a light touch, which might – from Eucherius – have been pleasant, but a hard, possessive grasp. 'I want you, Galla.'

Bile rushed up her throat, and she gagged. 'Move, please,' she croaked.

Her tone checked him. 'What is it?'

He did not see Elpidia behind him, one hand covering the other.

Galla did. Elpidia was about to stab him.

Her stomach could take no more, and propelled its contents upwards. She covered her mouth just in time, and the vomit sprayed out sideways from her clasping hand, onto the couch, the floor, and downwards, all over her dress. Another heave, and a fresh wave of hot liquid spattered. There were pieces of olive in it, and fish, cheese and sodden bits of what had once been bread.

Honorius lurched to his feet, repulsed. 'You are taken ill, sister.'

'I . . . I am sorry.' She wasn't, though; she was as glad as it was humanly possible to be.

'I shall send for my surgeon. His rooms are not far.' The major domus, who had been lurking within earshot, was already hurrying away.

'There is no need.' She stood, and let a glowering Elpidia, a cloth in her hands, wipe her face clean, and brush off the worst of the vomit.

'Was it the food?' Honorius' cheeks were reddening. 'I will have the cooks whipped, flogged within an inch of their lives!'

'No, brother, please. You ate almost everything I did, and are unaffected.'

'The wine then? The cellar master will pay!'

'I was feeling unwell before I came,' said Galla, praying he believed her. 'I was so looking forward to tonight, and did not want to cancel. Perhaps it would have been wiser, however.'

'Perhaps.' His face was stiff. 'Perhaps you would do better to stay unmarried also.'

'I am sorry, Honorius.' She was too, but not because of being sick. Head filled with the fantasy that he would help her, she had avoided the obvious truth. He had not changed. He did not wish her happiness. He was still a lecher who wanted to lie with his half-sister, and would never give his approval to her betrothal to Eucherius, unless she returned another night to give him what he wanted.

And, she realised, there was no way on this earth she could bring herself to do that.

She would rather die.

CHAPTER IX

North-west Italia

Vadomar's arse hurt. Leaving the rest of their companions to follow on at a more reasonable pace, he, Eriulf and Dog had been riding for four days solid, regularly changing mounts at the imperial *mutationes*. Many things had gone to rack and ruin in the western empire, but not the way stations. Honorius – or more likely Stilicho, Vadomar decided – had seen their many benefits to the official messengers who carried news to Italia from every part of the empire. A mutatio was to be found every ten miles on all larger roads. At each were fresh horses, good-quality oats and hay, clean water, and food for the messengers, or in this case, Vadomar and his two comrades. *Mansiones* had been built every twenty miles, state-run inns where they threw themselves down to sleep for a few hours before rising to take the road again.

Their need wasn't as great as the men tasked with carrying news of the horrific Clades Variana to the emperor four centuries prior, but as Vadomar said, Stilicho needed to know Constantinus meant business, and that his forces seemed capable of defeating any armies sent against them. If the usurper was not stopped, there was a risk of Italia being invaded. It meant riding as if the demons of both pagan and Christian hell were after them. Apart from the times, Dog drolly observed, when they were changing horses or asleep, which meant the demons needed rest as well. The shrewd observation had amused everyone.

Constant piss-taking did help, thought Vadomar wryly, shifting position on the saddle. His attempt made no difference – his arse cheeks, well used to riding, ached everywhere. He needed a day's rest, which was precisely what he could not have until they reached Roma.

As always, the unexpected changed his plans. Eriulf's horse suddenly went lame, and an examination of its hoof revealed nothing. With a mutatio perhaps two miles further on, Vadomar and Dog would gain little by leaving their companion behind here. Instead, they reduced their pace to that of the lame horse. Their enforced reduction in speed was both welcome and relaxing. There was time to take bread and cheese from bags and eat. To share around a skin of watered-down wine. To gossip with a passing imperial messenger, and hear of Honorius' visit to Roma. To exchange greetings with a farmer tilling his field, and comment under their breaths about how pretty his wife was.

It was in cheerful mood that they reached the mutatio, a large building with an attached walled yard, within which was located a smithy, stables and haybarn. They rode towards the open gateway, Dog loudly anticipating the cups of wine he'd have while Eriulf was picking out a new mount, Vadomar imagining the fresh bread that would replace the loaf he'd polished off. If he was in luck, there might be cooked meat on offer too.

'Busy, isn't it?' observed Eriulf.

The courtyard was full, more than a dozen horses tethered in a line before the stables. Good-quality beasts, well groomed and with fine fittings, they stood contentedly, nosebags fitted. There was no sign of their riders.

'Cavalry mounts,' said Vadomar, indicating the oval shields and spears stacked against a stable wall.

Eriulf scowled. 'What in God's name are cavalry doing in a mutatio? Only messengers are allowed to use the services, otherwise every arsehole would.'

It was a reasonable question. In enemy territory, messengers might need protection, but this was Italia. Dog opined that the cavalrymen were probably leaning on the supervisor of the mutatio to authorise wine and food as he would for any imperial messenger, and Vadomar found it hard to disagree. Mounted or on foot, soldiers were soldiers, and their tastes were simple. Food, wine and women, not necessarily in that order. If the cavalrymen were bending the rules, it wasn't for him to interfere, and as long as there was sufficient for him and his comrades, he didn't care.

Eriulf climbed down and fixed his reins to an iron ring in the wall. Ordering a yard slave to fetch water, he went in search of the ostler. In no particular hurry, Vadomar and Dog tied up their own mounts.

'Wine?' asked Dog.

'Why not?' One drink wouldn't hurt, thought Vadomar.

'Bring back a cup for me!' cried Eriulf.

The mutatio was like all of its kind, a simple rectangular one-storey building. The main room served as part cooking and living area for the supervisor and his family and slaves, and part rest area for messengers. The latter part was entirely filled with cavalrymen, seated on benches, leaning against the wall, watching a woman at the cooking fire. She, dandling a baby, a wooden spoon in the other hand, was stirring a pot of something, which by the smell was a stew of some kind. Dressed in a stola and apron, youngish, she was probably the supervisor's wife, Vadomar decided. Her expression was harassed, unsurprising given the still-awake baby, the ogling glances she was being given and the frequent enquiries about when the food would be ready.

He caught her eye and lifted his satchel, the leather front of which was embossed with a gold-painted imperial eagle. It proved he was a messenger. 'Any chance of three cups of wine?' he asked.

'I'll be with you in a moment. If I leave this stew, it will burn.'

'Don't let that happen!' This from a beefy-faced cavalryman, one of those standing watching her. Several of his comrades voiced loud agreement.

An officer might have stepped in at this point, but there didn't appear to be one with them. In Vadomar's experience, the wives of mutatio supervisors were more than capable of cutting discourteous customers down to size, but this woman said nothing. She gave Vadomar a nervous, apologetic smile, which told him all was not well.

'Let me help,' he said, striding over. 'We're parched. You get the wine.'

A nod of thanks. Handing over the spoon, shushing the babe, she hurried into the back room.

'Look at the arse on her,' said Beefy Face. 'I wouldn't mind giving her one.'

A lecherous rumble went up from his comrades. Vadomar hoped she hadn't heard.

'How's the stew looking?' demanded another cavalryman, this one a young buck with long curls and arrogant fat lips. 'Is it cooked?'

'Do I look like a slave?' Vadomar didn't turn his head from the fire. 'Come over here and see for yourself.'

Fat Lips sneered, but stayed where he was.

'Ho, listen to the barbarian!' cried Beefy Face.

Vadomar's jaw bunched. Few things got under his skin more than entitled Roman citizens, which by their dress and accents this lot appeared to be. Doubtless, he thought, their superior attitude was augmented by the fact that unlike most of their fellows, they had the balls to join the army.

'Here's the wine.' The young woman was carrying a tray with a clay jug and three beakers.

'I hope you're saving some for us and not giving it all to this barbarian,' said Fat Lips.

Vadomar tensed. This was fighting talk, but a fractional shake of Dog's head helped him to keep his composure. Only a lunatic backed two men against more than a dozen. Better to bite his lip and walk outside, he decided. Eriulf could choose his replacement mount, if he hadn't already, and they could drink their wine and leave.

Fat Lips was insistent. 'You're not going to deprive us?'

'There's plenty in the storeroom.' Another nervous smile. She gave the tray to Dog, then took the spoon back from Vadomar with a grateful nod.

'Are they paying for what they eat and drink?' he asked in an undertone.

She pursed her lips, which told him everything.

'Theft, that is.'

'It's the least of my worries,' she whispered. 'My husband had to go to the nearest town on official business. He will return this afternoon.'

Everything became clear, like clinging mist burned away by early-morning sun. If the woman protested, thought Vadomar, the cavalrymen's behaviour could worsen. Even if the slaves testified later, their word would not stand against that of a troop of citizen cavalry. He felt bad for her. 'I am sorry. Do you want us to stay until your husband gets back?'

'That won't be necessary. I'll serve up more food than they can eat and ply them with cheap wine. If any start to get frisky, I have a rolling pin on the counter that serves as a good deterrent.'

Under normal circumstances, she would have been right, Vadomar decided. Soldiers and messengers did not offer violence to the staff of mutationes or mansiones. This lot, though . . . He didn't like them, or their attitude. She was being brave, but not sensible. Action needed to be taken. He eyeballed Fat Lips on the way out, just to let him know he wasn't scared.

'There's trouble brewing, or I'm a good Christian,' said Dog when they were far enough away not to be heard.

'That is my thought also,' said Vadomar grimly. 'We should stay for a few hours. By the time the husband returns, the cavalrymen will all be shitfaced, easy to sort out if they start creating.'

'And if the fat-lipped prick comes outside wanting a fight, what then?'

'It won't go that far,' said Vadomar, hoping he was correct, 'but if it does, we will cross the bridge when it comes.'

'Fight, you mean.' Dog grinned. 'That would spice up this journey.'

'You're insane.'

'And you don't think the same thing? I see the glint in your eyes!'

Vadomar chuckled. A tiny part of him would also relish a brawl. Three of them, sober, against a gang of drunk cavalrymen wasn't so bad, he told himself, but his conscience spoke up at once. His task was to deliver the message to Stilicho, not get involved in unnecessary violence.

Eriulf, who had indeed picked out a horse, was ready to leave, but when the situation was explained and his wine poured, he was quite happy to delay their departure. They drank and made small talk, and kept their ears pricked for any indications of trouble inside the mutatio. There were none, thankfully. Some time later, their jug in need of a refill, Vadomar went back inside. There was no sign of the proprietress, which set an alarm bell ringing in his head, but a quiet word with a slave established she was in her private quarters, settling the baby down for a nap. Was she alone? Vadomar asked, and was relieved to be told she was. Jug replenished, he requested bread, cheese and olives, and meat if there was any. Turning towards the door, he found Fat Lips had risen from his bench.

'Messenger, are you?' Fat Lips' gaze was on his satchel.

'Aye.'

'Where are you headed?'

'Ravenna.'

'To the Imperator?'

'He's in Roma. Magister Militum Stilicho.'

A sneer. 'It's a sad day when the real power behind the throne is a semibarbarus.'

The term was just as derogatory as 'barbarian', and Vadomar was tempted to smash the jug of wine over Fat Lips' head. Instead he smiled. 'I'm a simple man. Far as I know, Imperator Honorius is the empire's ruler, not Stilicho.'

He could have predicted Fat Lips' snide answer.

'You would say that, being a barbarian yourself.'

Again Vadomar reined in his temper, although it was reaching boiling point. He smiled once more, all teeth. 'I took the sacramentum, same as you and your comrades. I fight for Roma. I have bled for her. I would die for her also.'

Fat Lips seemed a little taken aback by his passion. He glowered, and glanced at Beefy Face, but neither made any further comment.

Reaching his friends, Vadomar took a seat beside them, his back to the stable wall. 'One or two of them are spoiling for trouble.'

'We had best stay here and not go in,' said Eriulf.

'Unless the woman calls for help,' replied Vadomar.

Despite his earlier words, Dog made a face. 'There are a lot of them, and what's she to us?'

'Nothing,' said Eriulf.

They were right, thought Vadomar, and if it came to a fight, even if the cavalrymen were plastered, the odds were stacked against them. He grimaced. 'All right. But we're staying until the husband comes back. Our presence might be enough to hold them in check.'

His friends' faces told him they disagreed, but they didn't insist on leaving either. Good humour was restored by the arrival of a slave carrying a platter of bread, olives, cheese and thick slices of ham. Conversation ceased, and they fell to with a will. Plate emptied, they leaned back as one and closed their eyes. That was another soldier's need, thought Vadomar drowsily. Sleep.

He imagined delivering the message to Stilicho, first being praised and then questioned about Constantinus. The dream continued, Stilicho, army raised, marching into Viennensis and Gallia and inflicting a crushing defeat upon the usurper. His soldiers, Vadomar included, laden with booty taken from the field as the general returned in triumph to Italia. At the victory celebrations, Vadomar met a Roman woman. Exhibiting none of the usual antipathy towards his kind, she was fiercely admiring of his position in the bucellarii. Relishing the attention – something he was unused to from women – he made no protest. They went to bed.

Pressure against his foot – hers, touching his for contact. He pushed back.

This time, a kick. Startled, angry – why had she done that? – he opened his eyes.

Rather than a woman, he found one of the slaves, a slight-framed man of indeterminate age, standing over him. 'I am sorry, Domine, to wake you so, but the mistress needs you.'

Wine-foggy, his dream still bright in his mind, Vadomar did not immediately understand. 'What?'

'The mistress, Domine.' A filthy-nailed thumb jerked towards the mutatio. 'Some of those horse riders, they're molesting 'er.'

Shocked into wakefulness, Vadomar listened. Heard nothing, told himself the slave was imagining it. The sound of a ringing slap dispelled the lie. So did the anguished cry that followed, and the loud 'Bitch!' after.

Vadomar swarmed to his feet, mind suddenly clear, all thought of staying out of trouble vanished. With the nervous slave watching, he nudged Dog.

Nothing. He did it again, harder, bent down, hissed, '*Wake up!*'

A sour face, an irritated grunt.

Vadomar shook Eriulf's shoulder. 'Up! Get your shield and spear!' That worked better. Eriulf seized his outstretched hand. 'What is it?'

'Those bastard cavalrymen are about to rape the woman.'

As if on cue, a scream came from the mutatio, and was immediately muffled. Then a shout of pain, and laughter.

'He put a hand over her mouth and she bit him,' said Vadomar, any vestiges of doubt gone. Donar would be on his side – he had bought an ox in a village soon after leaving Constantius' camp, sacrificing it on the spot. Thanks offered up, he had presented the carcass back to the bemused peasant who'd sold the beast to him. Besides, he decided, it was not right to leave such a spirited woman to her fate. The sound of another blow, a meaty one this time, galvanised him further. 'Coming?' he asked Eriulf.

'This is a bad idea.'

'I didn't ask for your opinion, just whether you're with me.' Vadomar went through the ritual. Belt hitch, touch sword hilt, dagger.

'Of course I'm coming, fool. Think you can do this alone?' Eriulf kicked Dog, not gently. 'Up, you lazy fleabag. We need you.'

Dog, black-scowling, got up and peered towards the mutatio. 'How many of them are there?'

'Twelve who are awake, Domine,' said the slave. 'Two others are snoring fit to wake the dead.'

'You'll help,' said Vadomar.

The slave looked uncertain.

'Listen,' grated Vadomar. The sound of sobbing carried. 'She's a good mistress, eh? You cannot stand by and let this happen!'

A slight hesitation, then a nod. 'There's plenty of heavy crockery I can use. And the mistress' rolling pin.'

'Good.' Vadomar scooped up his shield and spear, and laid out his plan. There was no time to waste; they loped towards the mutatio, the slave following.

CHAPTER X

Roma

Peace reigned in the old capital. Spring was in full bloom. Mornings came cool, clear and dew-glistening, but the climbing sun soon brought welcome warmth. In Galla's courtyard, herbs sprang up anew from the raised beds. The fruit trees, lemon and plum, were budding. From their verdant branches a pair of courting doves flew, billing and cooing, to the roof tiles and back again. In the broken-down water trough in the street outside Galla's house, tadpoles swam in the stagnant green. The change came in people as well. Smiles and 'It looks to be a good year, this one' comments were replacing dour, survive-the-long-winter expressions, and the doleful, oft-heard 'Better weather can't be far off!'

Seeing Serena alight from a litter in the Forum Romanum recently, there had been an opportunity for Galla to offer sympathies again over the recent death of Maria, and a promise to see one another soon, but even as she had prepared herself to ask the question weighing her down, Serena had made her excuses and left. It could have been because she was grief-stricken, but it caused Galla to doubt once more that Stilicho's offer had been in earnest.

As Elpidia was arranging her hair, she said as much.

'Stilicho is worried,' said Elpidia, unsurprised. 'About his position, about how close – or distant – to the emperor he is. What with poor Maria dying childless, and him hell-bent on invading

Illyricum, is it any wonder they say Honorius favours him less and less?'

'What is his obsession with annexing that province?' Galla didn't understand. 'The real danger to Roma is to the west. The usurper Constantinus may have defeated the barbarians who crossed the Rhenus, but he and his son are a real threat. Gallia and Viennensis are his already; if he takes Hispania as well, he will have the strength to invade Italia.'

Elpidia clutched her Chi-Rho amulet. 'No.'

'I'm just saying what everyone else is.'

Elpidia tutted. 'As my mother used to opine, there's precious little point fretting about things you are powerless to prevent.'

'Do you practise what you preach?' Galla's question was arch.

'I do my best,' said Elpidia stoutly.

'Whether Stilicho was serious about my wedding Eucherius or not, it seems immaterial now,' Galla said. 'He is away for the foreseeable future and Serena remains silent on the matter. After what happened, Honorius isn't going to give his approval any time soon either. I can't see how the situation will change.'

'I agree,' said Elpidia with reluctance.

'If I am not to wed Eucherius, then who?' Galla hated the plaintive note in her voice. 'I do not want to become a nun!' Apart from marriage and spinsterhood, this was the only option available to young noblewomen.

'And you will not,' soothed Elpidia. 'You are beautiful and clever, and a senior member of the imperial family.' A slight pause. 'You could write to Honorius asking for his help in finding a husband.'

'What a stupid idea. I asked him in person for permission to marry Eucherius, and look what he did!'

'There may be a suitable nobleman at court.'

'No! I want nothing to do with Honorius.'

'That is a little like cutting one's nose off to spite one's face. In the absence of your parents, the emperor is the best person to arrange your marriage.'

'He might marry me off to some vile lackey of his out of spite.'

'Then do not complain about the lack of a husband!'

They stared at one another. Even from a friend of the same social stature, the comment would have been challenging. From a slave, it was sheer defiance. 'Be careful,' said Galla. 'If someone were to hear you address me in such a manner . . .' She did not continue, but both knew she would have no choice but to punish Elpidia severely.

'I am sorry.'

'I shall talk to my friends, see if they know of anyone in Roma who might be a match.'

'Do not give up on Eucherius. He may still wish to marry you.'

'And yet he has not demanded it of his parents,' said Galla sadly.

'You cannot be sure.'

'True. I think it unlikely, though. He is too . . . meek.' Determined not to lie down and accept her fate, Galla thought for a moment. 'Stilicho is not here, but I could visit Serena, see if she can be persuaded.'

'An excellent idea.' Elpidia beamed, lighting up her plain face.

Stilicho and Serena's grand residence was on the Palatine Hill, not far from the Forum Romanum. Until Honorius had decamped to Ravenna, it was the area where the emperors had lived for centuries. The streets were in good repair, potholes filled in, water troughs functioning, the plaster on houses' outer walls freshly painted. Stilicho's home was enormous, the size of a city block, and made Galla's, which was large, look tiny. A stone bench ran away to the right of the front door; this was for clients waiting to see their patron. Even with Stilicho absent, the bench was full. Climbing down from the rented litter – it would not give the right impression to arrive on foot – Galla counted fifteen clients at least. Togas had long been out of fashion, yet all wore one to denote their status. *Togati,* some called them, and it was not a compliment.

Her purpose was not dissimilar to that of the seated men, Galla concluded ruefully. She sought not protection, money or help in the courts, but a husband, and needed the help of Stilicho, or at the least, Serena. As the togati recognised her and rose, bowing to a man, she was glad they were ignorant of her situation. It was humiliating enough to come as a supplicant to Serena's door without the whole world knowing why.

Darme was with her. So too was Elpidia, proudly wearing her best dress, a deep blue reminiscent of the sea, and bought by Galla the year before. Reaching the door, Darme with a slight bow, stepped around Galla and thrice rapped the lion's head knocker off the timbers.

Sudden nerves took Galla. Her unannounced visit could be taken as discourteous. She glanced at Elpidia, who mouthed, 'God is watching over you.' Reassured, she firmed her chin.

The door creaked open. An annoyed voice said, 'How many times do I have to tell you? If anyone is to be admitted, it will not be—' A stout, officious man stood in the entrance, surprised not to find an impatient togatus. He looked at Darme, then Galla, and bowed low. 'Forgive me, Nobilissima Femina! I had no idea it was you.' He straightened, face rigid in anticipation of being reported to his mistress.

Darme registered the sharp jerk of Galla's chin, and snapped, 'Just admit us, you rude man.'

Serena's major domus knew when he was beaten, but another deep bow didn't quite hide his flash of resentment. He retreated inside, indicating they should enter. Bowing and scraping, promising to be back soon, he scurried up to the first floor. The burly slave guarding the front door stared until Darme's disapproving scowl made him drop his gaze.

Galla again went over in her head what she would say. First, an apology for calling in without warning. Next engage in polite, irrelevant conversation. Ask after Serena's health, and for news of Stilicho. Enquire how the defences at Ravenna and preparations for the campaign in Illyricum were going. Last, the real matter at hand, Stilicho's seemingly forgotten proposition that she wed Eucherius. Her heart beat faster. She was in the lion's den now. Her position was weak. She could not force Serena into agreement. Despite her prayers, and whatever she might have told herself in the hours leading up to this moment, her best hope was that the months of delay had not been deliberate, that Serena *did* want Eucherius to marry her.

The major domus reappeared, bidding them a warm welcome. If the nobilissima femina cared to follow, he said, he would escort her to the garden, where she could enjoy either the sunshine or shade, depending on her preference. His mistress would arrive presently. Darme remained in the atrium, but Elpidia came along, which made Galla glad. The nurse would not join in the conversation with Serena, but her mere presence would be reassuring.

Galla elected to sit in the cool of the wide covered walkway running around the magnificent rectangular courtyard garden. A bench was produced, placed against the wall and covered with richly designed cushions. She sat; Elpidia stood beside her. A slave appeared with a peacock feather fan, reminding Galla of her early childhood in her father's court. It also drove home the gulf between her relative poverty and Stilicho and Serena's immense wealth.

She was offered wine, but declined. A clear head was imperative. She accepted water, knowing the house had its own well.

Their wait continued. Galla wanted to ask Elpidia for her thoughts, but the fan-waving slave would hear. So might the slave weeding the beds, and the one pushing a broom along the footpaths. Don't be so suspicious, she told herself. Serena was selecting jewellery and applying make-up, or choosing clothes to wear.

More time passed. There was no sign of the major domus, and Galla was not about to ask the fan-waver or garden slaves when their mistress would deign to put in an appearance. To tell Darme to enquire would break protocol and appear weak. Elpidia was calm. She also had to stay put, Galla thought, Sphinx-like and outwardly content.

A musky perfume reached her an instant before the greeting. 'Nobilissima Femina, what a pleasure!' Serena swept along the walkway, preceded by the major domus and followed by two body slaves.

A younger Galla would have stood, out of respect. She did not want to do so now. She warred with herself, and almost got to her feet. Almost. Then stubbornness sparked. Serena had already been discourteous, making her wait for so long. As Theodosius' daughter, Galla outranked Serena, who had only been his niece. Remaining seated was her right.

Her pointed non-reaction made Serena briefly check, but her broad smile did not change, nor her welcome. 'Such a lovely surprise! It has been too long!'

Indeed it has, thought Galla, and not because of me. 'It is good to see you.'

Serena perched on the bench beside her, and gestured at the fan-waving slave, who moved to stand on her other side. Apparently innocuous, it made clear who held the power, if not the rank.

'Oh thank you,' said Galla, swift as an assassin's blade. 'I was getting cold.'

Serena was able for her. 'He was fanning you too much? I shall have him whipped.'

Galla felt a pang of sympathy for the slave, but to defend him could make his situation worse, so she acted oblivious. 'Are you well?'

A *pfff* of Serena's lips. 'As can be expected, with my husband away again.'

'How fares he?'

'His last letter, a week since, said all was going to plan. The army will march within the month. Arcadius has few garrisons in Illyricum; Stilicho expects to take the entire province before the harvest.' Another *pfff*.

'You do not think his plan wise?' Galla dared.

'In truth, I do not. If he invades, what will become of Arcadius' promise to send soldiers to aid Honorius? The answer is plain, and those men are sorely needed. That will be just the start.'

'Can you not dissuade him?'

A look. 'Oh, I have tried. Believe me, I have tried, but he can be ox-stubborn.'

'The emperor could order him not to go ahead with the invasion.'

'He may well do so.'

Galla waited, but Serena did not explain any further.

'Wine?'

She weakened. The pretence at friendship while throwing barbs at one another was proving more difficult than anticipated. 'I will, thank you.'

Serena glanced at the major domus, who shot towards the kitchen. 'It has been too long, Galla. I have missed you.'

Galla put on a beatific smile. 'I am glad to see you also.'

'Do you remember . . .' and Serena was off, soliloquising about the wonderful times they had enjoyed during Galla's childhood. Many of Galla's memories were quite different, but she kept silent. Much was made of the girth Serena had helped her to make for Honorius' horse. 'Do you remember?'

'I do.' Galla's tone was warm, because Serena had been involved, even kind, throughout the process. The good feeling didn't last, just as it hadn't back then. No doubt Serena had made sure Honorius knew it had been her idea to weave the girth, thought Galla, and also that it had been her supervision of Galla which saw it finished.

The wine arrived. When they had toasted each other, and Stilicho, and the emperor, conversation resumed. Galla expressed her genuine sadness over Maria's decline and death. Serena, sudden tears in her eyes, thanked her and changed the subject. Galla asked after Thermantia and Eucherius, and was told they were both well. Thermantia was at lessons with her tutor, Serena said, and Eucherius was probably still in bed. There was no suggestion of him and Galla meeting, which Galla found significant and disheartening.

Hesitant, therefore, of bringing up the thorny subject of marriage again, she let the discussion move on. They talked of the Senate, and the endless struggles between the various factions, and from there went on to the scarcity of silk from Seres, caused by an increase in banditry on the long road from the east. Both wondered if the outbreak of plague in the Suburra would spread. Eventually the conversation petered out, as it does between those who are not particular friends.

'A fresh cup of wine?' asked Serena.

'Thank you.' Galla wanted it to bolster her wavering resolve.

More salutations and good wishes; once more they drank.

A silence followed. For once, Serena did not break it. The peacock feather fan rose and fell; air moved. Elpidia coughed. Murmured conversation carried from the kitchen; Galla could hear Darme's voice, and her mood lightened briefly. No doubt he had sweet-talked the major domus into offering him wine, and was now holding forth on something or other.

I love Eucherius, she thought. It was time to speak or for ever hold her silence. 'I have a question.'

'What might that be?' Serena's tone was light.

Galla thought of Elpidia, and how strong she could be. 'For years there was talk of Eucherius and me marrying. It made me glad, because I love your son, and believe the feeling is reciprocated.' Serena's expression hardened, and Galla took a deep breath before continuing, 'All mention of it stopped, however, which saddened me. I also never understood why. My hopes were revived at the beginning of the year by Stilicho's visit – I am sure you will know of this – when he proposed our betrothal once again. I was in happy agreement with his suggestion. Since then, there has been only a resounding silence from your husband.' The implication was clear: and you.

'Child—'

'Nobilissima Femina.' The words burst from Galla's mouth. She would have respect at least.

'Nobilissima Femina.' Serena was smiling, but her eyes were not. 'Nothing would give me more pleasure than to see you and Eucherius wedded.'

Then why, Galla wanted to scream, have you not arranged it?

'Yet in the past, the time never seemed quite right.'

You are lying, thought Galla. There is more to it. She raised an eyebrow. 'I see. What about the most recent suggestion? Maria died childless, meaning Honorius continues to rule without an heir. This cannot continue. If Eucherius and I were man and wife, our son, God willing, would secure the future of the empire.' And I would be the mother of an emperor, she added silently, her passions stirring.

'You are right, Nobilissima Femina, but . . .' Serena's gaze went up to a window on the first floor, a window looking out onto the courtyard.

Suddenly, Galla knew the accusation she had levelled at Stilicho to be true. 'You mean to marry Thermantia, child though she is, to Honorius.'

Serena did not answer.

'Admit it!'

'You are perceptive, Nobilissima Femina.'

And you and your husband are leeches, thought Galla. Blood-sucking leeches. 'They will be committing incest. A man cannot marry his sister-in-law!'

'The papa has offered no objection to the union.' Despite her words, Serena looked a little discomfited.

The papa's coffers had been filled with silver and gold, thought Galla. People would talk about the unsavouriness of the marriage but do nothing about it. She breathed, regained composure. 'When is it to happen?'

'As soon as possible.'

She could not help herself. 'Of course it is.'

Again silence fell. Serena stared out into the garden. Galla pondered.

Her immediate reaction, that the proposed imperial nuptials need not stop her from marrying Eucherius, was followed by a stark realisation. Serena and her husband would never take such a risky path. Even before Honorius' marriage to Maria, gossip had been rife. Stilicho controlled the emperor. He coveted the imperial throne for himself. The upcoming wedding to Thermantia would create fresh rumours. If Eucherius were also to marry into the imperial family, the stories would have the ring of truth.

'You are already worried Honorius might dismiss your husband,' she said, noting the fear in Serena's face. 'For Eucherius to marry me would be a step too far!'

'It is nothing like that, I assure you, Nobilissima Femina.'

'Explain to me then why Eucherius and I cannot be betrothed.'

Serena was temporarily lost for words.

'It is as I thought.' Galla rose from the bench. 'I am grateful for your hospitality.' And nothing else, she thought.

'Please, you do not have to go!' Serena's sorrowful expression seemed to be genuine.

'I have no reason to stay.' Galla walked away, Elpidia behind her. She called for Darme, who came hurrying from the kitchen.

He took in the situation at a glance, and ran in order to reach the atrium before her.

'Galla, Nobilissima Femina, do not let us part like this!'

Galla did not answer. You have made your own bed, she thought, sadness tearing at her. Now lie in it. She glanced at Darme. 'Home.'

Ordering the slave to open the door, he slipped out into the street, calling for the litter.

Footsteps on the stair. She didn't turn.

'Galla!'

Her heart stopped. She looked up. Boyish mop of hair tousled, blue eyes dancing, clad in a simple belted tunic, it was Eucherius. Eucherius, whom she loved, whom she might have been happy with, raised a family with. And perhaps, through their son, ruled an empire with.

'I had no idea you were to visit!' he said. 'I would have risen earlier, come downstairs sooner.' His hand went to his hair; he looked embarrassed. 'Are you leaving?'

'Would you have married me, Eucherius?'

'I . . .' He hesitated, then said firmly, 'I would.'

'Did you ever say as much to your father? Your mother?'

In the silence, he reddened.

'I thought as much.' Galla's heart ached for what could never have been.

'They would have said no.'

'You could have argued with them, even gone against their wishes!' She was shouting now.

Eucherius' mouth opened. Closed.

'Well?' She heard Darme coming back to the front door.

'You are right. I am sorry, Galla.' His words sounded weak. Hollow.

'Goodbye, Eucherius.' She swept out, past Darme and climbed into the litter without a backward glance.

Elpidia was an instant behind her. 'Nothing more than he deserved,' she whispered.

Galla knew she was correct, but it didn't stop her heart from breaking.

CHAPTER XI

North-west Italia

Vadomar went through the door first, high-held spear angled forward, ready to stab. He took in the scene. Half a dozen cavalrymen, hammering cups and fists off the table they were seated around. Others standing close by. On the table beside it, the unfortunate proprietress, face bruised, dress ripped asunder, a cavalryman holding each of her arms, and between her open thighs, gloating, about to violate her, Fat Lips.

Vadomar didn't think. He threw. His spear flighted beautifully across the room. No one saw it coming, except the woman, whose eyes opened wide. The spear took Fat Lips in the side of his chest, punching him floorward, dead before he even realised. A roar of anger left Vadomar's lips, then he was charging at the astonished cavalrymen like a maddened bull. His sword sang from the scabbard. Reaching the table, he smashed a cavalryman's nose with his shield boss, and lopped the arm off another who came at him with a dagger. Whirling, he shield-slammed a third man, driving him back. Connecting with a stool, the man flailed and lost his balance. Vadomar stuck him in the belly on the way down. Four out of action, he thought, comprising one dead, two badly injured and Broken Nose, who could still fight if he was determined.

He saw someone coming at him from the corner of his eye, and turned. It was Beefy Face, purple with fury, wielding a cleaver and a vicious-looking narrow-bladed boning knife. Vadomar met a thrust of the first with his shield, and felt a nasty sting as the other connected with his upper right arm. He lashed out with a boot and caught Beefy Face smartly on the shin. It was distraction enough to ram his sword deep into his enemy's neck. A choking noise. He ripped the blade back. Red bubbles frothed at Beefy Face's lips, blood poured from the wound in his throat, cleaver and knife fell to the floor.

Vadomar spun in a circle, flesh crawling at the thought of sharp steel or a heavy platter being cracked over his head, but there was no one close.

Eriulf was finishing off a thin cavalryman. Dog was swearing as he hammered blows on a stool being used as a shield by another. The slave, grinning broadly, was moving from one sleeping cavalryman to a second, smacking each with the rolling pin. Remembering the proprietress, Vadomar glanced at the table. Clutching the remnants of her dress, she was sitting up, gazing in shock at the carnage.

He went to her side. 'Are you hurt?'

A sob.

'Did they . . . did he . . .?' Vadomar had seen it many times, had once to his shame even taken part, but now he couldn't say the words.

'No, thank all the saints. He was just about to when your spear—'

Rushed footsteps, and reacting out of instinct, Vadomar met Broken Nose's charge. He must have gone outside, because he was armed with a shield and spear. The latter's longer reach put Vadomar in a precarious position; he had to retreat to avoid taking a serious injury to the face. Broken Nose came after him rather than attacking the woman. It was fortunate, because as he and Vadomar traded blows, the proprietress stole in. Up went the cleaver discarded by Beefy Face, down it came, wielded with all her strength. It split Broken Nose's head like an overripe plum. Blood sprayed, brain matter oozed. Shards of white bone were visible in the cut-apart hair. Broken Nose, a standing corpse, his face surprised, folded and dropped.

Vadomar went to Dog's aid. Three cavalrymen were in a part-circle around him, only kept at bay because of his shield and their drunkenness. Vadomar rushed forward, stabbing one in the back and distracting another, which enabled Dog to stick him in the guts. Outnumbered two to one, the last ran for the door but, unsteady on his feet, tripped over the corpse of a comrade. The slave was on him in the blink of an eye. *Smack* went the rolling pin.

Vadomar had lost count of the enemy, of how many were down, dead, unconscious or injured. He cast about for Eriulf, couldn't see him. Felt a stab of raw fear. Saw three cavalrymen stooping over something, someone, their right arms jabbing up and down.

'Dog! With me!' The cry ripped free as Vadomar propelled himself across the room. The cavalrymen heard his pounding tread, straightened to face him. None had a shield, though, nor were they prepared for the force of his charge. His shield boss connected with the nearest man's chest; there was an 'oof' as the air was forced from his lungs. Ribs must have been broken also, for his face crumpled in pain, and he went down. Vadomar half turned, ready to tackle the others, but there was no need. Dog was all over the second man, stab-stabbing. Moans, a half-worded plea for mercy, which was ignored, and it was over. The third, attacked by the slave and his mistress, died in a hail of blows from rolling pin and cleaver.

Vadomar took one glance at Eriulf, lying ashen-faced on the floor, and a strange, cold anger seized him. The man he'd winded was close by his feet, dazed-looking, hands clutching his middle. Vadomar nudged him with his boot, and when he looked up, he rammed his sword right into the man's wide, terror-filled eye. A little spurt of watery fluid, then the steel sank home, breaking bone, slicing brain. Vadomar leaned until he heard a metallic noise as blade met tiled floor. He left the sword jutting upwards out of the corpse's skull, and kneeled by his friend.

'It's not too serious,' he said, willing his words to be true, asking Donar for his help, even asking the Roman god Aesculapius to intervene. 'There'll be a surgeon at the next mansio. He'll patch you up.'

'You're a terrible liar. I'm a dead man.' Eriulf's smile was weak.

Vadomar wanted to protest, but there was no point. He said nothing, fought back tears.

'Told you this was a bad idea.'

'It was. I am sorry.' A tear fell onto Eriulf's tunic.

'Don't be.'

Vadomar's watering eyes came up to meet Eriulf's.

'Better to go in a bloody fight we should never have won but did, eh? My shield brothers, you and Dog, you were with me, not to mention the slave and the she-wolf of a proprietress. And we won!' Eriulf sagged back, his breathing shallow. After a moment, he rallied himself. 'Tell me that's not a bad way to cross to the other side.'

'It is,' said Vadomar huskily.

Dog squatted down on Eriulf's other side and took his hand. 'I agree.'

'I'm going to linger, though.' A grimace. 'Can't have that.'

Vadomar realised what was coming, wished it wasn't the right thing to do, knew it was. Knew the price it would exact. In the same situation, he would want the same. He closed his eyes.

'Will you do it, Vadomar?' Eriulf whispered.

Vadomar and Dog did not continue their journey that day. They were grief-stricken, and Eriulf had to be buried. The proprietress, whose name was Julia, sent word to the local priest, who arrived a short while after. He said prayers over the body, and then declared that Eriulf needed to be anointed with myrrh and Sabean spices. Vadomar and Dog gave him a blank look, and Julia explained that these were expensive items and had to be paid for. Palm filled with silver, the priest prayed aloud as he performed the ritual, afterwards ordering the slaves to lave Eriulf's corpse and dress him in clean linen.

At this point, Vadomar told the priest his friend was to be buried with his armour and weapons. He wasn't sure if Christians allowed such things, but he knew Eriulf would have wanted it so. Dog's opinion later was that the priest's meek submission had had more to do with the way Vadomar toyed with his dagger hilt than with funeral protocols. Vadomar had felt a brief, black amusement, before his grief came surging back.

Julia's husband, a neat, dapper individual called Caius, arrived near sunset, and was horrified to hear what had happened. He wrung Vadomar and Dog's hands, thanking them over and again for saving his wife from harm. Eriulf must have been a good man too, he said, and his sacrifice would never be forgotten. They were kind words, but did little to ease the two friends' sorrow.

They sat by Eriulf until sunrise, talking about their time together, drinking and toasting his shade. They buried him the next morning, slaves from the mutatio helping Vadomar and Dog to carry the body a short distance along the road. His grave was to be in the narrow space between a red-brick mausoleum dedicated to a butcher and his family, and one of an ex-slave who had died with enough wealth to have a permanent tomb erected. Red-eyed and heads aching, Vadomar and Dog, used to burying comrades on battlefields, thought the location fitting, even humorous. Eriulf had been a butcher of men, after all, and as a barbarian serving in the imperial army had been looked upon by many Romans in the same light as a slave. Those commemorated on either side of him were suitable companions.

The only people present were Vadomar, Dog, the celebrant priest, Julia, Caius, the rolling-pin-wielding slave and the slaves who had helped bear Eriulf from the mutatio. The small number of mourners didn't matter, the priest said, nor that most had not known Eriulf. God and all His angels were waiting to welcome him into heaven. It sounded like pontificating claptrap to Vadomar; by the expression on his face, Dog felt the same. Their opinion didn't matter, however, because Eriulf, who had been quietly religious, would have liked the sentiment, and so Vadomar stood in respectful silence as the priest performed a mass and uttered blessings, waving an incense-filled thurible over the linen-wrapped body of their comrade.

The priest next spoke a few words of praise, about how Eriulf had given his life to save innocents from evil men. He then looked pointedly at Vadomar and Dog, who had already decided it would be Vadomar who would speak. He'd been ruminating on it since the previous night. There was so much to try and mention; he and Eriulf had served together for the entire time he had been in the army. They had marched and ridden to war together. Endured bitter winter cold and baking summer heat. Fought in the battle line side by side, saved each other's lives, dressed one another's wounds, and shed tears over fallen comrades. He had held Eriulf's forehead as his friend puked his guts up after a massive night on the town, and had Eriulf help him to the latrine when he'd been struck down by a life-threatening bout of dysentery. He had met Eriulf's wife, a stout, motherly type who lived in Bononia with their children, and stayed in their house more than once. Eriulf was part of his family, simple as that, which was what needed to be said.

'Eriulf was my brother, not in flesh and blood, but in spirit. Brave, loyal, unafraid of speaking the truth, he never took a backward step on the battlefield. He loved God, his wife and his sons. And let us not forget how he loved his horses. No matter how long the day, whether it was in barracks or on campaign, he did not eat or rest until he had fed and cared for them. When they were content, so was he. He was a good man and a true friend, and did not deserve to die, especially at the hands of men who were supposed to be on our side. He will be missed, always.' Vadomar's voice failed. As Dog squeezed his shoulder, he gestured for the priest to continue.

When it was time, he and Dog both kissed Eriulf on the lips, the final farewell. Leaning over so the priest could not see, Vadomar placed a coin in his mouth for the ferryman. He tied up the last laces then, encasing Eriulf entirely in linen, and with the slaves' help, they rope-lowered their friend into the grave. He faced east in the Christian tradition. The priest had explained earlier that this was to await the Parousia, the second coming of Christ.

'All go to the same place; all come from dust, and to dust all return,' said the priest.

Goose skin formed on Vadomar's arms. The simple words were powerful. That was how each of them would end up, he thought, imagining his own death. Flesh and bone eaten away by worms and time, until nothing was left except nutrient-rich soil. The finality, the inevitability made him wonder what life was about, what any of it was for.

Men and women, young and old, their lives came and went, sometimes quickly, sometimes at a slower pace. Illness took them, and hunger, and war. For a lucky few, it was sheer old age. It didn't matter how their lives ended, though, the world continued without pause. Vadomar could see it in the incurious stares of travellers going by on the road, mere steps away. When a person died, the only people who cared or remembered were those who had known the deceased. Everybody else went on with their daily business, as if nothing had changed.

Dog and I will remember you, Eriulf, thought Vadomar. And your comrades. Nonetheless, they would leave him behind in the ground when they departed. If Stilicho responded to the threat of Constantinus with military force, they might be able to visit soon, passing by on their way back to Viennensis. Otherwise there was no guarantee of being able to pay their respects until some unknown date in the future, perhaps after discharge from the army. If they lived that long.

'He will never be forgotten. We will make sure, not just in the construction of the mausoleum . . .' Julia looked at Vadomar, as if to reinforce the promise she had made when he'd handed over a weighty purse earlier, 'but on each anniversary of his passing.'

'Gratitude.' Vadomar's concern for Eriulf eased. Dog looked pleased too. They could not ask for more.

Vadomar had hoped to leave after Eriulf's funeral, but the incident had to be reported to the authorities. The four surviving cavalrymen had been incarcerated in a disused stable; someone would have to deal with them. It was all new to Vadomar. The battles he and Dog usually fought didn't require paperwork, or investigation by *beneficiarii*, the soldiers charged with security on the imperial roads. The matter needed to be handled correctly, however, for Julia's sake, and also in case the remaining cavalrymen went bleating lies to their commanding officer. Told a convincing enough story, he could make life awkward for them all. The safety of the rolling-pin-wielding slave needed to be established too; a slave who raised a hand to a citizen risked a swift execution.

'Where's the nearest unit of beneficiarii based?' Vadomar asked.

'About twenty miles north, towards Viennensis,' said Julia.

He glanced at Dog. 'That is not the direction we need to be going.'

'The message you carry is important?'

'It's for Stilicho himself.'

'You must go then. Do not tarry any longer. We will sort things out with the beneficiarii.' Caius didn't sound convincing.

Vadomar conferred with Dog. They agreed that the four remaining cavalrymen would swear blind they had done nothing wrong; that they had been attacked when asleep or some such. They would claim the perpetrators, out-of-control barbarian bucellarii, had fled the scene. The beneficiarii might take Julia's testimony with a pinch of salt, refuse to believe the cavalrymen had attempted to rape her. The slaves' account could be disparaged too. Slaves were untrustworthy.

'It would be best if Dog and I seek out the beneficiarii and bring them back here,' said Vadomar.

Caius and Julia both looked relieved.

They set out at once on a pair of fresh mounts. The road was quiet, birds singing in the trees, a farmer on a slow-moving ox cart. A short distance off to their left, two slaves were herding sheep from one field to another.

Their luck was in. Perhaps four miles on, they spied a patrol of beneficiarii. In Vadomar's experience, the soldiers tended to be officious and self-important, and quick to find fault. It was important to get off on a good footing, so he adopted a friendly expression as they drew near.

To his surprise, the patrol was made up of Visigoths like himself and Dog. Unlike many in the beneficiarii, the officer had served in Stilicho's field army. He was impressed to hear they had come from Viennensis with a message for Stilicho, but had the discretion not to ask more. Vadomar threw him a bone by mentioning it was to do with Constantinus and the threat he posed. The officer was most appreciative. Whether he realised it would be common knowledge soon enough didn't matter, Vadomar decided. It fostered goodwill, which meant the officer was more likely to believe their story, and Julia's. Sure enough, he listened attentively, asking questions now and again, before agreeing to return with them to the mutatio. A talk with Julia, a quick interrogation of the prisoners, the officer declared, and Vadomar and Dog would be free to continue their journey.

The two friends exchanged a pleased look. Nothing could bring Eriulf back, but justice would be done, and they had been delayed by less than a day.

CHAPTER XII

Some months later . . .

Roma; Mensis Iunius, AD 407

Although the sun was not yet in sight, the warm temperature gave an indication of the forthcoming day's heat. It was the height of summer, and the city had been baking in unpleasant temperatures for weeks. Elpidia, who tended to wake early anyway, rose from her bed – it was a mark of Galla's favour that she had her own little box room – and pulled on her second-best stola. She had no mirror to look into, instead running a wooden comb through her brown locks and knotting them up behind her head. Sandals on, wicker basket in hand, she was ready to sally forth.

Stealing to her mistress' part-open door, she peeked in. Galla was fast asleep, her expression peaceful. Elpidia's heart warmed. So beautiful and serene, she thought. What a formidable young woman Galla was, bright, intelligent, feisty. It was a scandal she still had no husband. Kind and decent, if ineffectual, Eucherius would have made a good match, but his parents had ensured it was never to be. As she had so often before, Elpidia was tempted to curse Stilicho and Serena for reneging on their promise. Christian values tugging at her, she refrained. It was altogether impossible to forgive them, however. In her mind, what Galla's foster parents had done was unpardonable.

Wishing to prolong the feeling of having the house to herself, she crept down to the atrium, avoiding the stairs that creaked. The two domestic slaves, young girls who stayed up late gossiping, would be asleep in the kitchen, but there was a chance Darme had also risen. He hadn't, she was pleased to see. His door was shut, and Fritigern, the last member of the household, was snoring on his pallet by the front door.

Used to her waking him, he slipped the bolts, yawning, and watched her leave.

The street was empty but for a scrawny cat. When Elpidia psss-psss-psssed in an attempt to coax it closer, it leaped gracefully up to a wall opposite. A short distance on, she cast a look back; it was watching her intently. A few scraps of gristle, she thought, or better, a fresh fish tail, and I'll win you over. Felicula won't mind.

There was no wind. Elpidia could already feel sweat in the small of her back. She slowed her pace; there was no need for haste. Keeping to the shade, she reached an old shrine to Castor and Pollux. The emperor Theodosius had ordered the closure of all pagan temples, but old ways died hard. It was too early for any worshippers, but there was a priest sweeping dust out of the open temple doors. He gave Elpidia a friendly nod, which she ignored. Pagans, especially pagan priests, were to be avoided whenever possible.

Reaching the Arch of Constantinus the Great, she took a left along a street leading between the Forum Romanum and the Mons Palatinus, where emperors had lived since, it was said, the time of Augustus. A patrol of *vigiles*, lounging by a water trough at an intersection, paid her no attention. Elpidia was content. Plain, amply girthed, and past childbearing age, it was rare that she had to endure unwanted approaches by men. There was another advantage to her relative invisibleness: listening in on conversations she would not otherwise have been party to.

Rather than squelch through the detritus at the back of the Basilica Julia, she cut into the Forum Romanum. The buildings on its western side, the Septimius Severus arch, the temples to Saturn and to Concordia, were orange-lit by the rising sun; the rest was in welcome shade. The forum, the pre-eminent space in the city, was busy. An ox cart, in breach of the regulations, was parked near the Curia, its builder owner shouting at his workers to get it unloaded faster or he risked a fine. Two frowning clerks stood, writing materials in hand, arguing a legal point. Slaves scurried to and fro on household errands. A homeless veteran with a stump for an arm watched the world go by, a black and white dog by his feet.

Elpidia turned left onto the Vicus Jugarius, the Street of the Yoke-Makers. Reputedly one of the oldest thoroughfares in Roma, it led along the shoulder of the Mons Capitolinus, atop which loomed the most important pagan temple, the shrine of Jupiter Optimus Maximus. Closed fifteen years prior, it was still revered. Even Elpidia could not help but feel awed by its sheer presence, its golden doors glittering in the sun.

She reached the Forum Olitorium not long after, a short distance outside the city's great defensive wall. Business was in full flow, as it had been since before dawn. Market farmers came here in their hundreds to sell produce. Lettuces stood in great mounds alongside piles of short, knobbly cucumbers. Rue leaves were on offer, and garlic, and early-harvested onions. One green-fingered farmer even had young leeks for sale. There were hen and goose eggs, and also honey in clay jars and glistening lumps on the comb. Young boys and girls stood over the last, waving palm fronds to keep wasps away.

This was one of Elpidia's favourite places in the city. She walked slowly between the carts, tables and stalls, buying some lettuce and cucumber, begging a taste of honey, pausing to watch a self-important workman complaining about the quality of some produce he'd not looked at until he was most of the way home. Noticing a cutpurse sidling closer, she stopped him dead with a black scowl before moving on.

'I tell you, the threat posed by Constantinus is real.'

A *pfff*. 'Don't fret! He's a savage from Britannia, a barbarian. How would you know anyway? You're just a farmer, like me. Ploughing the fields, weeding our plots, animal husbandry, that's our business, not war and politics.'

Elpidia casually turned her head. Two men in stained tunics and plain leather belts were leaning against the back of a cart, deep in conversation.

'Well in this case, I do know,' protested one, a stocky man in a straw hat.

'How?' His companion, a lot older, had sunburned nut-brown skin.

'An imperial messenger rode into my yard yesterday afternoon, asked if he could water his horse. Of course, I told him, and offered him a sup of my wine.'

A laugh. 'God above! Got him pissed, did you?'

'He made me water it down five to one, said he was on important business.'

'Aren't they all? How they love to push through crowds on a busy road, with their cries of "Let me past! I carry an important message from the Imperator himself!"'

'Do you want to hear or not?' The speaker's voice had taken on an irritated tone.

'Keep your hair on. I do!'

'Shut up and let me speak then. Forever interrupting, you are.'

You tell him, thought Elpidia. I want to hear as well.

'According to this messenger,' went on the man in the straw hat, 'Stilicho thinks Constantinus landing in Gallia wasn't all bad. He got rid of the barbarians who'd crossed the Rhenus last winter for a start.'

'Shame he didn't piss off back to Britannia afterwards.'

'Aye! But success breeds success, and his offer to rid Gallia of the bacaudae was always going to bear fruit. It's a wonder every local authority and garrison didn't go over to him. With Viennensis also falling into his lap, it was inevitable Hispania would follow suit.'

'Yes, yes, tell me something I don't know. Who cares? The trouble on the other side of the Alpes is nothing to do with me or you. Roma has endured worse; remember Brennus, who conquered the city, and Hannibal, who annihilated the entire Roman army at Cannae?' A cocky laugh. 'We'll survive this minor trouble, you'll see.'

He is a fool, thought Elpidia, a typical arrogant Roman fool. Has he forgotten the trouble Alaric and his Visigoths caused just a few years ago?

The other farmer wasn't impressed either. 'Do you not wonder where the money oiling Roma's cogs comes from? Britannia. Gallia.

Viennensis. Hispania. With those gone, only Africa is left. The coffers will soon empty, or my name isn't Gaius. Stilicho is worried, so I am too, and I'll pay more attention to him than you, a simple farmer.'

'If Stilicho is so concerned about Constantinus, why is he about to invade Illyricum? Because he's power-hungry, that's why. It's plain to see he wants to intimidate Imperator Arcadius. In turn, that will elevate his status with Honorius.'

A clodhopper like you couldn't know enough to formulate such an opinion, thought Elpidia, amused. You heard someone say it, a city official or a jurist, in conversation with a friend.

'Pah! Not if relations between the two brothers remain cordial, as they have these past couple of years. It's true what you say, though. Attacking Illyricum when there are enemies elsewhere makes no sense. The messenger said Stilicho has come to that realisation. He heard Stilicho tell a staff officer that the campaign into Illyricum would have to wait. He is concerned about Constantinus entering Italia via the coast.'

'Why?'

'One of his men got back from Viennensis not long ago, a Visigothic bucellarius. He met Constantinus, and was impressed by him and his army. Constantinus sent word with the bucellarius that unless Stilicho could guarantee an elevation to augustus by the autumn, he would advance into Italia.'

God help us, thought Elpidia. Alaric a few years ago. Radagaisus last year. Now this Constantinus. Will our persecution never end?

'Has Honorius agreed to make Constantinus co-emperor?'

'He doesn't know yet! The messenger was carrying the news to him at Ravenna.'

Incredulously, 'So *we* know what Constantinus wants before Honorius?'

'Isn't that something?'

'Aye!' Breathless, 'Will he grant Constantinus' demand?'

'Stilicho has advised him not to. Thousands of soldiers are being mobilised under the command of Sarus, one of his followers. They are to march into Viennensis at the first opportunity.'

'Good, good.' The previously sceptical farmer sounded relieved.

Elpidia was too; she offered up fervent thanks. Worry continued to niggle, however. Radagaisus' invasion was still fresh in her mind; now another serious threat to the empire's stability was at hand. This seemed to be the new norm. Weather one crisis, and another would raise its ugly head at once. She could do nothing about it except pray. She took solace from that. Thanks to decades of practice, praying came as naturally as breathing.

She could have stood and listened to the farmers all day, but the man in the straw hat announced that with his produce sold, he was for the road home. The two men shook hands and went their separate ways.

Conscious of the fast-climbing temperature, Elpidia's interest in browsing petered out. She bought a honey pastry for herself, and a chunk of the goat's cheese that Fritigern – and Felicula – liked, then set out for home. The pastry had vanished before she reached the Forum Romanum. Regretting that she had not bought two, she began to hum a favourite tune, one taught to her by her mother. In turn, Elpidia had sung it to Galla as a babe-in-arms. The tune came from Thracia, her grandmother's homeland. Enslaved after a tribal raid, she had been taken to Roma and auctioned on the block. Two generations later, Elpidia's only concept of freedom was the lilting, haunting song and a few words of Thracian. She wasn't bitter. Belonging to someone else was all she had ever known. She had mostly been treated well, and lived a life many citizens dreamed of. Even when Galla fulfilled her promise of manumission, Elpidia could imagine nothing other than continuing to serve her. She loved Galla as if she were her own daughter.

It was hours until midday, yet the heat was already growing intolerable. The warmth did not just come from the sun, but from the street surface and the buildings themselves. Heated daily for week upon week, the city's high ambient temperature prevented anything more than a slight cool-down at night. Elpidia felt as if she were in the *caldarium* of a bathhouse, and even in the depths of winter, that was not a place she enjoyed.

After a brief respite in the shade cast by the Basilica Julia, during which she drank some delicious pomegranate juice sold by a mobile vendor, she was ready to continue. Within twenty steps of leaving the shade, it felt as if she had never stopped. She was hot and uncomfortable. Salt stung her eyes; her clothing clung to every part of her. She considered her route back, along wider streets and thoroughfares. Areas of shade would be rare. By the time she reached Galla's house, she would be most of the way towards being cooked.

There was another option, an alleyway that would soon appear, half a dozen paces across, with three- and four-storey buildings on both sides. The thought of its intimidating Stygian gloom made Elpidia baulk. Such spaces were home to beggars and thieves, to the homeless and destitute, and no place for a God-fearing middle-aged woman. She trudged on through the baking heat, sweat running down her reddened face, annoyed she had spent so long eavesdropping on the farmers. If she were but a little less inquisitive, by now she could have been sitting in the cool shade of Galla's colonnaded garden, feeding dainty pieces of goat's cheese to Felicula.

She reached the alley. Her soles were burning up, the heat of the pavement penetrating her shoes' thin leather with ease. She glanced into the twilight leading off to her left. There was no one in sight. She took a few steps inside; the relief to her feet was instantaneous. I won't linger, she thought.

One moment became two. Two became three, and it went on from there. Soon she had been standing there longer than the halt for fruit juice, and felt no compulsion to move. She stared out into the street, squinting against the blinding light, then glanced down the alley. It was empty, and cool, and so tempting.

She took refuge in prayer. Mind calmed, sure that God had heard and would protect her, she determined to take the shortcut. Yet with the decision made, her fear resurged. Betrayed by her racing heart, she took a deep breath. Don't be stupid, she told herself. Nothing will happen.

Eyes accustomed to the dim light, she took a step deeper into the alley, and then several more. Broken pottery made her footing slow and uncertain. To her relief, however, she smelled nothing foul yet. She would soon, she was sure. The majority of the city's inhabitants lived in miserable one-room apartments with no sanitation. Not every building had easy access to the sewers; a simple solution was to empty one's chamber pot in an alleyway. Gaze searching the ground, Elpidia continued.

The only sign of life was rats, lithe dark shapes scurrying away from her tread, and once, a feral cat that hissed its alarm before fleeing whence it had come. Elpidia's spirits rose. If these creatures were all she encountered, the shortcut would prove to have been a wise choice.

Crunch. The sound, a little muffled, came from in front of her. Elpidia froze. Cats moved silently. It might have been a dog, she thought, hoped. She waited, unsure whether to go back or continue. The sound did not come again. At last, chiding herself for a nervous fool, placing her feet with the utmost care, she took another step. Stopped. Listened, the sound of her own breath louder than anything.

Silence.

She counted five steps. Ten. Saw, nearing her through the gloom on both sides, a vertical darker slit. It was a crossroads of sorts, she decided, probably the gap between buildings facing onto the street she had left behind and the one onto which she would emerge. The crunching noise must have come from one of those side alleys. Again she stopped. Pricked her ears. Heard nothing alarming.

She edged closer to the intersection, nerves taut. Still silence reigned. She poked her head forward, and saw to the right a heap of builder's rubble, cut-off pieces of timber and other detritus. The portion of the side alley visible to her left was empty. Relieved, deciding she had been fearful for nothing, she walked on. She had gone perhaps twenty paces when there was another crunch, this time from behind her. It took all her self-control not to cry out. She looked over her shoulder, seeing a large figure. A man, it had to be. He did not speak, but started to follow her.

Feeling a cold, naked fear, Elpidia hurried on. It had been foolishness of the worst kind to enter the alley. Her speed increased, first a fast walk, then a shambling run, the wicker basket knocking off her leg with each stride. The alleyway's end, a bright strip of hard-to-look-at light, seemed an enormous distance away.

At her back, the sound of running footsteps.

There was an acid taste in Elpidia's mouth. She would never get to the next street before her pursuer caught up.

Would rape precede her murder? she wondered. Her mother's words came to mind, that it was safer not to fight sexually aggressive men. Give them what they want, and they were less likely to harm you. Odd words, she had thought at the time, given how fond her mother was of recalling her Maedi tribal roots, and her long-distant warrior forebear, Spartacus. Later, aware of the predatory nature of some men, Elpidia had seen the survival mechanism for what it was, but thankfully had never had cause to deploy it. Until now, perhaps.

Imagining what Spartacus might have advised her to do, fierce anger sparked in her belly. She stopped. Turned.

The man was a dozen paces off. His pace slowed.

'What do you want?' Elpidia demanded.

'Whatever you've got. Coin. Your basket. A feel of your cunt.'

'Don't hurt me.' She pitched her voice just so.

A rasping chuckle. 'Maybe I will, maybe I won't. Depends how quick you make me come.'

You filth, thought Elpidia, emitting her best whimper.

Drawing near, he could have been any one of a thousand men from the depths of the Suburra. Bearded, barefoot, wearing an old, misshapen tunic, he held a blade in a way that suggested experience.

Elpidia's whimper was genuine this time. She prepared herself, asked God for his help.

The man reached out and pinched one of her breasts. Elpidia bit the inside of her cheek rather than give him the satisfaction of knowing it hurt. His hand moved across her chest. He stepped closer, clogging the air between them with his breath, a foul mixture of decay, onions and sour wine.

'Lie down,' he ordered.

'Kiss me first,' said Elpidia, tilting her head up.

Astonished, then delighted, he bent his mouth to hers.

She drove her knee into his groin with all the force she could muster. The connection was sweet, his genitalia crushed against the bone of his pelvis. Eyes bulging, making a strange oofing noise, he dropped like a sack of grain falling off the back of an ox cart.

Elpidia wanted to cut his throat, but even winded, he was dangerous, and her strength could never match his. Satisfying herself with a hefty kick to his midriff and the moan that brought forth, she ran towards the street.

'Bitch!' he called after her.

She emerged from the alley chest heaving. Never had sunlight and warmth and people been so welcome. Wary in case her attacker managed to give chase, she hurried away, soon blending with the crowd. A quarter of a mile further on, the sight of a church made inspiration strike. She could hit two birds with one stone now. The stone building's interior would be cool and welcoming, and she could offer thanks to God, who had ensured her safety.

Nonetheless, it had been a lucky escape.

CHAPTER XIII

Diocese of Viennensis; Mensis September, AD *407*

A short distance from the Roman road, amid the deep shade cast by downy evergreen oaks, hundreds of soldiers, Sarus' vanguard, were resting. The days were still hot, and respite from the heat was welcome. Sentries paced to and from the trees' eastern edge to the sinuous, glittering band of the mighty Rhodanus river. It was peaceful, even tranquil. Men had run out of conversation. They lay side by side on the mossy ground, clothing sweat-stained, eyes closed, weary from days of travel towards the city of Valentia, where Constantinus had holed up. Proper sleep was impossible, thanks to the horseflies. Attracted by the cavalry mounts but not averse to human blood either, the grey-brown insects alighted on every piece of exposed flesh.

Irritated from repeatedly nodding off only to be wakened by the stabbing pain of fresh bites, Vadomar gave up on slumber. He got to his feet, stepping over the prone forms of Dog and Wulfila, a young warrior they had taken under their wing. His name meant 'Little Wolf', and as Dog said, it was funny how a dog should care for a wolf.

Both men roused, the way men do on campaign when anything unexpected happens. 'Where you going?' asked Wulfila.

'For a walk. Maybe a dip in the river.'

'You'll drown,' said Dog.

'Who are you, my mother?' But Vadomar was grateful to be reminded of the deceptiveness of the Rhodanus. Its surface was sluggish, but the drop-off from the water's edge was steep, and the current much faster than it seemed from the bank. Not a day went by without stories of men who had gone for a swim and never returned.

He noticed a horsefly angling in towards his right forearm, and waited until it landed. *Slap*, and it fell earthwards. Protected by a thick carapace, the insect was only stunned, so Vadomar stood on it, finishing the job. He thought of Constantinus' subordinate, Justinianus, whose forces they had crushed like the horsefly, then of the usurper's main army. It would not be as easy to defeat, because Sarus' host numbered under twenty thousand men, which was a good deal fewer than followed Constantinus.

More men could have been summoned, but the summer was waning, and with it, the weather to wage war. As it was, they needed to bring Constantinus to bay fast, or supplies would run out. Then would come the risk of snow in the mountain passes, leaving the only way to Italia the coastal road, an easy way for Constantinus to give pursuit. They would therefore have to fashion a victory with what they had, Sarus told them. Confident to the point of cockiness, the new Magister Utriusque Militiae per Gallias led by example, first into battle and last to retreat. Vadomar, who had been mightily impressed by the victory over Justinianus, now felt Sarus was the right man for the job. Victory would be theirs.

Entering a sun-dappled, bramble-filled clearing, he began feasting on blackberries. Marching rations were never good at the best of times, often little more than bucellatum and *acetum*, sour, sediment-laden wine. The opportunity to hunt was also rare. Even bounty like blackberries, plentiful on the roadsides, was something to be eyed covetously rather than picked and consumed at leisure. Not now. Vadomar ate and ate until he could fit no more and the fingers of both hands were purple-stained. Sated, he took off his Pannonian cap and began to fill that too.

At length, his cap overflowing with blackberries, he walked back.

'Here 'e is!' cried Wulfila.

'He didn't drown, worse luck,' said Dog.

'Nice. You won't be getting any of these.' Vadomar handed the cap to a delighted Wulfila. In between mouthfuls, the young man waxed lyrical about how tasty they were, eyeing Dog all the while. His tactic worked: Dog scowled, and muttered under his breath.

'Go on, have some,' said Vadomar with a relenting grin. 'I know you'd be sad if I had gone to the bottom of the Rhodanus.'

Dog's black expression eased, and he took the cap from a purple-mouthed, still chuckling Wulfila.

None of the three realised it was the last occasion for light-hearted banter they would enjoy for quite some time.

Valentia was built on flat ground by the river, one side protected by the deep waters of the Rhodanus. A double wall comprised the rest of its perimeter, a formidable barrier to Sarus' army, which had no heavy artillery. Storming it was out of the question too, unless, as Dog dourly observed, their general wanted to throw away his men's lives for no reason.

He didn't, so they laid siege to the place. It was simple enough, for the city was small. Twenty thousand men quickly dug a ditch around the walls, and filled the bottom with tribuli. This done, they set up camp, neat tent lines stretching off to the north, east and south. Fires were kindled, and those who had wine got to drinking it.

Vadomar was disgruntled. He had wanted a battle, like the one against Justinianus. Wary of suffering defeat, however, Constantinus had withdrawn into the city. He could not have enough food and supplies to feed his army for long, but nor did Sarus, and with the usurper's other forces urgently summoned, time was on Constantinus' side.

Conversations around the fire each night centred on this topic and little else. Sarus ought to have gone after Gerontius and Edobichus, the usurper's other generals, before coming for Constantinus. He should have brought engineers, to build catapults. Three large ballistae would be enough, opined Wulfila; despite his youth, he had once seen a town's walls reduced to rubble. They discussed laying waste to the entire countryside around Valentia, so that when they withdrew, Constantinus' men might starve come the winter.

Risky, madcap ideas were mooted. Dog wanted to attack the city by boat. Scale the river walls at night, he claimed, and the defenders would be taken by complete surprise. Wulfila suggested that a select group could climb the ramparts in several different places, meet at an arranged location within and then open a gate. The army, waiting outside, would charge in and take the city.

The suggestions were either impossible, too risky or potentially disastrous for themselves. Morale, which had been high following the crushing defeat inflicted on Justinianus, began to diminish. No one wanted to retreat, or talk of giving up, but the solidity of the city's walls and the wind-carried insults of the defenders were stark evidence of their relative powerlessness.

Only one idea seemed viable: using ladders at night to enter Valentia. The night after one of their talks, Vadomar and his comrades crossed the ditch and walked all around the city's landward-facing walls, careful to keep out of missile range. Spears were thrown anyway, and an occasional speculative arrow was launched. If one came close, Dog would laugh and jeer, or bare his arse. The defenders were outraged, which amused him no end.

Two places suited an assault. One was close to the Rhodanus but quite far from any gates. There appeared to be few soldiers guarding it, possibly, as Vadomar said, because no one in their right mind would try to attack such a spot. The other was a section a little lower than the rest of the wall that from the look of it had been undergoing recent repairs. It would be, as Wulfila pointed out, well defended.

The mission was dangerous but achievable, they decided, and went to look for Sarus. Enquiries made at his large tent sent them to the area of flattened ground used by the cavalry to exercise their mounts. Watched by a group of staff officers and a couple of clerks, the magister militum was thundering up and down on his stallion, a magnificent black. Vadomar didn't hail him or call out; unless the need was great, senior officers were best left to their diversions.

They approached when Sarus had dismounted. A slave groom took the reins, and Sarus, a blocky figure in a fine tunic with patterned circles at the shoulders, basked in his staff officers' fawning comments. Vadomar, a skilled rider, didn't think much of Sarus' horsemanship. None of his amusement registered on his face. 'A word, if I might, Magister Militum,' he said politely.

Sarus raised an eyebrow. 'Who are you?'

'One of the bucellarii, Magister Militum.'

'Ah, yes, Stilicho's lapdogs, sent to watch over me.' Dutiful chuckles came from the staff officers.

Vadomar smiled; it wasn't too far from the truth, for Stilicho regarded Sarus as a rival. 'We are here to fight the usurper, Magister Militum, as you are. My comrades and I have an idea for taking the city.'

'Tell me.'

So Vadomar did.

'I had noted the repaired section, but not the other,' said Sarus when he was done. 'It must be some distance to the nearest gate?'

'A third of a mile, perhaps a little more.'

'To have any chance of success, the numbers involved will have to be small,' said Sarus, 'and the gate will doubtless be well guarded. Are you or your comrades familiar with Valentia?'

'No, Magister Militum.'

A sharp look. 'This mission is perilous indeed. First you would need to scale the wall undetected, then find your way to the gate through back streets none of you know. Lastly, you would have to overcome superior numbers in order to open the gate. Am I missing anything?' More amused laughter from his staff officers.

'I do not think so, Magister Militum,' replied Vadomar, pride pricking. 'But my friends and I are willing to give it a try.'

Sarus' attention was on him like a cat on a mouse. 'Even if you fight like the heroes of legend, three of you could never succeed. Will any of your comrades go with you on this suicide mission?'

Vadomar glanced at Dog and Wulfila, who seemed even more annoyed than he was by Sarus' arrogance, and was reassured by their fierce nods. 'I am sure of it, Magister Militum.'

'Well then, that's settled!' cried Sarus with a clap of his hands. 'The bucellarii will gain access to Valentia for us.'

Vadomar realised he had walked into a trap of his own devising. Sarus was sure they would fail. Being Stilicho's men and not his, he probably hoped they died in the process. If by some chance they succeeded, he would take the credit. Dog and Wulfila had seen through the magister militum too. Wulfila, whose idea it had been, bullishly maintained they would show Sarus what bucellarii were capable of. Dog seemed less sure, but when Vadomar asked if he still wanted to be part of it, he cursed him, saying, 'As if I'd let you two imbeciles try something like this without me!'

Vadomar didn't argue. Risky though it was, he wanted his closest friends by his side.

CHAPTER XIV

Roma

Galla was on her knees in her bedroom. Praying was a precious daily ritual. She would also give thanks for her good health, and that of Elpidia and her other slaves; and for life in the city, which proceeded as it always had. Of recent days, however, her devotions had taken on a real sense of urgency. Things she cared about were falling by the wayside. Nothing, she thought sadly, was going to plan.

In an effort to forget Eucherius, to move on, she had asked friends to suggest suitable husbands, and been in turn fascinated and appalled by the miserable selection on offer. Thus far, there had been chaperoned meetings with four middle-aged or elderly senators. They had been a combination of old-fashioned, insufferably arrogant and plain stupid, possessing either bad teeth, a paunch, receding hair or all three. There had been one younger nobleman, but his boorish manner and constant nail-biting had ruled him out of the equation. Galla wondered if she would ever find a husband.

Another failure, if it could be termed so, because it had been a fantasy, was her lack of success in establishing cordial relations with Honorius. Since the disastrous dinner and his return to Ravenna, there had been no contact, nor even an invitation to his wedding to Thermantia, which had gone ahead. It was sad to think she could never have a meaningful relationship with him, but it was for the best. His behaviour was sure proof that, as Elpidia was fond of saying, people did not change. She could only pray for Thermantia, barely a woman, to have the inner strength to resist his perverted desires.

The bad news wasn't confined to Galla's personal life. The campaign against the usurper Constantinus, which had appeared to be going well, had, according to the latest gossip, stalled. Stilicho's appointee, Sarus, was at Valentia in Viennensis, trying to force Constantinus to surrender. Galla hoped the siege ended soon. Once the snows came, the passes would close until the following spring, and the empire could ill afford to have Sarus and his army trapped on the wrong side of the mountains.

There was more. Roma's influence was diminishing by the month, it seemed. Britannia was lost, and most of Gallia and Viennensis, and unless Constantinus was defeated, Hispania would be too. Soon Africa, overseas, harder to defend if enemies threatened, might be the last tax-yielding region left to Roma. That did not bode well for Honorius, Stilicho, the army or the populace in general. It also augured badly for Galla. If the empire shrank and its power weakened, the likelihood of her finding a husband would decrease too. She had to do something.

Eyes closed, fingers interlaced, she prayed harder. Longer. Asked not just God, but every saint she could think of for help. Nothing happened. No golden light from above, or clamour of trumpets, no celestial voice telling her all would be well. The only thing she could hear was Darme lambasting one of the kitchen slaves for some reason or other. It was foolish to feel frustrated that she had not received a divine remedy, and sinful and arrogant to expect God to answer her prayers immediately, or even at all. She was one person, she told herself. Her concerns, while worrying, were not life-threatening. Many people were in far worse straits than she; no doubt God was helping them.

The prideful part of her spoke up. As empress, she could help so many. Was that not a reason for God to intervene on her behalf? Feeling guilty, she buried the idea, lest she bring down some form of retribution from above, but she could not completely kill it.

If she were given the opportunity, she felt sure Roma's fortunes would take a turn for the better.

Apart from prayer, which might or might not bring results, all she could do was to continue her search for a husband. Although Roma's population was small in comparison with its heyday, and the grandest families had decamped to the imperial court at Ravenna, there had to be some young men with good bloodlines left in the city. She confided later in Elpidia.

Pleased, Elpidia responded, 'I was in a perfume shop yesterday, looking for more rose water for you.'

Galla nodded; trying different scents was one of Elpidia's favourite activities. She could not afford to buy any for herself, but she made sure to tell every shop owner about her mistress. It meant she was treated with deference and allowed to sample every scent she wanted.

'I overheard a customer talking to her slave. Her son, who has been at the imperial court in Ravenna for more than a year, is returning to visit.'

Galla's ears pricked up.

'He is of marriageable age, it seems, and his mother thinks it is high time he found a wife. It is a wonder, she said, he hadn't already been ensnared in Ravenna by the daughter of an impoverished noble family seeking to renew their fortunes.'

'Does he have a physical impairment, maybe?' Galla didn't want to get her hopes up.

'She didn't mention anything like that, just what a fine-looking young man he is, and how she needed new perfume, not to mention a stola, to impress the possible brides who had been invited to their house.'

'Who is he, did you manage to find out?'

'I couldn't speak to her, obviously.' Elpidia looked smug. 'I waited until they had left, then asked the shopkeeper. Senator Maximianus is the woman's husband, and father to the boy. They are a well-bred family, he said, with strong loyalties to Honorius.'

Galla knew Maximianus to see, a portly type with receding hair. His bloodline was of good quality too, which opened the possibility of a potential match. She hoped, though, that son did not take after father. 'I should meet him – what is his name?'

Elpidia looked a little crestfallen. 'The shopkeeper wasn't sure.'

'I'll send Darme to the scribes in the forum with some coin. One of them is sure to know.'

Within a few hours, Darme having outdone himself, Galla had discovered that Maximianus and his son shared the same name, and the son was fond of chariot racing. This set her pulse to thumping. To have something she held so dear in common with a potential husband seemed a God-sent sign that he was suitable material. So did the fact that one scribe, his palm greased by Darme, claimed to have recently written out the details of a loan between the younger Maximianus and a certain moneylender. The monies were needed, it was rumoured, so Maximianus could place a large bet on the Blue charioteer Polyneices, due to race the next day.

'That's it!' she cried.

Elpidia looked confused.

'Maximianus will surely be at the Blues' stables this evening, you know, for the blessing of the horses.' This was a Christian tradition started some years before. Celebrated in private of old, it had ballooned into a large-scale event attended by supporters who wanted not just to pray for the success of their team, but also to meet the charioteers and the horses. Galla glanced at Elpidia. 'Help me to get ready – we will need to leave soon.'

'Are you sure this is a good idea?' asked Elpidia the instant Galla's bedroom door was shut.

Galla was a little surprised to be challenged. 'I am trying to find a husband. Does it matter?'

'I am talking about your possible choice of husband.'

'You haven't met him yet!' Galla suspected what was coming, knew Elpidia might have a point but did not want to admit it.

'A man who takes out a large loan to gamble on a chariot race is not the type I would wish my daughter wedded to. Maximianus must be a risk-taker, and not in a good way.'

'Polyneices' form of late has been excellent,' said Galla, calculating. 'He's won his last six races – it could be seven.'

'There is no such thing as a guaranteed winner on the track.'

It could not be denied that Elpidia's concern was a valid one. Maybe the younger Maximianus had been sent away to Ravenna because of a gambling problem. Galla hadn't considered that, but her desire to find a husband and Elpidia's mulish expression made her dig her heels in more. 'Say what you like. I am going to the ceremony. I shall make up my own mind about him.'

'Christ and all His saints!'

'Be careful! One day someone will hear you, and if they do, things will not go well for you.' This was Galla's concern, but with the words uttered, she realised they had sounded like a threat. 'You know what I mean,' she said.

Elpidia's scowl eased.

Galla couldn't help herself. Perhaps this was the day she met the man who would become her husband. With that achieved, she could plan for a child, a son, and if, God willing, Thermantia was as infertile as her poor dead sister, and Galla outlived her perverted half-brother, she might one day be mother to a child emperor. She could see it, could feel the power. When Elpidia tried again to dissuade her from going to the blessing of the horses, Galla snapped, said there had been enough debate. She was going, and if Elpidia didn't want to be left at home, she had better shut her mouth.

Elpidia's face fixed into a scowl that would make grown men hesitate.

For once Galla ignored her, and began to prepare.

With confined sides, the litter was small enough that Galla and Elpidia either had to close their eyes or stare at each other or the floor. With the atmosphere between them still tense, Elpidia went for the first option. Galla tried to divert herself by lifting the cloth aside to peer out at the street. Despite Darme's scolding, a leprous beggar spied her and darted in, waving a hand bereft of digits. Galla might normally have proffered a coin, but with her mind swirling with possibilities about how the evening might unfold, she let the fabric drop. When she turned her head, Elpidia was looking at her.

The nurse quickly closed her eyes again.

'This is childish,' said Galla.

No answer.

'I know you're not asleep.'

Elpidia opened one eye, suspicious.

'I do not like it when we fall out.'

'And I do not like it when you act foolishly,' whispered Elpidia.

Galla reined in her temper. She was not an empress yet, and Elpidia did have her best interests at heart. 'You could be wrong. He might not be an inveterate gambler. He may have wanted to place the bet because of some inside knowledge.'

'True. Let us give him the benefit of the doubt, and use the evening to find out what we can.' Elpidia smiled, and Galla smiled back.

Her spirits rose. Elpidia might find out much from other slaves. And it was not too much to ask that Maximianus would prove to be not just an upstanding young man who enjoyed an occasional big flutter, but someone she liked, and who in turn liked her. Last but not least, she hoped her bet on Polyneices, to be placed for her by Darme, would mean she won a large sum of money.

'How much are you going to wager?'

It was startling how often Elpidia seemed to be able to read her mind, thought Galla. 'Fifty solidi,' she lied.

'It's at least twice that then.' Elpidia's stare was piercing.

Galla coloured. 'What makes you so sure?'

An Elpidia look. 'I've known you from birth.'

'One hundred and fifty solidi.'

'Maybe it's you I should be worried about, and not Maximianus.' Elpidia's tone was serious.

Galla had no answer, and an uncomfortable silence fell, lasting until they arrived on the Campus Martius, where the stables of all four factiones were situated. As the rich smell of horse manure permeated the litter, Galla lifted the fabric again to look out. As might have been expected, the largest complexes were those of the Blues and Greens. Each had its own racetrack for practice and training; the Blues' one encircled the sprawl of buildings and stables. A set of banked wooden seating for trainers and spectators stood close to the arched entrance, its occupants three men in plain tunics, some of the trainers. They weren't the only ones watching. Several hundred spectators, diehard fans, had already arrived and were standing around the track.

The litter paused to let a pair of chariots thunder by, neck and neck with one another.

'It's Polyneices!' cried Galla.

Darme appeared. 'It must be a last bit of training, Nobilissima Femina, before the big race tomorrow.' He grinned, which told Galla he was gambling on Polyneices too.

'Heaven's sake,' said Elpidia. 'Put a solidus on for me, Darme.'

Darme gave her a solemn wink, and went to speak with the watchman at the entrance to the Blues' complex. A moment later, the great door was being pushed open, and Galla let the fabric fall again. It did not do to arrive peering out at the world like a yokel beholding Roma for the first time. The litter halted, was lowered to the ground. Galla checked her gossamer-meshed gold hairnet, touched her gold and garnet earrings fashioned in the shape of tiny doves, and smiled at Elpidia. 'Well?'

Elpidia's face softened. 'You are a vision.'

'Of what?'

A coy smile. 'You know – of beauty.'

'Do you think so?' asked Galla, worried that all her efforts would come to nothing, that Maximianus would not even notice her.

Elpidia's short-fingered, competent hands took one of hers and squeezed. 'I do. You are beautiful, Nobilissima Femina. Now go and see whether Maximianus is worthy of you.'

Galla had barely emerged from the litter when, alerted by a sharp-eyed slave, the *dominus factionis* appeared in the large rectangular courtyard. A tall, ascetic eques by the name of Lucius Petronius Volusianus, he was used to her visits. 'Nobilissima Femina,' he cried. 'What an unexpected pleasure!'

Galla inclined her head. 'Well met, Volusianus.' From the corner of her eye, she could see that men had paused in their work to glance in her direction. A young groom, curry comb in hand, stopped staring when his fellow cuffed him round the head. Galla gave no indication, but the attention boosted her confidence. Elpidia was telling the truth, she thought. I do look beautiful.

'It's not surprising to see you, I suppose,' Volusianus went on. 'Given your high opinion of Polyneices. Did you see him as you entered, Nobilissima Femina?'

'I did. Is he ready?'

'He says so, and there is no reason to disbelieve him. Three of his horses are in top shape; one is carrying a slight injury, but the *veterinarius* is sure it won't hold him back.' Explaining that the blessing ceremony would not start for a little while, Volusianus offered to guide her around the complex. Galla accepted with alacrity. She hadn't had a full tour for some time.

When they returned from walking the several avenues of stables, tack rooms, haybarns, storage sheds and sleeping quarters for the staff, the courtyard was much busier. Polyneices was standing by his chariot, having a word with the head trainer. Horses were being led out of stables and assembled in eight wide rows. When the priests were ready, Galla knew, the horses would be taken outside to stand in front of the wooden seating.

Volusianus escorted her through the archway. The crowd was now thousands strong, in the main comprised of ordinary people. There were sunburned farmers from the surrounding countryside, workmen with tools at their belts, and haughty-looking scribes with ink-stained fingers. Children ran about playing catch and pretend chariot races. Mobile vendors patrolled, selling wine, olives, bread, painted chariot and horse figurines. The well-to-do and the wealthy were also present, their ample rear ends planted on the banked wooden seating. The centre of the front row was empty, reserved for nobility such as Galla, and the dominus himself.

Seeing her, the crowd hushed. There were cries of 'Nobilissima Femina!' and 'Galla supports the Blues!' and a good deal of cheering. Everyone who was seated rose to their feet and bowed.

As taught by her father and Elpidia many years before, Galla raised her right arm and gave the half-turn of the wrist and hand signifying the imperial wave. To left and right she made the gesture, allowing her lips to curve upward just a little. Her eyes ran over the assembled nobility, searching for a young, handsome individual. There were several, all but two of whom she recognised and dismissed as unsuitable. Her gaze returned to the unfamiliar pair. Maximianus was either short with black hair, she decided, or taller and stockier with brown curly hair. She hoped he was the taller of the pair. It was better to look up at a man when kissing him, she thought.

When she was seated on a patterned cushion, Volusianus a little distance to her right, Elpidia sitting on the ground before her, an expectant hush fell. The children were summoned by their parents, or shooed away by attendants. Two priests, both wearing robes embroidered with the Chi-Rho symbol, paced out to stand in front of the seating. A trumpet sounded inside the Blues complex, and the procession began to emerge.

The ceremony wasn't long, the hundred or so horses and score of charioteers receiving the priests' blessings and promises of good fortune sent by God Himself. Holy water was thrown. There was a ripple of amusement as several horses, not realising what was happening, jerked their heads back in alarm as the droplets landed.

The ending was a special blessing for Polyneices and his team. Spontaneous applause broke out when the priests made their final gesture of the cross. Galla felt strangely moved, as if God was indeed watching from above, and wondered if she should tell Darme to add another hundred solidi to her wager.

Social custom, not to mention her elevated status, meant she could not approach Maximianus, and asking Volusianus to introduce him to her might cause gossip. Galla was at a slight loss about how to engineer a meeting until a short time later, in the courtyard, when she saw the pair of good-looking young nobles walking towards one of the avenues. Knowing that was the direction of Polyneices' team's stables, she decided they were going to take a private look at the horses. Volusianus was busy, explaining tactics to a red-faced senator and his equally red-faced wife, so she slipped away with just Elpidia for company.

Deep in conversation, the two men were oblivious to being followed.

'I'm not sure this is wise,' said Elpidia. 'You should have a chaperone.'

'You are my chaperone.'

'I am a slave.'

'And if either says or does anything, you can scream the place down. Happy?'

Elpidia glowered, but gave no further protest.

The pair entered a stable, roughly where Galla thought Polyneices' team were housed. It was a little surprising, but she concluded they wanted to see one of the horses close up. Their being out of sight meant she could move faster, and it wasn't long before the stable door drew near. Galla went over in her mind what she would say. An expression of surprise to see them inside. An understanding laugh, perhaps, and an admission that she too wanted to see the winning team for herself.

'Kiss me.' A man's voice.

Shocked, Galla stopped dead. Had the pair arranged a meeting with a female slave? Two female slaves?

'Like this?' A second male voice, silky, assured.

Galla couldn't believe, wouldn't believe what she had heard. No, she thought, it's not possible. Her head spun; she had to lean against the wall to steady herself.

'Yes, like that. Do it again, and do this as well, with your hand . . .'

A throaty laugh. 'This?'

Nausea bathed her.

'Come away.' It was Elpidia, calm, emotionless, taking charge as if Galla were a small girl again. 'You don't want a husband like him,' she muttered.

I will never find one, thought Galla. Never become a mother.

Never be empress.

CHAPTER XV

Diocese of Viennensis

Far away from Roma, Vadomar's existence was less upsetting, but far more dangerous. He, his friends and twelve comrades were lying in a slight hollow about sixty paces from the walls of Valentia. The night after his suggestion to Sarus, it was raining heavily, and they were all drenched to the bone. At first the bad weather had seemed a reason to postpone the attack, but their minds were changed by news brought in by scouts. Gerontius and Edobichus were two days' march away. There had been another meeting with Sarus, who was understandably far more enthusiastic. The city had to be taken at once.

Vadomar's hope was for the rain to mask their approach, and with luck, also their scaling of the defences and secretive journey through the darkened streets. Relentless downpours were the scourge of sentries, he said to Dog and Wulfila, whatever side they fought on. They had laughed, familiar with long nights spent in sodden clothing waiting for an enemy who never showed himself.

They had one ladder, fashioned from tree branches. Vadomar and two others had lengths of rope looped from one shoulder to the opposite hip. He would have preferred more rope, but sourcing what they were carrying had been hard enough. They would not need it, he told himself, ignoring the tiny, nagging doubt that it was pride that had him here in the mud rather than a genuine belief that they could succeed.

They'd left their camp a long time after darkness fell, inching their way to the hollow. He and Dog had been studying the battlements since. How long, he had no idea; it had to be hours. There had been no sign of movement there at any point. On a better night, Vadomar would have been able to spy out individual sentries, but the dark and the rain meant nothing was visible except the vast bulk of Valentia's walls. If there were sentries, they were huddled in their cloaks, and not paying attention to much.

He placed his lips against Wulfila's ear. 'Time to move, eh?'

Wulfila's head, an outline, nodded.

Quickly, Vadomar prayed. He wasn't sure if the gods ever heard him, still less answered, but he felt better for doing it. As his father had been fond of saying, if a man thinks he will survive a battle because the gods are with him, half the struggle is over. He performed his ritual. Belt, sword, dagger. Then he twisted, tapped the shoulder of the man behind and pointed. Without waiting for a response, he began to crawl. The ground was sodden, but he was so wet it didn't matter. He had no shield or armour, because of the risk of noise. He had no spear, it being too awkward to carry up a ladder.

They reached the bottom of the defences without incident, and after a short search, found the large, different-coloured piece of masonry marking the place to climb. Vadomar looked up the wall, wondering if the ladder would reach the top, and if there was a sentry up there. He would soon find out.

Wulfila had wanted to go first, but Dog and Vadomar had insisted they play dice to decide. To Wulfila's utter disgust, Vadomar had won. It didn't seem so wonderful now. They lifted the ladder, carefully leaning it against the wall. It seemed to be long enough, which was good, and there was no immediate alarm either. Vadomar waited for a dozen heartbeats, and still no alerting cry rang out. Wulfila gripped his arm by way of encouragement.

Vadomar swallowed, and put a foot on the first rung. It took his weight, so, gripping the ladder's sides, he climbed. Dog followed, Wulfila on his heels. Every third rung, Vadomar paused to listen.

At six rungs, he was halfway up. No sound came from above. At nine, he could see the ladder was too long. It was also in plain sight of anyone who came close. At once he began to climb faster. Instead of a straightforward jump off the top, he would have to step to one side, put a foot on the rampart and then launch himself onto the walkway beyond.

Eleven rungs and he was almost there. Stretch out, and he could grip the top of the wall with his hand.

Boots scuffed off stone.

Silent as a wraith, Vadomar climbed up one more rung and drew his dagger. He counted. *One. Two.* Reach ten, he thought, and the sentry hadn't seen the ladder. *Three. Four.*

A face appeared above him, a smooth-cheeked face. A boy sentry. He saw Vadomar crouched on the ladder, and his eyes went wide. His mouth began to open.

It was pure good fortune he looked over the right side of the ladder. Had it been the left, Vadomar would have been helpless to react. Instead, he rammed the dagger into the corner of the boy's jaw. Hot liquid drenched him as it came out. Again the scales tipped in his favour. The boy slumped, knees hitting the walkway, chin resting on the wall for an instant. There was a soft thump as his body landed.

Vadomar sprang down, heeling his eyes clear of blood, searching for another sentry, listening for the slightest sound.

Nothing.

He grinned at Dog and Wulfila, who had joined him. Relieved not to see another sentry, the three of them stripped the corpse of cloak, helmet and weapons, then lowered it down to the bottom of the wall. They'd already decided that if they had to kill a sentry, one of them would have to take his place in case his empty spot was noticed. Everyone wanted to be there when the gate was taken, so they had drawn lots. The chosen bucellarius, a greybeard who'd been old when Vadomar joined the army, was none too happy about being left behind, but he donned the slain sentry's cloak and helmet and took up his shield and spear. Mad as it seemed to remove a possible way of escape, the protruding ladder would have given the game away, so they lowered that down too. If needs be, the reasoning went, it could be hauled up again.

The veteran was one of the men carrying a length of rope, because it would be too dangerous for him to try and reach the gate alone, whether they succeeded or failed. Whatever happened, Vadomar told him, he would be able to climb to safety. If that was supposed to make him feel better, the veteran grumbled, it didn't. Telling him to stay alert, Vadomar left him to it.

The rain was growing heavier, dragging the temperature down further. The clouds felt low enough to touch. Now and again, a faint rumble of thunder echoed. It was, Vadomar decided, as miserable a night as the depths of winter, which favoured their mission. Sure enough, he encountered no one on the staircase down to street level. It was pitch black here, the only light the slightly less dark shade of the cloud-ridden sky above. He could make out the buildings that faced onto the wall, but no detail. Even if they'd had torches to light their way, the driving rain would soon have doused them. He was reminded of the myth of Theseus in the labyrinth, though they had no thread to trail behind them.

The scale of what they had to do seemed insurmountable, but to hesitate would allow the seeds of doubt to take root. Conferring with Dog and Wulfila, he elected to try and walk along the base of the wall. With luck, it might lead straight to the gate.

That hope ended with a large windowless building, a warehouse perhaps, which had been constructed so close to the wall only a rat could squeeze through. They worked their way around it and back to the wall again, but the flicker of light and the sound of voices had them retracing their steps to the nearest alleyway. Peering around the corner, Vadomar counted half a dozen sentries and an officer, a change of the guard or some such.

Part of him longed to attack, for they would surely overwhelm the enemy, but the risk was too great. The clash of weapons or an escaping sentry would bring reinforcements and ensure they never reached the gate.

The sudden appearance of another group of soldiers on the street forced them to skulk like thieves down the alleyway. That led onto an angling, narrow street which seemed to head the right way, but a wider thoroughfare never appeared. Nor did the gate. The three friends conferred again, agreeing to retrace their steps to the slanted street and go in the opposite direction.

That didn't work either, taking them to the town's forum, a large, open paved space empty of people and dominated by statues. Here the rain beat down in great blinding sheets. Water was overflowing from the gutters, running in streams along the pavement, splashing up with every footstep. Vadomar forced himself to stay calm. No one had seen them, there was plenty of time before sunrise, and it stood to reason one of the streets leading off the forum went to the main gate. He said as much to Dog and Wulfila, who agreed.

'This one?' He pointed. It was close to the alley they had arrived on, but running off to the left.

'Try it,' muttered one of the others. 'Anything's better than standing around in this downpour.'

Vadomar agreed, at least for as long as it took to cross the forum.

Then the door of the first building on the street opened, spilling warm yellow light over the shiny, wet paving. Vadomar stopped, as did the rest. There was nowhere to go, nowhere to hide, nothing to do other than to stand dead still amid the rainstorm. A man stumbled outside, complaining in a slurred voice that it was bucketing down, curse the gods, old and new. He was followed by four more drunkards. After came a huge doorman. 'No more, boys,' he declared. 'You've had enough for one night.'

'We're thirsty yet,' grumbled one.

'You drank enough to float a trireme between you,' said the amiable doorman. 'Go home!' His gaze moved past his protesting customers, through the sheeting rain, to Vadomar and his comrades, dark, unmoving, sinister figures. He puffed out his chest. 'Who's there?'

Vadomar's mind spun. Say nothing, and suspicions would be aroused. He shot a glance at Wulfila and saw the same realisation in his eyes. He *had* to respond.

'Going to relieve sentries, we are,' he answered loudly, striding towards the corner.

'Thought as much.' The doorman was already stepping back inside. *Bang* went the door; the bolts clunked one after another.

One of the four customers was puking, hunched over, strings of drool hanging. Another patted him on the back, saying, 'Let it all out.' The third was pissing against the tavern wall, but the fourth, swaying where he stood, watched the bucellarii approach.

Vadomar told himself the man was so rat-arsed drunk he wouldn't recognise his own hand if it wasn't on the end of his arm, but as they drew alongside, he couldn't help but look up.

A frown. A scowl. 'Y-you've no armour! No shields!'

His protest was ended by Vadomar's dagger, which buried itself in his throat. Emitting a horrible gurgling sound, the man dropped.

The three others died in a flurry of blows. There was little noise apart from the repeated wet thump of blades punching into flesh, and the gasps of effort from men who were killing with a ferocity born of desperation.

Chest heaving, standing over the body of the man he'd slain, Vadomar decided it could have gone a lot worse. It felt good, felt as if despite their experience thus far, they would succeed. His gaze went to the others, one by one. 'Come on. The cursed gate won't open itself,' he said.

Bolts were pulled back. The door creaked; light cascaded out onto the street again.

No, thought Vadomar. No!

A weaving shape emerged, another worse-for-wear customer. He goggled at Vadomar and his companions before his attention went to the corpses at their feet. His face worked, a picture of confusion. 'What . . .?'

The doorman loomed behind him. Being sober, he realised at once that foul murder was afoot. Being sober, he realised that a large group of armed men in dark clothing were up to no good. 'Awake!' His bellow could have been heard in Roma. 'Awake! The city is under attack!' He grabbed the customer by his belt and dragged him back inside, slamming the door. An instant's delay, and then a fearful clamour started up inside, a pot being beaten with a metal implement. Voices were also raised, the owner being woken and apprised of the situation. They would soon be banging pans from the first-floor windows, thought Vadomar.

'What should we do?' hissed Dog.

'We have to try for the gate,' said Vadomar. 'I will not skulk away like a cur.'

'Move then,' said Wulfila with a shove.

They ran.

The last street *did* go to the main gate, but it was some distance away. By the time they got close, half of Valentia was awake. Men shouted, a woman screamed, dogs joined in. The deep, sonorous clang of a church bell added to the noise. Vadomar was sure the only reason they hadn't been challenged was their ground-covering speed. Looking out onto the street, inhabitants would assume they were soldiers, responding to the alarm.

They spilled around a final corner. Vadomar took in the scene. Boarded-up shops to left and right. An abandoned ox cart, partly full of building materials. The gate, closed by a massive bar, and in front, in two neat ranks, thirty-odd soldiers. Shields high, spears held overhand, an officer in a crested helmet barking orders, they were ready for battle.

'Bastards,' said Wulfila.

'Bastard cunts,' said Dog.

Vadomar swore himself, long and hard. 'If we charge, we might break through.'

'Has the rain washed out your wits altogether?' cried Dog. 'Fifteen of us with no armour or shields against twice that number armed *properly*?'

Vadomar searched his comrades' faces and saw uncertainty and fear. He looked back at the men guarding the gate, and his heart sank as another half-dozen came pell-mell down the nearest staircase.

'Well?' growled Dog, and Vadomar realised he was being asked if they were to try, regardless of the stupid odds. His heart squeezed, and he thought, I cannot lead these men to certain death if failure is to be our result. Had there been more of them, they could have thrown caution to the wind, falling vengefully on the half-asleep, scared sentries. As it was, he valued their lives too much to throw them away on the roll of a weighted dice.

'Back! Back to where we climbed the wall!'

The bunched soldiers jeered and shouted. Before their officer could stop them, several spears were thrown. They landed short, skating along the wet paving. One planted itself in the back of the ox cart, where it stood, quivering.

'Retreat!' shouted Vadomar.

It was a grim journey back whence they had come. Men cursing. Colliding. Arguing over which street or alley to take. Boots slipping on the wet stones. There were falls, inevitably. Twisted ankles and bruised arses. A savage yelp left Dog's mouth as he went down, cracking a knee. Vadomar hauled him up. 'All right?'

'What would you do if I said no?'

Vadomar snorted. 'I'd say run!'

Dog didn't answer, but he had a bad limp.

Worried for his friend, but knowing he was too proud to accept help, Vadomar dropped to the back. Perhaps half the soldiers who'd been at the gate were on their tail. They weren't in any great rush, and from the noise they were making, hammering on doors, shouting, clashing weapons off iron shield rims, they were trying to wake every man of the garrison. It was a clever tactic. Doors were being pulled ajar, heads poking out. A window right above Vadomar opened, and a head peered up and down the street, assessing the situation. It popped back in, and an instant later, a large object came sailing through the air.

'Look out!' Vadomar shoved the man in front, and the object, a ceramic pot, smashed on the ground between them. He tried to leap over the contents, and failed. *Squelch* went his foot, even as his nostrils filled with the stench of human ordure.

Wulfila, just ahead, had twisted to look. 'Ha ha, I'll never let you forget that!'

'If I had the time, I'd go back for some shit to throw at you,' Vadomar retorted.

Their good humour lasted perhaps a dozen strides.

The men at the front slowed. 'There's light in the forum,' said one. 'Soldiers,' said another. Everyone stopped.

Vadomar pushed forward. The forum, still a distance off, was a different place to the one they'd left. Between the statues, bands of men were gathering, armed men. A trumpet sounded, summoning more. He wanted to rage at the gods, but he was the one to blame for being here. What had he been thinking?

'Our way back is cut off.' A note of fear was evident in the man's voice, one of the youngest present.

'It's a small city. A dozen alleyways probably lead there. Follow me!' With a confidence he did not feel, Vadomar plunged into the narrow space between two apartment buildings. Forced by the utter black, he slowed to a walk within a few steps, and felt his way forward. The footing was uneven, a mixture of hard – pottery shards and the like – and soft; he did not like to guess what. He tried to ignore the rats scurrying out of his path. 'Who's at the rear?'

'Me.' Dog's curt voice.

'Good.' No one would get past his comrade.

Covered in cobwebs, the shit stink filling his nose, Vadomar emerged onto a street. A small number of people had come out of their houses, some armed. The nearest, a simple-looking youth in nothing but a pair of trews, was staring at the bucellarii open-mouthed. He was perfect. Vadomar advanced and pricked the boy's throat with his dagger. 'Know the city well?' he asked in Latin.

'L-like the b-back of my hand. Don't hurt me, please!'

'I won't, if you do what I say.'

'Anything.'

Vadomar described the spot where they had climbed the wall, and the boy said he knew it. He seemed to be telling the truth. Vadomar spun him around and touched his daggerpoint to the small of his back. 'One false move, and I'll put this through your liver. You'll bleed to death inside, slowly. Understand?'

A terrified glance over his shoulder. 'Aye.'

'Move.' Vadomar used the dagger to push him. Within a few steps, the fresh tang of urine revealed the boy had soiled himself. If Vadomar felt anything, it was satisfaction. Consumed by fear, the boy would not play them false.

The inhabitants who saw them, no soldiers, were intimidated by the fierce expressions and ready blades of the bucellarii. Stepping back against the buildings, or even into their own doorways, they watched in silence as the fifteen men and the boy sped by.

'You still there, Dog?'

'You can't get rid of me so easily!'

'And our tail?'

'I've had to dodge a spear or two.' This was delivered in a conversational tone.

'Faster!' Vadomar jabbed the boy, who cried out in pain and fear. He did it again. 'How far?'

'We are close!'

'Better be, or . . .' *Jab. Jab.*

The boy was not lying. Reaching the end of the alley, they emerged about two dozen paces from a pair of staircases separated by a section of rampart. Vadomar wouldn't have known it from his own arsehole, but he'd have wagered his life the figure atop the walkway was the greybeard they'd left behind. Assailed from left and right, he was fighting a losing battle.

Vadomar shoved the halfwit boy out of the way and sprinted for the stairs. 'Hold on! We're coming!'

The others had seen too. Picking up stones, they hurled them at the men attacking their comrade, and screams rang out. One sentry toppled off the walkway, clutching his thigh. He hit the ground with a dreadful smack. Scrambling up the stairs, Vadomar hurled himself forward. A spear thrust at his belly, but he twisted sideways. He slid along the rough wall face, grabbing the shaft with his left hand and with his other sinking his dagger deep into its wielder's neck. Using his momentum, he propelled the dying man backwards into his comrade behind, who, hands trapped with shield and spear, stared in terror as the bloodied dagger came ramming down.

Wulfila, at Vadomar's back, slew the third sentry. The fourth lost his footing and went down, and that was the end of him. Heaving bodies aside, Vadomar found the greybeard leaning heavily against the wall. He was breathing with difficulty and holding his side. Beyond him, the remaining sentry was fighting a losing battle with Wulfila.

Vadomar reached out to support the greybeard. 'You should be long gone! Why didn't you use the rope, get away?'

'I wanted to make sure you could reach the walkway, you know, if taking the gate was a failure.' A bubbling cough, a knowing look. 'It was a failure?'

'Yes. The alarm was raised. They had time to get men to the gate.'

'A pity. I would have liked it said I was one of the men who took Valentia.'

'You will yet!' Vadomar could hear boots pounding along the walkway. Attracted by the noise, more sentries were coming. He slipped the rope from his shoulders and gave it to Wulfila, who lobbed one end over the wall and set to fastening the other end in place.

'You are a bad liar, Vadomar.' A pause, a grunt of pain. 'I am for the thunder god's feasting hall, if he will have me.'

'You will be welcomed with honour!'

'Aye, well, if you're not to join me, use this as well.' The greybeard tapped the stone beside him, and Vadomar saw the rope tied around the crenellation. 'Gratitude,' he said, powerfully moved. With two ropes, and if they moved fast, most of them had a good chance of escaping.

In the event, Vadomar was correct. The greybeard, who refused even to try to escape, died fighting a tide of sentries. The youngest of the bucellarii, who'd sounded scared at the forum, took a spear in the guts as he clambered up, rope in hand, and prepared to lower himself to safety. The pair were the only fatalities, however, for which Vadomar was grateful. Dog's knee was skinned to the bone, yet he made it out of the city. Two others had flesh wounds.

They were fortunate to have escaped, but their mission had been a resounding failure. When Vadomar went to speak with Sarus, the magister flew into an incandescent rage. Purple in the face, spittle flying from his fat lips, his words were inaudible apart from the frequent curses. At one point, he seemed about to draw his sword, but a staff officer stepped between them and with an urgent gesture indicated that Vadomar should leave.

'Sarus wasn't there!' Vadomar ranted to Dog and Wulfila a short time later. 'He didn't see how many men were guarding the gate! Does the cocksucker think we should have thrown away our lives?'

'Probably,' said Wulfila. 'I don't know why you're surprised.'

Vadomar's seething rage subsided enough for reason to return. 'Aye. Generals don't care about individual soldiers.'

'Never have, never will.' Dog spat on the ground.

Vadomar's mind was already turning to the next problem. 'Gerontius and Edobichus will be here soon. If we don't retreat, they will be the hammer and Constantinus the anvil.'

That wasn't a prospect any of the friends wanted to imagine.

Unexpected good news came the next morning. A messenger sent by Edobichus to Valentia was captured and brought to Sarus. The information he carried was cause for much celebration. To the south, which had also been affected by the heavy rain, the main road was washed away, and bridges destroyed. Constantinus' reinforcements would be delayed for some days at least, longer if the terrible weather persisted. Sarus allowed the messenger to enter Valentia, and had his engineers start working on the construction of catapults in full view of the city's walls. His ploy soon bore fruit. In the early afternoon, a herald came from Valentia, saying the magister militum, Nebiogastes, wanted to negotiate.

Sarus accepted, but he was unhappy. 'Constantinus is up to no good. Sending a mouse to nibble at the cheese in case it's a trap.'

Sensible enough, thought Vadomar. He was loitering outside with the sentries, hopeful of eavesdropping. Sarus' tendency to talk at the top of his voice meant he was rewarded.

'Tell him he will be welcome,' Sarus said, obviously talking to the herald. 'The sooner he comes, the better.'

Nebiogastes did not delay, emerging from Valentia by mid-afternoon. He came with a body of Alan cavalry, arrogant men, all shining armour and polished helmets. Their horses were dolled up too, chest harnesses gleaming and the flayed faces of slain enemies dangling on each side.

'They're the same lot as the bastard who tried to kill you,' said Wulfila, squint-eyed with anger.

Vadomar nodded, studying the riders. None seemed to recognise him, not that he cared.

Nebiogastes was in their midst, a pudgy, balding man who sat on his horse with the grace and ability of an overfull bag of grain.

His armour was expensive but ill-fitting, and Vadomar would have wagered ten silver coins his ornate sword was just that, a gewgaw not made for real combat. Although he kept company with soldiers, he looked completely out of place. He kept his gaze fixed straight ahead, ignoring the crowds of Sarus' soldiers who had come to witness the spectacle.

Sarus appeared in his finery, but unlike Nebiogastes, he was an imposing sight, polished armour well used, sword ivory-handled but in a plain scabbard. Despite Vadomar's poor opinion of his horsemanship, he looked as graceful as a Scyth beside the uncomfortable Nebiogastes.

'You are not Constantinus.'

It was an aggressive first move, designed to intimidate.

'It is beneath the Imperator's dignity to negotiate.' Nebiogastes did not need to add the words 'with his inferiors'. Before Sarus could speak, he continued, 'I am sent in his stead.'

'Will your emperor' – Sarus packed enormous contempt into the last word – 'open the gates? Order his soldiers to surrender? Give himself into my custody?'

Flustered, Nebiogastes hesitated.

Sarus' jaw set. 'Well?'

'I am not sure. I—'

'Not sure? What kind of herald comes to speak to his enemy in such an ill-prepared manner?'

Nebiogastes coloured. 'Imperator Constantinus wishes to know if Honorius will offer him the purple, make him co-emperor.'

'He has some balls to demand that even as he is besieged!'

'You might be saying something different when Edobichus and Gerontius arrive.'

'This is a waste of time.' Sarus' right arm chopped the air.

Vadomar blinked.

Nebiogastes gagged, courtesy of the arrow suddenly sprouting from his open mouth. A hand came up to clutch at the jutting shaft, and a second arrow skewered that arm. He emitted a horrible choking groan and fell from his horse. His Alani roared in anger, and laid hands to swords and spears.

'Move a muscle and you will all die!' Sarus indicated the archers who must have silently ringed the gathering. There were fifty at least, using powerful recurve bows.

The Alan in charge said something in his guttural tongue. None of his men moved.

'Take Nebiogastes back to Valentia,' Sarus shouted. 'Tell Constantinus he has until tomorrow morning to surrender. If he will not, I will take the town by storm!'

There was much muttering and glowering, but the Alani had little choice other than to obey. They left amid a barrage of jeers and abuse, Sarus' soldiers exulting in the humiliation of the embassy.

It was all well and good issuing such bold ultimatums, Vadomar said to Wulfila, but a man had to be able to back them up. In this case, it meant mounting an effective siege, something Sarus' army was not capable of in the short term. It might have worked out if time was on their side, but Edobichus and Gerontius could arrive any day, and autumn was well under way. The risk of defeat by Constantinus and his two generals, or of being trapped west of the Alpes, was real.

Nebiogastes' death changed nothing.

No more messengers were sent out from Valentia, and when Sarus dispatched an envoy to the main gate the next morning, so many arrows were loosed, he was lucky to escape with his life. Two days after, scouts brought the unwelcome news of the approach of none other than Edobichus and Gerontius with their armies. Sarus' gamble had not paid off. Furious, but no fool, he gave the order to break camp.

'This feels familiar,' declared Vadomar as they took the road south.

'Second time this year.' Wulfila had remained with the group when the three friends had gone on ahead and had the fight at the mutatio. That he had not insisted on coming with them was a regret, he said, he would carry to his grave.

'Eriulf is probably laughing at us,' said Dog.

'Probably he is.' Vadomar did not like retreating, but he would welcome the chance to pay his respects again at his friend's resting place.

'Do you think Stilicho will send us back to Viennensis in the spring?' Wulfila asked.

'I'd imagine so,' said Vadomar. 'Better to cut the viper's head off rather than let it slither into your bed. But let's get to Italia first, eh? The Alpes are a long way off still, and it's not just the usurper's soldiers who have to be evaded.'

They had to avoid the bacaudae as well.

CHAPTER XVI

Seven months later . . .

Roma; late Mensis Aprilis, AD *408*

Galla had spent hours getting ready. Her clinging stola was purple silk, her finest garment. Its cost would make a moneylender cry, Elpidia liked to say. A trace of kohl marked her eyes, adding years to her age. As was customary, her face was chalk-whitened; she did not like lead. The golden hairnet she was so fond of was in place. Pearls adorned her throat, the dove earrings nestled either side of her face. It was amusing, she thought, to have donned so much finery when it all had to be covered up. In the event of being discovered, however, the world would see her at her best.

Stilicho's address to the Senate was to take place at the Curia in the Forum Romanum later the same day, with her half-brother Honorius in attendance. Only the emperor, senators and relevant government officials were allowed inside during formal sessions, but Galla was determined to be present. The world was changing. Had already changed. She could not stay at home and weave or compose poetry.

The previous autumn in Viennensis, Sarus had been forced into an ignominious retreat from Valentia. Pursued by Constantinus' army into the foothills of the Alpes, his road to safety had been blocked by the bacaudae. It had taken every bit of the booty taken during the campaign to see safe passage granted through the snow-clad mountains. He had reached Italia with his tail between his legs, while Constantinus would have been in a far better mood. With his eastern border secured, he had set up court in Arelate, and according to rumour was planning further conquests. Gallia and Viennensis, it seemed, were entirely lost, and Hispania might soon follow. Italia would also be on his list.

Since the year's beginning, worrying news had continued to arrive in Roma. Alaric had moved his host from Epirus to the province of Noricum. This was well within striking distance of Italia, and a Hunnic war leader with thousands of followers was with him. There were widespread rumours that he had come in answer to Stilicho's summons. Whether this was true or not, Roma now had enemies and potential enemies to the west and east.

Even the slaves were saying it.

The empire's future hung in the balance.

Galla meanwhile had no husband still, but she was determined – by whatever means – to be involved in what happened next.

There were two political camps in the Senate, one favouring Stilicho, another loyal to Honorius. Through all the time Galla had been aware of politics, Stilicho's camp had been the largest and most influential. As she was realising, many of its members had joined wanting only to be part of the dominant faction. With Stilicho's power on the wane and the emperor back in Roma, they were revealing their true colours – dislike, disdain, condescension towards anyone who was not Roman. According to a contact of Darme's, a major domus to an influential senator, speech after speech was being made in the Senate about how there had been enough deferring and knee-bending to the barbarians. Roma was for the Romans, and so was its wealth. They were not for armies of fur-wearing brutes.

Stilicho had come to the city to speak with the Senate, and to persuade its members to agree to Alaric's latest demand. Quite what this was, no one knew: the message had been delivered to Stilicho, and he in turn would reveal all in the Curia. Honorius, perhaps the one person to have already been told, gauged the situation serious enough to be present also. In Galla's mind, it spoke volumes. It was her duty to be there too. Roma was her city. The empire was her empire.

An opportunity to rule might never come, she was well aware, but it would not be for want of trying. She could learn much in the Senate today, and knowledge was a form of power.

Elpidia came bustling in holding a heavy woollen hooded cloak. 'Put this on.'

Galla obeyed, and they went downstairs, where Darme was waiting. To Elpidia's disgust, he was an integral part of Galla's plan. Women weren't allowed inside the Curia when it was in session, she had explained. Elpidia's tart retort had been that Galla was female. Two women would be far easier to spot than one in a hooded cloak, Galla said. Elpidia had huffed and muttered, and now that they were ready to leave, she was again in bad humour over it.

'Yours is an important job.' Galla held out a bulging leather purse. 'You know what to do.'

Elpidia hefted it with an appraising expression, then tucked it away inside her dress. Galla had given a similar purse to Darme, his job to bribe the men at the door of the Curia.

The Syrian was waiting outside with his litter. He bowed and lifted the fabric so Galla could climb in. Elpidia followed, and Darme took up his usual position alongside the litter.

'Ready, Nobilissima Femina?' he called.

It was an apt question in more ways than one, thought Galla. She was as prepared as she would ever be.

Hood up, Galla was standing behind the rows of senators. Like them, her attention was focused on the low dais at the end of the long central walkway. It was perfect. No one paid her any heed. Not for the first time in her life, she was grateful to be taller than most women. Positioned about two thirds along the length of the Curia, she had a reasonable view of Honorius. A gold-leafed wreath encircling his head, he was seated on an ivory curule chair, a sign of office since Roma's earliest history. Candidati in red tunics and purple cloaks flanked him, and a richly garbed adviser with oily skin and a double chin stood a couple of steps to his rear. Beside the emperor was Stilicho, imposing in full military regalia, scale armour mirror-bright, sword in a magnificent silver-chased scabbard. Both men were eye-catching in their own way. It was a tragedy, with both so important to the empire, that they were on the verge of becoming enemies.

It was no surprise, however. Honorius had grown up being advised, directed, steered by Stilicho and, to a lesser extent, Serena. Marriage to their daughter had cemented the bond further, but her death and their lack of children combined with Honorius reaching a mature age – he was twenty-three – meant that if there was ever a time to grow a pair of balls, as Elpidia put it, it was now.

After the usual invocations and prayers to God, ignored by the small number of senators who were still pagan, the floor was opened. First to speak was none other than Maximianus, father to the young man Galla had gone to meet. He began with the usual fawning words of welcome to Honorius. Bored, for she had heard it all before, Galla wondered if he had any idea of his son's sexual proclivities. Even if he did, it wouldn't stop him trying to marry him off to some unfortunate girl. She was glad it wouldn't be her. Marriage didn't have to be all love and poetry, but in her mind, physical attraction was a must, and she could not have borne life with a man who preferred his own sex.

Her attention returned to the senator. He was waxing lyrical about Roma's might, its magnificent history and culture. For hundreds of years, it had brought civilisation, peace and prosperity to the world. Its armies had conquered every enemy there was. Much of the reason for Roma's success, Maximianus claimed with a look at Honorius, was the omnipotent, wise emperors it had been blessed with.

A ripple of agreement passed along the room.

Honorius smiled.

Stilicho remained impassive, far too wise to react to sycophancy.

Galla could have challenged Maximianus on any number of things. Roma's armies had not been invincible for more than half a century; defeat was as common as victory. As for Honorius, he was no warlike Julian, no hard-headed Theodosius. To Galla's knowledge, her half-brother had never made a single policy decision on his own. He might from this point onward, it was true, but whether his choices would be wise and beneficial to the empire remained to be seen.

Praise finally completed, Maximianus bowed to Honorius. His eyes moved to Stilicho. 'Magister Militum, as ever, you are welcome to Roma. I understand you come with a message from the barbarian Alaric.'

A weighty silence fell. Faces turned towards Stilicho. Galla felt simmering disapproval, read in the senators' expressions a latent hostility that threatened to be voiced. But no one said anything yet.

'Gratitude, Senator Maximianus. Imperator.' Stilicho bowed to Honorius, who acknowledged him with a slight inclination of his head. There was no smile. Unabashed, Stilicho turned towards the senators. His gaze travelled along those in front of Galla and she ducked her head, worried he might see her. When she looked up, he was scrutinising the senators on the other side of the room.

'I come to you with some news of import.' He paused. Senators glanced at one another. There were whispers. Heads shook, and not in a happy way.

They suspected, thought Galla, which wasn't a surprise. The dogs in the street knew that Stilicho had invited Alaric to move from Epirus to Noricum so his army could then march across northern Italia and, come the spring melt, cross the Alpes to vanquish the usurper Constantinus.

'News of import?' repeated Maximianus, managing to sound surprised.

'Even so. Will you hear it?'

Maximianus' eyes went to Honorius, who waved a hand in acceptance. 'Speak, Magister Militum.'

'Alaric occupied Epirus on behalf of the empire.' This was true, for since the death of Theodosius, the land belonged to the eastern emperor, Arcadius. Stilicho's eyes moved over the senators. 'Am I not correct?'

Silence. Men avoided his gaze, spoke quiet words to each other.

'Come now, are your memories gone altogether cloudy? The Imperator promised to pay Alaric to occupy Epirus, and this he did! If the Imperator had not sent a letter ordering Alaric not to invade the eastern empire, he would have continued his conquest of all Illyricum last year.' Stilicho pinned not Honorius – he did not dare do that – but Maximianus with his stare. 'Does this sound familiar, Senator?'

Maximianus cleared his throat. 'Yes, it does.'

'Good! I trust your colleagues can also recall these events.' Stilicho waited.

A couple of moments passed.

'Well?' he barked.

A few voices spoke in agreement, but the majority of the senators remained tight-lipped. Honorius was frowning.

Stilicho looked less than impressed, if unsurprised. 'And so Alaric wants to be paid.'

'He is a leech!' called a voice. 'And everyone knows what to do with a leech.'

'Alaric took his army to Epirus on behalf of Roma. The fact that the invasion of Illyricum was called off is irrelevant,' said Stilicho assuredly. 'Now he and his warriors are in Noricum, which also comes with its own price.'

'He will bleed us white!' cried the same voice, whose owner was not brave enough to show his face.

'You intend for him to march to Viennensis, I think?' said Maximianus to Stilicho.

'Indeed. But he needs to be paid first.'

'Or?' dared Maximianus.

'Draw your own conclusion.'

Stilicho wasn't going to say out loud that Alaric would bring war to Italia should the Senate refuse his demands, thought Galla, but it was what he meant.

'This is blackmail!' The second voice was close to the first, and just in front of Galla. 'It is shameful to buy peace from a barbarian like Alaric!'

A chorus of yeses went up. Maximianus looked to Honorius, who nodded.

Now he starts to show his position, thought Galla. It was underhand before, stopping Alaric from following Stilicho's plan of invading the eastern empire, in the process improving relations with his brother, the emperor Arcadius, but Honorius had grown tired of doing what he was told. The worm was beginning to turn.

Stilicho lifted a hand, and quiet fell. He still had power.

'Alaric's terms are these: four thousand pounds of gold, thirty thousand pounds of silver, two hundred bales of silk and various quantities of pepper and other spices.' The uproar was such that Stilicho could not continue. Stony-faced, he waited as the senators vented spleen.

The cries were heated, full of indignation. 'How much?' 'Extortion!' 'Outrageous!' 'It is an insult!' 'Roma will be shamed for ever if he is paid!'

A tiny smile played around Honorius' mouth, and Galla thought: he is with the senators, not Stilicho. He does not wish to deal with Alaric, even though it is the right thing to do, and it proves he and Stilicho are on divergent paths. Noticing the general's gaze linger on the emperor, she saw that Stilicho knew it too. It was in fact good, she concluded sadly, that she had not married Eucherius. Love him she might have done, but their union would have been akin to boarding a ship with a leak.

Stilicho was cunning, though, a fox with a thousand tricks. He was not done yet. Eventually he leaped into a momentary lull in the protests, and his force kept the senators silenced. 'You may not like Alaric's terms,' he thundered, 'but he and his men have not been paid these many months, even as they served the empire in good faith. Four thousand pounds of gold is not so large a sum. Unless I am mistaken, it is less than the average yearly income from a senator's estate! There are how many of you here – six hundred? All of a sudden, Alaric does not seem so unreasonable, eh?'

There were glowers and mutters, but no one shouted or protested, apart from one senator, a gaunt-faced individual whom Galla knew to be called Lampadius. Into the relative quiet, he shouted, 'This is not peace, Magister, but a pact of slavery!'

Stilicho's response was a flint-hard stare, which Lampadius could not meet. He hung his head, and the general seemed satisfied.

'Alaric merely wants what he has been promised,' he said. 'If we give it to him, he will serve as the hammer Roma uses to crush Constantinus. That is worth doing, is it not?'

A second bout of heated debate began, the crux of which was who presented the greater danger to the empire, Alaric or Constantinus. Take the emotion and pride out of it, and the problem was uncomplicated, Galla decided.

If Alaric was not paid, his army of Visigoths and Hunni would threaten Italia within weeks. It was by no means certain Stilicho could raise enough soldiers to see off both barbarian hordes. Choosing this path also meant that Constantinus remained undefeated; Alaric's presence in the empire's heartland would actively encourage him to invade as well. Pay Alaric, however, and the Visigoths and Huns would march westward to Viennensis, where they had a decent chance of defeating Constantinus.

In the end, a vote was taken. Two thirds of the senators voted to accept Alaric's demands. Lampadius did not linger after the result was announced. Galla heard him tell a neighbour he was going to take refuge in a church, lest Stilicho seek revenge for his comment. Honorius' displeasure was now plain. Muttering something uncomplimentary – by the look on his face – he stalked from the Curia. Stilicho watched him go, his own expression stony.

How you wish Thermantia were older, and fertile, thought Galla. If she were pregnant with Honorius' baby, things would not have come to this. But she was not, and if the rumours of the couple sleeping in separate beds were true, Thermantia would not find herself with child any time soon. Which meant, Galla realised with a thrill, that her own position close to the throne remained significant.

She could not make speeches or vote in the Senate, still less lead an army to war against the empire's enemies, but if God came to her aid, she could end up with immense power.

The power of life and death over ordinary people.

The power to stand in the shadows and manipulate from a distance.

The power to influence imperial policy.

A week later, Galla was in her courtyard, spinning wool. Elpidia was with her. They stood side by side, distaff and its ball of unspun wool in their left hands, weighted spindles thread-hanging from their right. Elpidia's actions were fast and graceful, the sign of decades of experience. The technique was second nature to Galla too; she had learned it from Elpidia when she was young.

Pull a short amount of fibre from the ball of wool on the distaff, twirl the thread to thicken it, and repeat. When the wool reached a certain length, reverse the spindle, wind the wool onto it, and then start over. It was a slow process, but the repetitive nature of the exercise was calming, even enjoyable. Hours could pass in this fashion. Galla didn't have to stay put; she could walk around the courtyard, and even upstairs, spinning all the while.

'Arcadius was thirty-one. Life can be so short,' said Elpidia.

News of the eastern emperor's sudden death had arrived in Roma the day before. Like most in the city, they had been talking about little else since.

'His son, Theodosius, is only seven years old,' said Galla. There were three daughters too, all older, but, being female, unable to take the throne alone. It was not dissimilar to her situation.

'Poor child. He cannot rule on his own, surely?' They had been through this more than once.

'No. From what I heard, Honorius and Stilicho have incarcerated themselves to discuss the best response. If they don't act, some eastern power-hungry general no one has ever heard of will seize the throne. They cannot both travel to Constantinopolis, however.'

'Not with Alaric roaming about, and Constantinus sharpening his knife on the other side of the Alpes.'

'Stilicho will want to go,' said Galla confidently. 'Honorius no longer listens to him. His refusal to pay Alaric after the Senate vote is proof enough. Stilicho is living on borrowed time here and must know it. In Constantinopolis, he can assume the guardianship of Theodosius, just as he did with Honorius at the same age. Succeed, and he could threaten Honorius next.'

'The Imperator will see that.'

'You would think so, but Stilicho can be persuasive.'

'What about the adviser who never leaves Honorius' side?'

'The Magister Scriniorum, Olympius.' This was the oily-skinned individual who had been standing behind Honorius in the Curia. Apparently helped by Stilicho to attain his high office – master of the imperial secretarial department – Olympius had fast-worked his way into Honorius' trust.

'I'd be suspicious of him.'

Galla knew why. Two days earlier, they had both attended the Circus Maximus. Honorius had been there; so had Olympius, forever whispering in his ear. At the time, Galla had been relieved that her half-brother's attention was entirely taken up so that he had no interest in her. Since then, however, she had seen Olympius and Honorius together a third time, at a religious service in the grand church close to the imperial palace, and the behaviour of the new Magister Scriniorum had been similar.

It occurred to her that she could send a message to Stilicho, warning him how Olympius seemed to have the emperor's ear, but a moment's consideration made her decide against it. After promising to agree to her betrothal to Eucherius, he had cut her loose. She owed him nothing. She wondered if she was being too ruthless, if she should think of the good of the empire, but in reality, Stilicho must know what Olympius was capable of, and could deal with him in his own way.

Events continued to move fast. A rebellion broke out among the imperial soldiers at Ravenna, incited by none other than Sarus, disgruntled that Alaric was to be paid vast sums while he, commander of the army that had fought valiantly against Constantinus the previous year, was overlooked. Galla thought he had a brass neck, given the undignified nature of his exit from Viennensis. The revolt was serious enough for Stilicho to have to deal with it. While he was away, Galla again saw Honorius with Olympius. Something was afoot, she was sure of it, and it wouldn't be good for Stilicho.

When the general returned, Sarus' revolt having been quelled, the thorny matter of who would travel to Constantinopolis to secure the throne for the young Theodosius II remained. Gossip raged through the city. Honorius was going to go. Stilicho was. They both were. Neither was. There was even an outlandish rumour of Sarus and Olympius being sent in their stead.

Whatever the truth, it seemed both emperor and general were more concerned about gaining control over the new eastern emperor than dealing with the problem of Constantinus. Matters were still undecided a few days later when Honorius and Stilicho travelled together to Bononia, there to supervise the assembling of the army, part to defend Italia, part to go west with Alaric.

How Galla wished she could have gone with them, but there was no reason for her to be present. Women, even those in the imperial family, did not plan campaigns or engage in war. So she languished in Roma, desperate for any news.

CHAPTER XVII

Four months later . . .

Ravenna; late Mensis Sextilis, AD *408*

It was a burning-hot day. Despite the number of Visigothic bucellarii within the octagonal church, five score at least, the thick red-brick walls and mosaic flooring kept the interior cool. The hundreds outside were less fortunate, seeking shade wherever they could. Vadomar had felt guilty at first, but as the gravity of Stilicho's predicament sank in, he soon disregarded his comrades' physical discomfort. He was in position by the locked and barred main doors, ready in case Honorius' men decided to force their way in. The jowly priest would be of no help, that was certain. He had vanished not long after their arrival the day before.

Time passed. Men slapped at mosquitoes and talked in low voices. The quiet inside and out saw drowsiness steal up on Vadomar. He shifted position, stretching his back and twisting his head from side to side, eavesdropping on the small talk. Dog declared himself hungry enough to eat the eucharist bread in the tabernacle. Scandalised, Wulfila announced he would be sent straight to hell. If his belly was full at least, Dog replied, he wouldn't mind. Watch out for the pagan, someone said, loud enough to be heard. Uncaring of Christian values, he had probably devoured the lot already. Everyone laughed, even Vadomar. Some men didn't like his loyalty to the old faith, and made occasional sniping comments, but most didn't care. The bonds forged in combat were strong enough.

With nothing to do, Vadomar began again to mull over the reasons he was here. Stilicho's proposal that Alaric be paid was a large part of it. The general had prevailed, the motion carried after a vote, but the bitter process had won him no friends. It had also hardened the opinions of his enemies – and, it seemed, the emperor himself.

More instability had been caused by the unexpected news from Constantinopolis of Arcadius' death. Deploying eloquence and persuasion, Stilicho had convinced the emperor to remain in Italia so his own throne was kept safe.

Until recent days, the arrangement had been for Honorius to stay and for Alaric, paid richly in imperial gold, to march to Viennensis, there to confront and bring to heel the usurper Constantinus. Stilicho, meanwhile, would travel to the empire's eastern capital. Vadomar and his comrades were to have gone too, a journey he had wanted to take all his life. He had even entertained dreams of becoming an imperial guard in Constantinopolis.

How he wished events had unfolded in such a way, or that Honorius had voyaged east instead and Stilicho remained to deal with the usurper in Viennensis.

Either would have been better than this, here, now.

A commotion outside. Barked orders. The sound of boots on stone, men moving, soldiers, surely. Vadomar touched belt, sword, dagger, then gripped his spear and lifted his shield from where it leaned against the stuccoed wall. Urged on by their commander, his nearest comrades were also preparing. They muttered prayers and shot quick glances at Christ on the cross, and at Stilicho on his knees in front of the altar below. Vadomar looked only at his general as he asked the old deities, Donar in particular, to send Stilicho guidance. He would have given several years' pay in that moment to be able to sacrifice an ox, even a sheep, to his gods.

Calm was restored outside. Men quietened. Vadomar heard shields thunk on the stone, soldiers' rest position. He waited, fear prodding, but no one approached the doors, or demanded for Stilicho to show himself. Hope sparked in his chest. Perhaps Honorius' head had cleared. Perhaps his snake of an adviser, Olympius, was dead, and no longer whispering poison in the imperial ear. For poison it must be. In the short time since Stilicho had spoken with Honorius at the city of Bononia, when matters appeared settled and the future bright, the world had turned upside down.

A rumour had surfaced and spread with alarming speed, of Stilicho's intentions to put his son, Eucherius, on the eastern throne. Vadomar could imagine the pompous toga-clad senators whispering and grousing at the idea. It was impossible to know the rumour's origins. Although Vadomar was not party to Stilicho's consultations with the senior officers, there had not been even a hint of such a plan from anyone else's lips.

While Stilicho prepared for his voyage east, Honorius had travelled to Ticinum, where the army was gathering for its campaign against Constantinus. Most of Stilicho's trusted supporters were in the town. Vadomar presumed the general had relied on his loyal men to see nothing untoward came to pass.

If he had, they had failed.

In an unexpected turn of events, the assembled soldiers mutinied. Over the course of several days, Ticinum was subjected to an organised orgy of bloodshed. To Stilicho, miles away, reliant on irregular messengers, it was unclear who had been slain, and whether his warriors or soldiers loyal to the emperor were behind the insurrection. Genuinely shocked, he had ordered Vadomar and his comrades to be ready to march on Ticinum in defence of the emperor. Then word had come that Honorius was unharmed, and about to return to Ravenna. Not long after, Stilicho's baggage train had been lost to a sudden attack by soldiers led by the army commander Sarus, once an ally, now an enemy of Stilicho. In the aftermath of this disaster, Vadomar had seen uncertainty for the first time in his general's face. Ticinum was no place to go, he declared. They would have to make for the new imperial capital at Ravenna, and there win over Sarus' warriors.

It felt like a huge gamble. Stilicho was possessed of a silver tongue, but his bucellarii numbered less than a thousand, while Sarus led perhaps thirty times that. Vadomar had heard men saying that only a simpleton would switch sides with those odds.

There had been lots of bullish talk too. Stilicho knew what he was about, said the old, wise heads. He'd been around, defeated Alaric on numerous occasions, and had saved the western empire many times also. Honorius, an indecisive weakling, would never harm his own father-in-law! Olympius might currently have the emperor's ear, but he was a sprung-from-nowhere traitor and would soon fall from favour. Sarus had taken their baggage train, yet he could be won over. Also a Visigoth, he would not murder his former leader.

Nearing the capital late the previous afternoon, the foundations of their world were shattered by a messenger on a sweat-lathered horse. Stilicho had been named a public enemy by the emperor; he was being sought everywhere. Brave as a lion, the general had declared it a terrible mistake. Honorius and Sarus were being fed lies. It could all be settled once he came face-to-face with the emperor.

Stilicho sought the safety of a church that night, though, which gave the lie to his confident words. And despite their sanctified surroundings, morale sank rapidly. There was little conversation as they set guards, ate what food remained and lay down on the bare stone floor to get what rest would come. Vadomar, who had never before set foot in a Christian place of worship, was mesmerised by the massive white marble font in the church's centre, and by the magnificent dome overhead depicting a man his comrades called John the Baptist immersing Jesus in the River Aulon. The dove fluttering over the two men was something bizarre called the Holy Spirit.

Out of sorts, he got not a wink of sleep. Late on in the night, he had ventured outside through a side door. A few of Honorius' soldiers had been watching the church, but heads bent, leaning against walls, they were either asleep or nearly so. No challenge rang out, granting Vadomar an unexpected option.

He imagined slipping into a side street, finding a boat on one of the myriad waterways criss-crossing the city and vanishing for ever. Ashamed even to think something so cowardly, he went back inside. Roused from sleep, Stilicho had refused to countenance doing the same. Honorius was part of his family, he said, and a reasonable man. They had nothing to fear.

Vadomar had been helpless before his general's determination. So had the rest. And now here they were, he brooded, a day later, cornered, outnumbered and without food. There was precious little water left either, and thanks to the marshy environs and the church's dim interior, mosquitoes were a constant, irritating presence.

A chuckle escaped him.

'What's funny?' This was Dog.

'Never thought I'd die in a Christian shrine, thirsty and covered in insect bites.'

'You think Stilicho will order us to fight our way out?'

'Maybe.'

Dog sucked air through his front teeth, which indicated he wasn't so sure.

Time passed. More soldiers assembled outside. Vadomar's commander, a block of a man with an evil temper who wore furs even in this heat, ordered the main doors opened a fraction so he could take a peek. There were hundreds of soldiers, he said, scowling. Sarus' warriors and *domestici*. Heavy-armoured front-rankers, mostly.

While Vadomar had a mail shirt and a decent helmet, many of his comrades only had leather caps, padded tunics and shields. His armour would make little difference in a fight, though. If there had been any hope of breaking out earlier, the presence of domestici, elite soldiers attached to the imperial household, had sealed off that avenue.

'Stilicho!'

Vadomar glanced at his general.

'Stilicho, come forth!' A pause. 'By order of Imperator Honorius, show yourself!'

'No!' The involuntary protest escaped Vadomar's lips.

Dog nodded. So did many others.

'You cannot go out there, Magister. They can't be trusted!'

Stilicho's smile was tired. 'Vadomar, isn't it?' He spoke in Gothic, his preferred tongue with soldiers.

'Yes, Magister.' Amid the dread, delight blossomed. Stilicho knew him.

'Go outside and see who is being so peremptory. I am accustomed to more courtesy.' Stilicho's lips twitched.

Vadomar saluted, wondering how the general could retain a sense of humour. Ritual performed, belt, sword, dagger, he readied his shield and took a white-knuckle grip on his spear, waited as the locking bar was lifted. He let his eyes adjust to the blinding sunlight, then walked through the doorway. A wall of heat struck, a physical blow. A throng of bucellarii comrades, some of those unlucky enough to remain outside, were waiting, faces red, tunic armpits dark with sweat. Furs lay in a pile, garments finally discarded thanks to the burning sun.

'What has Stilicho ordered?'

'Are we to fight?'

'Have you any water?'

'He wants to know who is summoning him,' said Vadomar, squinting against the brilliance of the glittering armour and helmets ranked two dozen paces away.

'The domestici were the last to get here. Got a priest with them.'

'He's a bishop.'

That was good, Vadomar thought. A Christ-lover might be able to moderate the behaviour of Honorius' men. He steeled his nerve and put his shoulders back. His pace was slow, measured. Despite the bishop's presence, he felt more exposed than he ever had in his life. Courage, he told himself. You are come in peace.

'I am Stilicho's messenger,' he shouted in his rough Latin.

'You're not him, it's plain!' barked an officer in golden scale mail. 'Where is he?'

Vadomar prickled. 'What do they call you, Domine?'

The officer drew himself up. 'What's it to you?'

'I would know your name.'

A sniff. 'Heraclianus.'

'Stilicho is inside, Domine. What message shall I carry to him?'

'He is to be arrested and taken to the Imperator.'

Vadomar baulked. 'Murdered, more like.'

'He is not to be harmed.'

'Why should I believe you?'

Heraclianus' irritation was clear. 'Your Eminence?' He was gazing at a man in an immaculate white robe edged with green, visible at the rear.

'It is as Heraclianus says. Stilicho is not to be harmed.' The bishop brandished a roll of parchment. 'Here is the emperor's letter.'

'Swear it,' said Vadomar.

The bishop took an oath. So did Heraclianus. Vadomar's Latin wasn't fluent, but they seemed genuine.

Offering up a heartfelt plea to his gods, Vadomar indicated he would relay the message. Every step of the way, he half expected a well-thrown spear to take him in the back.

Stilicho was waiting just inside, the familiar stocky figure who had been such an important part of his life. How had it come to this? wondered Vadomar, fighting a creeping helplessness.

'Well?' asked Stilicho.

'Imperator Honorius orders you arrested and conducted to his presence, Magister. That is all, they say.'

'They?'

'An officer of the domestici, Magister, Heraclianus by name, and a bishop who bears a letter from the emperor. Both swore they intended nothing more.'

Stilicho toyed with his short beard, but not for long. 'If a bishop has sworn Honorius means me no harm, who am I to doubt? Open the door.'

Vadomar's heart thump-thumped in his chest. 'Are you sure, Magister?'

'You're the one who went out there, heard their promises. Is there something else?' Stilicho's gaze, ever direct, bored into him.

'I don't trust them, Magister. I don't believe the emperor's letter.' He had said it. Vadomar didn't know Honorius well, but it was accepted he was weak. His opinion changed with the wind. It stuck in Vadomar's gullet like a fish bone that Stilicho, for so long the steering oar on imperial opinion, had been set aside in favour of Olympius, a glorified secretary.

'You are a valiant soldier, Vadomar, but state business is beyond you. I have known Honorius since he was a babe. He was family to me ere either of my daughters married him. He will cleave to me whatever bad advice he might have been given of recent days.' Stilicho clasped his shoulder.

Vadomar made the semblance of a smile and wished for the words to persuade Stilicho to remain in the relative safety of the church. He managed, 'If you say so, Magister.'

'I do!' Stilicho brushed specks of dust from the dark red roundels on the shoulders of his tunic, then hitched his belt and stepped up to the door. A glance at Vadomar's commander. 'Follow, if you will, but not too close. It must be clear I pose no threat.'

Again the blasting heat as the portal opened, again the blinding light.

Stilicho crossed himself, and walked out with the confidence of a man who knows his purpose.

Led by their commander, as uneasy-looking as Vadomar felt, the rest came out after, forming a six-man-wide file. They marched after Stilicho, already at the front rank of domestici.

Vadomar's tension was mirrored in the faces of the domestici closest to the general. Although he had come alone and in peace, they were edgy, and edgy men made stupid decisions. How Vadomar wished for a legion of Stilicho's veterans to appear and save them all, or for Sarus to be on their side, not Honorius'.

'Here I am,' Stilicho announced loudly in Latin. 'The emperor's loyal servant, come to surrender as ordered.'

His words broke the spell. Heraclianus barked an order. Domestici swarmed in. Stilicho's ivory-hilted sword and belt were stripped off him and brandished aloft. Vadomar reined in his fury, his desire to respond. There was hope yet. No one had laid a hand on the general.

'Take me to Honorius.' Captive or no, Stilicho's voice was commanding. He eyed Heraclianus.

The twitch of a smile. 'I have another letter from the emperor.'

Queasiness crept in to join Vadomar's anger. 'This is treachery!' he cried in Visigothic. 'We must protect Stilicho, Domine.'

Whether he wasn't heard or his commander didn't agree, there was no immediate response. Vadomar glanced at his comrades, but only Dog would meet his eye. He offered a what-can-you-and-I-do look, and so Vadomar did nothing.

Heraclianus accepted a parchment from the bishop, the latter firmly averting his gaze from Stilicho.

His worry made cold certainty by the religious' discomfort, Vadomar hissed, 'We have to help him!'

Nothing.

Another terrible moment dragged past.

'As a dangerous public enemy and threat to the empire, the magister militum Stilicho is to be executed.' There was a metal ring of finality to the Latin-spoken pronouncement.

Vadomar would remember afterwards the flicker of amusement from Heraclianus, who had obviously known, the utter shock on his commander's face, and most of all, Stilicho's composure.

He felt his comrades' outrage as his own. Bellowing war cries, intent on murder, they swarmed towards the domestici, who, nervous-faced, prepared to meet the charge.

'HOLD!' Stilicho could have been heard in Constantinopolis.

Good soldiers, Vadomar and the rest screeched to a halt, did not thrust spears at the vile, smirking domestici.

'Let the emperor's will be done! I command this as your general.' Stilicho's voice was iron-hard.

Vadomar was rooted to the spot. His attention, and his comrades', was fixed in horror on Stilicho.

Who had already bent his neck.

Heraclianus' sword whispered from its scabbard.

'Do not move, on pain of death!' Stilicho ordered.

Mesmerised, Vadomar watched the blade fall. Watched the magister militum's head leap from his neck. Watched the jets of blood after. Saw Stilicho's body, robbed of life, fall to the paving. Heard the terrible roar of delight from the domestici mix with his comrades' anguished cries.

Somehow, in the confusion, his eyes met those of Heraclianus. Gods grant me vengeance, Vadomar thought, and drew a finger across his throat. He saw fear in the other man's eyes, the tiniest of consolations, but then Heraclianus was shouting that they should leave Ravenna at once or share in their general's fate.

The domestici advanced a step, clear threat.

Grey-faced, Vadomar's commander gave the order to withdraw.

CHAPTER XVIII

Three months later . . .

Roma; Mensis November, AD *408*

Cobwebs around the window frame swayed to and fro. The cold air carried slaves' voices from the colonnaded garden, and from further away, the excited shouts of street urchins. In a small bedroom off the tablinum were two figures, one perched on a stool in front of a low table, the other standing behind.

'This feels like any other day,' said Galla. 'But it is not.'

Elpidia stared over Galla's head into the silvered mirror, where their gazes met.

'The Visigoths shouldn't be here,' said Galla. Alaric and his entire army surrounded the city.

'We both know why they are,' replied Elpidia.

'Because my half-brother the emperor has not fulfilled his obligations.'

Denied the promised four thousand pounds of gold after Stilicho's execution, Alaric had given Honorius one more chance to deliver gold and hostages. This too had been rebuffed, so before the mountain passes could close for the winter, the Visigothic leader had marched straight from his base in Illyricum to Roma.

'Are you done?'

Elpidia's fingers began to move faster, arranging the hair with a central parting, tied at the back, accentuating Galla's oval face. Reaching down, she picked up a pearl necklace from the table and fastened it around her mistress' throat. 'Shall I do the earrings?'

'No.' Galla fitted the pair, which matched the necklace. Standing, she tugged at her floor-length outer tunic, adjusting the jewelled belt under her bust so the light pink fabric lay better. Then she fussed with the tight long sleeves of her inner tunic, a darker shade of pink. She took a pose, putting one ankle-boot-clad foot in front of the other. 'Well?'

Elpidia's hands fluttered. 'You look beautiful.'

'You always say that.' But Galla's face had softened.

'Because it is true, as God is my witness.' Elpidia touched the Chi-Rho amulet at her throat. 'It's a scandal you're not married already.'

'We both know why.' Galla lowered her voice. 'The time wasn't right for "Empress" Serena.'

'Empress Serena!' This in a put-on accent, Elpidia tilting her nose in the air.

'Shh! One of the slaves might hear.'

'She's yesterday's news, and it's not as if I'm saying anything that everyone doesn't know. So full of airs and graces she is, your foster mother.'

'I mean your tone, with me.' It was an old theme, but still a valid one. Elpidia could not be too familiar with Galla, even in this house. If their close relationship became public knowledge, Galla would have no choice but to end it, most probably by selling her nurse.

Aware of this, humbled, Elpidia spoke more quietly. 'If you ask me, it was Serena who put the idea in Stilicho's head to put Eucherius on the eastern throne. She always had aspirations to the purple, for herself as well as her children. I am sorry Eucherius didn't become emperor in Constantinopolis. You would have made quite an imperial couple.'

'It was vile what was done to him. Honorius can be so cold-blooded.' Galla's expression was pained.

Not long after being spirited to Roma in the aftermath of his father's execution, Eucherius had been hunted down and slain by two eunuchs from the imperial household.

'At least his sister Thermantia didn't suffer the same fate. Being repudiated by the emperor and sent to live with her mother here in the city is preferable to a blade across the throat. Talking of Serena, do you think the latest rumours are true?' Elpidia stole to the door and checked there was no one close outside. She nodded at Galla.

'That she has offered to help Alaric the Visigoth?'

'Yes.'

'It wouldn't surprise me. It's what the people are saying.' Galla affected various gruff voices. '"Stilicho was practically a Visigoth himself." "He always favoured barbarians." "Look at the number of times he had Alaric at his mercy and let him go." "His wife is no different."'

'The people, phaugh! They would believe anything, especially with Alaric's host outside the city. You are prejudiced against Serena.'

'With good reason! She educated me, it's true, but I was never good enough for her. Could never know all the Christian principles, or show sufficient skill with distaff and spindle.'

'She was pleased with you once, when you helped her to weave the girth for Honorius' horse. She sent it to him, remember?'

'It was a once-off. It was always, "Oh, Maria this, and look, Thermantia that". To her, I was nothing more than a brood mare, to be married off to Eucherius.'

'That would have suited you well. You loved him, did you not?'

A sharp look, then a sad one. 'I did.'

Galla changed the subject. 'I need fresh air.' She threw on a dark green mantle with wide decorated borders. 'I am going to the garden.'

In the lararium, Elpidia paused to touch the reliquary, which contained a foot bone of St Paulus. She asked God to watch over Galla, to protect Roma from the barbarians and to ensure they continued to have enough food in the coming weeks. Her last request needed the most immediate solution.

Although not in the same straits as the poor, some of whom were starving, their kitchen stores were lower than Elpidia was comfortable with, and the markets, normally full of produce from the surrounding countryside and overseas, were close to empty. If a person needed fresh bread or safe-to-eat meat, it was all about which well-connected merchant or city councillor one knew. She began to compile a list of names in her head; once Galla was apprised of their need, she would write the necessary letters.

Watching her mistress, Elpidia felt a real sense of pride. Intelligent, educated and striking, and as determined as the most bullish man, Galla was a wonder. What an empress she would have made. It was hard to see how it would ever happen now. Honorius had no children, but nor was he showing any interest in marrying Galla off. Husbandless, childless, she could not take the throne even if her half-brother died.

Fritigern was pushing a broom along the mosaic floor of the colonnaded walkway fringing the garden. The arthritic house slave was also poor of hearing. Only sensing his mistress' presence when she was virtually on top of him, he startled like a deer with the first scent of hounds in its nostrils.

'A thousand apologies, Nobilissima Femina.' His voice quavered, the end of his broom twitched. 'I was just brushing the floor.'

'No need to stop on my account.'

'Nobilissima Femina.' Nervous, he got back to work.

His efforts were about as useful as a man trying to stop the flow of the tide, thought Elpidia. Her heart twinged. 'Maybe he thinks you're going to sell him,' she said when Fritigern was far enough away. This was the fate of slaves when they came to the end of their usefulness.

'Never,' said Galla. 'He has been with the family for decades. And it would be unchristian.'

'So you would never sell me, Nobilissima Femina?'

'Do not joke,' Galla chided. 'It is not funny.'

Elpidia smiled. The bond between them, forged in the time of Galla's infancy, was strong. She was body slave, friend and adviser rolled into one. When other slaves were about, she acted as they did, addressing Galla as 'Nobilissima Femina', but in private they were almost as familiar as mother and daughter. Elpidia's happiness clouded. Almost, she thought. She was at ease that she would never have her own children, but the yawning gap in social status between her and Galla stung. Even manumission would not make it vanish.

Stop, she admonished herself. She treats you well, and respects you too. She looks to you for advice. The majority of citizens have less influence than you.

'Visitors, Nobilissima Femina.' Darme filled the kitchen doorway. 'A pair of senators.'

Elpidia pricked her ears.

Galla lowered her spindle to her lap. She was sitting close to the oven, the warmest place in the house. She cocked her head. 'Senators?'

'Yes, Nobilissima Femina. They wanted to come in off the street, saying their message was urgent, but I refused. I told Fritigern to light the lamps in the office in case you receive them.'

'You did well. Admit the senators, and take their cloaks and boots. I will be with them soon.'

Galla's spinning could have been set aside at once, but she continued to work after Darme disappeared. Elpidia was pleased. Women, even those of the imperial family, occupied a secondary rank in society. For the senators to have come to Galla meant something of great importance was afoot. That she was wise enough to make them wait showed astuteness beyond her twenty years. Who had sent the pair was intriguing; the most influential senators would not have come themselves, but dispatched emissaries, men who owed political favours. They would have heard how Galla had exerted her power and taken note.

A while later – long enough to border on discourtesy, Elpidia thought, but said nothing – she shadowed her mistress to the office, which was on the left of the tablinum coming in from the street. A small, square room, it was dominated by a desk and leather-seated chair. A bookcase full of scrolls filled one wall, and the score of lamps hanging from a massive iron stand lit the room brightly.

Fritigern had done well, but Elpidia was already calculating the cost of the olive oil. With luck, she thought, the meeting would not last long.

The toga-clad senators bowed to Galla. They ignored Elpidia. She had been treated like this all her life, and it had its advantages. An unseen slave, she was often party to conversations no ordinary citizen would ever hear.

After polite enquiries about Galla's health, and confident declarations that the garrison was ready to repel any Visigothic attack, the senators got to the point of their visit. The larger, a rotund man in middle age with fleshy arms, who went by the name of Caecilianus, mentioned the uncertainty filling the city and the hunger being endured by the poor. The second senator, Maximianus, was the father of the young man Galla had once thought of marrying, and had combed-over hair that part-concealed his bald pate. He lamented the citizens' predicament. Things would only get worse. There were rumours of cannibalism in the Suburra.

It was not true, surely, said Caecilianus, but he looked worried – or wanted to appear so, thought Elpidia. One thing was certain, Maximianus continued, the city's streets were becoming more dangerous by the day. But for the presence of six slaves armed with cudgels, their journey to Galla's house could have been quite different and altogether more unpleasant. The mobs were seeking out traitors, people who were reputed to be sympathetic to Alaric, or even in league with him.

'Have you spoken to Stilicho's widow, Serena, of recent days, Nobilissima Femina?' asked Caecilianus.

There we have it, thought Elpidia, thinking of the conversation she'd had earlier with her mistress.

An emphatic shake of Galla's head. 'My foster mother and I are not on good terms.'

'You were once to have wed her son, were you not, Nobilissima Femina?'

'A person can be cordial with one member of a family and not with another. Do you like everyone in *your* family?'

A chuckle, an acknowledgement that this was true.

'Have you reason to be concerned about Serena?'

Being direct was one of Galla's qualities, but it could also act against her. Elpidia held her breath, watching the senators sidelong. If uncertain about Galla, this was when they might muddy the waters, pretend they had come about something else altogether.

After an exchange of tight nods with his companion, Maximianus said, 'We do have concerns, Nobilissima Femina, and of the most serious nature.'

'Roma herself is in great danger,' said Caecilianus.

'Is Serena in league with Alaric?'

'We have it on good authority that she is, Nobilissima Femina.'

For a moment, Elpidia thought Galla was going to demand more, but all she asked was if they had sent word to the emperor.

Chubby fingers worked the air. 'Indeed, yes, but there is no way of knowing if Honorius will receive our letter, Nobilissima Femina. Even if he does, his reply might not get through the Visigothic blockade.'

'You think immediate action needs to be taken?'

'Do you, Nobilissima Femina?' Maximianus countered, quick as a flash.

'If the city is at risk of being taken by treachery, it is true that waiting for my half-brother's answer could be perilous.'

Elpidia noted the glance shared by the two senators, and her nerves thrummed. This was dangerous ground. Avoid committing yourself further before they do. She willed the words into her mistress' mind.

'However, I would have to think long and hard about following such a path.'

Another look passed between the senators, a question from one to the other, and with a nod, a come-back answer.

'And if we were to say the Senate approves of taking action to safeguard Roma, Nobilissima Femina?' enquired Caecilianus.

'The entire Senate?'

'Even so.'

'Names?'

A little laugh. 'You ask much, Nobilissima Femina.'

'As do you,' countered Galla. 'You are clients of more powerful men. I would know who they are.'

Caecilianus looked discomfited; Maximianus muttered something. They conferred.

Galla folded her hands in her lap and waited. This was intelligent, thought Elpidia. She wanted to know who she was allying herself with before agreeing to anything.

'Priscus Attalus sent us, Nobilissima Femina.' Several other names were mentioned.

Attalus was the *comes sacrarum largitonium*, one of the most senior fiscal officials appointed by the emperor. The others were powerful men also. Elpidia knew of them, which meant her mistress would too.

Galla let them stew for a little longer, again, thought Elpidia, emphasising her power.

'Roma may no longer be the imperial capital, but it must not fall into barbarian hands,' said Galla. 'Serena has to be stopped.'

'She is a traitor.' Caecilianus' tongue worked its way around his lips. 'She must die, Nobilissima Femina.'

'Before she opens the gates at night or some such.' This was Maximianus.

The tense silence was broken by Darme calling from the courtyard to one of the kitchen slaves.

'I must think about this.' Galla had already made up her mind, but she wasn't going to admit it.

The senators' heads came close; they whispered together.

'You cannot give your approval now, Nobilissima Femina?' asked Caecilianus.

'It is no light decision to take.' Galla's tone was firm.

She asked the senators to return two days later. Disgruntled, but unable to say so, they took their leave.

Galla glanced at Elpidia. 'What are your thoughts?'

Elpidia didn't reply at once. She had never much liked Serena, who was haughty and prone to fits of temper. It was true she had treated Galla differently to her own children, but she had not been especially cruel. She and her husband had led Galla up the garden path when it came to Eucherius, however, and she was still scarred by the experience. 'You have no reason to love her, I know. She's also an easy one for the mob to hate, but she is no more about to give over the city than Fritigern can fly.'

'They seemed certain.'

'Yet they gave no evidence of her guilt.'

'Would the entire Senate act without proof?'

'The members of the Senate are among the last adherents to the old pagan deities. Like as not, they are thinking not of God's word but of the mob's bloodlust, and how it can be slaked. They have chosen Serena because she is Stilicho's widow and has fallen so far from grace.'

Galla gave Elpidia an appraising stare, but then she said, 'Given what they suggest, it is fair the senators offer something indicating that Serena is in league with Alaric. Happy?'

'Yes.' The fact that Galla would be content to see Serena, powerful for so long, removed from the scene made a horrible kind of sense, thought Elpidia. She had not considered it before, but if Serena were gone, Galla's position would be strengthened. Unless Honorius wed again, it would make her the most important noblewoman in the western empire.

Maybe it did not matter if Serena was innocent.

Two days later, Caecilianus and Maximianus returned. Again the pleasantries, asking after Galla's health and well-being. Wine was offered, and politely refused. Following Elpidia's advice, Galla did not bring up the matter of Serena, but left it to the two senators.

'We come, Nobilissima Femina,' said Caecilianus, a trifle nervously, 'to see if you have made up your mind about Serena and her treachery.'

'Have you any proof?'

A look between the pair. A nod from Maximianus.

'There is a Visigothic trader in the Forum Boarium who sells skins, Nobilissima Femina. He has been seen entering Serena's house several times.'

'The weather is cold. Perhaps she needed furs for her beds, for the house.'

'That is possible, but not all fur traders sneak out of the city at night. This one does.'

'How do you know?'

'You will be aware, Nobilissima Femina, of the coming and going after dark. In the Visigothic camp, for the right money, a man can buy meat. Cheese. Clothing and other staples.'

Galla glanced at Elpidia, who had to hide a smile. The senators would have no idea Vadomar engaged in the same behaviour at her behest.

'I had heard of this, yes.'

'The fur trader I speak of has left Roma on two occasions, Nobilissima Femina, both only hours after calling to Serena's house. This cannot be coincidence.'

'How do you know this?'

'A captain of the guard, a man I trust, swears it,' said Caecilianus earnestly.

'You can see this makes Serena guilty, Nobilissima Femina?' asked Maximianus.

Galla did not make immediate answer.

It was not definite proof, thought Elpidia, but it was suspicious. Whether it was sufficient to condemn Serena to death, she was less sure.

'Nobilissima Femina?'

'I say this with a heavy heart, and after giving the matter much thought: Serena must die.'

Smiles. Pleased looks.

Elpidia, who had known what Galla would say, kept her face blank. It was not for a slave to have an opinion on such things.

'It should be done at once,' announced Maximianus.

'I agree,' said Galla. 'How?'

A startled look. 'Strangulation, I would think.'

'She should not suffer.' Galla crossed herself.

So did Elpidia.

'No, of course not.'

'I am acquainted with someone . . . who knows the right type of people,' said Caecilianus, as if he were referring to a good builder or tradesman.

And that was that. Expressing profuse gratitude, and promising Serena would soon be dealt with, the senators departed.

With Elpidia following, Galla went back to the kitchen as if nothing untoward had happened. 'We will go to the church later and offer prayers for Serena's soul,' she said quietly.

Elpidia's admiration for her mistress grew. She was ruthless but not without sympathy, useful qualities that were only part of her considerable talent. Elpidia asked God to grant Galla the opportunity to take power one day.

What an empress she would make.

CHAPTER XIX

Unaware of the momentous decisions facing Galla, Vadomar was propped up against the counter of a *thermopolium* in the Suburra. Even by the standards of the neighbourhood, it was run-down. The floor was dirt, the tables rickety, the seating a few ill-made stools. The wine was abominable, and to consume any food risked explosive vomiting and diarrhoea. As for the whores, even a drunk blind man would hesitate about taking one upstairs. Vadomar wasn't interested anyway. He was plastered. Legless. Stocious. Rat-arsed.

His inebriation was an attempt to drown his blood-soaked memories. Ravenna had only been the start. Soon after, in Bononia, he had witnessed the Roman soldiery's brutal response to Stilicho's execution. If the stories were true, it had happened in garrison towns all over northern Italia, tens of thousands of innocents butchered, the families of the foederati, the Visigoths and other tribes who served the empire. Narrowly escaping with his own life, losing Dog and Wulfila in the chaos, burning for revenge, he had considered returning to Ravenna to assassinate the emperor. Cognisant of Honorius' day-and-night protection, however, he had decided Stilicho's enemies in the Senate would be easier prey. He had reached Roma not long before the arrival of Alaric's host.

The scale of the metropolis, which Vadomar had never visited, made his jaw drop. It had started outside Roma, with magnificent tombs on either side of the road for miles, mausolea dwarfing any house he had ever entered. It went on. Thirty-foot-high walls surrounded the city. Five-storey apartment blocks lined narrow streets. At every junction, there were great temples and huge painted statues of emperors and great men from the past. His grievances momentarily set aside, interest kindled, he went to the forum, about which he had heard so much, saw the great basilicae, the Rostrum, the Curia where the Senate met. Wandering past massive decorated triumphal arches, his feet took him to the amphitheatre where, until banned by Honorius a few years prior, gladiator fights had been held for more than three hundred years.

Although the grandeur brought home the power and wealth of Roma and its empire, it was a faded majesty. Some of the impressive buildings were in poor repair, others had been pillaged for *spolia*, construction materials. The paint on older statues was peeling, cracked or vanished altogether. Roma's power had greatly diminished, he decided. The decay was proof.

Even if the empire's time in the sun was over, those in power were far greater than he, and immune to his vengeance. Vadomar sank into a deep gloom. Ignorant of the names of those he wished to kill, not wishing to draw any more attention to himself, a Visigothic soldier inside the city, his hunt ended before it even started. Disconsolate, despairing, he used wine to forget. One day had become two. Two became three, had become a week. Soon all that mattered was getting drunk and staying drunk. It meant he didn't have to think about Stilicho, think about the massacres, think about his failures.

He drained his wooden beaker of its last sour, sediment-laden drops, and more in hope than expectation picked up the jug by his elbow. A thin dribble poured down his throat, a mouthful, no more. Better than nothing, he thought muzzily.

He had no money left on the counter, having consumed three jugs already. There were a few coins in the bronze purse nestled in his right armpit. He could slide it down to his wrist without drawing attention from anyone to his rear, but this approach would not stop the proprietor and the two waitresses behind the bar from noticing. Vadomar trusted them as little as the other customers. His money didn't total much, but it *was* worth slitting his throat for.

He pictured the alleyway beside the thermopolium where men went to piss, but he was so far gone the coins would fall into the foul mire underfoot, never to be found again. The purse had to stay where it was, which meant no refill. He was thirsty, though. A hand went to his sword hilt, then reluctantly came up again. His shield, spear and helmet were long gone, yet he had not sunk low enough to sell his blade. The scrape of scale against the counter as he shifted position reminded him of his armour, rarely taken off since the dreadful day in Ravenna. Despite its wine- and piss-caused rust spots, it was still worth a considerable sum, but he could not bear to part with it.

When his purse was empty, though, he would have nothing else to sell but his sword and armour. Catching sight at the door of a pretty-faced youth who trawled the local thermopolia for customers, he silently added his arse. A cynical chuckle escaped him. He didn't care if men lay with other men, but he felt no desire to do so himself.

'Another?' The weak-chinned proprietor had materialised in front of him and lifted the empty jug.

'No.'

'Food?'

'Do I look as if I want to get ill?'

The proprietor's face reddened. A short pause ensued, during which Vadomar decided he was wondering whether to issue a protest or a rebuke, or even to try and throw him onto the street. In the end, the man opted for discretion over valour. Muttering imprecations under his breath, some of which included 'barbarian' and 'pagan savage', he stumped towards the other end of the bar.

'Call me those to my face and I will open you from balls to brisket,' said Vadomar. All his life he had been on the end of contemptuous stares and snide comments from Roman citizens. Even those who were dirt-poor looked down on Visigoths and other tribesmen. They were careful not to do it too obviously, or too loudly, in particular if the Visigoths, say, were in large groups, but when a man was on his own or the worse for wear, out came the real sentiments.

Barbarian. Savage. Fur-wearer. Stinking brute. It was worse than ever now thanks to Alaric's siege. Alone, sleeping on the street, Vadomar had decided a long time ago that the gods must be watching over him. He could think of no other reason he hadn't been murdered in his sleep. They would not help his situation, but they hadn't let Roman lowlifes do him in, until now anyway.

Having resolved not to have another drink, he was left with nothing to do. It was a bizarre feeling, and not one he much liked. Of course his first instinct was to rummage for a coin, consequences be damned, and order another jug. He managed not to, realising in the same moment that removing himself from temptation was the best policy.

He wandered the Suburra for a time, declining the offers of gaunt-faced women reduced to selling their bodies, and watchful for cutpurses or men who would offer violence. No one barred his path. It was his sword and scale shirt, he decided, that kept the greedy-eyed individuals on every corner at bay. These were not always enough, though. Not long after, he had to lose a bunch of lowlifes who dogged his trail the length of two streets. Soberer than in an age, he decided he did not want to end his existence face-down in the mud, bleeding out.

Taking control was a new, heartening feeling, and when a tavern keeper recognised him and issued a fulsome invitation to enter his premises, Vadomar was able to refuse politely. Belly rumbling for food, another forgotten sensation, he stepped into a timber yard, and unseen amid the stacked planks took a bronze from his arm purse. When he protested in a bakery at the quarter-loaf proffered in return, the bread was withdrawn and he was sourly told prices had risen, did he want it or not?

He handed over the coin, checking the part-loaf was fresh – it was – and went out into the street again. Taking a bite, marvelling at the deliciousness, he resolved to eat as slowly as possible.

A tug on his scale armour.

Alarmed, Vadomar took a step back, preparing to draw his sword.

'Spare a little for a comrade?' The speaker's broad shoulders were stooped, and his right arm ended in a stump at the elbow. Perhaps a decade older than Vadomar, he had an unkempt beard and a greasy leather Pannonian cap. 'I haven't eaten in days.'

'You're a veteran,' Vadomar replied in Gothic. He didn't offer any bread – crippled soldiers were common as sparrows.

The stump waggled. 'Obvious, eh?'

'And your size gives it away. Who did you serve under?'

'Stilicho, back in the day. Fought Alaric twice or three times, and defeated him. You?'

'I was at those battles also. I am – was – a bucellarius.'

A whistle of respect. 'One of the magister militum's household warriors?'

'Yes.' Vadomar's pride stirred; it was not dead.

'Was you at Ravenna when . . .?'

'Sadly, aye.'

'I heard he surrendered, meek as a lamb. Why didn't you fight for him?'

'He commanded us not to!' Vadomar's spittle hit the veteran's face. 'Would you disobey a direct order from the magister militum?'

'I . . . No.'

'Save your scorn.' Vadomar stalked off, shame biting that he hadn't yet taken revenge on Stilicho's enemies in the Senate.

The veteran hurried after him. 'Friend!'

'You're no friend of mine.'

'I meant no insult.' The footsteps came to a halt.

Vadomar went another ten paces. Then, conscience needling, he turned. The maimed veteran had retreated to the doorway of a boarded-up shop. Crouched on his haunches, eyes downcast, his good hand was outstretched in entreaty towards anyone passing by. It was a piteous sight.

Vadomar broke his bread in two and placed the larger piece in the veteran's palm.

A cry of grateful thanks, and when he looked up, astonishment.

'Eat it quick, before I change my mind.'

A brief silence followed as they both ate.

'An ordinary *pedes*, were you?' It had been Vadomar's rank.

'No. I was a *circitor*, not that you'd know to look at me.'

Vadomar's lips twisted. 'By rights I should call you "Domine".'

'Not serving any more, am I?' The stump was raised. 'I'm nothing now, with this.'

'Wife? Family?'

A shake of the head. 'You?'

'No, thank the gods.' Vadomar could hear the screams, the cries for help. See the murder, rape, the buildings aflame. He hoped Dog and Wulfila had somehow made it out.

'I heard about the foederati massacres. Bastard Romans, killing women and children.' The veteran spat. 'Why did you come to Roma? I thought most men had joined Alaric.'

'I had the mad idea of killing Stilicho's enemies in the Senate.'

'All of them? There are a lot.'

'Every last one. The trouble was, I didn't know where to start. Ended up drowning my sorrows, and well, you know how it can go.'

'I spent a month pissed out of my head after this.' The stump was brandished. 'When I sobered up, I still had no hand.'

They both laughed.

'It was vile what happened to Stilicho. How did it ever come to pass?'

'The Senate and people hadn't trusted him for years,' said Vadomar.

A snort. 'All those dealings with Alaric can't have helped. The dogs in the street could see they were scratching each other's backs for a time.'

'So it was easy to blame him for the tribes coming over the Rhenus.' Vadomar had talked this to death with his comrades.

He remembered the great river, and the tens of thousands of Vandali, Alani and Suebi who had been waiting to cross over. Repercussions from the mass incursion were still being felt, with Britannia abandoned by its garrison and much of the dioceses of Gallia and Viennensis under the control of barbarians or usurpers such as Constantinus. What a pity they had not taken Valentia, he thought. Things might have been different.

'Stilicho was busy fighting Radagaisus at the time. I should know. That's where I got this.' The stump waved.

'I was there too,' said Vadomar. 'Stilicho was powerless to stop the crossing of the Rhenus, but he was the magister militum, he was supposed to defend the entire empire. Every Roman soldier hated him anyway; it just added fuel to the fire.'

'And if the ordinary riff-raff don't like him, you can bet the nobility and the Senate feel even more strongly.'

'Ticinum was proof of involvement at the highest level; it was so well planned and orchestrated. The massacre wiped out almost every ally and supporter Stilicho had.' Bitterness filled Vadomar. 'The writing was on the wall then, even if he didn't admit it to us. He hoped to win over the soldiers at Ravenna, but never got the chance.'

'Honorius had Eucherius murdered as well. Bastard. It's a wonder he didn't do away with Thermantia and Serena too. At least they're safe here.' A laugh. 'I say safe, as long as Roma holds out. Speaking of which, you heard the rumours?'

'Rumours?'

'About Serena.'

Vadomar thought of the state he'd been in over the previous weeks. 'No.'

'They say she is in league with Alaric. They say she will let his soldiers into the city.'

'Horseshit! Why would she do such a thing?'

'Don't seem right to me either, but it's what the people are saying. Must have heard it a hundred times.'

'Let us hope she stays at home and keeps the door barred.' Serena had seen enough misfortune for a lifetime, Vadomar thought, losing first a daughter, then her husband and son in quick succession. Her second daughter was alive, but had been discarded by the emperor like an unwanted plaything. Theirs could not be a happy household. Maybe he should seek her out and offer his protection, such as it was.

Their conversation was interrupted by loud shouts, which spread along the street like an out-of-control house fire. Cries of thanks rose, to God and all His saints, and to Laeta, the widowed second wife of the long-dead emperor Gratian. Apparently there was to be a distribution of food in the Forum Romanum. Quite when wasn't clear, but people were already moving towards the city centre. Vadomar and the veteran needed no encouragement. It seemed natural to walk together.

Unease pricked at Vadomar, though. Gratian had been devout; his widow would be too. It was easy to imagine having to be a believer to receive food. 'I am no Christian. Are you?'

'I keep a foot in both camps,' replied the veteran, unashamed. 'It don't matter to Laeta anyway. Kind-hearted she is. Turn up is all you have to do, and look hungry. There's no questions asked.'

The crowds wanting food in the Forum Romanum were huge. It took an age to reach the front of the line. To Vadomar's surprise, there had been no queue-jumping, even where it would have been easy, around the temple of Ianus, the altar of the divine Iulius or the great statues of Camillus and Constantinus. The civilised behaviour came about thanks to Laeta's patrolling slaves, who advised there was food for all. Their presence – and the famished state of the population – reduced any hostility towards the two barbarians to a few dark looks.

The line ended in front of the temple to Julius Caesar, where Vadomar was astonished to find Laeta herself handing out bags of flour with a friendly word for everyone. There was olive oil too; his companion had come prepared, holding out a grimy wooden beaker when his turn came.

They planned to go to the veteran's accommodation in the Circus Maximus, described in his own words as 'a flea-infested armpit of a place', and use a metal sheet atop his brazier to cook flatbreads. They wouldn't be as tasty as if they'd paid for them to be baked in a bakery, but Vadomar didn't care; his belly was growling in anticipation.

The veteran had said he could stay if he wished. It was cramped, he added, and there was no bed, just space on the floorboards, but it was worlds better than the street. Vadomar gratefully accepted. By now they had exchanged names; the veteran was called Theodrid. As they left with their food, Vadomar felt a friendship beginning. It felt good.

Theodrid lifted his cup of oil. 'We're going to have full bellies soon!'

Vadomar grinned. 'A sup of wine to go with the bread would top it all. Is there a thermopolium on the way?'

'I have no coin.'

'Leave it to me.'

Theodrid protested for politeness' sake, but soon gave up.

Reminiscing about Stilicho's victories over Alaric, lamenting how these had never been followed through, agreeing that he had been a good military leader but indecisive at critical moments, the pair made their way past the Vicus Tuscus to a great arch on the edge of the cattle market, the Forum Boarium, and onwards. Nearing the Circus Maximus, Vadomar stopped mid sentence.

'Impressive, eh?' Theodrid was pleased enough he could have been the original architect.

'It's so big!'

The veteran waxed lyrical. First constructed half a millennium before, it had been enlarged by the emperor Constantinus, and could apparently accommodate two hundred thousand spectators. Chariot races were held every three days or so throughout the year. Large-scale beast hunts and foot races also took place in the hippodrome.

'I didn't know people lived in it,' said Vadomar.

'Course they do. There are businesses on the ground floor, around the whole structure, and shopkeepers and tradesmen often live at the back of their premises.' Theodrid anticipated the next question. 'Me, I don't have a trade, not anything useful in civilian life anyways, but an ex-soldier I know, a basket-maker now, he lets me sleep in the attic over his shop. Tells his wife I guard the place, which I do, much as I can.' A scowl. 'Luckily, not too many latrones want to rob a basket-maker's.'

'He's not going to be appreciative of me staying, nor his wife from the sound of her.'

'She's a right cow. Don't worry, though, Gaius is decent. Quarter Visigoth, and proud of it. He won't mind, especially when he hears you were in Stilicho's bucellarii.'

Vadomar winced inwardly, but decided that disclosing a few details about his previous life would be a small price to pay for a roof over his head.

'Get off me!' A female voice.

A low, guttural reply. Coarse laughter.

A scream, cut off.

Gut instinct told Vadomar what was happening. His head turned, searching. Perhaps half a hundred paces down a narrow street to his left stood a small group of figures, in the midst of which lay another, slender form. His stomach turned.

'Leave it.' Theodrid's tone was brusque. 'None of our business. 'Sides, there's more of them than us.'

'Stay here.' Dropping one of his bags of flour, fingertips brushing belt, sword, dagger, Vadomar broke into a loping run. He took care to stay close to the buildings on the right, which were in the shade.

'Are you mad?' Theodrid called.

Maybe, thought Vadomar, and kept running. Afterwards, he would put his reaction down to talking about Stilicho. Stilicho, who he had seen walk to his death while he stood by and did nothing.

His well-oiled sword whispered free. He had forgotten how good it felt to have a blade in his fist. He counted the men. Seven. Six really, because one was bare-arsed on top of their sobbing victim. The rest had their backs to him, or were side-on. Oblivious with lust, none registered his approach. It was stupid odds regardless, yet Vadomar was beyond caring. Die here, or die some night with his head caved in by a brick, it did not matter.

He closed half the distance, and still had no plan.

Three quarters.

He was going to stab the first man in the back. After that, he would see.

A section of paving shifted underfoot. Vadomar checked, didn't lose his balance, but the sound of the stone clicking back into place echoed in the narrow space.

An unshaven, hard-eyed man saw him. 'Lads!'

Heads turned. Snarls. Daggers were produced, clubs hefted.

Inspired, Vadomar swung the bag of flour in his left hand and let fly. It shot through the air, smacking into a skinny man's chest. The thing weighed as much as a year-old babe. With an oof of surprise, the man went down on his arse.

The rest spread out, blocking the street.

Vadomar came in hard and fast, his reach far longer than that of any of his enemies. *Stab.* A second ruffian fell, mortally wounded. Vadomar danced away, hacking at a lunging arm and knowing his victim's shocked scream meant the odds had reduced again. He was going to die, though, there could be no other outcome against five men. Five, not four, because the would-be rapist was on his feet, sorting out his tunic. From the encouragement being shouted at his companions, he was the ringleader.

Something arced in overhead, struck a man on the shoulder. He stumbled and went to one knee, oil splashing everywhere. Vadomar could have cheered. It was Theodrid's wooden beaker, and here was Theodrid himself, a rusty knife in his hand and a gleam in his eyes that hadn't been there before.

'Looks like you need help,' he said.

'Now who's mad?'

'Both of us, I'd say.'

The lowlifes advanced. Three had daggers, but one looked winded still from the bag of flour. The other two were armed with clubs. They spread out, aiming to come from every side.

'Sure about this?' asked Theodrid.

'We can't leave the girl.' Whether she had been punched half-senseless or was merely traumatised, Vadomar wasn't certain, but all she had done was sit up. She wasn't capable of running.

'Backs against the wall, quick,' said Theodrid, and they retreated to the stuccoed frontage of a large house. Its iron-studded door was shut, the building's occupants uncaring or, Vadomar thought, too wise to come out and see what was going on.

Leering, laughing in anticipation, the lowlifes closed in.

'The first man to reach me will die, you know,' declared Vadomar. 'Theodrid will gut the second. After that, we'll see!' Brave words, fighting words, designed to sow the seeds of fear.

A long pause. Uncertainty in the gaunt faces. Curses. Hissed rebukes from the ringleader, then threats. Vadomar prepared himself. He had seen it before, enemy officers forcing their wary men to charge. It would only take one, and they would swarm forward like a pack of dogs.

Wood creaked above. Focused on the ruffians, Vadomar paid no heed. He would have given several years' pay for his shield.

Four charged. One hung back, the man who'd been winded by the bag of flour. The wily leader and one other made for Theodrid, leaving Vadomar to a strapping youth with crossed eyes and an older man with a determined scowl.

'Now!' shouted a voice overhead.

Pieces of roof tile, half-bricks and a ceramic bowl rained down, more objects than one person could hurl. Not enough to kill, they were nonetheless a real and painful distraction. The latrones' charge faltered, and Vadomar took his chance. Three steps forward, *stab*, and back to the wall.

His scowl transformed into a rictus of agony, the older man dropped. Dismayed, the youth gawped, so Vadomar darted in and stuck him too.

A hiss of pain. A cry of delight.

From above, 'More tiles, Fritigern!'

Vadomar went to Theodrid's aid, slashing at the ringleader, who dodged back nimbly.

A fresh onslaught of pieces of tile. The majority missed, but several struck the ringleader and his companion, eliciting yelps of pain. Vadomar stepped in front of Theodrid, sword raised, and advanced towards the pair. He and the ringleader locked eyes, each recognising that the other was capable of killing, neither prepared to back down.

The spell was broken when a tile fragment cracked off the ringleader's skull. With a savage curse, he turned and ran. His companion did the same; so did the winded man, albeit more slowly. They left behind a corpse, a man with a spraying bloody stump for an arm and two others with serious injuries. As the last three hobbled and dragged themselves away, Vadomar became aware of two things: the girl's loud prayers of thanks and Theodrid softly grunting.

'You're hurt,' he said, concerned.

'It's my own fault. Can't move like I used to.' Theodrid's stump was clasping his belly. His gaze came upwards. 'Gut wound. I'm done.'

'Don't say that,' said Vadomar, fear surging. 'Maybe the blade didn't go in deep.'

CHAPTER XX

The hinges screeched as Fritigern, grunting with effort, eased the heavy door open.

Elpidia heard someone speaking in Gothic, one of the two men who had come to the girl's aid. Barbarians, she thought. It was no surprise. The city was full of them, soldiers, ex-soldiers, criminals, slaves, escaped slaves. It was impossible to tell one from another. 'It might be safer not to go into the street, Nobilissima Femina,' she said, suspecting how Galla might act next.

Clearly thinking the same, Darme glanced at their mistress. His face was unhappy. 'Nobilissima Femina, please stay inside. Please.'

Galla did not reply, and Darme sighed. He held an old battered shield that had been in the house so long no one knew its origins; in his right fist was a meat cleaver. He was scared but resolute, and as Fritigern pulled the door ajar, Darme at once poked his head out.

'They're gone.' The barbarian addressed him in Latin rather than Gothic, heavily accented but intelligible.

One at least speaks our language, thought Elpidia. He's a soldier.

The major domus walked outside. Fritigern tottered determinedly after, his weapon a kitchen knife.

Before Elpidia could react, Galla picked up a jagged piece of roof tile and slipped through the doorway as well.

'Nobilissima Femina!' Hurrying after her, Elpidia took in the scene. Closest, almost on the doorstep, was the girl who'd been attacked. She was the slave of a neighbour, and a confident type, which was probably why she had been out alone. She gaped at Galla, though, dumbstruck in the presence of someone so far above her in social status.

'Are you injured?' asked Galla.

'N-no, Nobilissima Femina.' Brushing down her tunic, she stood.

'Did they . . .?' Galla paused.

'H-he nearly did, Nobilissima Femina, the leader, but then . . .' The girl's voice failed as the degree of good fortune granted her sank in.

'Get yourself home. Fritigern will accompany you.' Galla jerked her head, and the old Goth, delighted with the responsibility, began fussing over the girl like a grandparent. Galla's attention moved to the two men who had come to her aid. Elpidia was also evaluating them.

The sword-wielder was a young man, tall and broad-shouldered as Visigoths were, and wearing a rust-spotted scale-mail shirt. He had a mass of long, curly brown hair and a scraggy beard; his eyes were bloodshot. He looked and smelled, Elpidia decided, as if he'd been drinking for a month solid. Despite this, he was handsome, in a barbarian kind of way.

'You are a brave man,' said Galla.

An awkward duck of his head. 'I was only trying to help.'

'And you did.'

'My friend, he's injured. It's serious.' The Visigoth turned to his companion, who was slumped against the front of the house, face ashen.

'Bring him inside. I can send for a surgeon.'

'I need a Christ-miracle.' A rasping laugh from the wounded man, also a Visigoth.

Elpidia saw Galla's eyes drop to the injured man's stump, which was cradling his stomach. There was a telltale crimson stain on his tunic, and the disapproving retort at his blasphemy died in her throat.

'Come into the house. We can take care of you.' Galla's tone was commanding, but laced with genuine concern.

'Are you sure?' asked the sword-wielder. 'You don't know us.'

'You will address her as "Nobilissima Femina"!' Darme was scandalised. 'She is sister to Imperator Honorius!'

To Elpidia's astonishment, the Visigoth sneered. 'The same Honorius who had Stilicho executed? His son Eucherius tracked to Roma and murdered?'

Darme, rarely discomfited, was struck dumb.

'Stilicho's killing was wrong,' said Galla, emphasising the last word. 'He was loyal, and no public brigand. As for Eucherius . . .' Her voice caught.

The Visigoth gave her a blank look, and Elpidia thought, he has no idea Galla and Eucherius were once to be married. She wondered uncharitably what he would think of Galla's involvement in Serena's murder, which, according to a coded letter sent by Maximianus, was to take place today. Elpidia felt terrible thinking about it. She hoped God would forgive her mistress for supporting the senators' baseless but rabble-pleasing plan.

Regaining control of her emotions, Galla repeated that Stilicho had been a good servant to the empire. The emperor had been ill-advised to take such a drastic course of action.

Placated, the sword-wielder submitted to her insistence, and helped his friend through the doorway. Casting wary glances up and down the street – it wasn't impossible that the latrones would return with reinforcements – Elpidia urged her mistress after them. The door slammed shut, Darme's way of protesting.

The bedrooms were on the first floor. As Galla said to Elpidia, the injured Visigoth would never climb the stairs. Brisk and efficient, she threw wide the door to her office and took a stool from behind the desk. He sagged down onto it with a groan. But for the wall behind, Elpidia judged he would have toppled backwards. Commanded by Galla to fetch blankets, she muttered to Darme not to leave the mistress alone with the two barbarians, and received a withering do-you-think-I-don't-know-that look.

When Elpidia returned, the sword-wielding Visigoth was supporting his friend, whose eyes were closed. Laying down the blankets, together they eased the wounded man onto the floor. One look at his midriff was enough. The knife had gone into his belly. It might take a few days, but unless a miracle could be worked, the poor soul's fate was certain. Catching the other Visigoth's eye, Elpidia saw that he also knew. Galla must have too, but it did not stop her sending Darme to fetch a surgeon.

With the wounded Visigoth dozing, his friend relaxed a little and accepted a drink of watered-down wine, brought by a kitchen slave.

'What is your name?' asked Galla.

'Vadomar.' A slight hesitation, then, 'Nobilissima Femina.'

'You are a soldier?'

Elpidia noted how Vadomar seemed relieved to tell his story. Born in northern Italia, the son of a domesticus, he'd entered the army at the first opportunity. After distinguishing himself in battle, he had been invited to join Stilicho's bucellarii. Year in, year out he had followed the magister militum, until the recent fateful journey to Ravenna and the church outside which Stilicho had been slain.

'That was bad enough,' Vadomar said, 'but you will have heard how the families of the foederati were murdered soon after. I saw comrades' wives and children being butchered like animals, Nobilissima Femina. Somehow I escaped and came to Roma. I wanted to avenge the general, but I didn't know who his enemies were and had no real way of finding out. I started drinking to forget. Drank myself stupid for a month or more. Then today I met Theodrid here' – he indicated his friend – 'and thought my luck had changed. How wrong I was.'

Elpidia's heart went out to him.

'You saved the girl,' said Galla.

'I suppose, but if I'd known the price was Theodrid's life . . .'

'He may yet survive.'

Vadomar pitched his voice lower. 'I have seen a hundred wounds like his, Nobilissima Femina. Perhaps three lived.'

'A mass shall be celebrated for him every day. We will pray also, ask God to be merciful.' Seeing something in his face, she asked, 'You are a Christian?'

'I am not.' Proud words. No 'Nobilissima Femina'.

It was a challenge.

'You will see the light one day,' said Galla.

They stared at one another, the emperor's half-sister and the sweaty-faced, wine-reeking barbarian. In this moment, Galla had no power over him.

'I am not here to debate theology,' Galla said eventually. 'What are your plans after your friend recovers' – her eyes went to Theodrid – 'or not, from his injuries?'

'I am in debt to you, Nobilissima Femina. But for your intervention, it wouldn't just have been Theodrid who got hurt.'

Galla looked pleased.

'Have you any need of protection, Nobilissima Femina? The city is dangerous at this time. Your major domus is brave, I saw that, but he wouldn't last a dozen heartbeats in a real fight. As for the old Goth, well . . .' Vadomar chuckled.

'I might have more slaves who can use weapons.'

'If you had, Nobilissima Femina, you would have sent them out onto the street.'

It was Galla's turn to be amused. 'A shrewd observation. Although Honorius is my half-brother, my funds are not limitless. How much would you expect to be paid?'

'The same as a bucellarius.'

He appeared to be honest too, thought Elpidia.

'How much is that?'

He named a yearly sum.

Galla looked surprised. 'I thought you would ask for more. It is more than acceptable.'

Vadomar dropped to his knees. 'I would speak the oath, Nobilissima Femina.'

He did not see Galla's quickly masked shock, but Elpidia did. Making a vow such as the military sacramentum, to serve the emperor, clashed with the Christian belief that baptism was the only acceptable ritual.

'Very well.'

'I will faithfully execute everything you command, Nobilissima Femina. I will never desert your service. I will not seek to avoid death in your cause,' Vadomar declared, adding, 'May I die before you.'

'I accept your service.' Galla's reply was gracious. 'Rise.'

Vadomar did, and their eyes met. He bent his head in respect.

Elpidia watched him, and thought: despite Theodrid's mortal wound, today will not have been all bad. You have found a purpose.

He was not alone either.

She hoped that in accepting his service, Galla Placidia had also been fortunate.

A month later . . .

Vadomar's eyes roved round the fire. Conversation had been dying; the only replies to his last mention of how long it might take for Roma's defenders to open the gates had been sleepy mutters. It would be time to move soon. He was outside the city, sent by Galla to find out what he could about Alaric's intentions.

Negotiations had been going on for a while, but nothing had come of them thus far. To her frustration, Galla had been able to find out little. The Senate's delegates at the talks were keeping their lips sealed. It was probable that Alaric's demands hadn't been met, she had declared, and once the Senate gave in, the siege would end. A slim possibility existed, however, that he was planning an all-out assault. Knowing this would mean she could plan her escape, hence Vadomar's mission tonight.

This was the third; the previous occasions had gone smoothly, slipping through an open gate as night fell, stealing close to the Visigothic lines, then walking in among them as a man does after he's answered a call of nature. The encampment was large; no one gave him a second glance.

There was no reason to; he was one of their own, and as he often thought, but for his encounter with Galla, he might well have been a member of Alaric's horde, come to besiege Roma. He felt no animosity towards any of the warriors, but it went without saying that they did not feel the same about him. He had taken an opposite side to theirs, and sworn allegiance to a member of the imperial family. It was strange, he had thought more than once, given that Galla was half-sister to the emperor, who had ordered

Stilicho's execution. And yet it was not, for she and Honorius were like chalk and cheese. She did not speak of him, but having asked Elpidia, Vadomar knew relations between the half-siblings were not cordial.

He had sworn to serve Galla because it returned purpose to his directionless life. If he admitted it, she was also perilously attractive. He had thought it from the moment he set eyes on her. She was courageous also, getting involved in the clash with the latrones. Not that she would ever have anything to do with him, a lowly soldier. There was a third, darker reason behind his taking the sacramentum. Stay close to Galla, and an opportunity to reach Heraclianus, the officer who had murdered Stilicho, might one day present itself.

His attention returned to the here and now, and the snoring warriors by the fire. If they had had even an inkling of who he was, thought Vadomar, there would have been no sleeping tonight. They would have spent the hours of darkness torturing and killing him.

It was for this reason that he had been careful each time he entered the Visigothic camp to have a reason for wandering about, asking questions. A worn-out shoe in need of replacing, an oilstone required to sharpen his weapons, or, like tonight, a genuine desire to find cheese. This last was somewhat bizarre, a request made by a baker in the city who had been tasked with making an elaborate dinner-party dish for a rich matron. The baker knew about Vadomar's sallies from the city thanks to his fondness for fresh bread and pastries, both things hard to come by unless one walked in with a joint of meat, say, purloined from a Visigothic supply wagon. Joint of meat exchanged for a week's worth of bread, the baker had put two and two together, and mentioned his failure to source the necessary cheese.

Vadomar had promised to see what he could do, and his luck had been in; the cheese had come from one of the sleeping warriors, who had spent the day scouring the countryside. The price had not been outrageous. He touched the bulky half-wheel secreted in a fold of his cloak, and hoped his body heat wasn't softening it overmuch.

Orange-red sparks lifted as a piece of wood slipped off another and landed in the embers. The fire was low; delay any longer, and one of the men dozing around him might wake to put on another log. He would then have to wait until everyone was asleep again. Again his gaze roved, and he decided it was safe to move.

Unbending stiff knees – he had been sitting for hours – he stood, one hand on the cheese, the other holding his sword tight against his middle so the metal fittings didn't shink. He waited, motionless, in case a warrior stirred. Thirty heartbeats went by, and none had. Fifty. Nothing. Content, Vadomar turned on the spot. Gaze taken from the dull glow of the fire, he let his vision adjust to the darkness.

A loud fart ripped the air. It had come from the corpulent man nearest him, who had downed a large amount of wine. Vadomar twisted, watching, wary, in case anyone woke. They did not, to his relief. Once more he delayed, counting his pulse. Peace continued to reign.

He walked away. One careful step after another, he padded west, through the irregular mass of tents. There was no order; even if many of Alaric's men had previously fought for the empire, they had forsaken the neatness of the Roman military. It was a pity, he thought, because it made finding a way out difficult. Thanks to his meandering path through the camp, he had also lost his sense of direction somewhat. He searched the heavens for the Dog's Tail, at the end of the Ursa Major constellation. It was the only star not to move through the sky as night progressed. Locating it, he dropped his gaze straight down to the horizon. That was north. He had come out of the east of the city, so he had to head off to his right.

Although sentries were rare – their host was so large, and Roma's defenders so few, the Visigoths could not be blamed – Vadomar remained alert. He moved slowly and stopped at regular intervals to be sure no one was following. At one point he stood statue still as a quartet of drunken warriors loudly argued about who was the strongest. The demands to be quiet from men woken from sleep were met with insults and aggression. It took a furious chieftain, also roused, to tell the four that if they didn't piss off somewhere else, they would all be torn apart by horses in the morning. There were muttered apologies, belches, and the warriors weaved away.

The tension in Vadomar's spine eased. With a careful grip on the cheese and an eye out for the inebriated warriors, he continued his journey. All went well until he tripped over an oddly placed guy rope and went sprawling onto the muddy ground. The cheese fell from his cloak. The hilt of his sword dug into his hip. He cursed. The disturbed men inside the tent did too, and advised that if they came outside and he was still there, he'd be sorry. Vadomar apologised, slurring his words so it appeared he had overindulged. The replies he received advised him to move, fast.

Fumbling for the cheese, he was relieved to find only a little mud on it. Wrapping it in his cloak once more, he got to his feet. The edge of the camp was close; the gaps between the tents were larger, and the occasional stink of shit marked the spots where lazier men had emptied their bowels. Grateful he hadn't dropped the cheese here, Vadomar did his best to sidestep the piles of faeces.

It was an impossible task, of course, and sooner rather than later, something squelched underfoot. In the same instant, his nostrils were assailed by an unmistakable stink. Vadomar cursed silently. It was too dark to try and clean his boot, and he was not quite out of danger. Trying to ignore the stench, he walked on.

'Who's there?' The challenge, in Gothic, came from in front.

'No one,' said Vadomar, again slurring his speech. 'Just a man in need of a dump.' Seeing a figure loom out of the darkness a little to his left, he angled his walk to ensure they would not pass close to each other.

'Don't go that way – there's shit everywhere.'

Vadomar flailed for an answer that would not cause suspicion. 'Donar's arse crack! Here will have to do then.' He stopped, laying down the cheese to his left, the opposite side to which the warrior was coming from. Shrugging off his cloak and placing it on top of the cheese, he rummaged at his waist as if to open his trousers.

'Strange hour to need a crap.'

Vadomar didn't like the man's tone. 'When nature calls, it calls.'

The warrior came closer. 'Who did you say your chieftain was?'

He suspects something, thought Vadomar, belly tight with fear. Down on his haunches, he was at the other's mercy. 'Eh? Can't you leave a man in peace?'

'It's a simple question.'

The warrior was close, Vadomar saw from the corner of his eye, but his spear wasn't aimed at him. Yet. 'Simple it might be,' he said, groaning. 'My guts are killing me, though. I haven't had a shit in four days.'

'Give me a name and I'll leave you in peace.'

Vadomar cursed himself silently. It had been overoptimistic to imagine he could forever steal in and out of Alaric's camp without being challenged, and foolish to bury his head in the sand to avoid thinking about what would have to be done when it happened. He groaned, trying to delay the inevitable.

'A name.' Now the tone was markedly hostile.

He waited until the last moment before leaping up off his haunches. Wrapping both hands around the startled warrior's throat, he squeezed with all his might. Throttle the man unconscious, went his reasoning, and he could escape. Shield and spear discarded, the warrior ripped at Vadomar's fingers, and when that didn't work, thumb-gouged at his eyes. Vadomar twisted his face to the side and tightened his grip. Nails tore flesh from his cheek. A fist struck his head once, twice. Desperation blossomed in his chest. A few more blows and he would have to let go. *Bang*. Stars burst across his vision. His grasp weakened.

'Theudis? Are you taken ill?'

Vadomar's opponent made a choking sound.

'Theudis?' Feet pounded the earth.

Decision forced on him, Vadomar let go and drew his dagger as the warrior staggered back, coughing and retching. Then, quickly, he stabbed. Hard, because he had to be sure. The warrior went down. Cloak and cheese scooped up, the shouts of his victim's comrade ringing in his ears, Vadomar sprinted away into the gloom.

CHAPTER XXI

Elpidia was in the kitchen, stoking the embers in the still-warm oven. It was early; the sky above the frost-rimed courtyard was dark. Used to her habits, the floor-resting kitchen slaves had peered drowsily at her, readjusted their blankets and gone back to sleep. There was time. Darme had not yet appeared, and Galla would not stir until the morning was well under way. Her only company was the household cat, which was winding itself around her legs in a winsome attempt to be offered some food.

'I have nothing for you, Felicula sweetheart,' said Elpidia regretfully, stooping to rub behind the cat's ears. 'Go and kill a rat, there are enough about.'

'You're up.'

Startled and embarrassed – her back was to the door – Elpidia snapped, 'What does it look like?'

'That's a nice welcome for someone who comes with fresh *speusticus*.' Vadomar was brandishing three loaves.

The rich, delicious smell filling her nostrils – 'hurry' bread, made quickly, was one of Elpidia's great weaknesses – she said, 'I did not mean to be rude. I was surprised.' She noticed the blood marking his fingers, the reddened side of his face, and asked, concerned, 'Are you hurt?'

His eyes followed hers to his hand. He set the bread on the counter. 'I . . . No.'

'It is someone else's blood.'

'Yes.'

'I do not think it was the baker, unless you have taken to robbery.' A poor attempt at humour, it was all Elpidia could come up with.

A long breath out. 'I killed a warrior in Alaric's camp.'

'He realised you had come from inside the city?'

'More or less. I didn't have much choice.'

'It was him or you.'

'Yes.'

'God will forgive you.'

His lips twisted. 'I do not care what your God thinks.' He said no more, but went to wash his hands and boots in the courtyard, where there was a bucket.

Uncomfortable with how matter-of-fact he had been, Elpidia decided not to bring up the topic again. 'You did well to get the bread,' she said when he returned. 'Where is it from?'

Her question was apposite. The situation in Roma was desperate; Serena's strangulation had made no difference. The grain dole had almost stopped. People were dying of starvation, disease and violence. Thousands of slaves had fled the city to join Alaric's horde. Every day the churches were full to overflowing with people praying for salvation from the Visigoths. Extraordinarily, the papa, Innocent, had given permission to celebrate pagan rites in private.

It didn't matter which god you prayed to, Elpidia had decided, none of them filled your belly. Guilt pricking at such a blasphemous thought, she silently asked for forgiveness.

Vadomar hadn't answered.

'Well?'

'It's all about who you know,' he said with a wink.

They were back to their sparring. She threw him an Elpidian glare.

'There's a bakery close to the gate I use. The owner needed some cheese, something for a fancy dinner party. I managed to get half a wheel in Alaric's camp.' An amused snort. 'It was a little muddy, but he wasn't going to get it anywhere else, so he couldn't complain.'

Cheese was far harder to obtain than hurry bread, thought Elpidia. 'All he gave you was three loaves?'

'I could have had a dozen, but I'll need a favour in the future. When I go asking, he will look after me.'

Stomach growling, Elpidia wanted to grab a loaf and devour the lot. Instead she set two small chunks of wood atop the glowing cinders and turned so her back benefited from the resulting heat. 'Hear anything interesting?'

'Plenty.'

It was a constant competition between them. Never reply to a question with enough information. If the other person asked for more, they had lost.

And so Elpidia ignored him, picking up Felicula and fussing her.

Nonchalant, Vadomar set the loaves on the counter, and broke off three of the scored pieces. 'Mm,' he said, chewing, his mouth full. 'It's so good.'

She gave in. 'Tell me what you found out.'

He grinned. 'Are you sure?'

'Yes, curse you!'

'Alaric is prepared to lift the siege. I told you Serena didn't need to be killed.' Like most of the population, Vadomar had been outraged to hear of her murder by order of the Senate. He was none the wiser about Galla's involvement either, a state of affairs Elpidia hoped would never change. She gave a non-committal grunt.

'His terms are these: five thousand pounds of gold, thirty thousand of silver, four thousand silk tunics, enough leather to make shoes for his entire army for a year or more, and three thousand pounds of pepper.'

Elpidia whistled. 'That will mean extra taxes.'

'Ordinary people will be bled dry, the same old story, but the rich will have to dip into their coffers too.'

'The Senate won't have much choice.'

'It's not as if Honorius has helped in any way, the useless prick. The entire army is sitting on its hands at Ticinum instead of marching to the city's aid!'

'Shh.' Elpidia motioned at the blanket-wrapped slaves on the floor; they were stirring.

'The mistress probably thinks the same thing.' Vadomar sniffed, but his next words were quieter. 'If Honorius didn't have someone to pull his strings, he'd fall over.'

One of the two slaves on the floor opened an eye.

Elpidia's stomach tightened. 'It is not for you and me to have opinions about the emperor,' she said loudly. It didn't do to speak ill of the most powerful person in the empire, even here, in Galla's house.

'Aye, well, he won't be using the treasury to pay off Alaric any time soon, will he?' Vadomar's face twisted.

The emperor's method of disposal of Stilicho had left a raw, bleeding wound in Vadomar's soul, thought Elpidia. A simple, honourable man, he would not forget what had been done to his master. But he was Galla's man now, he had said so more than once after a little too much wine; Galla's man until death took him. Unless, she thought with a tickle of dread, he discovered her part in Serena's killing.

It might have been thought odd during a siege that there was wine for hired soldiers like Vadomar, but there was an impressive collection of amphorae in the storage rooms off the courtyard. They were there thanks to Darme. If he drank plenty himself on the sly, it didn't matter, so numerous were the amphorae. There was wine from Gallia and Viennensis, Iberia, every region of Italia and places Elpidia had only a vague awareness of: Judaea, Carthage and Thracia.

'Best keep this warm, eh?' Vadomar was proffering an untouched loaf.

Elpidia huffed; it was beneath her to do something so lowly. She kicked one of the shapes on the floor. 'Up! Get the bread in the oven, lest it go cold before the mistress wakes.'

The younger of the two kitchen slaves, a none-too-bright girl by the name of Iovina, scrambled up, apologising. She put the bread into a specially shaped clay case and placed it in the oven.

'Not too close to the embers,' warned Elpidia.

Seeing Vadomar taking more bread, she broke off a piece for herself, then two smaller wedges for the kitchen slaves. 'The rest is for

Darme and Fritigern. Make sure no crumbs are left on the counter,' she said, and got a happy nod from Iovina. None of them, Vadomar aside perhaps, were supposed to eat bread, but what Galla didn't know about, Elpidia decided, she couldn't mete out punishment for.

Galla called for Vadomar the moment she was up and dressed. He found her at a table in the courtyard, a trap for sunshine. It was warm enough, just, to sit outside. A pair of sparrows twittered from the branches of a lemon tree.

There was no one else about but Elpidia, so no 'Nobilissima Femina'. Elpidia didn't mind; she didn't think Galla did either. She had caught her mistress watching Vadomar more than once, and suspected she had feelings for him, physical feelings. She wasn't stupid enough to fall in love with a Visigothic soldier, or at least Elpidia didn't think she was.

Vadomar had changed his clothing, and was in a fine tunic with roundels on the upper arms and purple bands around the wrists. 'You wanted to hear about my mission?'

'The speusticus is delicious,' Galla said, wiping a drop of honey off her plate.

Vadomar's lips quirked. 'How many pieces did you have?'

This was being overfamiliar, thought Elpidia.

Galla smiled. 'Three.'

'You really do like it.'

'As I said, it is good. Iovina says there is another loaf also. Where did you get them, and how?'

Again Elpidia heard the tale. Vadomar mentioned the mud on the cheese, which made Galla laugh. She asked next if he had found out anything in the Visigothic camp; he related Alaric's terms for the siege to be lifted.

Galla sat thinking, then said, 'It would have been reasonable to ask for a great deal more. He is still owed thousands of pounds of gold from the settlement made with Stilicho. The Senate is so short-sighted, my half-brother too. I do not understand. They should just pay him and have done.'

'They cannot see past their hatred of barbarians,' said Vadomar with some feeling.

Galla studied him. 'I think you are right, and therein lies the problem. Treat a man badly for long enough, and he will react in the end. Alaric's patience thus far has been considerable, but the siege is only a taste of what he is capable of.'

Elpidia stirred. 'You think he would sack the city?'

'Perhaps.'

She shuddered. It did not bear thinking about.

'Let us hope the Senate realises he cannot be brushed off like an annoying pedlar on the street,' said Galla.

Elpidia waited to see if Vadomar would mention the warrior he had slain, but he did not. She told Galla about it when he had gone.

'He is loyal then,' said Galla, a little shocked.

'You may be sure of that,' replied Elpidia with feeling.

In the days following, Alaric's demands saw ornaments seized from pagan temples and melted down to provide the required silver and gold. Vadomar raged silently up and down the courtyard when he heard, telling the slaves the deities would be rendered inanimate and inefficacious. When Elpidia, a devout Christian, asked him why, he explained that the decorations made the statues of the gods sacred. Worse, he declared, the statues of Bellona and Virtus themselves had been destroyed, leaving the Romans with neither courage nor strength.

Elpidia could have said that was already the case. She had gleaned enough history listening to Galla's tutor, and had made a practice of eavesdropping on Stilicho and Serena in the time when she and Galla had lived with them. The Senate pontificated and blustered, and the emperor pretended he ruled the world from his gilded palace in Ravenna, Stilicho had been fond of saying, but the glory days were long gone. Roma was a city built on sand. Its territories were shrunken, and large areas were under the control of barbarians or usurpers. His declarations had been an education to Elpidia, who like many slaves had thought of the empire as all-powerful.

If not for men like Stilicho and Vadomar, she thought now, the Roman army would barely exist. The days of antiquity when ordinary citizens had taken pride in military service were not just long gone but forgotten. One only had to look at the sparsely defended walls to realise Roman men had no desire to serve in the army; they preferred others be paid to fight instead. It didn't matter who: Visigoth, Goth, Vandal, Suebi or a dozen other tribes. Rather than strengthen the empire, it resulted in warlike hordes wandering its territories, wreaking havoc. Roma itself being besieged by Alaric, Elpidia concluded, was the most extreme example thus far.

True to his word, however, the Visigothic warlord had withdrawn his soldiers after his demands were first approved by Honorius and then met by the Senate. The siege lifted, the ports again open to grain freighters from Africa and thousands of Gothic slaves fled the city to join Alaric, life had returned to a semblance of normality. It did not mean the threat had gone. Alaric was at Ariminum, not far away. He still wanted land for his people, as he had all these years of being bought off by the Senate. Negotiations with the emperor – another of his demands – were to take place at Ravenna.

Whether they would come to anything was another matter altogether, Galla confided to Elpidia. Olympius, the man who had orchestrated Stilicho's downfall and execution, was rabidly opposed to giving Alaric any more concessions than were necessary. 'It's well for him, safe in Ravenna,' Galla said. 'Roma's one real protection is its walls. If Alaric doesn't get what he wants . . .'

'He'll come straight back,' Elpidia finished. 'A second siege would be terrible. He's not scared. Remember what he said about the city's population being ready to fight? "The thicker grass is more easy to mow than the thinner."'

Galla frowned. 'If relations between me and the emperor were not strained . . .'

'He won't have changed,' said Elpidia.

A sigh. 'I know. I will not go to Ravenna, even if it is safer than Roma.'

'In that case, let us pray Olympius and the emperor agree to Alaric's demands.'

They both knew it was improbable, but an illusion of hope when one is powerless is better than the bitter truth, so the pretence continued.

Time would tell, thought Elpidia grimly.

CHAPTER XXII

One month later . . .

Via Popilia, south of Ravenna; Mensis Ianuarius, AD *409*

Vadomar hunched his shoulders against the cold north wind, which felt as if it came from the Alpes mountains. The leftmost man, midway along the column of fifty horsemen, the chill air found every little gap in the folds of his fur cloak. He squinted at the orange ball of the sun, which was fast dropping to the horizon. 'It will be dark ere long,' he said. 'How far to Ravenna?'

'The last milestone said four miles.'

It was easy to see why men called Gnaeus, the individual riding beside Vadomar, Jupiter's messenger. The white streak in his pitch-black hair resembled a thunderbolt. It amused Vadomar to hear Christians use such a name. Old traditions died hard; another example had been the return to pagan worship during the recent siege of Roma.

Gnaeus jibed, 'You saw the milestone too.'

'I suppose I did. My bones ache with the cold, though. Can't think straight. I need a roaring fire and a cup of warmed wine.'

'Going soft, you are.'

'A Roman calls a barbarian soft? You're treading on dangerous ground.'

'Fur-wearer.'

'Who wouldn't, in weather like this? More fool you not to.'

Gnaeus laughed. So did Vadomar.

This kind of verbal sparring had bonded them since meeting in Roma more than a week before. They had both been selected to accompany the senatorial embassy journeying to Ravenna, its aim to try to pressure Honorius into acceptance of Alaric's still outstanding terms. The transfer of hostages was not of much importance, but the central pillar of Alaric's demands, lands for his years-homeless people, had not been acknowledged by the emperor in any way. Everyone knew Alaric would not wait for ever, so the Senate had taken action. The principal members of the party were Attalus, the senior fiscal official, Caecilianus and Maximianus.

Guards were needed for the embassy, men of fighting age being in scant supply in Roma. A letter of recommendation from Galla had been more than enough for Vadomar to be taken on. Tasked to bring back as much information as he could, he had relished the opportunity to leave the city. Falling in with Gnaeus, a regular soldier, had been extra good fortune.

Gnaeus was a rare beast, a dyed-in-the-wool Roman veteran. Stubborn, unwilling to fawn or curry favour, he called a spade a spade, and horseshit horseshit. Lowly born, he had never been promoted to the heights possible with noble support. Another reason, Vadomar had concluded, was because of his willingness to be comrades with barbarians. As Gnaeus declared within an hour of their meeting, it didn't matter what race a man was if he was loyal and could fight. 'Are you loyal?' he'd asked.

'I am,' Vadomar had replied, adding quietly, 'To Galla Placidia. Took the sacramentum on my knees in front of her.'

Gnaeus seemed pleased. He'd jerked his chin at the carriage in front of them. 'Do those nose-in-the-air senators know?'

Vadomar had wavered. It wouldn't be the end of the world if the senators found out who he was, but Galla had asked him to keep a low profile. There was no need for anyone in the Senate to know she had spies, she'd said; Vadomar thought it sensible. He hadn't wanted to lie to a new comrade, though. 'No,' he'd replied.

To his relief, Gnaeus didn't make further comment, and although Vadomar couldn't be sure his new friend hadn't told the senators about him, nothing during the journey occurred to change his opinion.

It was full dark by the time they reached the walls of Ravenna and the principal entrance, the Porta Aurea, a magnificent marble-faced double triumphal arch built centuries before in honour of the emperor Claudius. It was shut and barred, and was only opened after Attalus threatened dire punishment for the guards who refused to admit a delegation from the Senate. Vadomar and Gnaeus followed the carriage over a bridge spanning the moonlit moat.

Vadomar nodded his thanks at a sentry who was watching them pass. 'Gratitude. It's not a night to spend outdoors.'

A grunt. 'Embassy from Roma, eh?'

'Yes. We come to seek the emperor's support against Alaric.'

Another disinterested grunt. 'Dunno what it is about today. You're the second embassy to enter Ravenna. The other one was full of eunuchs.' The sentry hawked and spat.

Vadomar's interest pricked. 'Who sent them?'

'Constantinus, the usurper who calls himself the Third.'

Vadomar and Gnaeus shared a look.

They had spoken about Constantinus several times on their journey. Since his invasion the previous year with the entire garrison of Britannia, he had ruled most of Gallia and Viennensis. Hispania had also risen in support of his cause. A serious threat, he had survived Sarus' attempts to defeat him. Dark memories returned to Vadomar, of the failed night-time attempt to take Valentia, and the humiliating retreat to the Alpes, where they were robbed blind by the bacaudae.

Constantinus was to have been dealt with the previous summer, but the uncertainties following the downfall and execution of Stilicho had kept the imperial army in Italia. There was every possibility he would finally invade come the spring, another army to threaten Roma, not to mention Ravenna itself.

The fact that his embassy had been received, rather than refused entry to the city, was alarming. Despite his position as ultimate ruler, Honorius' position was weak and unstable. Vadomar's veins thrummed with fresh anger. If Stilicho had still been alive, the emperor would not have been in this situation, for despite the general's faults and mistakes, he had been a strong and capable military leader. At this moment, there seemed no one to replace him. Even if Honorius had been prepared to go to war himself, which he was not, the auguries would have been inauspicious. Julian, the last emperor to take the field, had died in battle more than forty years prior.

Vadomar briefly considered Olympius as a general, but Honorius' current favourite was a soft-handed, scheming politician rather than a man who would pick up a sword. It was a pity, he thought, that Galla Placidia had been born female. Intelligent, determined, decisive, she would have made a better fist of things than her dithering half-brother.

Late the next morning, having spent the night at the bishop's residence, the embassy made its way to the emperor's palace. Built within an extended loop of the walls, it was a massive villa in the old style. The candidati on duty were a stark contrast to the soldiers accompanying the embassy. The imperial insignia on their shields were fresh-painted; their scale armour and helmets were not dusty from the road, but shone in the watery sunshine.

Their attitude was polite but superior, as might have been expected. The official letters carried by Attalus and his companions were carefully examined, and the senators were searched for weapons. Three soldiers were allowed to enter with the embassy, one for each of its members. The rest, a lip-curling officer announced, could wait outside. Gnaeus, Vadomar and another were chosen, and were ordered to hand over their swords and daggers.

Remembering the deceit surrounding Stilicho's death, Vadomar bridled. The candidatus tasked with taking his weapons responded by laying a hand to his sword hilt. Vadomar took a deep breath. Conflict was not only unnecessary but stupid, he thought, and unbuckled his belt. 'Take care of this,' he said in a friendly tone. 'It has served me well for years.'

'No one will touch it,' said the candidatus. 'You have my word.'

'My thanks.' Curiosity and a desire for revenge pricking, he asked, 'Does Heraclianus still serve in the emperor's household?'

'You know him?'

'We met once,' replied Vadomar, casual as if it had been in a tavern.

'He's long gone,' the candidatus said. 'After the traitor Stilicho's execution, Heraclianus was rewarded with the post of Comes Africae. That's where he has been since.'

'An important position.' The job of the official in charge of Africa was vital, ensuring the grain supply upon which the empire relied. Vadomar nodded and smiled, but inside, impotent fury bubbled. If the chance of revenge on Stilicho's murderer had been small before, it was impossible now. As they followed the senators inside, he had to content himself with a prayer, asking his gods that Heraclianus be disgraced or fall from office, or die in an unhappy hunting accident.

The three waited in the atrium as Attalus, Caecilianus and Maximianus were escorted through into the peristyle courtyard beyond. Watched over by half a dozen candidati, Vadomar took in the room, three times the size of the atrium in Galla's house. Painted busts of the emperor's ancestors fringed the walls. Offices and storerooms opened off the main space. The mosaic floor was the grandest part of it. Chariot scenes dominated. Each corner had a panel with a horse and driver from one of the four teams, Blue, White, Green and Red. The central panel depicted a Green chariot in the midst of a race, the dolphin lap counters and banks of seating visible above and to either side. It was magnificent, the finest mosaic Vadomar had ever seen.

He wasn't stopped as he walked around the room admiring the mosaic. This encouraged him to move closer to the tablinum, which led onto the courtyard. Of course his hope was to see the emperor, about whom he had heard so much. It was all in vain. He got a glimpse of the courtyard, of bare-branched fruit trees, a pattering fountain, statues, but of Honorius there was no sign. Then one of the candidati flanking the entrance to the tablinum ordered him away. Vadomar rejoined Gnaeus, rolling his eyes as he did.

'Fur-wearing fool. Did you think he would let you walk through?'

'If a man doesn't try, he doesn't get.'

'Stand still. Wait for the senators to come out. They won't be long.'

Instead Vadomar walked to the front door, from beyond which he could hear raised voices. He gleaned that the members of Constantinus' embassy, arriving a little late, were unhappy about the senators having already been admitted. His amusement at this would have vanished had he known the senators would soon emerge empty-handed, while Constantinus' minions received a promise of imperial insignia for their master. Honorius' motives were easy to understand, if infuriating. Constantinus, it seemed, had offered to march into Italia and crush Alaric's host, and so the emperor had given him official recognition.

'Constantinus won't be here until the spring at the earliest,' Gnaeus grumbled later. They had procured a small amphora of decent wine from the major domus and were drinking it in their room.

'Alaric will not wait that long. Why should he?'

'I cannot argue with you,' said Gnaeus with a frustrated shake of his head. 'Which is why I do not understand Honorius. He could make peace with Alaric with ease. Give him Illyricum as he asks, and settle this dispute at one pass. Tens of thousands of Alaric's warriors would then join the army, men who are badly needed. If the emperor doesn't like it, there are other options. He could form an alliance with Sarus, and use him to defeat Alaric.' Sarus' host was massive, and its leader currently sat on the fence in the struggle for power.

'Honorius hates all barbarians with a passion, as does Olympius,' said Vadomar. 'There can be no other rational explanation.'

'I think you are right, sadly.'

And it was the empire that would suffer, thought Vadomar. He did not care, but Galla's future was entwined with that of Roma, and that gave him an interest. He had never seen evidence of the gods deigning to answer his prayers, but he offered them up anyway.

There was not much else he could do.

Several days later, Vadomar and Gnaeus had changed their minds somewhat. Honorius – through Olympius – had declined to grant lands to Alaric. Nor had he agreed to supply hostages, but he had put five legions, fresh from Dalmatia, at the disposal of the Senate. Commanded by a self-assured general by the name of Valens, these six thousand soldiers were to accompany the embassy back to Roma. To arrive with such a force would break the terms of the truce agreed by Alaric, but once within, it would strengthen the garrison, allowing the city to wait for Constantinus, now Honorius' ally.

The major problem, they agreed on the first evening of their journey, was to enter Roma without being seen. Although Alaric had withdrawn the majority of his army to Etruria, he had left plenty of warriors to keep watch over the city. It would be incredibly difficult to bypass all of those.

'Valens seems like a bold man,' said Gnaeus. 'He won't like subterfuge.'

'Five legions can't exactly hide their presence either.'

They were both relieved, therefore, by an announcement the following morning. They would halt a day's march from Roma and use nearby forests as concealment. The scouts would determine the best route to take, whereupon the legions would advance under cover of darkness, punching through any Visigothic warriors in the way. Alaric would have no chance to assemble his entire host. It was a reasonable tactic, Vadomar and Gnaeus agreed, as long as Alaric remained unaware of their presence. Vadomar found it amusing but unsurprising how the three senators, with their minimal knowledge of military matters, were breezily confident about Valens' plan.

Even they could not help but notice the tension developing as the army's journey continued. All eyes were on the horizon, searching for Visigothic horsemen. Men rode and marched with their hands on their weapons, and slept badly. Remarkably, nothing happened. There was no sign of the enemy. Gnaeus said that after the heartfelt prayers of Roma's people, maybe God had decided to reach out His hand and help. Vadomar didn't believe in Gnaeus' God, but chose not to blaspheme. He would leave off giving judgement, he told Gnaeus, until they and the five legions were safe within the city's walls.

The dream, the hope that they would succeed continued for eight days. Covering considerably more than the daily average of twenty miles, the usual journey time had been cut by four days. This was to their advantage, for Alaric would not expect an enemy to move with such rapidity.

On the ninth morning, having spent the night in a forest of beech and oak on high ground, the army moved out. Spirits were high thanks to the scouts, who had returned at sunrise. Perhaps two thousand warriors lay between them and Roma, but they appeared to have no idea of Valens' army's proximity. It seemed the rest of Alaric's host was still in Etruria. It was a God-sent sign, Valens had declared jubilantly. They would march at the double to the enemy positions, smash through, and be inside the city before midday. It was good to think like that, thought Vadomar, but despite their easy progress and Valens' certainty, he would not be happy until the gates slammed behind him.

As guards for the Senate embassy, he and Gnaeus were in the safest part of the army column, the middle. They had little idea of what was going on in the vanguard, and relied on mounted messengers who came past at regular intervals. The sun rose, and was obscured by banked cloud. It was a chill morning, damp and dewy. Vadomar was grateful to be descending; from the feel of the wind, snow was a possibility. He hoped the inclement weather continued, because it would dull the Visigothic sentries' attention, and keep their comrades longer in the comfort of their blankets.

Perhaps two hours passed before the column ground to a halt. This was a common enough occurrence, nothing to get alarmed about. Men climbed down from their horses, emptied their bladders, talked among themselves. As time dragged on without the march starting up again, however, Vadomar began to feel uneasy.

'What if the Visigoths know we're coming?'

'There will be an ambush on the vanguard,' said Gnaeus.

'If so, we should withdraw, find another way to get in.'

'Valens will want to attack.'

'Then he's a fool.'

'I am not arguing with you.'

'It's an obvious choice,' said Vadomar. 'Why wouldn't he see that?'

'Hubris.' Noticing Vadomar's blank expression, Gnaeus explained, 'It means exaggerated pride. In ancient Greece, men used to say those guilty of hubris would bring down the wrath of the gods upon themselves.'

'Ha! If we're right about Valens, and Alaric's warriors *are* ready and waiting for us, it will prove the Greeks of old knew what they were talking about.'

'For both our sakes, I hope you are wrong,' said Gnaeus.

Gnaeus did not get his wish. Not long after, a messenger on a wild-eyed, sweat-lathered horse came galloping along the column. Alaric must have known of their coming, because the Visigoths had sprung an enormous surprise attack on the vanguard. Outnumbering Valens' legions by a substantial margin, they were wreaking fearful damage. Valens had ordered the entire army forward. A full-scale advance, the messenger shouted, and they would smash their way through to the city walls.

Vadomar and Gnaeus conferred. Alaric's host numbered in the tens of thousands. Both would have preferred to retreat, but when they asked Attalus, Caecilianus and Maximianus, they were told in no uncertain manner that they were but ordinary soldiers and Valens knew what he was doing. Vadomar protested, and was shouted down. Short of deserting the ambassadors, which neither he nor Gnaeus was prepared to contemplate, there was little else to do but obey orders. They rode with ready spears, and the gut-sure knowledge that if they were attacked, the fight would be short indeed.

Valens' plan went awry from the start. Impatient to reach their beleaguered comrades, entire units broke away from the column and began advancing. Their formations broken up by the trees and scrubby ground, men moving at different speeds soon saw any sense of organisation vanish. Vadomar and his companions, with the embassy as their responsibility, stayed on the road. It was far slower, but at least they were going forward. Which in itself did not feel good. Approaching a battlefield escorting three unarmed senators felt monstrously stupid.

Again they slowed to a crawl. There was time to brood, to dwell on things. That it had been so easy to get this close to Roma without their enemies appearing to notice was warning enough, Vadomar grumbled. Alaric was a seasoned campaigner, not one to be caught unawares. Visigothic scouts had probably been on their trail since Ravenna. The more he thought about it, the more impossible Valens' orders seemed, and the harder it became to see how the five legions could ever have found a way into Roma that did not involve horrific loss of life.

Gnaeus was of the same opinion. The stark truth brought them to another realisation. It was one thing to protect the senators from bandits, quite another to bring them unharmed through a battle. They were debating how to tell the trio this when the first signs of disaster became apparent. Movement on the road ground to a complete halt. Disconcerted, men to the left and right slowed up. Questions were hurled to and fro, arguments began. What was the reason for stopping? Had fresh orders from Valens come through? Was the battle going well? Badly?

No one had answers to be relied upon. No one sounded convincing. Uncertainty and fear, two of a soldier's greatest enemies, took root with frightening speed. Vadomar saw it in men's faces and posture. Heard it in their voices. Officers shouted for the advance to continue, which worked for some, but when panicked shouts and cries carried back, movement again ceased.

There was a short lull before events began to move at breakneck speed.

An injured messenger came galloping back, shouting that all was lost. He did not stop to explain, just thundered by, focused on saving his own skin. Individual soldiers began to retrace their steps. A comrade here and there would join them. Then another, and another. A few officers tried to intervene, but they were ignored. One who struck out at a couple of soldiers was cut down from behind. That silenced any officers who saw; most quietly joined the retreating mob.

More shouts and cries from in front. A rendition of the barritus, ending with a chorus of triumphant shouts. Men began to walk faster. Faces paled; there was muttering and shaking of heads. Many soldiers threw away their shields, others their spears. Some dropped everything and ran.

Vadomar and Gnaeus knew how it would play out from here on in. The senators were instructed to look out of the carriage and see what was happening, and were told that they were about to retreat. If they didn't like it, Vadomar instructed, they could continue on without their escort. Attalus blustered and threatened, Caecilianus swore and cursed. Only Maximianus seemed to understand.

Very soon, Vadomar knew, the retreat would become a rout. That was dangerous enough, a time when to stumble and fall meant being trampled by one's own, when to lag behind resulted in a violent death at the hands of the enemy. If the senators would not listen, he told Gnaeus in an undertone, they could fend for themselves. Fortunately, Attalus and Caecilianus heeded Maximianus' counsel. Refuse to agree, he told them, and they would end up like lambs at Eastertime, butchered. None protested as Vadomar ordered the carriage driver to turn it around.

Late that night, Vadomar was lying flat on his belly in the mud on the fringes of a wooded area perhaps three quarters of a mile from Roma's south-western defences. The coast was a few miles away. Between him and the city lay the Visigothic camp. A short distance to his rear were Gnaeus, four of the other guards and the trio of unhappy senators.

Their party was small because he and Gnaeus had split up the escort's fifty soldiers hours before. They were too many to continue travelling together. Each group would attempt to make its own way into Roma under the cover of darkness. Vadomar and Gnaeus had decided their best option was to go as far as possible from the battlefield.

Thus far, it seemed like a good decision. No one had come anywhere near them from the Visigothic encampment. There was no sign of sentries either. If the celebrations he could see were anything to go by, Valens' army had been annihilated. Orange-red flames rose from huge fires. There was singing, dancing and much carousal. It was Vadomar and Gnaeus' hope that the Visigoths would eventually fall into a drunken stupor, uncaring of Roman soldiers still intent on reaching the city. This would be their chance, their opportunity to steal through unseen.

Vadomar had been watching the enemy camp for a good three hours. He was stiff and cold, but convinced the time was right. He offered up a quick prayer to Donar, then, rustling the dead fallen leaves, he belly-crawled back to the others, huddled in a circle at the bottom of a hollow.

The senators jumped liked scared children. Gnaeus and the other guards stared expectantly.

'W-well?' Attalus' teeth were chattering.

Despite how rude he had been throughout the journey, Vadomar felt a trace of sympathy for the portly senator, who had probably never spent a night outdoors, let alone one with thousands of bloodthirsty Visigoths in the immediate vicinity. Gone was the bluster and arrogance of before. Attalus' expression and tone were those of a frightened boy.

'I think it's time to move,' said Vadomar. 'Things are quiet.'

'Will there be sentries?' asked Maximianus. He too looked scared, but there was a calmness about him also.

'I cannot see any,' Vadomar replied. 'We must not let down our guard, however. One shout of alarm, and a host of Visigoths will wake. Drunk or not, they will slaughter us.' His gaze travelled from senator to senator, to Gnaeus, to the other soldiers. 'We must be as silent as wraiths. Not a clink of metal on metal, not a cough or a sneeze. I do not want to hear as much as a fart, understand?'

Wry smiles from the guards. Meek nods from the senators. The role reversal from earlier, thought Vadomar, could not have been more complete. His amusement didn't last long.

Attempting to traverse the Visigothic camp felt stupid. As if he was about to throw all their lives away. But the other option, going back to Ravenna in the hope of more aid from Honorius, felt even more hopeless. Having just lost five legions, the emperor would be in no mood to waste more of his already scarce military resources.

Vadomar had an even more important reason to succeed.

Galla Placidia was inside Roma.

He could not abandon her.

CHAPTER XXIII

A year and a half later . . .

Roma; Mensis Sextilis, AD *410*

Galla laid a hand on her growling stomach, grateful to be alone. Everyone in the house was hungry, but it was unseemly to be betrayed by her body. A feeling of guilt stole into her mind. She wasn't starving, like the poor in the Suburra. Alaric's third siege was a week old, and already the old rumours of cannibalism had surfaced. Galla wasn't sure they were true – nothing got tongues wagging like hardship – but her situation, secure in her large house, was worlds better than a family of ten with no income, crammed into an ill-lit room at the top of a run-down apartment block.

Other than helping Gratian's widow, Laeta, with her distribution of food to the poor, there was not much to be done. More important matters were at hand. The siege would not last long. Morale was at an all-time low, not just in the population, but within the garrison also. Understrength, inexperienced – most were not regular soldiers – and lacking good officers, it would crumble under the first serious assault. Fantastical it might seem, thought Galla sadly, but Roma was about to fall for the first time in almost eight hundred years. Hunger forgotten, her belly flip-flopped at the thought of Alaric's warriors swarming into the city. Her strong front door would be no barrier to a dozen men with a battering ram, and as for what would happen when the Visigoths crossed the threshold . . .

She shoved away the disquieting images, composed herself. Her life would not end in such violent fashion. The members of her household would not die defending her, or be sold on the block to a new owner when all was done. She was unsure how these outcomes could be achieved, but with God's help, she would find a way.

A thought came: Vadomar could be sent in secret to treat with Alaric.

She opened her bedroom door and called his name.

He came pounding up the stairs from the atrium, slowing his pace along the corridor. A respectful knock on the door and he came in. 'Nobilissima Femina?'

How he had changed, thought Galla. His mass of curly brown hair tied back in a ponytail, beard short and trimmed, dressed in embroidered tunic and trousers, he was an altogether different sight than the filthy, wine-reeking individual he'd been on the occasion of their first meeting, or the gaunt, mud-spattered figure who had returned from Ravenna in Ianuarius of the previous year. She remembered with a little thrill his words to her then, how every Visigoth in existence could not have stopped him from getting into the city to make sure she was safe. It had been the first occasion she had really wished he was a well-placed Roman noble. She was thinking it again now. Had he not been a lowly Visigoth, things might have been different between them.

Elpidia appeared in the doorway behind him. It helped Galla to refocus, to return to the matter at hand.

'Come in, both of you. Close the door.'

Elpidia obeyed, giving the slightly surprised Vadomar a nod.

'Things are bad in the city,' said Galla.

'They are, Nobilissima Femina,' said Vadomar. 'It won't be long before Alaric's warriors get in. Have you given any thought to my suggestions?' These were either to embark at Portus and sail for Ravenna, or, riskier, to escape at night through the Visigoth lines, then head to the imperial capital overland.

'I have.'

'Taking passage on a ship would be my recommendation, Nobilissima Femina.'

'I will not leave Roma.'

Vadomar didn't see Elpidia pull a face, but he was also disconcerted. 'If this is your decision, Nobilissima Femina, so be it. I will fight to the end. You can count on Fritigern and Darme, I am sure, but we will all die. That is unimportant. What matters is *your* life. You must not fall into Alaric's warriors' hands. Do you mean to commit suicide?'

'No.' Touched by the concern her answer brought leaping into his eyes – and Elpidia's – Galla said, 'I have another idea.'

'I am much relieved, Nobilissima Femina.' His voice was gruff.

'And I,' said Elpidia archly.

'I want you to meet with Alaric, tell him I will surrender myself into his safe keeping.' She caught Elpidia's glower. 'Fortunately, he appears unaware of how little Honorius cares for me. In his eyes, I am too valuable a gaming piece to be lost.'

She was referring to her meeting with Alaric the previous year, after his second siege had ended with the city's capitulation and his appointment of Attalus as a puppet emperor. Unlike many of the wealthy inhabitants, Galla had not fled. At the time, she could not have given any explanation except stubbornness. She had done her best to avoid meeting the Visigothic warlord, who was famously unwed, but in the end had felt obliged to accede to his never-ending requests for an appointment. Her gut instinct had been correct. Alaric, half his lifetime spent making threatening moves and countermoves, forging alliances and walking away from them, swearing and breaking oaths, had shown a keen interest in marrying her. The benefits of becoming a brother-in-law to Honorius were not lost on him.

Acutely aware of her vulnerability, Galla had been sweet and demure, and made frequent mention of her intention to become a nun. Elpidia, eavesdropping nearby, then arrived full of apologies, and the revelation that a kitchen slave had been taken seriously ill. It had been a lie of course, and a flimsy reason to abandon a meeting, but Galla, tears in her eyes, had explained that her slaves were like family. She would have to go.

Alaric, unhappy, but loath to shatter the pretence that their meeting was one of equals, had taken his leave. By some miracle, Galla managed to avoid further contact during the rest of his tenure in the city. It had been an immense relief when the thrusts and counterthrusts between him and Honorius had seen him leave Roma and advance upon Ravenna with Attalus in tow.

The surprise arrival of thousands of soldiers from the east under the command of an experienced general by the name of Flavius Constantius had put an end to Alaric's potential siege, however. Now he was back, his patience with Honorius spent, and if the opinions of the warriors overheard by Vadomar during his spying missions were correct, he had no intention of accepting Roma's surrender and installing another puppet emperor. His previous experiment had been a dismal failure – Attalus had been stripped of his insignia of office and was Alaric's prisoner. The talk in the Visigothic encampment was of rape and pillage, burning and bloodshed.

It would be wiser, Galla decided, to make the first move.

She was suddenly aware that Vadomar and Elpidia were both waiting for her to speak again. 'I do not mean to marry him.' She said this for Elpidia's benefit rather than Vadomar's, but she did not miss the relief in his eyes, nor fail to savour it. 'Even if it would ensure my safety.'

'And if he carries you off from the city afterwards?' demanded Elpidia.

'There will not be much I can do about it.'

Elpidia scowled. 'I suppose so. He will continue to bully you to marry him, you realise?'

'I do. You will have to help me keep him at bay.'

'I will kill him before he lays a hand on you!' Vadomar looked visibly upset.

'You would die soon after,' said Galla, holding up a hand to silence his instant protest. 'And he would force me to wed him anyway. It will not come to that. I will find a way to be Alaric's prisoner, but not his wife.'

That night, the twenty-second of the month, Vadomar succeeded in creeping out of the beleaguered city and into the Visigothic camp.

Revealing himself and his mission to a chieftain, he was escorted under heavy guard into the presence of the man who threatened Roma's existence. Alaric, he reported later, seemed delighted that Galla had sent a personal message, and willingly swore an oath to God and all His saints to protect her from harm.

'He wanted to know if you would arrange for a gate to be opened, Nobilissima Femina,' he added.

'Did you agree?' Galla was horrified, and furious not to have thought of this request, and a response for Vadomar to have given.

'No, Nobilissima Femina.'

'Why not?' Relief spilled into curiosity.

He met her gaze. 'I was certain you would not betray Roma to an enemy, Nobilissima Femina.'

Galla gave him a dazzling smile. 'You know me well, Vadomar.' He bent his head, and she saw his cheeks colouring. She had long suspected he had feelings for her; this was proof. She filed away the information. 'What words did you use?'

'I said you knew he would take Roma regardless, that he did not need anyone's help, Nobilissima Femina.'

'Did he believe you?'

'I think so. His chest puffed out, and he laughed and said his warriors *would* triumph.' Vadomar put on a deeper voice. '"I will be remembered for eternity as the general who took the greatest city in the world."'

Galla was dismayed. It drove home brutal truths. Honorius was a bad emperor and leader. Roma's time in the sun had ended. For hundreds of years its empire had stretched from Syria and Judaea to Britannia and the far reaches of Africa. Soon, however, it would come under the rule of the Visigoth Alaric. It was reminiscent of a fall from the glorious, angel-filled heights of heaven to the burning pits of hell. She composed herself. 'You did well, Vadomar. I am grateful. Was there anything else?'

'Alaric said his warriors are under strict instruction not to harm any priests or nuns, Nobilissima Femina. The churches in the city are to be spared, and their riches left unplundered. He has also forbidden bloodshed, although he admitted the impossibility of wholly avoiding it.'

'Welcome news nonetheless. Once more he shows how restrained he can be.' She was referring to the demands Alaric had made of Roma and Honorius over the previous few years. Despite the senators' outraged protestations, they had in her opinion been quite moderate in comparison to what he could have demanded.

'I would still be cautious, Nobilissima Femina.'

'What do you mean?'

'I have been there.' He wouldn't look at her. 'I have taken part in the sacking of a city, Nobilissima Femina. Reason leaves a man's mind. The animal takes hold. In other words, Alaric's promise may well be genuine, but it does not mean that some of his warriors, if they did not know who lived here, would not . . .'

'I understand,' said Galla, trying not to imagine Vadomar on the rampage. 'You told him where the house is, gave clear directions, though?'

'I did, Nobilissima Femina. He will send a strong party of warriors here. I am to paint a symbol on the front door, a cipher that will mean nothing to your neighbours but will be recognised by Visigoths.'

'I am grateful.' His eyes lifted to hers, and she said it again.

'It is my honour, Nobilissima Femina.' His head bent.

Galla glanced at Elpidia and saw she also knew about Vadomar's feelings for her. It was no surprise; her nurse had a keen intuition. All the better, she thought. Elpidia can help me to utilise him best.

The tension in Roma grew with every passing hour. By the second day after Vadomar's meeting with Alaric, it could have been cut with a knife. Everyone, old and young, male and female, noble and plebeian, freeborn and slave, knew the city would soon fall. Knew tens of thousands of Visigothic warriors would charge through the streets, taking whatever they wanted and, despite Alaric's orders, acting however they pleased.

With the vigiles drafted into the city garrison, public unrest swelled. Shops were broken into and looted. Bands of criminals wandered about, setting upon anyone unlucky enough to cross their path. After Elpidia, out to look for supplies, was forced to take refuge in a church for several hours, Vadomar suggested to Galla that until the situation improved, he should be the only member of the household to venture abroad.

Galla took his advice in as far as she forbade the slaves from leaving, but she made an exception for herself. Vadomar served as her escort as she called in to the houses on either side and opposite hers. Explaining that she had a guarantee of safety from Alaric, she invited the neighbours and their households, slaves included, to stay. She sent Vadomar with a message to her two closest friends, but neither took her up on the offer. One intended to flee to the basilica of St Peter, and the other told Vadomar she would not be forced from her home by barbarians. The neighbours were less picky. By the second evening, more than forty people filled Galla's atrium and the walkway around the colonnaded courtyard. Thanks to the fine, warm weather, it was possible to sleep in the open air.

Galla was amused by Darme and Fritigern's reactions to the upsetting of the norm. Darme walked about with his nose in the air, quietly sniffing with disapproval. Any time he was asked to do something by one of the visitors, he would let out a theatrical sigh, agree, but then take for ever to fulfil the request. Fritigern's deafness became total; he also appeared to lose most of his vision. To get his attention – Galla, Darme and Elpidia were the exceptions – one had to stand right in front of him and wave a hand six inches in front of his face. Even then, he feigned complete incomprehension at what was said, cupping an ear and making apologetic noises. Soon the guests knew to leave him alone; it was far easier to deal with the martyrlike Darme or the more biddable kitchen slaves.

Given authority by Galla, Vadomar picked out the male slaves who looked capable of a fight. There were five, three youthful, two older. None seemed happy being given hunting spears and put on sentry duty at the door, but the combative glint in Vadomar's eyes prevented protest. Galla wasn't sure whether they would make any difference if the Visigoths smashed their way in, and she suspected Vadomar felt similarly, but it was better than doing nothing. She kept thinking of her stubborn friend Metella, who lived like herself, with only a few slaves for company. Galla had tried again to persuade her to come to stay, sending a message with Vadomar, but he had come back empty-handed. God be with her, she prayed, thinking guiltily how her prayer would not save Metella's virtue or life.

A warm westerly wind carried in great banks of black cloud as darkness fell. The air thickened, humid and close. Torrential rain came after, drumming off the roof, pouring through the downspouts and spilling out into the garden. Thunder rumbled and crashed over the city, and lightning illuminated the world in dazzling yellow-white.

On a different night Galla would have enjoyed sitting by her open window, listening to the rumbling noise and waiting for the next brilliant flash of light. This evening was different. Her stomach was in knots, and there was a tightness in her neck and shoulders. She recognised it of old; when her worries grew too great, those muscles tensed, often leading to an intense, prolonged headache. Unable to relax, she busied herself supervising Iovina and the other kitchen slave as they prepared a meal for their guests.

Everyone had brought supplies from their own homes, Elpidia reminded her; there was enough food for a week if they were careful. She went on to suggest in an undertone that the two kitchen slaves would be better left to their own devices. Their mistress' presence was making them flustered. Galla had the insight to recognise this was true.

Making for the stairs and her bedroom, she saw Vadomar on a stool by the front door. Clad in his scale armour, he had a sword laid across his knees; his shield and helmet were beside him. It was a bizarre but reassuring sight to have a veteran soldier on guard in her house.

'Nobilissima Femina.' He bent his neck. The two slaves on duty with him got to their feet and bowed. As Galla drew nearer, he jumped up and also bowed.

'Is all well?'

'Yes, Nobilissima Femina. I went up and down the street before the rain started, didn't hear or see anything of concern.'

Galla felt a little better. Quietly, she said, 'The rain means Alaric won't attack tonight, doesn't it?'

Silence. A grim look.

A knot formed in her stomach. 'It will be tonight?'

Vadomar spoke in an undertone. 'If I were giving orders, Nobilissima Femina, yes.'

Suddenly light-headed, Galla swayed. Despite everything that had happened – the new siege, the deprivation throughout the city, Vadomar's mission, Alaric's agreement and what that meant, Metella left on her own while her neighbours packed into her house like salted fish in a barrel – she had hoped it was a dream, a nightmare from which she would eventually wake. She had been wrong. If Vadomar said the Visigoths were attacking Roma tonight, it was going to happen.

Vadomar set down his sword. One of his hands went around her waist, the other gripped her shoulder. 'You are taken unwell, Nobilissima Femina. Let me help you to your room.'

Galla did not protest, and was grateful for his support climbing the stairs. By the top, she had regained her balance. Intensely aware of his touch, she stopped. 'Thank you, Vadomar. I am all right.'

His hands fell away as if he had been holding red-hot metal. 'Are you sure?'

Her cheeks warmed, and she could not meet his gaze. 'Yes.'

Elpidia came bustling out of nowhere, her plain face creased with worry. 'What happened?'

'The mistress had a dizzy spell.' Vadomar took a step down the stairs, as if to emphasise the distance between him and Galla.

Elpidia rushed in, fussing, taking her arm.

Annoyed by her momentary weakness, Galla pulled away, stood up straight. 'There is nothing wrong with me.'

Elpidia knew the warning signs. 'As you say.'

Galla did not look back as she walked into her bedroom and shut the door. She let out a shuddering sigh. The night was just beginning, she thought. It was hard not to lose hope. Dropping to her knees by the bed, she closed her eyes and began to pray. After a time, some calm returned. She kept praying. It helped.

There was always hope, she decided.

Hope.

CHAPTER XXIV

Back against the wall, comfortable on his stool, content that there was no immediate threat, Vadomar let his eyes close. Thoughts of Galla filled his mind, but tired from the preparations and the late hour, he fell into a deep, dreamless slumber. He jerked awake a while later, white-knuckled grip on his sword, convinced the house was under attack. Peace reigned, however. The slaves he had chosen to guard the door were asleep on the floor nearby. Loud snores carried from the courtyard. Not a sound came from the first floor, where Galla and Elpidia slept. Only Felicula was awake, coming down the stairs as grandly as an empress of Roma. She approached, rubbing her face against his outstretched hand, purring as he scooped her up into his lap.

'Will you help in the fight, Felicula?' he whispered.

She purred louder, and pushed her whiskers against his fingers.

'I agree. It would be far better to hide away until it is all done.'

Perhaps he was worrying too much, thought Vadomar. Alaric had been earnest and seemingly genuine. His entire army would be told about the house on the Aventine Hill with the chalked mark on its front door. A hand-picked group would come to secure Galla's safety.

All would be well, he decided.

His certainty did not last long. He knew warriors, knew their nature. Familiar also with war, he had tasted sour defeat, and drunk deep from the cup of victory. Trying to moderate the sack of a city was akin to expecting a fox in a coop to kill a few hens, not every last one. He had to remain vigilant and prepared until Galla was brought into Alaric's presence. Nerves taut, giving up on rest, he prowled around the atrium, watching, waiting, listening for anything untoward.

The eastern sky was paling when Vadomar heard the first sounds suggesting his intuition had been correct. First it was muffled shouting, excited voices some distance away. In a different situation, he might have taken the noise to be inebriated revellers wandering home. Not now, here. Still the only person awake, he listened with bated breath. The shouting reduced in volume, but did not stop. Then he heard yelling from another direction.

Guts tightening, he thought: so it begins.

A scream reached his ears, and was cut short.

Vadomar shook the nearest slave's shoulder. 'Up!' he hissed, moving on to the next. 'Get up. Make no noise!' Silence was important. The longer those in the courtyard slept on, the better. They would only panic, and be of no help whatsoever to the defence of the house.

The slaves roused and armed, Vadomar decided to have a quick look outside. Locking bar lifted, he eased open the door. He had oiled the hinges the day before; it did not make a sound. Poking his head out, he peered left and right. The street was empty. He could hear the shouts and cries better. The screaming was more frequent now too. He could imagine only too well what was happening, but there was nothing he could do to help the city's inhabitants. Or, for that matter, the people in the house. It was bitter medicine to swallow, but if enough Visigoths made an assault, it did not matter how heroic his defence was. It did not matter if the five slaves fought like warriors out of legend either. They would be overwhelmed by sheer weight of numbers.

He gritted his teeth. Knowing his fate did not mean he would lie down and feel sorry for himself. He would sell his life dearly, and the Visigoths who survived would long remember the battle. If he were fortunate, Galla might one day reach the same afterlife.

Dawn arrived. The temperature began to rise. Galla came downstairs, her face tight. She had heard the commotion, but Vadomar was relieved to see she was composed, going out to reassure her neighbours in the courtyard, ordering the kitchen slaves to prepare breakfast. Upon her return, she beckoned him into her office.

'It has started.'

'Aye, Nobilissima Femina. With luck, the warriors sent by Alaric will arrive soon.'

A preoccupied nod.

There was something else on her mind, thought Vadomar. He waited.

'You know my friend Metella, the one who would not leave her house?'

'Yes, Nobilissima Femina.'

'I want you to go and fetch her here.'

'I tried that yesterday, and she refused,' said Vadomar, thinking: this mission will be my death.

'Today you will not take no for an answer.'

'I swore to protect you. I cannot do that if I leave.'

'You and I both know that if the house is attacked, there will only be one outcome.' She stared.

'Yes, Nobilissima Femina.'

'So your presence is immaterial.'

'True,' he admitted.

'On the other hand, there is a chance you could save Metella's life.'

'I suppose so.'

'Please, Vadomar.' Her voice was soft, entreating.

His heart clenched. 'I will do it, Nobilissima Femina.'

'God bless you.'

He ducked his head, uncomfortable not just with her mention of the Christian deity, but with the way she had looked at him. He itched to get out of the house, into the open air, away from Galla, before he said something that would for ever change their relationship.

He would go alone. Galla had suggested taking one or two of the armed slaves, but Vadomar refused. It would be quicker moving on his own, he'd told her. He didn't want their deaths on his conscience.

He had left his scale armour on; any Visigothic warrior with enough coin wore similar. Nor would anyone pass comment about his helmet. The telltale bucellarii markings on the outer face of his shield were more problematic, but he was not prepared to leave it behind. His solution, an old blanket tied in place with leather thongs, worked, but looked odd. He had no time to do anything better. He'd be moving so fast no one would notice, he told himself, and would snatch up a shield from a fallen warrior at the first opportunity.

Galla told him she would pray for his swift return, with Metella. Then, tears welling, she vanished upstairs.

'Be careful.' This was Elpidia, standing by the front door.

'I will.'

To Vadomar's utter surprise, she wrapped her arms around him.

'Come back safely,' she said.

Awkward, he patted her back, grateful to know she cared.

She stepped away, face unusually soft. 'God be with you.'

Vadomar nodded. He had already asked Donar to watch over him, but he would take her blessing, and Galla's prayers too. This was not the time to ponder religion.

A moment later, the door eased shut behind him. The locking bar thunked into place with a finality Vadomar liked not at all. He set off without looking back, every sense on alert.

But for the shouts and cries reaching his ears, he might have been in a ghost city. The streets were empty, doors closed, every window shuttered. No limbless veterans or lepers begged at the first crossroads, no slaves filled amphorae at the water trough at the next. There were no vigiles lounging in the shade, or loud-voiced vendors of fruit juice and watered-down wine. It was disquieting, but would soon change. Tens of thousands of warriors could not hide from sight.

Apart from a couple of terrified-looking inhabitants, who both ran when they saw him, Vadomar encountered no one on the entire journey. If anything, this increased his sense of urgency; when the Visigoths appeared, it would be in real force. Metella lived in a decent-sized house not far from the bathing complex built by the emperor Traianus. The street leading to the baths' front entrance, usually jammed with people, was abandoned, and Metella's door, like everyone else's, was shut.

Vadomar hammered on it with his spear butt. *Boom, boom, boom.*

There was no answer, which didn't surprise him. Metella would not be expecting anyone she knew.

He did it again.

Nothing.

'I seek Metella!' he called out, wanting his voice to carry within, but no further.

No response.

His anger stirred. Here he was, announcing his presence to one and all, more or less inviting those Visigoths nearby to come and kill him. The least Metella could do was reply. He thumped on the timbers for a third time, and harder. 'Metella!'

'Who is it?' The voice was quavering, old.

'My name is Vadomar. I am sent by Galla Placidia. Let me in!'

The slave who admitted him, a frail man with wispy grey hair, was old enough to be his grandfather. He led Vadomar to the kitchen, which was warm and smelled tantalisingly of fresh bread. Metella was there, bustling about as if this day were no different to any other.

She brushed wayward hair from her forehead, leaving a smudge of flour. 'Vadomar, isn't it?'

'Yes, Domina.'

'Hungry?' She indicated the loaves cooling on the worktop.

'I . . . No, thank you, Domina.' Vadomar wondered if she had taken leave of her senses. 'I have come to take you to Galla Placidia's house.'

'I am going nowhere.' Her chin jutted.

'You will die, Domina, if you stay.'

'I know—'

He cut her off. 'It will not be pleasant. You will be ravished, many times. You will long for death.' Her mouth was a shocked 'O', but he continued, laying out the fate of a captive woman in bald, brutal terms until she began to cry. 'Your only chance of surviving, Domina,' he said gently, 'is to accompany me. Now.'

Her chin trembled. 'My slaves?'

Vadomar's eyes went to the old man who'd let him in, and the dumpy little woman who was helping Metella. 'They come also. If they fall behind, though, I will not be held responsible.'

Metella considered this.

'I will stay, Domina,' said the old man.

'And I.' The dumpy woman had taken the old man's arm, which allowed Vadomar to see the resemblance. They were father and daughter.

Metella gave him a 'You see?' look, and said, 'I cannot leave them.'

'You are coming, Domina, even if I have to tie you up and carry you like a sack of grain.' He buried his pity, and added, 'Whether your slaves come as well is not my concern.'

Metella held his stare, saw he was serious, and started to cry.

The two slaves began to weep too, quietly.

Vadomar waited a couple of moments, asked, 'Well?'

Metella's tear-filled eyes went to her slaves, who were embracing. They both shook their heads, refusing, and Metella looked at Vadomar. 'I will come.'

They set off at once, exiting onto the still empty street, the old slave barring the door behind them. Vadomar threw up a prayer asking that he and his daughter survive, then put them from his mind. He set a murderous pace, away from the baths, choosing alleyways and smaller thoroughfares rather than the more direct avenues. It worked well until he had to cross a street leading towards the Circus Maximus.

There was a wine shop on a corner opposite. Its shutters lay in ruins, and loud voices emanated from within. He glanced at Metella, pointed, then mimed going across to the next alley. She nodded, understanding that the warriors in the shop were fully occupied in drinking everything they could lay their hands on.

They were halfway across the street when a Visigoth sauntered out of the doorway, belching and wiping his mouth with the back of his hand. He saw Vadomar, who instinctively slowed.

'Ho, friend!' called the warrior. 'Found yourself a woman?'

'Aye.' Vadomar kept walking, Metella staying close.

'Come and have a drink! There's more than enough for me and my mates. The price: a turn with her each.' He cupped his groin.

'No.' Vadomar increased his pace.

'Why not?' Suddenly the warrior was truculent.

Vadomar had slipped his dagger into his hand, and now he threw it. It took the warrior in the throat, as fine a kill as he'd ever made. Choking, eyes a-bulge, his victim dropped.

'Run!' Vadomar took to his heels, trusting Metella would follow.

She did.

At the far end of the alley, he stopped and looked back. There was no one in pursuit, nor any shouts of outrage. The warrior's companions were oblivious to his fate, he decided, palming away sweat. Concentration lapsing, he stepped out into the next street.

Feet pounded. Jubilant whoops split the air.

His head turned. Two figures, both female, young, well dressed, were running towards him. Mouths open, arms flailing, they were weary. Behind them came a group of warriors, perhaps twenty. From the back-and-forth banter and occasional lobbed spear, it was clear this was sport for the wolf pack, not an all-out pursuit.

'Christ on the cross,' said Metella. 'You have to help them!'

They had been seen, Vadomar was sure. If they ran, they would be chased down. He glanced along the alley whence they had come. There was no one in sight. Seizing Metella's hand, he dragged her into the gloom.

'What are you doing?' she cried.

He shushed her, and shoved her against the nearest cobweb-covered wall.

The women went past, wailing and crying to each other. A few warriors were next, calling out in awful, accented Latin that the women had nothing to fear. Stop, one said, and they could have a nice kiss and cuddle.

Metella's eyes were full of horror.

Vadomar placed a finger on his lips, mouthed, 'Be quiet.'

Two of the warriors slowed. One ambled to the alley's opening. He was short, bearded and, true to his origins, uncaring of the summer's heat, wearing a fur cloak. He stared in. At once, Vadomar hoicked up the hem of Metella's dress and fumbled with the front of his trousers. She let out a cry of pure fear.

'Piss off,' he snarled. 'Looks as if you have your own meat to pound, when you catch it.'

The warrior seemed about to answer, but a shout from a comrade and a despairing woman's cry drew his attention away. He walked off.

Vadomar let go of Metella's dress, stepped back. 'My apologies, Domina. Our act had to be convincing.'

She was crying silently, but nodded to show she understood. She made no protest as he led her to the alley mouth, took a look beyond. A circle of warriors had formed a short distance along the street. Their cheers and roars did not quite drown out the piteous screams.

An inarticulate sob escaped Metella.

'Be quiet, unless you want the same fate!' hissed Vadomar, steeling his heart against her upset and what was unfolding in the warriors' midst.

Metella obeyed.

They stole across the street, gaze averted, into a narrow lane lined with pottery workshops. At the far end, preceded by the stink of urine, was a fuller's premises. Vadomar knew where he was now, and led them unerringly towards Galla's house.

About a quarter of a mile remained when he began to relax, to decide he'd been over-pessimistic thinking he would die during the attempt to rescue Metella. Safety was at hand, and the warriors sent by Alaric to find Galla would soon arrive. What would happen after, he wasn't sure, but the woman he had sworn to serve would be safe. He could ask for nothing more.

The stuccoed walls and red-ridged roof tiles of Galla's house were visible now. Vadomar's belly rumbled; he had not eaten for hours. He hoped there was hurry bread, indeed any bread, left.

'There they are!' The shout was in Gothic.

He looked behind him, and his spirits sank. Like a bird to its nest, he thought, ill fortune comes home to roost. Out in front of a large group of his fellows was the bearded, fur-cloaked warrior. He pointed at Metella. 'Told you she was worth hunting down!'

Baying like a pack of hounds on the trail of a wild boar, the warriors charged.

'Run!' Vadomar cried.

Metella was physically fit; she kept pace all the way to Galla's door.

Vadomar banged, one, two, two, one, the agreed signal.

There was no immediate response.

The warriors were about a hundred and fifty paces away, but Fur Cloak was a good two-score paces out in front. His right arm was cocked back, ready to launch his spear.

'Open up, in Donar's name!' cried Vadomar.

'All right, all right.' For some reason, it was Fritigern on the other side of the door, not one of the much younger slaves. A rasping noise, a heave and a grunt, and the portal opened.

Shoving Metella in first, Vadomar threw himself inside and slammed the door shut. He lifted the locking bar and set it in place, thinking: it will only hold for so long.

'Someone after you?' wheezed Fritigern.

'Yes. Why are you here and not the others?'

'It was quiet. The mistress told them to get food in the kitchen.'

Vadomar swallowed down the 'All five?' that came rushing to his lips. Galla was no soldier. 'Go and get them, *now*. Quickly.'

Fritigern made a face, and shuffled off at his best speed, which wasn't fast.

'I'll go.' It was Metella.

Vadomar muttered his thanks and, setting down shield and spear, upended the heavy table he'd had carried into the atrium earlier. Stooping low, using the power of his leg muscles, he had it in place by the time the five slaves, still chewing, returned.

'We're about to have company,' he said. 'A large group of warriors.'

'How many?' asked the youngest slave, a burly lad with jet-black hair.

'Too many. We will have to try and hold out, and hope Alaric's men get here before—'

'OPEN UP!' Poor Latin, but understandable. Metal hammered on the front door, sword blades, iron shield rims, spear butts. 'OPEN!'

The five slaves' faces were a picture of indecision, fear and pure terror.

'They can't get in immediately. The door is solid, and the table is too,' Vadomar barked. 'If they do get in, the first half-dozen, more maybe, will die if we stand fast. That will give the rest something to think about, and if I had to guess, they will hold back. We will have a chance to close the gap again.' He didn't know how it would be possible, but the slaves didn't seem to realise that. Their expressions brightened, and the burly lad stabbed his spear back and forth. 'We'll show them!'

'It will be better for everyone if you let us in.' This was better Latin, less accented, a warrior who had served in the legions, maybe. 'We will be merciful.'

'Liar!' Vadomar shouted, adding the worst insult he could think of in Gothic.

'You're one of us? Traitor! Kiss-arse! Whore's get!' Amid the barrage of insults, the door was subjected to more and more force. It held firm.

'You found Metella.' Galla had appeared, was looking nervously at the front door, and at her friend, who had returned from the kitchen. They embraced.

'Yes, Nobilissima Femina, but I also brought back some unwanted visitors.' It was a lame joke, but she smiled nonetheless.

'If not these ones, others would have come anyway.'

'You shouldn't stay in the atrium, Nobilissima Femina. Nor you, Domina. If the door . . . when the door is broken down, it will get dangerous.'

'We will be in my room with Elpidia.' Another smile. 'I have stockpiled broken roof tiles by the windows. I hope they are all wearing helmets. And before you say it, I know they have spears. We will be careful.'

She would do it even if he told her not to, thought Vadomar. A wry smile creased his lips.

The battering on the door ceased.

Vadomar listened. Waited.

Thunk. A heartbeat's delay. *Thunk*.

'They have an axe,' he said grimly. This was happening faster than he'd thought it would. Donar had turned his face against him. He eyed Galla. 'Go, please, Nobilissima Femina, now.'

CHAPTER XXV

Elpidia met Galla at the top of the stairs. 'Did I hear Vadomar say "axe"?'

'Yes.' Galla wanted to curse, to swear, to blaspheme. After all her planning of a future in Alaric's host, her life was going to end in the bloodiest, most violent fashion possible. Anger surfaced. If that was how it was going to be, she would not go easily. 'Come with me,' she said to Metella.

'What will they do when they . . .' The words died in her friend's throat.

'It will not come to that,' said Galla, entering her bedroom and showing Metella the daggers lying beside her silver mirror and cosmetics. 'No Visigoth will lay his filthy hands on me, or you.'

'Or me,' added Elpidia, glowering.

Galla hoped God would forgive her. To kill oneself was to break the sixth commandment, but given the suffering and degradation that would follow being taken captive, she felt as if there was little other choice. She had already warned her neighbours what might happen; they could decide their own fates. Iovina and the other kitchen slave had said they would take their chances with the warriors. They were young enough and sufficiently attractive to warrant being left alive. Despite the inevitable rapes, one had said to Galla, life was better than death. She had not argued. In desperate situations, each person had to choose their own destiny.

'Before they get in, we can make a few of them sorry they ever darkened my door.' Galla tiptoed to the window and selected a chunky piece of red tile with a jagged edge. Cradling it in her right hand, she sneaked a look down onto the street. A smile brightened her expression; her wish had been granted. Perhaps half of the warriors were not wearing helmets. Without further ado, she leaned out, selected a target and threw. Even as she ducked back out of sight, she heard a dull crack, then shouts of rage and surprise.

No cry of pain, she thought. I knocked him out. Maybe even killed him. She felt no guilt hoping it was the latter. This was not cold-blooded murder; she was defending her house, her life, and those of her slaves and neighbours.

Elpidia, a fragment of tile in her hand, gave her an enquiring look. When Galla nodded, she stepped forward, peered carefully to make sure it was safe, and flung. A crack followed, and straight after, a bellow of pain and a litany of curses in Gothic.

Galla made ready to throw again.

'Wait, Nobilissima Femina.' Elpidia was more formal with Metella present.

'Why?' Galla was eager. She wondered if this was what it felt like to go into battle.

'They will be ready this time.' Elpidia took up one of the spears she had brought upstairs, and skewered a cushion. Motioning Galla to prepare herself, she eased the cushion out at head height. Two spears shot up, both just missing it. A third came an instant after, tugging one of the cushion's corners and forcing Elpidia to tighten her grip on the shaft.

'Now,' she hissed.

Galla took the most cautious of glances. Seeing only upward-peering faces, she leaned out and flung the tile, catching a warrior right in the mouth. He screamed and clutched at his face, and she darted back inside. Spears hummed past the window. Curses and threats filled the air.

'Move to the other window, Nobilissima Femina,' said Elpidia. 'They'll be watching this one now.'

Emboldened by their actions, Metella took a shot next, splitting open the forehead of the fur-cloak-wearing warrior. They managed a couple more throws before the warriors set a watch on both windows. From that point, if any of the women showed as much as a hair, volleys of spears and stones came shooting upward. Because many spears fell back into the street, there was no shortage of missiles either.

Galla sent Elpidia to see what was happening in the atrium. She came back reporting that the axeman had cut through a tiny part of the door, but the criss-cross metal strips were doing an excellent job of holding it together. 'Vadomar said to be careful, Nobilissima Femina.'

Galla had a fresh idea, although Vadomar would not approve. They could climb on top of the roof, two men's height above the street, and throw tiles from there. The footing would be precarious, she thought, but they would also be a lot harder to hit with spears. She was about to issue orders, but Elpidia was pointing at the first window, beyond which scuffling and whispers were audible.

Galla realised with visceral horror that the warriors were climbing up the wall.

Before she could react, Elpidia had picked up a spear. Cat-soft, she padded to the side of the window, mouthing, 'Tell me when.'

Galla's throat closed with fear. Eyes fixed on the sill, she waited. There was more scuffling and muttering, and a grunt such as men give when boosted onto another's shoulders. A head appeared outside the window, a sharp, angled face with an ugly cicatrice on the chin. The warrior's hands were next, gripping the wooden frame. He leered at Galla, who screamed, 'Now!'

Spear held in both hands, Elpidia stepped to the left, blocking Galla's view. She rammed the weapon forward. An awful gurgling sound followed.

'The other window!' cried Metella.

It was Galla's turn. She didn't hesitate, stabbing a fresh-faced warrior in the throat. An astonishing amount of blood chased the blade out, bathing the window ledge, the floor, her shoes, the bottom of her stola. As the warrior fell from sight, she staggered back, repulsed. Acid surged up her throat, and she was sick. But she did not lose her reason. Wiping her mouth, she ordered Metella to run downstairs and tell Vadomar.

In the time that took, the warriors tried again, a man appearing at each window simultaneously. Galla and Elpidia were waiting. More blood flowed. Two more corpses fell to the street. Galla retched again, bringing up a little bile, but she did not back away from the opening. There was only so long they could keep this up, she saw with sinking dread. Warriors had broken down the door of the house opposite, and a moment later had clambered on top of its garden wall. They weren't quite at the same height as Galla, but they had a good line of sight to the windows. The street was narrow too, perhaps fifteen paces wide: an easy spear shot. Each time she or Elpidia prepared to meet the next man climbing, they would be exposed from the waist upwards.

'Are you hurt, Nobilissima Femina?' Vadomar bounded into the room, spear ready. The burly young slave was with him.

'No.' She indicated her dress. 'This is not my blood.'

There was respect in his eyes. 'You killed a man.'

'Two,' said Elpidia, adding proudly, 'As did I.'

'You did well, Nobilissima Femina, and you, Elpidia.' Vadomar laughed. 'There has been no fighting downstairs yet. I was waiting for the door to give way!'

Elated by his recognition, Galla brought his attention to the warriors on the wall opposite. Vadomar acted at once. Using his shield as protection, he leaned out and closed both sets of shutters.

'Now they can climb up unhindered,' said Galla.

'And seeing movement through the gaps in the shutters, we can stab them.' He took a step forward, sliding his spear tip into position. 'See?'

'I do. How is it in the atrium?'

'They have two axes now, Nobilissima Femina.' His expression was grim.

The windows didn't matter then, thought Galla wearily. 'How long?'

'It's hard to say.'

'Vadomar.'

'Not long.'

She wanted to tell him he was a good man, how she valued his service, his bravery. She pushed away the words.

'When they break in, Nobilissima Femina . . .' His eyes were full of sorrow.

'I will open my veins with a dagger. So will Metella. Elpidia will help, before doing the same to herself.'

A stiff nod. 'That would be best. It has been an honour to serve you.' There was more, clearly, but he did not say it.

'You have my gratitude, Vadomar,' she replied, unable to keep the emotion from her voice. 'Go now, and die valiantly.'

He saluted her then, as he would have an officer, and, calling the slave, vanished downstairs with a clatter of hobnails.

Galla realised Elpidia was studying her. There had been no impropriety, but her cheeks flamed nonetheless. She lifted her spear. 'Are you ready?'

'It has been my honour to care for you. To serve you. To love you as I would my own child, Nobilissima Femina. If I am to die, I am glad it is by your side.'

Tears pricked Galla's eyes. 'I am glad you are here, Elpidia, so glad. And you, Metella.'

Metella began to sob.

Galla made no move to comfort her, because the familiar scuffling and muttering was audible through the shutters. She readied herself, waited until there was movement on the other side of the slats, paused another moment for the warrior to lift himself up a bit more, then shoved with all her strength. The spear slid between the shutters and into something. Something that groaned and bucked away from the steel. She shoved harder, and the spear sank home. A drawn-out cry of pain, a sudden wrench carrying up through her arms. The warrior had grabbed the spear shaft, she realised, and was trying to free himself. She pushed even harder, and the resistance against her effort weakened and stopped. She tugged the spear back. It came free. Something – a body – slumped against the shutters. Shouts carried up from the street, angry, frustrated, redoubling as the warrior's corpse fell down among them.

Her triumph did not last long.

There was cheering below. Cries of encouragement. Feet stamping. The thudding of the two axes increased. Perhaps a third axeman had joined in, she thought. The door must be close to falling asunder, and when it did, the warriors would charge inside, where Vadomar would be waiting with the armed slaves. Galla did not want to be unfair to the slaves, but they would be easy prey for the Visigoths. Vadomar was a different proposition. He would fight like a man possessed, but what could one do against so many?

'Nobilissima Femina.' Elpidia's voice brought her back to the bedroom.

Galla stared at the dagger Elpidia was offering. Ivory-handled with an engraved silver scabbard, it had been her father's. She accepted it and, drawing the blade, set the scabbard back on her make-up table. She laid the cold metal on the inside of her left wrist, studying the blue network of veins under the skin. It was better to cut along the length of her forearm, she knew, rather than across the wrist as might have been thought. It was something Elpidia, somehow versed in these things, had taught her. She looked up. Her nurse was watching, face solemn.

'When I have cut the veins in my left arm,' Galla said, 'I might not have the strength for the right.'

'I will do it, Nobilissima Femina.' Elpidia's tone was husky.

'Gratitude.'

'I will need help too,' said Metella.

'Of course, Domina,' said Elpidia.

'And you?' asked Galla.

'I am going to die fighting, Nobilissima Femina.' Elpidia lifted her spear. 'The first warrior up the stairs will get this in the face. And the second. Maybe even the third.'

'This is not how I wanted our lives to end,' said Galla sadly, aware that Metella was crying again.

'Nor I, but this is what God has decided for us.'

There had to be a greater meaning to their sorry end, Galla thought, but she could not see it.

Amid the thudding of the axes, shouts on the street. The heavy tramp of feet. Barked commands. An angry response from outside Galla's house, then another. More shouts. A deep, commanding voice. Although she could not understand the Gothic, there was no mistaking that this was someone in authority, someone who was used to being obeyed.

The axes stopped. There was angry muttering, and more loud orders.

Galla set aside her spear and eased open the shutters.

'What are you doing?' asked Metella, alarmed.

'The attack has stopped, and I want to know why.' Galla peered outside. A large body of warriors in scale mail filled the street. In their midst, shoving his way forward, distinctive because of a magnificent crested helmet, was a thickset figure with a bushy beard. Seeing him, the warriors stepped back, called out a name.

'Alaric is come.' It was ironic, Galla thought, to feel such relief at the sight of a man who had taken Roma, humiliating its people as they had not been in eight hundred years. 'Let us meet him,' she said.

Downstairs, Vadomar was still ready for the warriors to come smashing in, but he too had noted the commotion. When Galla explained, his grim expression eased. 'I hope you're right, Nobilissima Femina.'

Noise outside, men stepping away.

'Is this the house of Galla Placidia?' shouted a voice in accented Latin.

'It is,' Vadomar replied. 'Who comes to her door?'

'Alaric, king of the Visigoths,' came the answer. 'He would see that Galla Placidia is safe.'

'He arrived just in time,' said Vadomar under his breath.

This was an intervention by God Himself, Galla decided. It had to be. She gave silent thanks, and resolved to make a generous offering in the basilica of St Petrus at the earliest opportunity.

A few moments later, the table had been pulled aside. The shattered door sagged open, and Galla saw Vadomar tense. He was worried that a wave of attackers would come charging in, she realised, her own stomach knotting.

Warriors did enter, but in disciplined fashion, well turned out in scale mail and polished helmets. They gave no acknowledgement to

Galla or anyone else. Forming up in two lines on either side of the doorway, they waited.

In stalked the bushy-bearded man she had seen from upstairs. Beady, calculating eyes took in everyone, but mostly her and Metella. Elpidia got barely a look, being the wrong age. Galla took a step forward. 'You are welcome, Alaric.'

'Nobilissima Femina.' He performed a deep bow. Straightening, his face was concerned. 'Are you hurt?'

'No, fortunately. If you had come a little later, though, things would have been different.'

A black scowl. 'I apologise, Nobilissima Femina. My warriors were under strict instructions to leave your house untouched and not to lay a finger on anyone inside.' He barked an order, and Fur Cloak and three others were dragged in. Their hands had been tied. They already had the appearance of men who had been badly treated: black eyes, cuts, bruises.

'These are the ringleaders, Nobilissima Femina.'

'I recognise at least one.'

'They have been told their crime. Now they will pay.'

It was plain what he meant. Galla saw that the warriors knew it too. The first emotion she felt was pleasure, that they who would have raped and slaughtered would instead be put to death. Quick to follow, however, was pity. Disarmed, wrists tethered, beaten, they were pathetic. And yet she did not speak. Those who attempted to murder a member of the imperial family had to be made an example of.

Alaric issued another command. As the warriors were being shepherded away, Fur Cloak fell to his knees, wringing his hands and speaking in Gothic. His eyes were fixed on Galla.

No one made an immediate move to force him to his feet.

Again he voiced his entreaty.

Galla was aware of Alaric studying her. 'What is he saying?' she asked.

'He had no idea this was your house – none of them did, Nobilissima Femina. He would never have attacked it had he known. He begs for his life, and those of his companions.'

Fur Cloak was young, thought Galla, about her own age. 'Is he married?'

Alaric looked surprised, but asked the question. A vigorous nod, more voluble Gothic. 'Yes. He has two children also, the first three years of age, the other a babe.'

It was easy to think of the warrior with his wife and family. He was probably a decent man in many ways, Galla decided, but her mind was still full of horrific images. If Alaric had not appeared, the inside of her house would by now be a charnel house filled with the screams of the wounded and of the women being violated.

'Let him die,' she said, staring into Fur Cloak's face. She didn't know if he spoke Latin, but he understood her meaning. His face paled, and he fell silent. Galla brought her gaze back to Alaric. 'Let him die,' she repeated. 'Him and every single man who attacked this house.'

Alaric's surprise was replaced by respect. 'As you wish, Nobilissima Femina. It will deliver a succinct message: you are not to be harmed.' He issued a string of orders, and the four warriors were hustled outside.

Killing in cold blood, Galla realised with some surprise, could be quite a silent business. The only sounds carrying in from the street were plaintive cries, cut short, and the wet, hacking sound of blades cleaving flesh. Her stomach protested, as it had upstairs, but she refused to allow it to control her. She had taken a decision worthy of an empress; it would not be appropriate to vomit. Alaric was also watching her like a hawk, no doubt wanting her resolve to weaken, to hear her demand that the executions end. Instead, she slowly breathed in through her nose and out through her mouth, then did it again. The trick was one taught to her long ago by Elpidia.

Silence fell outside at last. A warrior came in, bloody sword in hand, and spoke to Alaric.

'It is done, Nobilissima Femina.'

She dipped her chin in acknowledgement.

Alaric bowed again.

Galla was delighted by his respect, and asked that the restraint he had ordered during the taking of the city be strictly observed.

Risking a jab to his pride, she warned that if innocents were slaughtered and churches ransacked, he would go down in history as a monster. Although he seemed surprised by her demand, he agreed to it. Messengers were sent out to every quarter of the city at once. They would succeed only in part, Galla knew, but lives might be saved, and some properties protected from the worst of the pillaging.

To find Alaric a little awed by her confidence gave her strength. There must always be an air of formality between them, she decided. He was the one with all the power, so it was important her status remained a barrier between them. He was the conqueror of Roma, and the self-styled scourge of the empire, but he must bear in mind that she was the daughter and sister of emperors.

Remembering the size of his army, the impunity with which he had taken the empire's greatest city, her self-assurance faltered. In reality, she was at his mercy. Telling him she wished to become a nun might work for a while, but he was unlikely to be dissuaded from trying to win her hand for long. Then there was the matter of Honorius. Alaric had no idea of the bad relations between him and Galla, and of how improbable it was the emperor would agree to ransom his half-sister. If he found out, he would have no reason to treat her with respect. He could force her to marry him.

Desperate, she prayed to God. Asked Him for help. For strength.

Calmness returned.

Despite what was going on throughout the city, Galla told herself, she was alive. Unhurt. She had not been ravished. None of her household had been harmed, not Elpidia or Vadomar, Darme or Fritigern. Not her kitchen slaves or any of her neighbours. True, she was Alaric's captive, but she was being treated with great respect. The only casualty, she thought with amusement, was her front door, which was irreparably damaged.

Given the enormity of the day's events, it was a small price to pay.

CHAPTER XXVI

Four months later . . .

Near Consentia, central Italia; Mensis December, AD *410*

Vadomar hunched forward, holding out his hands to the fire. It was late, but he knew from the sound of low voices inside the large tent that Galla and Elpidia had not yet retired. Even when they were asleep, he could not rest. Honoured guest she might be, ring of protective warriors around the tent regardless, he did not trust her care to anyone else.

Since leaving Roma, his routine had been to stand watch over his mistress, and to lie across the tent's entrance overnight like a hound. If the temperatures were warm, it was pleasant. Cold and damp did not stop him, though, nor did frost. Two ox skins, stitched together and heavily waxed, served as protection from the rain. When he slept, it was lightly, coming awake at the slightest sound. He could not have kept it up for ever. No man can do without sufficient rest, Darme told him, and Vadomar had been forced to concede. For some time now, he had let Darme take his place every second night, lying down a few paces away, grateful for deep, dreamless sleep.

Vadomar had seen more of Italia on this journey than ever before. Roma had been bare of food and supplies after the siege, and with the harvest nigh, it was an obvious choice for Alaric to head for Campania. Fertile land, full of large latifundia, it had provided plenty of grain, wine and cattle. As summer became autumn, the host had moved on to plunder Lucania and Rhegium. In the far south, with Sicilia visible over the narrow straits, Alaric's intentions became plain. Italia could not feed his army all year round, but the farms of Sicilia produced vast quantities of grain. A short voyage beyond the large island lay the breadbasket of the empire, Africa.

There had been much celebration, and several nights of feasting and drinking. The delay was to prove costly, unsettled weather arriving out of the blue, and with it, strong winds and heavy rain. The passage was short and Sicilia was ripe for the taking, Alaric had declared, ordering the first of his ships to set sail. To the horror of everyone watching, the heavy seas and strong currents had sent a number of ships to the bottom. Several thousand warriors drowned. Faced with the loss of even more of his host, Alaric decided to march north again. The Visigoths' decades-long search for a homeland continued.

The roads north were clear of Roman armies. It was not altogether surprising, given Galla's hostage status, the fractures in the imperial court at Ravenna and the scarcity of good generals. There was also a need to defend the passes through the Alpes against an incursion by Constantinus. Although Alaric did not announce it, most said Illyricum was their destination. It made sense, the location that had succoured his host for so many years, but to return there would mean the ire of Honorius, and also those who advised Theodosius, the child emperor in the east. It might take time, but joint action by the two rulers against Alaric was possible.

Vadomar would have to engineer Galla's escape before they left Italia, but he was unsure where they would go. Few options offered themselves. Roma, her home for so long, would not be safe: Alaric would have the city turned upside down to find her. There was her half-brother, the emperor, but her relationship with Honorius was poor. The mere mention of his name caused an immediate change in her demeanour, while Elpidia's mood turned savage. Seeking refuge in Ravenna, therefore, was not a desirable solution to Galla's dilemma.

Unless she became a nun – unlikely – her best chance of security was to find a husband. The knowledge grated because he, Vadomar, could never be that man. Not for the first time, he wondered about persuading her, with Elpidia's help, to wed Alaric. He was old enough to be her father, but he was not evil, and he regarded her highly. An image of Alaric heaving on top of her appeared, and Vadomar shuddered. Even if the match made sense, he could not be party to it. There had to be a more suitable candidate.

The next morning, the world changed again. Alaric, whose habit was to rise with the dawn, was nowhere to be seen. A rumour that he was ill spread with lightning speed. Any moves to strike camp ceased. Men gathered in groups, talking, gesticulating. Crowds assembled outside his tent, ignoring orders to move on. Curious, and also conscious of a nagging concern in his belly, Vadomar went to see for himself.

The Visigoths' impatience did not take long to boil over.

A warrior with a burnished Roman helmet was the boldest. 'Show yourself, Alaric!'

Others took up the cry. 'Come and speak to us, Alaric!' 'When are we to leave?' 'Whither are we bound?'

The sentries exchanged unhappy looks. One went inside the tent, reappearing soon after, his expression grim.

'Well?' roared the helmet-wearer. 'Is Alaric still abed?'

The sentry muttered something in the ear of a comrade.

Vadomar lip-read the reply. 'Tell them.'

'Alaric is taken ill,' announced the sentry. 'He has a fever. And the flux.'

Bedlam. Roars of concern. Anger.

'How ill?' 'Can he stand?' 'Will he die?'

The crowd pressed closer, right up to the sentries, but no one quite dared to try and enter the tent.

'This helps no one, least of all Alaric,' shouted the lead sentry, but no one paid any heed.

It was not like Alaric to allow this kind of disorder. He must be very unwell, Vadomar decided. Immediate concern for Galla stabbed. If Alaric did not recover, her fate would be in the hands of whichever individual took the reins of power.

*

Alaric died in the afternoon. He was buried with great secrecy several days later, in the stony bed of a nearby dammed watercourse. When the dam was dismantled and the river flowing again, the captive Romans who had dug the grave were executed. Alaric's grave was hidden from sight for ever.

The entire host gathered in the evening and voted for a new leader. While two of Alaric's sons were considered, it was his brother-in-law, Athaulf, who won. The announcement was accompanied by a pounding of spears on shields that would have woken a sleeping man in Ravenna. Vadomar was glad. An intelligent, great-spirited man, Athaulf's lack of stature was compensated for by beauty of face and form. He did not seem the type to treat Galla badly. Vadomar could not be sure, however, and so it was with a good deal of nervousness a day later that he saw Athaulf approach Galla's tent, a dozen warriors at his back.

Vadomar squared his shoulders and hooked his thumbs into his belt. The gesture said: I am the gatekeeper, and I will fight if I have to.

Although many of his men scowled, Athaulf did not react to the obvious gesture. 'Greetings.'

Vadomar dipped his chin, showing respect. 'Lord Athaulf.'

'I am come to speak with Galla Placidia. Is she receiving visitors?'

This was a pleasing level of courtesy. 'I shall ask.'

He ducked inside the spacious tent to be met by Felicula. He gave her an absent-minded stroke and regarded Galla. Sitting in front of her table, perfume bottle in hand, she had clearly heard every word. She was in one of her finest dresses, eyes kohled, tasteful earrings and pearl necklace marking her status. She was a vision. Despite her circumstances, thought Vadomar, she radiated imperial authority. What an empress she would make.

'Nobilissima Femina, Athaulf is outside,' he said. 'He wishes to speak with you.'

Galla glanced at Elpidia, who was hovering nearby, and inclined her head. 'Send him in.'

Vadomar bowed and withdrew, silently asking both Donar and Galla's Christian God to watch over her in the moments that would follow. 'She will see you,' he told Athaulf.

Athaulf smiled. He made no attempt to take his warriors inside, another good omen. In he went.

It was not Vadomar's habit to eavesdrop on Galla, but today was an exception. Athaulf's intentions would impact them all, in particular if he showed an interest in marriage. Frustratingly, both he and Galla pitched their voices low. Little conversation could be discerned. Vadomar reassured himself with the knowledge that Elpidia was party to it. He would find out later; since the attack on Galla's house, any differences between the two had been set aside.

Sniggering. Half-suppressed laughter.

Vadomar's gaze went to Athaulf's bodyguards. They were talking between themselves, combing their beards, scratching their balls, looking bored the way men who wait on others do. Two, however, were staring straight at him, the first a lanky figure whose scale armour hung off him like a too-large tunic, the second a corpulent prospect with a fur-trimmed cloak.

'No need to wonder what Athaulf is doing with your mistress.' Lanky made a ring of forefinger and thumb, and lasciviously slid the forefinger of his other hand in and out.

'Shut your mouth,' said Vadomar. 'I don't want to hear your lies.'

'I'd wager she's loving it,' said Fatso, hips moving back and forth. 'The haughtier they are, the dirtier they like it. I found that out during the sack of Roma.'

'Aye. Roman noblewomen like a bit of rough,' Lanky agreed.

Vadomar's fury erupted. 'Say another word, and I'll—'

'Do what?' Lanky puffed out his chest. 'There are twelve of us, one of you.'

Vadomar didn't hear. Before either man could react, his blade was snugged under Lanky's chin. 'Take back what you said.'

Lanky's eyes bulged. 'Kill me, and you're a dead man.'

Vadomar was beyond caring. No filthy Visigoth was going to insult his mistress so. 'Apologise.'

A lip-curl. 'Go and screw yourself.'

'Let him go.' This was Fatso, whose sword was aimed at Vadomar's face.

Vadomar could sense the bodyguards spreading out to left and right. They'd be behind him as well. Kill Lanky, and he wouldn't take another breath. Even if he released his victim, the result would be the same. Galla would be powerless to avenge his murder too. He had been foolish, let emotion take control.

'Let. Him. Go.' Fatso's voice was chilly as dawn fog.

'You heard him, arse-licker,' said Lanky.

Vadomar thought of the instances since Galla had been taken prisoner. There must have been hundreds. He had bitten his tongue, said nothing. Acted as if he hadn't heard the insults, insinuations and innuendoes. Pretended not to see the lewd gestures. Now he had had enough, and the consequences be damned.

'Let me go.' Lanky sounded confident. Arrogant.

'I will.' A jerk of Vadomar's right hand opened Lanky's throat. Hot red poured, soaking Vadomar's front. Lanky's face paled; his eyes went wide. His mouth worked like a fish out of water. Vadomar seized his tunic, and heaved him at Fatso. One-handed, it didn't have much strength, but Fatso's attack was blocked. Vadomar spun, sword outstretched, and kept – just – the four warriors who'd been behind him at bay. They laughed, and his skin crawled, for he'd turned his back on the rest. One heartbeat, two, and he would be pierced through and through.

'HOLD!' The shout was full of authority.

Vadomar froze. So did the warriors, but the hatred in their eyes showed there was nothing more they would like to do than butcher him where he stood.

It was Athaulf who had prevented his death. The chieftain came out of Galla's tent; she was a step behind, Elpidia at her back. The two women looked shocked. Horrified.

'What in the name of Christ is going on?' Athaulf thundered.

A dozen voices – eleven bodyguards' and Vadomar's – answered.

'SILENCE!' The veins in Athaulf's forehead and neck were throbbing. He was angry, deeply angry. He jabbed a forefinger at Fatso. 'You! Speak!'

'Galla's man attacked us for no reason, lord – killed him.' Fatso pointed at Lanky's corpse.

Athaulf was frowning. 'Only a simpleton would do that.' His attention moved to Vadomar. 'How do you answer?'

'Two of your men were saying foul things about you and the

nobilissima femina, lord. Filthy, depraved lies. I lost my temper, slew the first who had uttered the insults.' Behind Athaulf, Vadomar saw Galla's expression tighten, Elpidia taking her arm in support.

'This sounds far more like the truth,' said Athaulf. 'Does anyone contest this warrior's word?'

A few bodyguards seemed about to speak but thought better of it. The rest hung their heads.

'You said two insulted the nobilissima femina. Who was the other?' demanded Athaulf.

Vadomar pointed. 'Him, lord.'

Athaulf's face was granite-hard as he walked to Fatso. 'You thought I was rutting with the nobilissima femina, did you?'

'No, lord, I—' Fatso stopped, gasped. Athaulf's dagger was hilt-deep in his neck. He tugged it out as dispassionately as he might have from a hunk of roasted meat, and as Fatso fell dying at his feet, he pinned his remaining bodyguards with an implacable gaze. 'Galla Placidia is my captive, but she is also an honoured guest who should be treated with the utmost respect. The next man who talks ill of her in any way will be first flayed and then torn apart by horses.'

His warriors looked chastened. The two bodies were carried away, by Athaulf's order to be displayed at the camp's main entrance. A sentry was to stand by the corpses, announcing to one and all the punishment meted out for insulting Galla Placidia.

'If I had not come outside, you would be dead,' Athaulf said sternly to Vadomar. 'If there is a next time, curb your temper and summon help. You are no use to your mistress dead.'

'Yes, lord,' said Vadomar, annoyed to have acted like a callow youth.

Next Athaulf apologised to Galla.

'I trust it will not happen again.' Her voice was cold.

Looking a little uncomfortable, and promising he would do his best, Athaulf took his leave.

Galla went back into her tent, leaving Vadomar to brood. His life was at risk from this point onwards. Athaulf could kill one of his bodyguards and get away with it, but not someone like him. He knew this in the marrow of his bones, because if the boot were on the other foot, he would act in the same way.

CHAPTER XXVII

Elpidia was brushing the floor with quick to-and-fro strokes. 'I think he would make a good husband.'

'Shh!' This had been on Galla's mind too, but she felt uncomfortable hearing it spoken out loud.

Elpidia peered out of the tent's entrance. 'All is well. He is far enough away, as I thought.'

Elpidia's smugness was annoying, but scolding her further would make no difference. Galla rolled her eyes. 'He gave no indication of being interested.'

'Athaulf is a proud man. Besides, only a fool or a boor, and he seems like neither, would make overtures the first time he came to see you.'

It was true, Galla thought, and yet there had been nothing. Not an up-and-down look, typical of so many men, nor a gaze-drop to her chest. Not even a sideways glance, or anything in his tone other than polite formality. 'Maybe he prefers men.'

A *pfff* from Elpidia. 'He doesn't.'

'How can you be sure? What do you know of Athaulf and his habits?'

'It's possible, I suppose,' admitted Elpidia. 'Even if you're right, he will still need an heir.'

Memories of Maximianus surfaced. 'God willing, he is not like that. I could never be wife to such a man.'

'And you won't be, rest assured.' Elpidia had noted her mood. 'You *will* have a husband. Children.'

Galla longed to believe Elpidia, but her inner doubt, fuelled by long years of solitude and the absence of suitable men, would not go away. She fought it with her faith, the belief that God had a purpose for her. It was surely not being hostage to the leader of a wandering horde of Visigoths. That seemed like a sick joke. No, she decided, strength and determination beginning to flow again, God's design seemed obscure because as an ordinary mortal she was not possessed of divine insight. His purpose for her would become clear in time, when He wished it to happen. Until then, she had to trust in Him, and continue to live her life in the best and most Christian way possible.

And, she thought with a trace of mischievousness, winning Athaulf's affections was not sinful.

'It is not like Vadomar to lose his temper,' said Elpidia in a low voice.

'You think he acted so because of his feelings for me?'

'Don't you?'

Galla could not help but wonder again what life might have been like if Vadomar's social rank had been sufficient. Rebuking herself – it was childish fantasy to think of marrying him – she said, 'It seems probable.'

'Athaulf's bodyguards will not let the killing of their comrade lie.'

Galla sighed. She knew where Elpidia was going but did not want to say the words herself.

'Vadomar is at risk of being murdered from this point on.'

Galla could not bring herself to answer.

'You know it is true. He might be slain at night, a rush of men with blades. When he is at the latrine trench, defenceless, or simply walking through a quiet part of the camp. It *will* happen sooner or later.'

'Other than you and Darme, there is no one more important to me in this life.'

'All the more reason to send him away.' Elpidia's tone was gentle. Understanding.

'Where? He has no family. His former comrades are dead or gone with the four winds.'

'Ravenna?'

'To my lecherous half-brother? Vadomar is no silver-tongued courtier. He wouldn't last a week.'

'It was a poor suggestion,' Elpidia admitted.

'Flavius Constantius,' said Galla, inspired.

'You mean to send Vadomar to serve the general from the east? Is that wise? You have never met Flavius Constantius; you have no idea what he is like.'

'Where else can I send him?'

No answer.

'I do not want to discharge him from my service. He would feel, rightly, that he had been ill-treated. Sending him to Flavius Constantius makes sense! Flavius Constantius is loyal to the empire. He is also determined and combative, by all accounts, and a successful general. Last summer, he defeated Constantinus' former commander Gerontius, and besieged Constantinus himself in the city of Arelate. God willing, that siege will end in another momentous victory.'

'You hope Flavius Constantius will find use for a man like Vadomar, and that he will be impressed by his valour,' said Elpidia, nodding.

'Exactly, which might lead to me having the ear of a man whose rise to power has been rapid.'

'The stories haven't just been from Gallia and Viennensis. Honorius favours him too,' said Elpidia. 'In Ravenna, it's Flavius Constantius this, Flavius Constantius that, Flavius Constantius the other.'

'Think of the sycophants who crowded around Honorius of recent years. Olympius was recently mutilated and executed. Heraclianus is in Africa, far away from the centre of power. Sarus, who murdered Stilicho at Honorius' behest, seems to be lying low. Flavius Constantius is the Magister Utriusque Militiae, master of both branches of the soldiery – he is in complete charge of Honorius' armies. The future of the empire is wrapped up with him.'

'I think you are being shrewd. If Vadomar can persuade some old comrades to tag along, Flavius Constantius might look favourably on him,' said Elpidia.

Galla smiled. 'Vadomar!' she called.

'He won't be happy,' Elpidia warned.

'I know.'

Elpidia was correct, as she so often was, but Vadomar deferred to Galla, as both women knew he would. He did not manage to hide the momentary trace of relief in his eyes either. Being sent away meant he would not always have to look over his shoulder. And as Galla said, and Vadomar had to agree, she was such a valuable hostage that Athaulf would never let harm come to her. With this knowledge, and the danger to Vadomar ever present, it made sense to start building a relationship with Flavius Constantius.

Despite knowing she was acting for the best, it pained Galla to send Vadomar away. It would have been easier to let him leave without a goodbye, but she could not be so cold-hearted. Waking from fitful sleep, she dressed without waking Elpidia, and unlaced the tent flap. Vadomar leaped up; he had been sitting on his already rolled-up ox skins. He was dressed in his war gear, weapons and kit lying close by.

'You are ready.' It was a stupid thing to say, but Galla could think of nothing else.

'Yes, Nobilissima Femina.' The words came out more formal than usual.

He felt awkward too, thought Galla. 'Where will you go first?'

'Bononia and the surrounding area, Nobilissima Femina.'

'To try and find your old comrades?'

'Yes, Nobilissima Femina.'

'And then to Flavius Constantius' camp?'

A nod. He patted his tunic. 'I have your letter of introduction.'

'That is well.' Galla's emotions were a maelstrom. Part of her wanted to kiss Vadomar. Part of her wanted to beg him not to leave. Part wanted to turn her back on him, not even say goodbye. Part wanted to wish him Godspeed and a safe journey, to tell him she knew he would do his utmost to win over Flavius Constantius. That he would fight with courage, risking his life to do what she had asked. She wanted to say she knew he would willingly die for her, and she valued this above all else.

'I had best go.'

'Yes, of course,' said Galla, realising they had been staring at one another. 'Take care of yourself, Vadomar. Send word when you can.'

'I will, Galla.' Scooping up his gear and weapons, he walked away without a backward glance.

There was a lump in Galla's throat. He had not used the formal 'Nobilissima Femina', she realised, but her name.

'It is as well he has left.' Elpidia, who had been eavesdropping, emerged from the tent.

'Why?' Galla asked defensively.

'Do you want me to say the reason?'

To do so would speak the unutterable secret. Galla broke her gaze from Elpidia's, muttered, 'No.' Then she went into the tent, wanting privacy for the tears she could no longer hold back.

Early in the new year, Roma was plundered by the Visigoths for the second time in less than six months. Galla had done her best to dissuade Athaulf beforehand, but he had been implacable. The alternative was to let his people starve. Why should they go without, he challenged her, while the citizens, whose Senate had so many times refused to grant lands to the Visigoths, lived in plenty? Unable to sway his mind, Galla had retired to her tent and spent the three days of the sack on her knees, praying for the homeless, the ravaged, the beggared and the slain.

On up the western coast of Italia the horde continued. Towns emptied, farms were abandoned as the local populations fled before the invaders. Whether the Visigoths would venture into Viennensis and Gallia or cut eastwards towards Ravenna and the emperor was unclear. Finding large stores of grain in the towns of Etruria, Athaulf halted his advance. Several days turned into a week, which extended to two, and then a month. Marauding parties continued to source grain and transport it back to the main body of the army. One month became two, two became four. Galla was relieved. Her tent was large and capacious, and decorated with the best of carpets, beds, tables and stools, but constantly being on the move was no kind of existence. She bore it because she had to, but any change from a daily juddering wagon ride was to be welcomed.

Sitting in the warm spring sunshine one morning, distaff and spindle in hand, Elpidia beside her doing the same and Felicula dozing at her feet, Galla counted her blessings. She had not been able to buy her freedom as Metella and so many others had done, nor was she free. She was healthy, however, and Elpidia and Darme – and Felicula – were with her. Athaulf had not yet shown any romantic feelings, but he seemed to enjoy her company, and liked learning about imperial politics, who was who and which nobles belonged to which faction. Attalus had taught him much, Athaulf reported, but it was good to gain information from more than one source, and as the emperor's half-sister, she seemed to have a better understanding of Honorius.

'Look.'

Galla's eyes followed Elpidia's gaze. The warriors set to guard her had long since learned – in the main, from Elpidia's tongue-lashings – that she did not like them too close. Thirty to forty paces from her tent had become an unspoken, agreed norm. It was at this distance, his way barred by two warriors, that a young man stood, wearing a wolfskin over his helmet. This in itself was unusual, Visigoths and other tribes preferring to use pelts as cloaks. What also drew attention was his belligerent manner, and the gestures indicating he wished to approach Galla's tent. This too was out of the ordinary. In the first weeks of her captivity, thousands of warriors had come to gawp, and gossip, and share tall tales about her, but Galla's curiosity value had long since palled. Along with the other high-ranking noble hostages, she was simply another member of the host.

'Is he drunk?' asked Elpidia.

'He seems sober enough.' Hope sparked in Galla's heart. 'Vadomar might have sent him. Go and see.'

She watched as Elpidia spoke to the sentries and asked the wolfskin wearer a few questions. Then, to her delight, Elpidia issued a brusque order to let the young man through, which was obeyed, albeit reluctantly and after he had been disarmed. He came limping after Elpidia, who was beaming from ear to ear.

'He's a comrade of Vadomar's,' she announced. 'Wulfila, they call him.'

Rising from a deep bow, Wulfila indicated his wolfskin headdress. 'My name's on account of this, Nobilissima Femina.'

'I see,' said Galla, affecting surprise. 'And you come from Vadomar?'

'Yes, Nobilissima Femina.'

Emotion overrode composure. 'He did not come himself?'

''E would have done, Nobilissima Femina, but Flavius Constantius values him too much.'

'I see. Is he well?' Galla didn't trust her voice to say more.

A broad smile. ''E's in the finest of health, Nobilissima Femina. 'E sends greetings and salutations.'

Galla could have shouted for joy. 'Before you tell me everything, are you thirsty? Hungry?' She made an impatient gesture. 'Stupid question. Elpidia?'

A plate of bread, cheese and cured meat and two cups of watered-down wine later, Wulfila began. Vadomar had found him and Dog near Bononia, delighted they had survived the massacres after Stilicho's execution. It had been easy enough to gather together a hundred warriors, all of whom had previously served in the imperial army. Retired soldiers make poor farmers, so the saying went, Wulfila pronounced with a philosopher's sagacity, and Visigoths were no different. Even though Vadomar had been able to promise no more than the possibility of a position in Flavius Constantius' army, the comradeship that went with his offer was far more appealing than the backbreaking drudgery of life on a small farm.

Vadomar and his band were numerous enough to avoid the attention of the bacaudae on their march to Arelate. Encountering a group of Flavius Constantius' cavalry scouts, they made their identity known and were escorted to his camp. After being interrogated by several suspicious officers, and having produced Galla's letter, Vadomar was brought into Flavius Constantius' presence. At this point, Wulfila paused.

Elpidia read his mind and refilled his cup, receiving a grateful grin in reply.

'Flavius Constantius, 'e was wary, Nobilissima Femina, but 'e was grateful you would send him soldiers, even if it were only an 'undred. A couple of days later, 'e put us in with the lads who were to lead the next assault on Arelate.'

Of course he did, thought Galla. She knew Vadomar was well, but her stomach twisted anyway. 'Were many men killed?'

'A few, Nobilissima Femina. I was lucky only to take an arrow 'ere.' Wulfila pulled up a trouser leg, exposing a fresh red-purple scar on each side of his right calf. He grinned as Galla made a face.

'Was the attack successful?'

'It was not, Nobilissima Femina.' As Galla and Elpidia gave each other a disappointed look, Wulfila continued, 'But thanks to Vadomar, our retreat did not become a rout. Flavius Constantius were proper impressed.'

'Does Arelate still resist?'

'The story gets more involved, Nobilissima Femina.' Wulfila went on to explain how news had come of the impending arrival from the north of a massive army of Franks and Alamanni under the command of Constantinus' general Edobichus. Rather than be caught between the walls of Arelate and this new force, Flavius Constantius had set up an ambush a short distance from the city. Edobichus and his warriors were taken by surprise. Some were killed, but most of his men laid down their arms, the news spreading fast that any who did would be pardoned.

'And Edobichus himself?' asked Galla.

''E fled to the estates of 'is friend Ecdicus, but it didn't do 'im no good. Ecdicus cut 'is 'ead off and sent it to Flavius Constantius, 'oping for a reward. Didn't work, mind. Flavius Constantius thanked him for his service to the state and dismissed 'im.'

'Hearing of the defeat must have affected Constantinus.'

'The city gates were opened the next day, Nobilissima Femina. Constantinus was so downhearted, 'e took off the purple, entered a church and was ordained as a priest.'

Coward, thought Galla. 'Didn't he have one son living still?' The other had been killed by Gerontius.

'Aye, Nobilissima Femina. 'E asked for sanctuary in the same church 'is father was in. Flavius Constantius was 'aving none of 'is claims – ain't legal yet, is it? 'E took both prisoner and sent them to Ravenna under guard.' A chuckle.

'What happened?'

'"Killed while trying to escape", I think you calls it, Nobilissima Femina. Thirty miles from Ravenna, it was. Only part of either of 'em what reached the Imperator was their 'eads on poles.'

Galla could imagine an isolated section of road, a shared look between the captors. A simultaneous drawing of weapons, the looks of surprise and terror on the faces of the usurper and his son. Given how many former enemies had been accepted into Flavius Constantius' ranks, she thought, it made sense to order the pair slain far away from his army. Living, they would have continued to present a threat to the empire. Dead, they were just two more names on a long list.

'With the usurpers gone, Flavius Constantius can now regain control of Viennensis and Gallia. The bacaudae won't stop him,' she said.

''Cept there's another usurper, Nobilissima Femina.' Wulfila looked embarrassed, as if it was his fault.

'What is it about Gallia and Viennensis?' cried Galla. 'Usurpers spring up there like mushrooms. Who is he?'

'Iovinus, 'is name is, Nobilissima Femina, one of Constantinus' followers. 'E's formed an alliance with two tribal rulers what followed Constantinus until 'e bent their ears. The king of the Burgundi is one. The other is king of the Alanni.'

'His army will be large then.'

'Tens of thousands strong, the spies said, Nobilissima Femina. There was talk of Flavius Constantius pulling back to Italia when I was leaving.'

'He doesn't want to be caught between Iovinus and Athaulf's Visigoth host.'

An impudent grin. 'You'd make a good general, Nobilissima Femina!'

Wulfila was verging on being overfamiliar, but Galla was amused by his boyish, irrepressible manner. She also liked the compliment.

Given another life – as a man – she would have leaped at the opportunity to command an army.

She set aside the pleasant fantasy. Athaulf would hear the news about Flavius Constantius' tactical withdrawal before long. When he did, it would make sense to advance north, perhaps even forge an alliance with Iovinus. Together they stood an excellent chance of defeating Flavius Constantius, which would be disastrous for the empire.

She would ask to see Athaulf this day, she decided, to try and gain an idea of his intentions. Regardless of what she discovered, Wulfila would carry a message back to Vadomar, to be passed on to Flavius Constantius.

Beware the road to Italia.

CHAPTER XXVIII

More than two and a half years later . . .

Genua, north-western Italia; Mensis Sextilis, AD *413*

Vadomar was outside the tent he shared with Wulfila and Dog, deep in Flavius Constantius' camp. Left to his own devices – his comrades were off hunting – he was organising his kit, cleaning and re-oiling leather, putting an edge to weapons. The repetitive behaviour afforded an opportunity to think. He chafed to do something, anything for Galla Placidia. The long-familiar feeling had been birthed when Alaric made her a captive, and grew worse when she sent Vadomar away. It had continued ever since. Sometimes it was a restless sensation in his legs, such as a man feels when he has done no physical activity for a time. That could be resolved by a brisk walk, or a sparring session. But at other times, his inability to do anything meaningful for her was an acid sensation in his solar plexus, a dull ache often lasting for hours. Dwelling on it made it worse, often to the point of significant discomfort. It was like that now.

He downed several mouthfuls of water. It helped ease the pain. The only other thing that did was news of Galla. Wulfila had succeeded in bringing messages to her three times and returning with information, the most recent being a month prior. She was doing well, and for the moment, staying in one area, southern Viennensis.

According to Wulfila, who fancied himself when it came to the opposite sex, Galla had intentions towards Athaulf. He had witnessed a meeting between the two, and also noticed how Elpidia, Galla's 'fearsome slave' – Wulfila's words – had spoken to her mistress afterwards. 'Thick as thieves, they were,' he reported. The news hadn't surprised Vadomar, nor had the jealousy he had felt upon hearing it. He had wrung every last detail from Wulfila. Had Athaulf seemed interested in Galla? Did he compliment her, or offer her gifts? How did she respond when he spoke to her? Did she smile? Laugh? It hadn't taken long for Wulfila to see through Vadomar, who, rather than deny it, had muttered that whatever his feelings, he knew his place.

Wulfila had confirmed a lot of the information that had reached Vadomar – and of course Flavius Constantius – via messengers and spies. Having spent a year wandering northern and north-western Italia, the Visigoths had entered Viennensis late the previous year. Not long after, Athaulf forged a shaky alliance with the usurper Iovinus. It had been threatened almost at once by the arrival from Italia of Sarus, recently fallen out with Honorius, another old enemy of both Alaric and Athaulf. Sarus was taken captive and killed by Athaulf in short order. Enraged, Iovinus elevated his brother to the rank of co-emperor, reducing Athaulf's importance and alienating him in the process.

Vadomar's thought on hearing the news had been that Athaulf might change sides. Honorius and Flavius Constantius did not have the military strength to take on both him and Iovinus. Offering to deal with Iovinus and his army would be a powerful bargaining tool. Thanks to Galla and Wulfila, Vadomar had learned that this was indeed Athaulf's intention; revealing the information before the messengers sent by Athaulf arrived had seen his standing with Flavius Constantius rise immeasurably.

In order to come to an agreement with Honorius, Athaulf's main demand was the same as Alaric's, for lands to be granted to his people. He wanted grain supplied for the foreseeable future too, until the Visigoths were settled enough to grow their own. The offer was sent to Ravenna, with Flavius Constantius' firm advice that Honorius accept. As well as requiring the Visigoths to serve as part of the imperial army, ensuring Viennensis and Gallia could once again be ruled by Roma, Flavius Constantius also recommended Galla Placidia be set free. The emperor had agreed, overjoying Vadomar.

Athaulf had not wasted any time, attacking and defeating Iovinus and his brother. Like Constantinus and his son, both were murdered while being sent to Ravenna, and their pole-spiked heads presented to the emperor. His side of the bargain fulfilled, Athaulf was waiting for Honorius to honour his.

The pain in Vadomar's midriff increased, and he winced. Despite his prayers, the likelihood of Athaulf releasing Galla had withered away. The failure had not been because Honorius intended to double-cross Athaulf. Nor was Flavius Constantius at fault. The reason was altogether more random. Remembering the fateful August afternoon when he had been trapped in a church with Stilicho, Vadomar cursed Heraclianus long and hard.

Rewarded for his treachery with the post of Comes Africae, commander of the troops in Africa, Heraclianus had decided to make his claim to the imperial throne in the spring, setting himself up as yet another usurper. His control of Africa meant the grain shipments so vital for the feeding of Roma's population were no longer being transported to Italia. It also meant the Visigoths would receive no grain either, breaching the terms of the treaty between Honorius and Athaulf.

If he had slain Heraclianus in Ravenna, thought Vadomar, there would have been no rebellion in Africa. The grain would have flowed, and Galla would have been freed. His wish was fanciful. Of recent times, usurpers appeared like new heads on the mythical Hydra. If not Heraclianus, it would have been someone else.

Even if the rebellion in Africa were put down by the end of the year – improbable – the grain would not reach the Visigoths when promised. Even if Athaulf could be persuaded that Honorius and Flavius Constantius were in no way responsible for the situation, he would be understandably reluctant to enter into agreements in the future. Vadomar sighed. Almost three years had passed since Galla's capture at Roma, and her situation seemed set to continue.

This bitter realisation caused him to question what he was doing in Flavius Constantius' army. It was a familiar quandary. While helping to put down rebellions, there had been merit in remaining where he was. For more than a year, however, he had been in camp, with nothing better to do than care for his weapons and kit and stand on sentry duty. Flavius Constantius might want to play the long game, but Vadomar was sick of it. He would be risking his life returning to Galla. Athaulf's bodyguards would not have forgotten what he'd done.

It was still an easy decision to make.

Dog and Wulfila returned in jubilant mood, a wild boar swinging between them from a spear shaft. Vadomar set about building up the fire; it would take many hours to cook all the meat. Knowing their comrades would be drawn in by the delicious smell, he decided to act at once. Take the bull by the horns and deal with it that way, his father had been fond of saying, otherwise it will jab you in the arse.

'We need to leave,' he said quietly, placing a thick length of branch into the flames.

'What are you talking about?' cried Wulfila. 'There's a boar to cook, in case you hadn't noticed.'

Dog, cunning, knew there was more to Vadomar's words. 'Why?'

'We're doing nothing here.'

'Other than eating well,' countered Wulfila, slicing around the top of a hind leg to begin parting it from the pelvis.

'Nothing important.'

Wulfila tutted. 'Since when is filling your belly not important?'

'Flavius Constantius has shown no inclination to enter Viennensis in the last year. He isn't going to this year either, because the grain promised to Athaulf isn't going to materialise. The Visigoths will be spoiling for a fight. True?'

Wulfila shrugged, pretending not to care.

'You're probably right,' said Dog. 'I'm also thinking Galla Placidia won't be released once Athaulf discovers there'll be no grain. Which means you want to go back to her.'

'I'm of no use to her in Flavius Constantius' camp.'

'Athaulf and his warriors will look dimly on us turning up.'

It was Vadomar's turn to shrug. 'Galla Placidia is a member of the imperial family. They treat her with huge respect. That should be good enough for the warriors she chooses to guard her.'

'*Should* be. Doesn't mean it *will* be,' said Wulfila. 'I've met the men set by Athaulf to watch over her thrice now. They're not friendly.'

'I don't imagine Flavius Constantius will be too pleased by our sudden departure either.' Dog's tone was dry.

'Which is why I'm going to go and talk to him.' Vadomar was taking a risk, but it seemed cowardly to skulk away under cover of darkness when he was doing nothing wrong.

'And the rest of the lads?' Dog jerked his head, indicating the tents around them. 'Do you think they'll want to follow us?'

Vadomar grinned; Dog had just confirmed his presence. 'They can make up their own minds. Are you coming, Wulfila?'

A scowl. 'I'm not being left behind.'

Vadomar's spirits rose. His most important comrades would accompany him.

In the end, two others agreed to go with them: both cousins of Wulfila's, near-identical twins who answered to Nosy and Big Nose. They had real names, of course, but Big Nose had been called that for ever, thanks to his massive nose. Nosy was similarly blessed, but not to the same extent. The pair didn't possess huge amounts of intelligence, but they were tough, brave and loyal. Blood was thicker than water, Big Nose had told Vadomar, and if Wulfila was leaving, so were he and Nosy. The other warriors, some seventy-odd, had been less receptive. 'Easy for you, Vadomar,' one of the oldest had commented. 'Galla Placidia knows you. Trusts you. You can vouch for Wulfila, who she's met already, and he for his cousins, but she don't know me from a hole in the ground, or any of the rest. It's different with Flavius Constantius. We've fought for him, bled and died for him.' His reasoning made sense. Vadomar didn't argue.

Wulfila wasn't happy that he intended to speak with Flavius Constantius before they left. The general wouldn't like it, he said; fearful punishments would follow. Vadomar wouldn't be dissuaded. Dog asked why he was doing it. On being told it was the right thing to do, and that in all likelihood one of their comrades, currying favour, would tell Flavius Constantius if he didn't, Dog grunted and asked if Vadomar wanted him to go along as well. Vadomar said he didn't. 'If he loses his temper, I hope it will only be me who is disciplined.'

The soldiers on guard outside Flavius Constantius' large command tent recognised him. 'Bit late to be calling on the general,' said the officer in charge.

'It's important.'

A sniff, an up-and-down glance. 'You'd better not be wasting his time, or mine.'

Vadomar folded his arms.

The officer came back soon enough. 'Flavius Constantius will see you.'

Vadomar made to walk in, but was prevented by the officer.

'Your sword. Dagger too.'

Vadomar hesitated. This was new. It meant that dying within the next few moments was a distinct possibility. To resist would be pointless, and would make it seem perhaps that he had come to assassinate Flavius Constantius. The truth will be enough, he told himself. Donar had looked after him in a situation like this once before. He unbuckled his belt and handed it over.

The officer passed the belt to one of his men, and indicated Vadomar should enter. He obeyed, acutely conscious of the officer walking close behind.

The interior was brightly lit by oil lamps, the floor carpeted, the furnishings as grand as a nobleman's house in Roma. Flavius Constantius was sprawled on a couch, an open scroll on his lap, a cup in his right hand. With a long neck and a rather flat head, he was not a prepossessing man, and in public was prone to keeping his gaze fixed on the ground. He rode a horse in odd fashion too, sitting forward, bent over the animal's neck and shooting glances to left and right.

Now though, his eyes, unusually large, came up to meet Vadomar's. The stare reminded him of those who said Flavius Constantius' appearance resembled a usurper or tyrant. Vadomar bowed. 'Magister.'

'It is good you came. Part of me thought you might steal away in the night.'

'You heard of my plan then, Magister.' It was unsurprising, but Vadomar did feel a little let down by whichever comrade had told tales.

'I did. You wish to return to Galla Placidia.'

'Yes, Magister.'

'Why?'

One word, loaded with importance and meaning. Say the wrong thing now, thought Vadomar, and Flavius Constantius would make a gesture to the officer to slit his throat.

'I was Stilicho's man for years, Magister.' Vadomar had revealed this before, but it didn't hurt to remind Flavius Constantius, who had been loyal to Stilicho also. His revenge for the latter's killing had seen Olympius' ears cut off in advance of his execution. 'Entering Galla Placidia's service, I took the sacramentum for a second time, swore to be loyal to her. I came to you because she commanded me to do so, no other reason.'

'Those words might cause a lesser man to accuse you of disloyalty now. You are one of my warriors, part of my army.'

'I have served you valiantly, Magister.' Vadomar stared at the general.

A heartbeat's hesitation, then, 'True.'

'You have good reason to stay in Italia, Magister, especially if the rumours of Heraclianus crossing over from Africa are correct. In the meantime, Galla Placidia remains Athaulf's captive. I am her man, first and foremost, and I can do nothing for her here.'

'You and your four friends cannot fight Athaulf's host either,' Flavius Constantius challenged. 'Nor could you spirit her away, or you would have done so before.'

'In Viennensis, at least we can be of service to her, Magister, and if her situation worsens, we can die protecting her. Better to do that than to stay in your camp.' Vadomar swallowed the words 'doing nothing', but he might as well have spoken them. He sensed the officer behind him shift position, and his skin crawled.

Flavius Constantius regarded him in silence.

Vadomar knew his life was on a knife edge, but did not drop his gaze. He did not want to die, but he had nothing to lose.

'You are a brave man, and remarkably loyal. It is admirable.'

'Thank you, Magister.'

Another silence. Vadomar's palms were sweaty; he was unsure whether Flavius Constantius would damn or exonerate him with his next breath. Whatever fate befalls me, he thought, I will accept it.

'I have a letter for Athaulf. I want you to give it to him.' Vadomar must have shown his surprise, because Flavius Constantius laughed. 'I was never going to kill you. Men like you are rare enough as it is.'

Vadomar grinned.

'You must wonder what is in the letter.'

'It would be a lie if I said I did not, Magister.'

'I have promised Athaulf that Roma will honour the treaty. Heraclianus' revolt means a significant delay, but the grain will be sent to the Visigoths. In return for my sworn oath on this, I ask for Galla Placidia to be released forthwith.'

Vadomar's heart sang. 'I am grateful that you continue to fight for her freedom, Magister.' He thought it politic not to say that Flavius Constantius was doing more than her own brother.

'It is cruel how long she has suffered. Even if Honorius doesn't realise it, she is important to the future of the empire.'

Flavius Constantius wanted to make Galla his wife, thought Vadomar, feeling foolish for not intuiting it sooner. If his military career continued to advance, he would be nominated as a consul before long. To become Galla's husband, however, would significantly strengthen his position. A male child born of such a marriage would in likelihood become Honorius' heir. Common sense would dictate both his parents be of full imperatorial rank, making it probable Honorius would appoint Flavius Constantius as augustus, co-emperor. These ideas flashed through Vadomar's mind in the time it took him to blink, and reply, 'She is, Magister, which is why I wish to return to her side.'

'I also have a letter for Galla Placidia.' Flavius Constantius clicked his fingers and a scribe standing unobtrusively nearby hurried forward with two wax-sealed wooden tablets. One was etched with the letters 'G. P.', the other with a simple 'A'.

'Make sure you give the correct one to each person,' said Flavius Constantius, with a smile suggesting it would be a bad idea to fail this command.

'Of course, Magister.'

Vadomar was free to go.

CHAPTER XXIX

Narbo, Diocese of Viennensis; Mensis September, AD *413*

Galla walked the thronged shop-lined streets, her spirits exultant. Narbo wasn't large and it was overcrowded, but to be in a town again – to live in one, she corrected herself – felt like a dream come true. She had seen a bakery, a fish shop, a dressmaker's and even a jeweller's. Women stood and gossiped while their small children played chase. A carter argued with a workman over whose job it was to unload the bricks in his wagon. A stray dog lingered by the door of a butcher's, hoping to steal a scrap. It was ordinary life as she had not seen in two years, and she drank it in. The tent-living she had endured was over, and would never return. So she hoped.

Yet her happiness stemmed from more than that. Elpidia remained a font of good advice and support. Vadomar was safely back with four comrades – they were a couple of steps behind Elpidia – and although Athaulf's treaty with Honorius had foundered, the Visigoth host had seized control of parts of southern Viennensis and Gallia, including this town, Tolosa and Burdigala. It would once have appeared strange to approve of these conquests, thought Galla, but her outlook had changed. Roma continued to fail her, as it had these many years. Despite her troubled relationship with Honorius, she had expected to hear from him after her capture. Not once had he written, causing her support for him as emperor to cool significantly. Athaulf, on the other hand, who had for so long played neutral, seemed to be developing feelings for her. And she for him, if she admitted it. Having spent considerable time together, it was a natural outcome. Thinking of him put a smile on her face each morning, and gave her endless reason to talk to Elpidia.

She had another suitor too, in the form of Flavius Constantius. In his letter, recently delivered by Vadomar, he had declared that he held her in high regard and was doing everything in his power to free her. When that was achieved, he promised to ask her to become his wife. It was flattering to know he regarded her in such light, but Galla had no interest in marrying a man she had never met, who was much older than she, and whose obvious motivation was to become a member of the imperial family.

No, she thought, Athaulf, her own age, brave, attractive, interesting, was far more suitable. Her hopes seemed to be bearing fruit. For months now, it was a rare day when he did not find a reason to visit. Most often it was to talk about Roma, its empire and army, its long, illustrious history or the legal and political system. Barbarian or not, uneducated or not, he was an avid student of how the world worked, and while he might have been reluctant to say as much, he was also an admirer of the empire.

At other times, however, he would bring a gift – wine, fresh bread, blackberries, even wild flowers once. They would take walks together, through his camp, and sometimes into the surrounding countryside, accompanied at a discreet distance by his bodyguards. Athaulf talked about his childhood, stories of rough-and-tumble with his brothers, his father teaching him to hunt and to use a spear, and about the battles he had fought since becoming a man. He said little of his first wife, Alaric's sister, but spoke with fondness of their six young daughters. Little by little, Galla found herself warming to him. He was straightforward, courageous and loyal.

In return she told him of the parents she dimly remembered, and of Stilicho and Serena. She mentioned how she had fallen for Eucherius on the brink of womanhood, and he for her. How the union had never been realised, in the main because of his parents' scheming. Athaulf's silence when she had finished made her worry, but when he declared he was glad she and Eucherius had never wed, the risk in revealing it was proven to have been worthwhile.

A definite turning point in their relationship, it had given Galla confidence. Two days into the brief siege of Narbo, she had demanded a house, a decent-sized house with a courtyard and a toilet and a dining room and at least three bedrooms. She was also insistent that the owners were to be well recompensed. No one was to be manhandled, assaulted or thrown out on the street, still less murdered.

Athaulf had taken her at her word. Her new home was villa-like in size, old-fashioned in the way provincial buildings often were, but its large, airy rooms, mosaic floors, and courtyard complete with fruit trees and a pattering fountain had caused her to fall in love with it at first sight. The owner was Ingenuus, a prominent local noble. Athaulf said he had been delighted to move out so Galla Placidia, half-sister of the emperor Honorius, had somewhere suitable to live. When it came to payment, Athaulf had refused to take no for an answer. Despite initial protestations, he reported later, Ingenuus had seemed quite relieved.

Galla paused by a shop door. Her nostrils filled with various perfumes: the familiar rose water, musky olibanum, deep, rich myrrh. There were other smells she was unfamiliar with too, intriguing, exotic. At once Athaulf came to mind. Men loved perfume, she thought, and she hadn't bought a new one in years. She walked in. Elpidia followed; Vadomar and the rest stayed outside.

'Domina, welcome!' The amply stomached proprietor was possessed of a fawning attitude and overexpansive smile. 'You honour my shop!'

Galla gave him a courteous nod.

'How can I be of service, Domina? Is there a perfume you seek?'

Galla wasn't sure, but she didn't want to give him anything to go on either. Mention of a particular perfume would cause its price to double, more if he realised who she was. 'No,' she lied blithely. 'I just came in for a look.'

'You are most welcome, Domina.' A greasy smile, a grand wave encompassing the small interior with its wooden counter and shelf-lined walls.

Elpidia bristled, as was her wont when people did not use the correct method of address. Galla shot her a 'stay quiet' look. 'Show me a variety of your best perfumes.'

'Of course, Domina.' The proprietor unrolled a rectangular piece of linen on the counter and, reaching behind him, took down a selection of slender glass phials. He carefully laid them in a neat line. 'Please try these, Domina.'

The first was rose water, which Galla used every day. She set it down without comment. The next phial held olibanum, but other smells were part of the mixture. She liked it, and dabbed a little on one wrist, holding it up to Elpidia.

'Lovely.' Elpidia smiled.

'Olibanum is dominant, but there is more.' Galla sniffed gently. 'Ah, cinnabar.'

'You have an excellent nose, Domina.'

'What else is in it?'

'A light olive oil is the carrier, Domina.'

'As it is in all perfumes,' Galla retorted. 'I meant the secondary scents.'

'My apologies, Domina, I cannot say. Secrets of the trade, you understand.'

She nodded, used to this response from perfume sellers in Roma. She tried a couple more phials, but they were not to her liking. The last vessel caught her eye, being different to the rest. It was made of a clear stone, with a stopper of a second darker stone. 'This is what the Greeks called *krystallos*.'

The proprietor's mouth, a neat 'O', closed. He coughed. 'Indeed, Domina. You are a fountain of knowledge, if I may be bold enough to say so.'

Galla was pleased. 'And the top?'

'I believe the stone was quarried in the mountains north of Italia, Domina.'

Galla pulled out the stopper, releasing a rich, musky and unfamiliar scent. Dense, spicy and blended with several different aromas, it had a sensual feel she had not experienced with other perfumes.

'Do you like it, Domina?'

'It's unusual.' She did like the perfume, a lot, but to admit it would cost her more. The krystallos phial had already revealed its value.

'Have you smelled it before, Domina?'

'No.' Galla held the phial up to Elpidia, who shook her head.

A self-satisfied smile. 'It comes from the other side of the world, Domina.'

'Was it bought in Barbaricum?' This was the port on the western coast of India from which spices, tortoise shells and other exotic goods were traded, making their way around Arabia to Aegyptus and thence to Roma.

'Yes, Domina, but I am told the region the plant grows in is far to the east of India.'

'In the land of the Seres, where silk comes from?'

'Even further perhaps.'

His claim sounded fanciful, an exaggeration to justify the inflated price that would be revealed, but it might be true, thought Galla, remembering the worlds she had heard described by a well-travelled merchant: dense forests, overwhelming, prickly heat, clouds of mosquitoes, savage wild animals: big cats and elephants. 'What is it called?'

'Pa-choo-lee, Domina. I believe it translates as "green leaf", an ordinary name for something possessing such a wondrous smell, don't you agree?'

'I do,' Galla replied, realising a heartbeat later how her admission had handed the advantage to the proprietor.

A prolonged bout of bargaining saw the perfume's eye-watering initial price drop in increments to a level Galla judged expensive but worth it.

Elpidia did not. 'Sixteen *miliarensia*?' she hissed in her ear. 'That's more than a solidus. He'll go lower – I know it.'

Galla had been about to agree to the price, but noting the proprietor watching her like a hawk, she decided Elpidia was correct. 'A solidus,' she said.

His expression grew anguished. 'I have gone as low as I can, just for you, Domina, but I have a family, children to feed.'

'I understand. Thirteen miliarensia is my final offer.'

A regretful clasping of his hands. 'I am sorry, Domina.'

He was bluffing, thought Galla. 'So am I,' she said, and made for the door, Elpidia a step behind.

She reached the threshold.

'Domina, please!' His anguish sounded convincing.

Galla turned, arched an eyebrow.

'Thirteen miliarensia is the price, Domina. I will make almost no profit, but it does not matter. You must have this perfume.' As he bowed and scraped, waxing lyrical about how the scent would increase her beauty, the two women exchanged a satisfied look. Elpidia, who carried Galla's purse, paid him.

Coins stashed away in the blink of an eye, carefully wrapped phial handed over, the proprietor grew curious. 'Narbo is a small town, and I have never seen you before, Domina.'

A glance from Galla was the permission Elpidia needed. 'She is the nobilissima femina Galla Placidia, daughter of Imperator Theodosius and half-sister of Imperator Honorius.'

The proprietor's jaw dropped, but he had the wits to bow deeply. Speechless, his gaze shot between Elpidia and Galla.

'If you don't close your mouth, flies will go in,' said Elpidia.

Galla hid a smile.

'I-I-I had no idea, Nobilissima Femina,' wailed the proprietor. 'Please forgive me!'

'You treated me with courtesy. There is nothing to forgive,' said Galla.

A tremulous smile played around his lips.

'Besides, I paid a fairer price than I would have if you had known my true identity.'

Leaving the stunned proprietor speechless for the second time in as many moments, Galla left.

'Neatly done,' whispered Elpidia. 'He will be regretting his mistake for a long time.'

A laugh escaped Galla. 'No doubt he will tell a different story when he spreads the news that I came into his shop. A tidy profit he will have made, and no doubt I was happy to pay it. I'm tempted to have you stand by the door for an hour and eavesdrop.'

'We have more important business to attend to.' At Galla's

curious glance, Elpidia winked. 'You must prepare to meet Athaulf, wearing your new perfume.'

'Was it that obvious?'

A conspiratorial smile. 'It was a shrewd purchase. Now he will truly fall under your spell.'

Galla's heart skipped a beat, and she asked God and all His saints to help see it was so.

Athaulf did not visit in the afternoon or evening, which set Galla, done up in her finest, wearing her new perfume, to worrying. He no longer wanted to see her, she said to Elpidia, he had never been interested in her in the first place, he was probably lying with the most expensive whore in Narbo. Elpidia listened without comment, and when Galla had finished, put a glass of wine in her hands and told her calmly how she tended to worry just before her time of the month. Something must have come up. Athaulf was interested in her. He would soon return.

Partly appeased, Galla drank the wine, took off her jewellery and best dress, and went to bed early. Her worries returned; it took her an age to fall asleep, and when she did, her night was full of vivid, disturbing dreams. Athaulf discarding her, allowing one of his chieftains to take her as his wife. Freed, transferred to Honorius' care, only to have her half-brother force her to marry him. Birthing a male child, father unknown, and have it die within a day.

She woke feeling terrible. Her silver mirror revealed deep purple lines under her eyes. It did not matter, she thought, sinking into an uncustomary gloom. Athaulf had tired of her.

It was therefore even more of a shock when Vadomar came upstairs, knocked on her bedroom door and announced that Athaulf was come.

'Now?' Galla eyed Elpidia, who gave her a lips-pursed, what-did-I-tell-you look.

'Yes, Nobilissima Femina,' said Vadomar. 'Thinking you were still abed, I did not admit him. I hope I did right?'

Panic flooded Galla's veins. Rebuffed, Athaulf might leave and never return. She was about to shout at Vadomar, but Elpidia was by her side, murmuring, 'Calm. He will be keener for being kept at the door. He can wait while I help you get ready. Darme will serve him wine. All will be well.'

Galla breathed in deeply. Grateful for the wise counsel, she gave Elpidia a grateful look. 'Thank you, Vadomar. You may let Athaulf in. Explain I will be with him soon. Convey him to the courtyard, have Darme offer my best wine, and anything else he wishes.'

A heartbeat's pause. 'Yes, Nobilissima Femina.'

He knows, or suspects, thought Galla with a pang. Vadomar's return had been a great relief, but she had ruthlessly quelled her feelings for him. She shoved him from her mind. His sentiments were unimportant, and what was left of hers.

'The same dress as yesterday?' she asked.

'I think so,' replied Elpidia. 'You were stunning in it. Athaulf will not know what has hit him.'

Nervous, Galla powdered her face to mask her tired eyes, and dressed as fast as possible. Elpidia slowed her down. 'He is here. He is keen. Better to let him wait.' Galla calmed, and told herself Elpidia was correct.

A while later, as ready as she would ever be, wearing her best jewellery and a minute application of the new perfume, Galla sent Elpidia downstairs. Returning, Elpidia informed her that Athaulf's bodyguards were in the atrium, while he himself was walking around the courtyard garden, glass of wine in hand. He seemed relaxed, not impatient at all.

Inspired, Galla kneeled on a cushion and, closing her eyes, offered up the same heartfelt plea she had for some time now. Standing, she smiled as Elpidia smoothed down the skirt of her dress. 'I am ready.'

She glided past the bodyguards, taking great satisfaction from their unabashed gaping, and entering the courtyard, saw Athaulf in the far corner. Darme was refilling his wine, which allowed her to cross half the intervening space before Athaulf saw her.

'You are welcome, Athaulf,' she called out. But for Elpidia's advice, she would have followed this with an apology for making him wait. Instead she continued, 'I hope the wine is palatable.'

'More than palatable, Nobilissima Femina! I am certain it is better than anything in my possession.'

Darme glided over to Galla. 'Wine, Nobilissima Femina?'

'Yes.' She accepted the glass, admiring the multicoloured flowers within it. 'Ingenuus has good taste, does he not?'

'Indeed, Nobilissima Femina.' Athaulf cleared his throat. 'You are looking radiant today, so beautiful. The gold hairnet, I have not seen that before, I don't think.'

'It was my mother's, God rest her.'

'She must also have been beautiful.'

'From what I remember, yes.'

'I remember you said she died when you were young.' Athaulf was much closer now. Darme retreated, affording them privacy.

'Sadly, yes.' Galla wanted to move the conversation on, and decided to take a risk. 'I missed you yesterday.'

'I am sorry,' Athaulf said at once. 'I was taken away from Narbo for the entire day. Cavalry scouts had brought unexpected word of Flavius Constantius' army, and I wanted to see for myself.'

Elpidia had been right, thought Galla, feeling foolish. Athaulf had had matters of real importance to deal with. It was unsettling news. 'Flavius Constantius has entered Viennensis?'

'He has.' A grim smile. 'He wants to push us into Hispania, or I am no judge.'

'That sounds ominous.' Her first thought was for Athaulf's – and Vadomar's – safety.

'Only if he is victorious, which I cannot see happening.' A tight smile. 'I am sorry to bring such a matter up. Of course you want Flavius Constantius to defeat my army; it would help the chances of you being freed.'

'Roma has scarcely been my friend these last two years.' Part of Galla felt traitorous to say this to the leader of the Visigoths, the empire's enemy, but more of her wanted him to come closer.

'True. And I hope that despite his advance, I can still come to terms with Flavius Constantius. All I have ever wanted is lands for my people, which is not unreasonable. There is plenty of space here in Viennensis, and in Gallia. I do not understand why Honorius refuses to see it. The Visigoths would be loyal to the empire and defend its territory against further incursions.'

Galla believed him. Noted that he had not mentioned releasing her. Liked being this close to him. Thought, as she had from the start, how attractive he was.

He came even closer. 'Forgive me, Galla – may I call you Galla?'

She had thought he would never ask. 'You may.'

'We have spent a lot of time together over the past three years.'

'We have.'

'Thanks to you, I have learned much about Roma and its empire.' He chuckled. 'I make it sound like history lessons. They were far from that. I enjoy your company – which is why I kept coming back.'

'I enjoy our conversations too.' Galla didn't want to risk more, in case he didn't reciprocate. 'They helped a lot, given my . . . situation.' There it was, she thought, laid out between them. Was she to be held captive for the rest of her life, in the faint hope that Roma would eventually offer good enough terms to secure her release, or could there be something more?

The silence continued, she waiting for him to speak, he deep in thought. Nervous, worrying she had read too much into his behaviour, Galla pretended to take interest in the detail of her wine glass.

'About your situation.'

Startled, she asked, 'What?'

'Your situation. It could change.'

'I am not sure what you mean.' Her heart was hammering.

Athaulf hesitated, then blurted, 'Would you take me as your husband?'

She stared.

'Am I being too forward? Forgive me, Galla, I—'

'Yes. Yes, I will marry you.'

He stood right in front of her, looking down. They were face to face, very close. 'This is wondrous news, Galla. You have made me a happy man.'

'I am happy too,' she said, and meant it.

He bent towards her. His breath smelled of wine. 'May I . . .?'

Standing on tiptoe, Galla kissed him.

CHAPTER XXX

Four months later . . .

Narbo; Mensis Ianuarius, AD *414*

Vadomar upended the leather flask, swallowing the bitter wine dregs. He needed another. It was a long way until midday, when the wedding would take place, and he didn't want to have to think.

'Early to be drinking, isn't it?' Elpidia had her arms folded, and it wasn't because of the cold, frosty air.

'That's not your business.'

'It is if you are pissed at our mistress' wedding.'

He snorted. 'I can hold my wine. Nobody will know.'

'Says the man who has emptied a full skin and it not long after sunrise. You're setting a bad example.'

Vadomar glowered, knowing she had a point. He cast around, self-conscious. The house was a hubbub of activity, Darme overseeing dozens of slaves as the preparations for the ceremony reached fever pitch. To his relief, no one appeared to be paying any attention, standing as they were in a quiet corner of the colonnaded walkway around the garden.

Elpidia came closer, her tone calm, sympathetic. 'Even if she would have you, and there is no certainty of that, you could *never* marry her. The gap in social rank is too great. Admit it: I am right.'

He stared, as much astonished by her awareness of his feelings for Galla as her ability to put her finger on the pulse. 'You knew?'

Her laugh wasn't unkind. 'Do I have a nose on the end of my face?'

Vadomar coloured. 'I have tried never to show it, always.'

'You cannot conceal anything, Vadomar. If you are angry, it is obvious. If you are sad, it is written all over your face. Your love for Galla shines out, to a woman at least.'

Vadomar didn't know how to respond.

'Drunk, it will be even more obvious. You don't want to ruin her special day. She has been waiting years for this.'

'No, of course not,' he replied. 'I am a fool.'

She took his hand, something she had never done. 'You are not, Vadomar. You are a good man, and a loyal, valiant one too. Galla needs you. She relies on you.'

The esteem in which Elpidia held him saw his chin lift. 'I won't drink any more.'

'Several large cups of water would do you the world of good.' And Elpidia was off, calling out to Darme to move those flowers a little to one side, just so, yes, and to have a bowl of hot water brought to the mistress' bedroom. Last came a warning. Before long, Galla herself would be down to inspect his progress. Darme huffed, but began to issue orders faster, and with more force.

Vadomar made for the kitchen, where he could deposit the wineskin without being noticed, filch a loaf of hurry bread and, if his luck was in, some honey to go with it. Belly rumbling in anticipation, he decided there was nothing to be done about Galla Placidia's impending wedding to Athaulf other than to wish them well. His feelings were of no consequence.

Sensing someone was watching, he spotted a woman in the kitchen doorway and recognised her as one of Ingenuus' house slaves. Curly-haired, her nose a little long, a trifle flared, fair-skinned, she had a round face. It wasn't the first time he had seen her stare. He hadn't bothered acknowledging her attention before, but stinging still at the knowledge that Galla would soon be beyond his reach for ever, he nodded a greeting.

'Ready for the wedding?' she asked. Her accent was odd; he didn't recognise it.

'As I'll ever be.'

'Need more wine?' She had seen the skin.

'Hurry bread is what I'm after.' Peering into the kitchen, Vadomar's hopes fell. Although he could see a rack of fresh-baked loaves near the oven, the head cook, a no-nonsense woman with all of Elpidia's attitude and more, was close by. Charging a line of enemies was preferable to securing his breakfast, he decided.

'I'll get you some. Honey as well?'

'That would be nice.'

'Wait for me over there.'

Bemused, Vadomar obeyed. She returned not long after, bearing a plate with stacked slices from a still-warm loaf. It had been thick-cut, and each piece generously covered in honey. 'How did you get away with it?' he demanded.

A coy smile. 'I said it was for the nobilissima femina.'

'Which is a lie.'

'Who's going to check?'

Vadomar chuckled, and busied himself with the bread and honey.

'I don't even know your name,' he said through a mouthful.

'Keturah.' An appraising glance. 'You have never heard it before.'

'I am sorry, I have not.'

'It is Hebrew.'

'You're from Judaea.'

'My mother was.'

'And your father?'

Without looking at him, 'A Roman. He owned my mother.'

Kicking himself for not anticipating the all-too-common story – she had been born into slavery, the child of a woman who had doubtless been forced to lie with her master – Vadomar said, 'Keturah. I like that.'

'Do you?'

'Yes.' A little uncomfortable with her eagerness, Vadomar thanked her for the food and made his excuses. Deep in thought, he did not see her watch him walk away.

It was good that Elpidia had intervened, he decided. The chance of committing some kind of impropriety during the wedding ceremony or afterwards was small, but he needed to be sober. First and foremost, he was Galla's protector, and inebriated, he was no good to anyone.

Several hours later, Vadomar was in a better mood. Taking a message up to Galla, sequestered in a large room given over to her wedding preparations, he had caught sight of the bride. Arrayed in magnificent silk imperial robes and a specially knotted belt, she sat while Elpidia parted her hair with a spear and tied it into six lengths. The ancient martial tradition appealed to Vadomar, who also thought Galla looked beyond compare. She seemed happy, talking with animation about the ceremony and how handsome Athaulf would look. There was giggling, and mention of children. It was not Vadomar's place to say anything, but he lingered in the doorway until Elpidia shot him a black look that took him off, rueful but accepting.

He would not stand comparison to Athaulf, who was wearing the apparel of a Roman general, but Vadomar did look good. His hair and beard were washed, oiled and combed, and his tunic and trousers, newly tailored, were of the finest quality. His helmet, armour and equipment, polished for hours, had never shone as bright. Even the warriors of Athaulf's bodyguard, a group of whom had arrived before their master, looked dull by comparison.

Not that Galla would notice. He told himself off for the thought. To keep his mind focused, he decided to treat the wedding as a gathering of people he didn't know. All were to be closely watched. His guard could not be let down until the end of the night, when Galla and Athaulf retired to their bedroom.

Ingenuus, a slight individual with combed-over hair and an annoying habit of ending people's sentences for them, had arrived early. He fussed around, asking Darme endless questions and getting in the way of the table-carrying, bench-moving slaves. Attalus, elevated to the purple by Athaulf, appeared with two powerful local Gallo-Romans who had allied themselves to the Visigothic cause. The three had been charged with singing the marriage chants, the *epithalamia*. Vadomar, unaware of this tradition, had asked Elpidia about it. Usually professional poets were given the task, she had reported tartly, but none were available. Listening to the three men practice, Vadomar agreed the singing would not be the ceremony's highlight.

The tolling of bells at midday brought Athaulf to the house, by which point most guests – a mixture of Visigothic chieftains and leaders, and local Gallo-Roman nobility and politicians – had entered. Athaulf looked every inch the prospective husband of a high-ranking member of the imperial family, wearing over his silk garments a *paludamentum*, worn by generals and emperors, which was fastened with a gold brooch inset with precious stones. He smiled at Vadomar, who snapped off a salute, and made his way to the garden.

The statues had been moved, creating an open space between the fruit trees large enough for the crowd. A passage opened, the guests bowing and greeting Athaulf as he took his place in the centre of the courtyard. Attalus spoke with him, then retreated to stand again with the two Gallo-Romans. Next Ingenuus approached, and Athaulf smiled and thanked him for the use of his house. Simpering, bowing, Ingenuus replied that the honour was all his.

Athaulf had a score of bodyguards with him now. A few nodded at Vadomar; there was no love lost between them still, but following Athaulf's direct orders, they had accepted he was not to be harmed. It meant he didn't have to worry about the bodyguards spreading out around the courtyard and mingling with the extra guests filling the colonnaded walkway.

Spying Elpidia, come to see that everyone was ready, Vadomar banged his spear butt on the floor. Athaulf's bodyguards copied him, and the crowd hushed. He gave Elpidia a nod, and she vanished.

An expectant silence grew.

Vadomar felt his heart thudding faster. Stop it, he told himself.

Galla appeared in the doorway from the tablinum, head covered in a flame-coloured veil, Elpidia six steps behind her, carrying flowers. The guests peered, and whispered to each other. Reaching Athaulf, Galla held out her right hand, and he took it. Athaulf spoke the vow of fidelity; she repeated it. He lifted her veil and kissed her. Vadomar felt a pang, but joined in the subsequent cheering.

The simple marriage complete, Athaulf gestured to his men. Vadomar heard the front door opening, and a moment later, a procession of young, handsome, silk-wearing warriors entered the garden and approached the marital couple. There were audible gasps. Each bore two large salvers, one piled with gold, the other with precious stones. This, thought Vadomar, was wealth plundered from Roma during the Visigothic sackings. The warriors kept coming, two by two, up to Galla, bowing a little then retreating whence they came. Vadomar counted fifty. Athaulf had given his wife a wedding gift worthy of an empress.

The epithalamia followed. Attalus didn't make a bad fist of it, and the Gallo-Roman pair's passion made up for their lack of vocal talent. A huge roar went up when they were done. It was as much in relief as a gesture of gratitude, Vadomar decided. The guests were no doubt also hungry and thirsty.

With tables set up in the courtyard and the crowd seated, the wine began to flow. Vadomar was amused to see Darme, the oenophile, watching for reactions. Vadomar did too. The Gallo-Romans tended to nod in appreciation at one another, while the Visigoths drained the glass in a single draught, often belching at the end.

'It's going down well,' said Vadomar. 'A good vintage, no doubt.'

Darme's *hmph* was happier than his usual one.

It would have been nice to join in, but Vadomar was content to wait until the festivities had ended. He looked at Galla and Athaulf, receiving toasts from the guests all around them. Chieftains were seizing Athaulf in bear hugs and bowing to Galla. The Gallo-Romans were more formal, offering the couple congratulations and wishes for a long life and a healthy family.

Food was served, a feast such as Vadomar had never seen. The house kitchen was not nearly large enough to cater for hundreds of guests, so the owners of neighbouring villas had been paid for the use of their facilities. Handcarts were wheeled in, each bearing a spit-roasted pig. There were platters of beef, venison and every fish from turbot to bream. Farmed eels were on the menu too, and oysters, clams, mussels and sea urchins. There was duck, goose, fattened fowl in pastry and, for the Gallo-Romans with old-fashioned palates, cooked sow's udders and vulvas. To mop up the juices, speusticus and wheaten bread were served in addition to bread baked with cheese or honey. Slaves moved through the throng, offering apples, candied fruit and sweetmeats.

The feast went on for a long time. Vadomar, by now hungry, had to ignore his grumbling belly. There would be time for that later as well, he told himself.

The drumming of Visigothic feet on the floor caused the general hubbub to die down. Athaulf stood, glass in hand. Uproarious cheering broke out. Even the Gallo-Romans joined in, their social inhibitions loosened by wine.

'For many years, I ardently desired to eradicate the Roman name. I intended to make all Roman territory an empire of the Visigoths in fact as well as in name. In my mind, Gothia should have been what Romania had been, and I should have become what Caesar Augustus had once been.' Stalling the shouts of agreement this elicited, Athaulf continued, 'But long experience taught me my people are not capable of obeying laws.' Loud guffaws. 'The Romans say it is because of our barbarism, but I say it is our free, fighting spirit!'

When the applause abated, he went on, 'A state and a people should not be deprived of law, because without it, a state is not a state, and its people are half-savages. Marrying Galla Placidia, I choose to restore the Roman name, tarnished of recent years, using the power of the Visigoths!'

Uproar. Pandemonium. Banging fists, glasses falling from tables, boots stamping the ground. Cheers. Shouts. Cries. And one discernible word, repeated over and again.

'Imperator!'

Vadomar's gaze went to Galla. A faint smile played around her lips.

If Athaulf became emperor, he thought, she would be by his side as empress. It wouldn't be surprising if she had planned it all.

'Imperatrix!' he shouted into the wall of noise. 'Imperatrix!'

Early afternoon passed into late afternoon. The sun dropped below the level of the roof, seeing a sharp fall in the temperature. Clear skies meant a frost, and to combat the growing chill, braziers were placed throughout the courtyard. Vadomar, who had been standing all day, was grateful, and walked about slowly, lingering by each in turn. The guests had thinned out, lighter drinkers and the more elderly taking their leave. Most of the Visigoths remained, as well as the more dedicated, some might have said sycophantic, Gallo-Romans. Furs had been brought out for those who needed them, and the wine continued to flow.

Keturah materialised by Vadomar's side. 'Not long until Athaulf and Galla retire to their bedroom.'

'True.' He had seen her throughout the day, and been aware on each occasion how she had nodded, or whispered hello. The attention was flattering, and helped to take his thoughts away from Galla.

Small talk blossomed into full conversation. His career as a bucellarius under Stilicho, the battles and campaigns, his dearly beloved comrades. How he had come to serve Galla Placidia, and the unfolding of his life since. Her growing up in Narbo, loved by her mother and indulged – a little – by her father, also their owner. The death of her father's wife when she was six, and his taking soon after of a second, who noticed Keturah's mother's special position at once. Sold a week later, separately, Keturah had been 'lucky' to be bought by Ingenuus, a kind man. Her mother, less fortunate, was purchased by the vilicus of a local estate.

'Did you ever see her again?' asked Vadomar, horrified, knowing she would shake her head, no.

Tears welled in Keturah's eyes.

'No one should have to suffer so,' said Vadomar, genuinely upset.

'I am a slave.'

Vadomar didn't know what to say to the bald fact. Not for the first time, he was grateful to be free. True, he had to obey Galla, who might order him to do something that would end in his death, but he would do it willingly, not because he had to. Keturah had a few rights, but not many. 'Ingenuus is a good man, though, you said?'

Keturah palmed her eyes. 'He is kind, yes, and does not . . . touch the female slaves.'

'That is good.'

'He turns a blind eye as well,' murmured Keturah.

Vadomar had an idea of what she meant, but his attention had been drawn to a warrior in a Pannonian cap. It wasn't unusual to be wearing one; he might be one of Athaulf's bodyguards, who had taken off his helmet. He wasn't carrying a helmet, however. The cap was pulled down low, too, making it hard to see his face. He was walking with measured step towards Athaulf.

Cold certainty stabbed at Vadomar. 'By your leave,' he said to Keturah, and began to run. He was a little closer to Athaulf and Galla than the warrior, which afforded a slight advantage. He hadn't gone far when the other noticed him and broke into a sprint; there was a sword in his fist now too.

'Assassin!' roared Vadomar, skidding around the open-mouthed nobles at a table. 'Assassin!'

Cries of alarm rose. Men lumbered to their feet, drunk. Pointed. Swayed.

Athaulf was on his feet, saw the warrior coming. Warning Galla to stay behind him, he picked up a three-legged stool in one hand and made ready to fight.

Vadomar came in from the side, forcing the assassin to a stop. They feinted at one another, the assassin with sword, Vadomar with spear. He jabbed, ducked behind his shield, probed again. He was calm. A shield gave him a massive advantage. The assassin would soon be dead.

Galla screamed.

Vadomar twisted to the left, fear surging.

A second assassin had approached unseen. Trying to get to Athaulf – the intended target – he was being blocked by Galla, who was brandishing a bunch of flowers at him.

'Get out of the way!' Vadomar roared.

Galla either didn't hear, or ignored him.

The assassin lunged, twisting her around and wrapping an arm around her neck. The dagger in his other hand came up, moving towards her chin.

Vadomar was perhaps ten paces away. The risk was enormous, but if he did not act . . .

He threw.

His spear buried itself in the assassin's open mouth, punching him backwards. Galla ripped at the dagger-wielding hand and ducked down and away. Relief flooded Vadomar. She was saved.

'Look out!' Athaulf's voice.

The first assassin, thought Vadomar. He turned to the left, bringing his shield up, knowing he was slow, too slow. A hammer blow struck the lower edge, the blade skidding downwards. Robbed of force, it nonetheless sliced through his trouser leg to connect with his shin. Vadomar screamed. Survival instinct to the fore, he punched with the shield. The metal boss hit the assassin in the midriff, a solid blow that winded him. He staggered, and was skewered by two of Athaulf's bodyguards.

'Nobilissima Femina, are you hurt?' Vadomar's left leg would not bear weight. There was warm liquid running down his shin, and he had to grit his teeth not to scream again. His gaze fixed on hers.

Her face was twisted with concern. 'I have not been injured, but you . . .'

Vadomar's world spun, and he fell.

CHAPTER XXXI

Galla paused outside Vadomar's door, praying for his recovery. All would be well, she told herself. The surgeon said so. She lifted the latch and went in. The room was sparsely furnished: a wardrobe, a table, the bed Vadomar was lying on, a carpet. He was asleep, but Keturah, his constant companion since the assassination attempt, was perched on a stool by his side. She jumped up.

'Nobilissima Femina.'

'How is he?' Galla asked quietly.

'He hasn't woken for some hours, Nobilissima Femina.'

'Leave us.' Galla wanted to be alone with Vadomar.

Keturah obeyed, closing the door behind her.

Galla took her place, studying him. Although his injury had only been sustained the day before, his face was gaunt and lined. God above, she thought, keep Your hand over him, I beg you. Let him heal completely.

As if he sensed her prayers, Vadomar's eyes opened. They came into focus, and he noticed her. 'Forgive me for not getting up.'

'It is good to see you awake, Vadomar.'

'Are you all right? There were no more assassins?'

'No. Athaulf and I are unhurt, thanks to you. It was just the two.'

'Who were they?'

'One was a disgruntled kinsman of Sarus. Athaulf's men are trying to discover if there were any more.'

Vadomar grimaced. 'What day is it?'

'The wedding was yesterday.'

'So I wasn't unconscious for long,' he said, relieved.

'No. Is the pain bad?' She held out a cup. 'I have poppy juice here, from the surgeon.'

'What did he say?' His worry was evident.

'Your leg bone is damaged, but not broken. You lost a lot of skin down your shin. It will take time to heal.'

'Was there talk of amputation?'

'No.'

'Thank the gods.'

'Keturah has been with you constantly.' She thought he would like that; she had noticed them talking during the wedding.

'My leg has to heal. I don't want to be one of the hopalongs begging on the streets. What use would I be to you then?'

She squeezed his hand. 'The surgeon who treated you is the best in Narbo. He is to visit later.'

Vadomar managed a smile, but it was clear he couldn't shed his worries. When she offered the poppy juice again, he threw it back.

A week went by, and his wound remained clean. The surgeon visited once daily, sometimes twice, and changed the dressing every other day, first applying honey to the raw surface of the shin. Vadomar, used to brusque but efficient military surgeons, told Galla this one reminded him of a mother doting over a newborn. Amused, she revealed she had threatened dire punishment if the patient did not do well.

Galla noted Keturah was present from morning until evening, bringing Vadomar's food and drink, emptying his chamber pot, helping as he took his first steps around the upper floor. She had appointed herself to his care, proving she had an ulterior motive. It was of no concern, Galla decided, and Elpidia agreed. It would be good for Vadomar to forget her, and perhaps to find a woman of his own.

Her own relationship with Athaulf grew. He was kind and generous, and attentive when they lay together. When Galla talked of children, he was enthusiastic, waxing lyrical about how strong their sons would be, and how beautiful their daughters. Their conversations ranged far and wide, now taking in what it might mean to topple Honorius and for them both to take the throne. It would be a long and difficult road, but Athaulf was convinced that in the right circumstances, he could defeat Flavius Constantius. At first Galla had felt guilt talking about deposing the rightful emperor, but as time went by, the feeling was replaced by a sense of entitlement. She was Honorius' half-sister after all. He had no children, and showed no signs of having any these many years. The way she came to power was inconsequential compared to the importance of maintaining their family's imperial status.

Although duty took Athaulf away most days – riding out with his scouts, meetings with his chieftains and leaders, not to mention hunting – he made sure to return each evening to Ingenuus' house, which had become their semi-permanent home. Ingenuus did not complain, no doubt because of the large amount of coin given him by Athaulf. Nor did Galla, who coaxed her husband to bed at every opportunity.

She missed her bleed a month after the wedding, and was quietly joyful. Wary of tempting fate, she did not mention it even to Elpidia, but her nurse, used to her cycle, asked her about it some days later. Galla came clean; they hugged, and shed tears of happiness together. The pregnancy would go well, Elpidia reassured her, and her baby would be a boy.

A week became a month, and Galla missed another bleed. She told Athaulf, whose whoop of delight reverberated throughout the house. At her urging – pregnancies, especially first ones, often failed before the third month – he said nothing of the exciting news to anyone else. They celebrated together over dinner that evening, bandying about boys' names, Elpidia watching indulgently. Galla decided her nurse was as happy as she was about the baby. She was glad. If not a real grandparent, Elpidia would serve as a proxy doting grandmother.

There was more good news. Vadomar's wound continued to progress well. A huge scab extended from his upper shin almost to his ankle: it would leave a nasty scar. He told Galla he didn't care, as long as he regained full use of the leg. With the surgeon's blessing, he began to walk up and down the stairs. She saw how frustrating the simple exercise was; his confinement to bed had taken more from him than he realised. He spoke about returning to training with his comrades, but informed by Galla, Athaulf told him how men set themselves back by doing too much too soon. Vadomar was disgruntled, but did not argue.

Keturah continued to minister to him, changing his dressings and cooking his favourite foods. Galla saw how Vadomar warmed to her, caring and attentive, and suspected that before long, their relationship would become intimate. She was surprised to feel a pang of jealousy, but her own contentment with Athaulf could not be denied, and the feeling did not linger.

Spring arrived, and the surgeon allowed Vadomar to commence training in the courtyard with Dog, Wulfila and the twins. He was stiff and out of practice, but with Darme's help – an unexpected font of knowledge when it came to stretching – after a while Galla noticed he was acting more like his old self. Elpidia told her how he went for walks in the town with Keturah, their arms linked, and how he rode out with his comrades, watching as they hunted boar in a nearby forest. Galla was happy for him; sometimes during his recuperation, he had reminded her of a caged wild beast.

In Iunius, Athaulf announced to the world that Galla was pregnant. The household slaves were happy for the woman they had come to call mistress, but it was Darme's tears that moved Galla the most. She embraced the old major domus, telling him he would always be a part of her family. Vadomar joined in the widespread celebration, saying he was happy for her and Athaulf. There was more in his eyes, but Galla did not ask, and he did not say. That time had gone.

Troubling news came soon after of Flavius Constantius' army, which had entered Viennensis and was making for Narbo. Galla suspected that Athaulf's appointment of Attalus as emperor – following Alaric's example – might have been the cause, but there was no need to say so. Athaulf had already realised that Attalus, with even less power than he had had in Roma some years prior, was a useless puppet. He sent out spies, Dog and Wulfila among them, and they returned with alarming intelligence. Honorius' Magister Utriusque Militiae meant business this time. His forces were not large enough to envelop the town, but the powerful fleet accompanying them along the coast would easily blockade Narbo's port. Since the destruction of the ships trying to reach Sicilia, the Visigoths had had few seaworthy craft. To Galla's relief, Athaulf saw how a shortage of food and supplies would force him to surrender without a battle.

They had no option, he said, jaw bunching, but to abandon Narbo. There was no more talk of invading Italia and deposing Honorius – the size of Flavius Constantius' host precluded it. Retreat to Hispania was the obvious, the only option. Since the invasions of the Alans, Suebi and Vandali and the fall of the various usurpers there, a clear opportunity had opened for an organised army to claim a territory for its own. Galla suggested this might be the long-awaited chance that had evaded Alaric all his life, and Athaulf until now. He conceded with a rueful smile. 'It would be odd indeed if the Visigoths find a permanent home thanks to Flavius Constantius.'

Galla told him that as long as they had one before the baby was born, she didn't mind where it was or who was responsible.

On this they were both agreed.

Flavius Constantius did not pursue the Visigoths, seeming content to set up his headquarters in Arelate. A vengeful Athaulf led his people to Burdigala and other towns that had capitulated. To Galla's horror, widespread slaughter followed. She remonstrated to no avail. Trying to prevent such things, he told her, would lead to his being deposed or even murdered. He added that if Honorius had given the Visigoths their own lands years before, the pillaging – not to mention countless other bloody episodes – could have been prevented. Galla had had to accept, as she had with the murder of Serena, that the path to power was lengthy and tortuous, and bloody.

It did not always have to be so. When Athaulf decided to rid himself of Attalus, Galla argued that there was no need to kill him, he being powerless and almost friendless in the world. The unfortunate Attalus, who had helped to sing the epithalamia at their wedding, was expelled from the camp. Other than his clothing, his possessions were a horse, a spear, food to last a month, and, at Galla's insistence, enough coin to last the same period. Athaulf had also shown mercy to Sarus' brother Sigeric, who had come to ask forgiveness for Sarus' actions. Not only had Athaulf embraced him, he had accepted him and his followers into his army. Galla didn't think it wise, and said as much. Athaulf explained that if he wasn't prepared to rebuild relationships after arguments, he would have no allies at all. Sigeric and his warriors were few in number, moreover, and posed no threat. Athaulf was not to be moved on the matter; Galla prayed it never came back to haunt him.

Vadomar returned to full health during the following months also, which gladdened Galla's heart. His relationship with Keturah burgeoned; she moved into the house he shared with Dog, Wulfila and the twins. He did not speak of her to Galla, but if asked, he reported that she was well. He enquired once if she could help with the nursing of Galla's baby when it was born. Surprised by the vehemence of her negative reaction to this innocuous suggestion, Galla had kept a blank face and taken a moment to think.

Her answer, that Elpidia would suffer no one else to care for the babe, seemed to relieve Vadomar, which meant Keturah had put him up to asking. It did not surprise Galla, who was well used to sycophants. She said nothing to Vadomar, but resolved not to place too much trust in Keturah from then on. She noted that he continued to sleep outside her door, except for the occasional night when he suffered Dog to do it. Keturah, who would not like him absent from her bed, did not have complete control, Galla decided.

Despite the months of constant travel, her pregnancy was uneventful. She vomited each morning for a time, and had food cravings – apples – but that was the extent of it. She had not expected her acceptance among the Visigoths to grow during this time. Although no one had protested her marrying Athaulf, their union had been coolly received by some factions within the host.

But as she walked through the camp on summer evenings, or went for a ride with Athaulf, men noticed her swelling belly and there were loud compliments, shouts to Athaulf that his son was growing fast, and smiles and encouraging words for Galla. When Athaulf, delighted, placed a hand on her stomach, spontaneous cheering would erupt, and requests made of God to see the baby – a boy, naturally – arrive safely and in good health.

Galla and Athaulf's son was born not long before the year's end, in the town of Barcino in north-eastern Hispania. His name, Theodosius, was chosen with care. It had been her father's, and was carried by the young ruler of the eastern empire, who was also a semibarbarus. It was an emphatic statement to the world of his imperial bloodline. While unrecognised by Honorius – as yet – the baby had a clear claim to the throne at Ravenna.

Motherhood suited Galla. The first time she saw Theodosius, placed on her chest by a beaming Elpidia, she thought her joyful heart would burst. Despite her exhaustion from the labour, she had been unable to fall asleep. Athaulf, sitting by her, one hand on her belly, fingers just touching Theodosius, had been overjoyed. 'What a son he will be,' he whispered. 'King of the Visigoths and Imperator of the western empire.'

Theodosius' first months were uneventful. He slept most of the time, waking to nurse, which he did well, and to fill his linen loin-wrappings. Galla could not believe how he did so straight after every feed. Elpidia laughed. 'Sleep. Eat. Shit. Babies do little else,' she said. A smiling, content infant, he grew steadily through the spring and summer. When he began to roll over, Elpidia warned he would crawl before long, and then they would have to watch him closely. 'They have no sense,' she told Galla. 'He'll put anything and everything in his mouth, fall down the stairs, whatever you can and can't imagine.' When Galla, laughing, asked if he would soon start to walk, Elpidia advised that with two such wonderful parents, she wouldn't be surprised. Galla was filled with joy, picturing Athaulf there as she helped Theodosius take his first, tottering steps.

About eight months after his birth, Galla was woken early one morning by a strident, mewling cry. It was different from Theodosius' usual noises, and sent panic knifing through her every fibre.

'Elpidia!' she called, scooping up her swaddled son. 'There, there, my love,' she murmured. 'All is well. Mother is here.'

Elpidia, who had slept in the hallway beside Vadomar since Galla and Athaulf's wedding, came sweeping into the room with an oil lamp. 'What is it?'

'I don't know. He just started crying.' Galla glanced at Athaulf, who had not woken.

Elpidia saw. 'Typical man, as my mother used to say.' She placed the back of a hand against Theodosius' cheek. 'The poor mite is burning up. We need a surgeon.'

Nausea washed the back of Galla's throat. 'Will he get better?'

'You soothe him,' said Elpidia calmly. 'I will send Darme.' She disappeared.

Galla walked the room, caressed Theodosius, rocked him, relived over and over how Elpidia had not answered her question. It meant nothing, she told herself, but her nurse always had been direct to the point of rudeness. Elpidia was worried, and with Theodosius refusing to settle, so was Galla.

'Galla?' Athaulf's voice, half sleeping, half waking.

'Yes?'

'Is the babe well?'

'N-no.' Her voice cracked. 'He has a fever. Elpidia said we need the surgeon.'

Athaulf was off the bed in one leap and by her side. His hand rested on Theodosius' forehead. 'He *is* hot. I will have the *lekeis* attend as well.'

A Visigoth word, it meant one who cast spells on disease. If it had been anyone but Theodosius, Galla would have scorned the services of such person, but now she nodded gratefully.

Athaulf's summons saw Vadomar come in, his face concerned. It was clear he had been waiting outside but not wanted to intrude. 'Elpidia said the babe was unwell, Nobilissima Femina?'

'Yes.' Galla didn't know what else to say.

'Send one of my warriors for the lekeis,' said Athaulf.

'At once, lord.' Vadomar hesitated, then said to Galla, 'I will ask the gods to intervene on Theodosius' behalf, Nobilissima Femina.'

Again Galla accepted with gratitude.

It seemed a lifetime before the surgeon arrived, and a short time after him, the lekeis. After examining the wailing Theodosius, the surgeon pronounced he had a build-up of black bile.

Galla gave him a blank look.

'He needs to be bled, Nobilissima Femina.'

Horrified, Galla shot a glance at Athaulf, who muttered, 'If he thinks so . . .'

'No! He is a baby! You are not going to cut open his veins. Do something else,' Galla ordered.

'He has a temperature, and his belly is tight. Like as not, he has colic as well as whatever else ails him,' said Elpidia.

'Extract of pomegranate is good for colic,' the surgeon declared, looking relieved. 'So is rhubarb.'

Vadomar hastened to the kitchen to see what could be found, and the surgeon produced a stone from his leather bag. 'Green jasper,' he said. 'It is good for stomach problems.' Galla nodded, and allowed him to slide it under the baby's swaddling cloth to lie on his abdomen.

The lekeis looked at Theodosius next, and said the fever was being caused by an evil spirit. Galla did not interfere as, holding a hand over the baby, he chanted a spell. She spoke Visigothic reasonably well, but many of the words, arcane or little-known, were unintelligible to her. Theodosius' crying eased as the chant came to an end, however, which gave her hope.

'See?' whispered Athaulf. 'All will be well.'

It wasn't.

Theodosius' tears soon began again. Nothing he was given made any difference. Not pomegranate extract, not the liquid from boiled rhubarb, not a foul potion the lekeis had brought with him. Elpidia suggested removing the swaddling cloths and laying him on a sheet on the floor – 'He will cool down, Nobilissima Femina.' Galla agreed with reluctance. Theodosius' temperature did drop, but he would not take the breast, and he continued to gripe, his tiny fists bunching in seeming pain, frustration or a combination of both.

Time passed, Galla had no idea how long, and his condition worsened. He had malodorous brown-green diarrhoea now, his loincloths filling with terrifying rapidity. His eyes sank into his skull, and when Elpidia pulled on the skin over his ribs, the tent she formed stayed in place for two heartbeats.

'What does it mean?' Galla whispered.

Elpidia's face was grim. 'He is losing fluid fast. He must drink.'

But no matter how Galla tried, she could not get Theodosius to accept the nipple. She expressed a little milk into a clay baby's bottle, but he refused to suckle from that either, pursing his tiny lips in disgust.

Theodosius died sometime around nightfall. Galla knew it was then because, dazed, barely taking in Elpidia's soothing words, a vague awareness of Athaulf's arm around her shoulders, looking down into his still, red face, she heard a slave in the corridor ask another what time it was, and the answer came, 'It's getting dark.'

Galla shrieked. A visceral torrent of pain, it shredded the back of her throat and did not stop until her lungs were empty. She staggered, light-headed, and would have fallen if Athaulf had not been there. She shook Theodosius, gently. 'Wake up, my darling. Wake up.'

His staring eyes did not move. A line of dribble ran from the corner of his mouth.

'Theodosius,' said Galla, louder.

'He is gone, my love.' Athaulf's voice was tender.

Right then, Galla would have given Athaulf's life, Vadomar's, Elpidia's, Darme's, her own, *anyone's*, to have Theodosius alive and healthy again. Blasphemous it was, no doubt, but she didn't care. Again and again she asked God to strike down one of them, all of them, just to let her baby son live.

Nothing happened.

She screamed, a scream she wanted to kill her.

It did not. Theodosius, cradled in her arms, was dead.

Grief consumed her.

CHAPTER XXXII

Vadomar knew from Galla's scream that Theodosius was dead. Sadness clenching his heart, for Galla, but also for Athaulf, he ran from the front door where he'd been on guard to their bedroom. He did not go in, and made sure no one else did either. When Darme, alerted by one of the other slaves, came to see what had happened, Vadomar confirmed the terrible news. The old major domus' face crumpled, and he seemed to shrink in on himself. 'No, please,' he whispered. 'Poor little Theodosius.'

Vadomar patted his shoulder. 'It is brutal. So sad.' It was unimaginably cruel for a baby to be taken away in such a manner, he thought. The gods' reasoning was impenetrable. He could make no sense of it, and doubted Galla and Athaulf, both Christians, would either.

Elpidia emerged a moment later, her face a mask. She was followed by the surgeon and the lekeis, both sombre. They walked away, leaving Elpidia. There were tears in her eyes.

'How is the mistress?' Vadomar asked. Darme echoed his words.

'She fainted. Athaulf is caring for her.'

'It is not fair.'

'No. Life seldom is.'

It was so true, thought Vadomar, thinking of Stilicho's end. Eriulf's. Theodrid's. The list went on. So few people got to die in their beds, of old age. 'The funeral will be soon?'

'Darme is to organise it,' said Elpidia.

Darme nodded.

It was fitting, thought Vadomar. The old major domus had loved Theodosius.

Darme wandered off, ticking off on his fingers a list of things to be done.

'The mistress needs water.' Elpidia left him by the door.

Vadomar tried to imagine losing a baby of his own, and could not. Not for the first time, he was glad not to have any children. It wasn't that he did not want them as such; he was unsure if he wanted to have babies with Keturah. It was an uncomfortable feeling, because from the way she talked, she *did* want children. Wary of her falling pregnant, he had taken to emptying his seed on her belly when they lay together.

Nothing was said about it. Thus the status quo continued. Vadomar was glad. He had entered into the relationship with Keturah because she had chased him so hard. Her attentions had helped to salve his pride, wounded by Galla's betrothal to Athaulf. They also allowed him to bury his love for the woman he still served.

Hearing Galla's sobs through the door, he knew his love had not gone away. Would not go away. He shoved it to the back of his mind. Now was not the time. There would never be a time. Did it mean he should stay with Keturah? He wasn't sure. He wondered if having a baby might improve her mental state, but his gut reaction was no, pregnancy would not solve her problems.

'I came the instant I heard.' Keturah's chest was heaving; she had run from the house they shared a short distance away. 'The baby, Theodosius – he is dead?'

'Aye.'

'Poor thing. Poor Galla, Athaulf. Can I go in?'

'It is not your place!'

Startled by his vehemence, she pouted. 'I would like to express my sympathies, as you did.'

'I have not been within since the babe passed on,' Vadomar grated. 'No one is to enter, save Elpidia and Darme.'

Another pout.

Vadomar had had enough. It was all about her, as usual. 'You had best leave.'

Keturah's face turned hard. 'Very well.' She walked away.

Angry, Vadomar did not try to stop her. He would be paying for this for a long while. Hearing Galla wail again, he chided himself. A trivial argument between him and Keturah didn't matter. What mattered was helping his mistress and Athaulf to grieve the loss of their little boy in whatever small way he could.

Theodosius' funeral took place three days later. Thousands of people lined the road to the church dedicated to the martyr Cucuphas, which lay twelve miles from Barcino. Warriors carrying lighted torches preceded the carriage in which the babe, encased in a solid silver coffin, was borne. Behind walked Galla and Athaulf, heads bowed. In acknowledgement of the regard in which they were held, Elpidia and Darme followed the couple. Vadomar and his comrades were there as guards, along with a dozen of Athaulf's warriors. After came the Visigothic chieftains and leaders, their wives, and the entirety of Barcino's ruling class, then thousands of others, Visigoths, and locals come to see what the fuss was about.

Keturah was not in attendance. She and Vadomar had still not made up. Besides, she had said snidely when he challenged her, Galla wouldn't notice whether she was there or not. That was not the point, he had declared, but she had turned away. He wasn't about to apologise for what he'd said outside Galla and Athaulf's bedroom, so he left her to it and went to pay his own respects to the dead boy.

Vadomar had buried his mother and father, and countless friends and comrades over the years, and had thought himself inured to grief. Theodosius' funeral was different. The tiny silver coffin broke his heart, and the idea, however improbable, that the baby might in other circumstances have been his and Galla's. As it was placed in the brick mausoleum, he began to weep, managing by supreme effort not to make a sound. Dog's strong arm around his shoulders helped him to regain control, and the fierce, tears-in-his-eyes nod his friend gave him.

They got rat-arsed drunk that night, Vadomar forgetting about lying on guard outside Galla's bedroom door. When he returned, late, to the house he shared with Keturah, and she put her arms around him, and whispered in his ear, and coaxed him to hardness, he did not protest.

The next day, head pounding, praying Keturah did not fall with child thanks to his stupidity, he put on his gear and returned to his post at Galla and Athaulf's house. He was relieved and humbled to find Wulfila and Nosy standing watch at the front gate.

'Here he is,' jibed Wulfila.

'Finally,' said Nosy.

'Thank you,' said Vadomar, from the heart. 'I drank to forget last night.'

'We know,' said Wulfila. 'Go back to bed. Dog and Big Nose can relieve us later.'

'I'd feel better here,' said Vadomar, who didn't want Keturah, smug from the previous night, winding herself around him. He didn't have the strength just then to end it with her, so shoved the matter to the back of his mind.

Wulfila handed him a skin of water, which Vadomar drained in a few swallows. He was feeling a little bit more human an hour later, when Athaulf emerged, his bodyguards following. The three saluted.

Athaulf, deep bags under his eyes, breath laden with wine fumes, gave Vadomar a friendly nod. 'I am going for a ride. Galla said it would be good for me, would clear my head. I tried to persuade her to come, but she refused.'

'I see, lord.' She wanted to grieve in private, and with someone who wasn't drinking to drown his sorrows. It was understandable, Vadomar decided. 'Is Elpidia with her?'

'She is.' A tight smile. 'Until later.'

'I'm not surprised Galla told him to go out. Life must continue,' said Wulfila as Athaulf made for the stables, which were down a side street.

'It must,' said Vadomar, wishing to see Galla, but knowing that if he did, he would not have the words. He doubted if any existed that could help her. He said as much to Wulfila, who in the uncanny way he had of saying the right thing when it mattered, replied that it wasn't about words, it was about being there. Being there showed you cared, which was what people remembered. 'You are always there for her,' he said. 'She won't forget.'

The advice was better than nothing, Vadomar supposed. He offered up a prayer to the gods for no more sorrow to come Galla and Athaulf's way. They had had enough for a lifetime. He drank more water, and hoped his headache would disappear soon.

'Had too much last night?' Elpidia's tone was arch.

Surprised to see her outside, Vadomar wiped his sweaty brow. 'I did. Trying to forget.'

'Aye. I drank a lot too.' Despite her admission, Elpidia looked no different to normal. She held out a skin. 'Athaulf did as well, and he forgot this. The mistress wants him reminded to drink it. Otherwise he might fall off his horse, the way he is behaving. Will you take it?'

'Of course.'

'I'll stay with Wulfila.'

Grinning, for Elpidia made as fearsome a guard as anyone, Vadomar headed for the stables, skin in hand.

Gravel scuffed beneath his boots. A lizard sunning itself on a paving stone darted away. A mule pulling a cart down the street brayed its irritation at the world in general. Vadomar hefted his own skin, which was almost empty. He could refill it from the stable well. He wondered if Athaulf would ride out to Cucuphas' church, and Theodosius' mausoleum. Vadomar intended to go there himself in the coming days, to offer his respects again, and to pray for Galla and Athaulf.

He turned into the archway that gave onto the stable courtyard. It was a natural sun trap, and already baking hot. There was Athaulf, talking with his warriors, drinking deep from a fresh wineskin. Grooms were readying a dozen horses, fitting bits and saddles, adjusting girths. A skinny cat watched proceedings from atop a wooden barrel.

A burst of laughter carried from the semicircle of men around Athaulf. Warriors glanced at the grooms, and at one in particular, who had ducked under the belly of the horse he was readying rather than go around its head or tail. It was easy to see why; although stockily built, he was short. Vadomar recognised him as Dubius, a Visigoth who followed Sigeric, Sarus' brother. A surly loner, he preferred the company of animals. Vadomar had never spoken to him.

'Do it again, Dubius,' Athaulf called out.

Dubius stopped what he was doing. 'What, lord?'

'Your trick of going under the horse – it's hilarious.'

Dubius scowled. 'Why is it so funny?'

'I couldn't do it. None of us could,' said Athaulf, gesturing at his warriors, each of whom was three to four handspans taller than Dubius.

A ripple of unkind laughter and comments. 'Short-arse.' 'Dwarf.'

This was not like Athaulf, thought Vadomar. The wine was talking, and his grief.

Dubius did not move.

'Do it, Dubius!' Athaulf's tone was sharp.

Dubius ducked under the horse's belly, turned and came back again.

The warriors applauded. 'Wasn't so hard, eh?' said Athaulf.

Dubius made no answer, just stood holding the horse's bridle.

'We had best get on the road. Cucuphas' church will not come to us,' said Athaulf. Noticing Vadomar, he gestured. 'Have you a message for me?'

Vadomar came forward, and said in a quiet voice, 'Galla Placidia wanted you to have this. It is a hot day.'

Athaulf gruffly took the waterskin; he knew what the real message was. 'Will you come with us, Vadomar?'

'Thank you, lord, not today. I need to stand guard outside your house.' Vadomar took a step back.

Another nod, this one with a trace of gratitude. Athaulf took the reins from Dubius. 'Let us go,' he cried.

'Short-arse, am I?' Dubius' voice, full of fury. There was a dagger in his hand.

Vadomar, who was closest, snatched for his sword.

Athaulf gaped. 'Dubius—'

'That is for Sarus!' Dubius plunged the dagger deep into Athaulf's groin. 'And for mocking me!'

A terrible groan left Athaulf's lips.

Vadomar's sword took Dubius in the side of the neck, almost severing his head. Blood showered, Dubius fell. So did Athaulf, clutching at his groin, muttering foul oaths.

Warriors swarmed in, hacking at Dubius' body, shouting, panicking.

Vadomar dropped to his knees. 'Lie back, lord. Let me look!'

Athaulf sagged down.

The flow of blood was immense; a major vessel had been severed. Speed was of the essence, thought Vadomar, pulling at the dagger-rent in Athaulf's trousers. Horror filled him. Blood was pouring from a deep, wet-lipped cut at the top of the thigh. Hastily Vadomar cut away a large section of trouser leg and, rolling it up, pressed it deep into the wound. Athaulf roared in pain, and pawed at Vadomar's hands.

'Hold his arms, someone!' Vadomar shouted.

Men obeyed. Athaulf lay back, face ashen.

Vadomar's rough dressing was already soaked through. 'Give me a bandage – cloth, a blanket, anything! Someone tie a thong around the top of his leg – fast!'

A frantic period of time passed, Vadomar remaining where he was, directing the thong to be put in place and twisted tight using a piece of wood. The bleeding slowed but did not stop, Vadomar able to see this by periodically lifting away the dressing. 'Tighter!' he ordered, not content until the blood flow had been stemmed. It wasn't clear if they had done enough. The ground beneath Athaulf was deep red in colour; three sodden dressings lay close by, and Athaulf's complexion was sickly grey.

Vadomar, in charge by dint of his confident manner, ordered a stretcher fashioned from spears and a blanket, and sent someone for both the surgeon and the lekeis. Dressing exchanged for a grip on the wood holding the tight-wound leather in place around Athaulf's thigh, he walked, stoop-backed, alongside the stretcher as it was carried to the Visigothic leader's house.

Vadomar saw Athaulf's lips move. Ordering the warriors to stop, he leaned down close. 'Sire?'

'Vadomar . . . Galla must be cared for.'

'Of course, lord. I will see to it, on my life.'

The suggestion of a smile. 'My brother should rule. My people . . . must have a homeland.'

The nearest warriors rumbled agreement.

'Galla must go to Ravenna, to her brother. Vadomar, do you hear me?'

'I do, lord.'

'Honorius will make peace then. He will give us the territory . . .' Athaulf's voice died away; his eyes closed.

Those were the last words he spoke.

They laid Athaulf down in the courtyard of the house. His warriors, dumbstruck, stood in numbed silence around his corpse. All the slaves appeared, attracted by an awareness of the second great sorrow to befall Galla. Vadomar went to tell her. Elpidia answered his knock, saw his face, knew instantly something was wrong.

'What is it?' she whispered.

'Athaulf . . .' Vadomar's voice failed.

She came out and closed the door behind her. *'Tell me!'*

'He's dead. Murdered.' The whole story came out.

Elpidia listened, a hand covering her mouth. There was fear, real fear in her eyes.

The same fear had Vadomar's belly clenched in a knot. Queen of the Visigoths an hour ago, Galla was now nothing more than a grieving mother and widow, and, as she had been until her marriage to Athaulf, a hostage.

'Who will take the king's place?' Elpidia asked. 'Athaulf had no boys with his first wife.' None of his six daughters had yet reached womanhood either, and thus were not married.

'Athaulf named his brother, but it has to be put to a vote. Alaric's sons were not elected when he died. I doubt Athaulf's brother will succeed either.' Vadomar paused. 'Wallia is fierce but honourable.' Wallia was a prominent, well-respected noble. 'And then there is

Sigeric, whom Dubius followed. It may well have been Sigeric's plan to assassinate Athaulf.'

'What should we do?' It was the first time Elpidia had ever posed such a question of him.

'Athaulf's faction will remain loyal to Galla, I am certain. I shall fill the house with warriors, in case the new king, whoever he is, decides to take her prisoner.'

'We cannot stay here for ever.'

'No indeed. As soon as I can persuade Galla, we will leave Barcino, preferably by ship, and make for the nearest Roman-held town in Viennensis.'

Elpidia nodded. 'That seems like wise counsel.'

'There is little left for her here.' Hearing the heavy tramp of feet on the street outside, Vadomar laid a hand to his sword.

CHAPTER XXXIII

Galla had been encased in a fog of grief since Theodosius' death. Had not left his little body alone for a moment. Had watched, numb, as Elpidia wrapped him in his funeral shroud. Had, prompted by Athaulf, kissed him before the cloth covered his eyes for the last time. The funeral passed in a daze, Galla barely aware of the crowds, the loud exclamations of anguish, the interment of the tiny silver coffin in the mausoleum. Athaulf, deep in his own world of sorrow, drank himself into a stupor afterwards. Galla had lain awake all night, staring at the ceiling, wishing she could turn back time, bring back her baby boy.

Today, she had mouthed a goodbye to Athaulf, but said no more. She was too broken-hearted. It was Elpidia's suggestion to go after him with the waterskin. Since then, Galla had stared at the walls, which was what she had done for days. Time and again, she had tried prayer, but could muster no fervour, no passion. God had taken away Theodosius, her darling boy, when he was not even a year old. There was a divine reason behind his death, but what it was, she had no idea – other than that it was the cruellest blow she had ever taken. The grief would continue for the rest of her life.

Elpidia came back into the room; she had gone out a couple of moments earlier in response to a knock.

Galla paid no attention.

'Galla.'

It was most unusual for Elpidia to call her this. Her head turned. 'Yes?'

'Athaulf is dead.'

Galla laughed. This was too much. It was a joke, it had to be. 'Dead?'

Elpidia came close, took her hand. 'He was murdered at the stables, by one of Sigeric's followers.'

Galla stared, slowly took in that Elpidia was serious. Her world spun. 'H-how? When?'

'He was attacked as he was about to mount up. Vadomar slew the assassin and tried to stop the bleeding, but he could not. Athaulf died soon after.'

'The surgeon . . .' said Galla.

'He did not arrive in time. According to Vadomar, it would have made no difference.'

Theodosius was gone. Athaulf too, thought Galla dully. She might as well be dead also. She had nothing to live for.

'There is more, dear heart.'

Galla almost laughed again. What could come after this? 'Explain.'

'It is uncertain who will be king. Vadomar was about to send for Athaulf's warriors so they might protect you, but a warband has come to the house.'

'Whose men are they?'

'Vadomar has gone to see. Sigeric's, he thinks.'

There was only one way to rule, thought Galla. To be ruthless when it mattered. She had thought Athaulf unwise to accept Sigeric into his ranks, but wanting to be Christian about it, she had not argued. She had been a fool. Kill your enemies when necessary, she thought, and repent later.

'What will you do?' asked Elpidia.

Galla sat at her low table and picked up her mirror. 'Deal with these interlopers outside my door the way a queen would.' She busied herself with make-up, disguising the lines and bags caused by grief and lack of sleep. 'Fetch my pearls.'

Not long after, dressed as if to attend the imperial court, Galla emerged from her room. Elpidia accompanied her. Vadomar was in the courtyard, speaking to the dozen or so warriors. Galla suppressed a sob at the sight of Athaulf's blanket-covered body, but gave no other overt sign of emotion.

'Nobilissima Femina.' Vadomar bowed. The warriors, copying, murmured respectful greetings. 'I am sorely grieved by your husband's murder. I did what I could, but—'

'He slew the assassin, your majesty,' interjected Reccared, who had served Athaulf for decades. 'He tried to stop the bleeding, but it was impossible.' He hung his head.

'You have my thanks,' said Galla, her eyes lingering on Vadomar, then moving to each warrior in turn. 'I know you would all have died rather than let harm come to Athaulf, but we have more important matters to deal with. Who is outside?'

Vadomar's face hardened. 'Sigeric, Nobilissima Femina, with two hundred warriors at his back. He claims to be the new king. He bids you surrender yourself into his custody.'

An animal roar went up. 'Never!' 'Let them try!' 'We will fight to the last man!'

Galla's heart swelled with pride; they meant it. Not just Vadomar and Reccared, but every one of them. Elpidia's fierce expression showed she would fight too. Darme also would, Galla knew, maybe even some of the house slaves. She considered how the attack on the house would go after the front door was smashed in, and her spirits, having risen, fell. Perhaps thirty in total, her followers were no match for Sigeric's warriors.

'Say the word, Nobilissima Femina.' Vadomar's voice was eager. 'I will go and tell Sigeric to shove his demand—' Embarrassed, he stopped.

'Where the sun doesn't shine?' Galla finished, laughing at Vadomar's shock. 'That will not be necessary.'

'What is your intention, Nobilissima Femina?'

The question hung in the air. Their fates hung in the balance.

Galla made a decision. 'I will accept Sigeric's demand . . .' she held up a hand, and the wave of protests died away, 'because I will not have your deaths on my conscience.'

'But Nobilissima Femina—' Vadomar began.

'This is my command!'

Not a warrior argued. Only Vadomar met her eyes, defiant, angry. 'Sigeric may well order you slain the instant he has you!'

'He will take me prisoner whether you fight or not, and your death – and the deaths of everyone here – would be in vain,' said Galla. 'I will *not* allow it.'

'And if Sigeric murders you, Nobilissima Femina?'

Vadomar had everyone's attention.

'I am far too valuable a hostage,' Galla declared, conveying a confidence she did not feel inside.

She was correct, though. Sigeric took her prisoner; she was treated well. There was much mention of how much grain and gold Honorius would pay for her release. Vadomar and Athaulf's bodyguards were permitted to keep their daggers. All other weapons were confiscated, to be returned, Sigeric said, at a later stage. More than fifty warriors remained on guard outside the house, and no one was allowed to leave without permission.

Galla held an immediate council of war with Vadomar and Reccared. Elpidia was present, standing unobtrusively behind her mistress.

'How much support does Sigeric have?' asked Galla.

'That remains to be seen, your majesty,' said Reccared. 'Some of the chieftains won't care that he murdered Athaulf, if it helps them, but I think the majority will disapprove. Athaulf was popular, and a good leader. Sigeric is, and always has been, a firebrand.'

'You think someone else may try to seize power?' asked Galla, hope sparking.

'Perhaps,' replied Reccared.

'Who? One of Alaric's sons? Wallia?'

'If I had to wager, your majesty, I would say Wallia. He is fierce, brave and well regarded by most.'

Vadomar nodded. So did Elpidia.

'He is no friend to Roma, but my husband liked him; trusted him too. We shall wait, and ask God to send Wallia a sign. In the meantime, there is a funeral to arrange.' Galla's voice was even, but her heart was breaking.

*

Sigeric was ruthless when it came to Athaulf's children with his first wife. She had fled with them to the house of a local bishop. She was left alive, but all six daughters were dragged onto the street and slain. Sigeric wasn't a complete fool, though, ordering a massive funeral for Athaulf. Galla, grateful at least that the Visigoths would have an opportunity to grieve for their slain king, sent Vadomar with a request for Athaulf to be interred with Theodosius in the mausoleum at Cucuphas' church. Sigeric agreed, which, after his murder of Athaulf's daughters, came as a pleasant surprise.

On the morning of the funeral, there was a hammering on the front door, so loud and continuous that it sent Felicula, ears down, under her bed. Galla, up for some time, had been praying for Athaulf and Theodosius. Unable to continue because of the racket, she went into the courtyard.

Loud voices carried from the atrium – demands, angry answers, more demands – and then the front door slammed shut.

Galla's mouth was dry. This was not what she needed today. It would soon be time to leave for the funeral; the carriage and horses were ready in the stables.

Vadomar, exiting the tablinum, saw her. He crossed the courtyard, his expression grim. 'Nobilissima Femina, Sigeric is outside. He wanted to enter, but I refused.'

'What does he want?'

'He orders you to come out and accompany him to Cucuphas' church, Nobilissima Femina.'

This was rude, but not impossible to deal with, thought Galla. 'The carriage will need to be fetched.'

'No, Nobilissima Femina. You are to walk there.' Vadomar's expression was thunderous.

'How did you reply?'

Now he looked miserable. 'I wanted to insult him, Nobilissima Femina, to name him a treacherous dog, but I bit my tongue and said I would tell you. I hope I did right.'

'You did.' Galla stood up straight. 'Tell him that if I am to be humiliated in this fashion, he can wait until I am ready.'

'And if he refuses, Nobilissima Femina?'

'Kill him and as many of his warriors as you can.'

A fierce grin, a bow, and Vadomar made himself scarce.

'I trust you would approve, husband,' Galla said quietly, raising her eyes to the heavens.

She made Sigeric wait for an hour. He had tried to make her move faster, his warriors repeatedly banging on the door and demanding entrance, but Vadomar, enjoying his role, responded each time that the queen was almost ready. Sigeric, perhaps realising a bloodbath would follow if he forced an entrance, had given in.

'He will be furious,' Elpidia again warned as Vadomar prepared to open the front door. She had been harping on about it.

'I am well aware. What else can he do to me?' Galla knew there was more, plenty more, but she was gambling on the presence of thousands of Visigoths, many of whom did not support Sigeric, saving her from further punishment.

Elpidia pursed her lips and said no more.

Vadomar, in full armour, dagger on his belt, glanced at Galla, who nodded. He slid back the bolts and heaved on the door.

Sigeric, astride a grey stallion, was prominent in the mob outside. As his warriors milled about, cursing and shouting, he lifted a hand. Silence fell. Sigeric, a podgy-faced individual with bulging eyes, gave Galla a baleful stare. 'You show yourself at last.' There was no 'your majesty'.

'Sigeric.' Galla sallied out with the confidence of a champion charioteer entering the Circus Maximus for the thousandth time. 'My maid and bodyguards will accompany me.' She did not wait for permission. Elpidia, with Vadomar beside her, came out, then Darme; half the warriors, their armour winking in the sun, followed two by two.

'It is twelve miles to the church. Can you walk that far?' Sigeric's tone was mocking.

'I would walk ten times the distance and more to attend my husband's funeral,' Galla replied.

Sigeric curled his lip. 'And your nurse? If her girth is anything to go by, she will not manage it.'

Galla shot a keep-your-mouth-shut look at a furious Elpidia, and said calmly, 'She is made of stern stuff, you will see.'

Resentful, Sigeric seemed about to say more, but the assembled Visigoths began chanting, 'Ath-aulf! Ath-aulf!' With a scowl, he indicated that the waiting wagon be drawn up by the front door. The warriors who had remained inside bore out Athaulf's magnificent, gilded wood coffin and laid it on the vehicle's bed.

I am with you, husband, Galla thought, as the wagon led off. I will be with you every step of the way. Taking a deep breath, she began to walk. She had not gone ten steps before the first shout.

'God be with you, your majesty!'

Sigeric scowled, but the speaker was in the depths of the crowd.

'God bless you, Galla Placidia!' Another voice.

And another. 'Sigeric is no king!'

Sigeric's face grew choleric, but the crowd, Visigoths all, was armed. Any attempt by his warriors to find the speakers would be futile, and would probably end in bloodshed. 'Keep moving!' he roared.

They continued walking, the wagon in front, then Galla and her followers, Sigeric and his retainers, and the throng of Visigoths who wished to attend their king's funeral.

'The king would be proud of you, Nobilissima Femina,' said Vadomar.

Galla threw him a grateful glance, and thought how lucky she was to have him, ever present, ever loyal, close by. She had Elpidia too, and Darme, Reccared and the other bodyguards, not to mention a large chunk of Athaulf's faction, who had sent secret messages pledging their allegiance.

She was not alone.

Stony-faced, determined to give Sigeric nothing, Galla walked to Cucuphas' church and saw Athaulf interred beside Theodosius. Elpidia, purple-faced and sweating, was there; she wept the tears Galla did not allow herself to. Sigeric, ruthless, did not provide a carriage back to Barcino. His victim Athaulf disposed of, his humiliation of Galla complete, he left her to walk back.

His plan went awry the moment he and his large group of allies and followers were out of sight. A local dignitary offered Galla his carriage; would not take no for an answer. Galla didn't care what anyone thought, and insisted Elpidia and a quite exhausted Darme join her. They were driven away with the crowd's prayers and cries of acclaim filling the air. Vadomar and the bodyguards marched behind, Sigeric's escort sullenly following.

Cloth blinds in the carriage's window openings offered privacy; this in turn allowed Galla's grief to surface. She wept most of the way back to Barcino, Darme, self-conscious, pretending to sleep, Elpidia rubbing her back, just as she had when Galla was upset as a small girl.

Reaching the town, she wiped away her tears, and alighted from the carriage a little red in the face, but composed. Entering the house, she told Vadomar that no one was to leave or to be admitted without her express permission.

'I have a good feeling,' she said. 'Sigeric is unpopular. His reign will not last.'

Less than a week later, Galla's prediction came true. Sigeric was murdered in a drunken brawl. That the warrior who took his life was sworn to Wallia was much commented on, but quietly. Sigeric would not be missed. An election was held the next day, Wallia the clear victor. A fierce warrior, he came to power with a mandate to continue the war with Roma, and to win for his people the homeland they had sought so long. Despite his animosity towards the Romans, he was respectful of Galla. Much as he wished to set her free, she was too valuable. Without her as a captive, he maintained, Honorius and Flavius Constantius would have little reason ever to accept a treaty.

A treaty seemed unlikely, however. As summer turned into autumn, Wallia resurrected the idea of crossing to Africa, whose fertile lands would feed his people. Heraclianus, long since defeated and killed, had been replaced, but the imperial forces there would be no match for tens of thousands of Visigothic warriors. So went Wallia's thinking, as he admitted to Galla during the long journey to the south of Hispania. Despair often threatened to overwhelm her at these times; still grieving the deaths of Theodosius and Athaulf, her position seemed even worse than it had been five years before.

She continued to pray several times daily, and at every opportunity stopped to worship in churches on their route. Eventually her devotion, or as Elpidia wryly opined, her refusal to stop until God answered, paid off. Brutal storms ended Wallia's hope of crossing to Africa that year. Staying put was an option, but the Visigoths' position was precarious, firstly thanks to the shortage of winter food, and secondly because their bitter enemies, the Alani, Suebi and Vandali, were not far away.

And so, to Galla's secret delight and in seeming answer to her prayers, Wallia ordered his people to retrace their steps towards Viennensis. The war with Roma would be resumed in the spring, he declared. With Flavius Constantius vanquished, and Galla Placidia as a bargaining chip, they would be granted not just grain by Honorius, but the lands occupied by Athaulf two years prior. His decision was a popular one.

His prediction that Flavius Constantius would be defeated proved naïve, however. Anticipating the arrival of Wallia's host, the Roman general led a lightning-quick raid through the mountains, catching the Visigoths unaware. Driven back into Hispania with heavy losses, forced to buy grain from the Vandali at extortionate prices, Wallia had the winter to consider his next move.

The Visigoth defeat gave Galla cause to rejoice. Few of Athaulf's faction, loyal to her, had been killed; in her mind, those who had were expendable. Wallia's position, now weaker than it had been, meant he would have to give serious consideration to hammering out a treaty with Flavius Constantius and Honorius. Before Athaulf's death, Galla would have been against this, wanting the Visigoths to forge their own strong future, but her predicament necessitated an about-face.

A formal agreement with Roma would ensure grain supplies from Africa, as well as land in Viennensis or Gallia. In return, it was probable the Visigoth warriors would be required to serve as foederati with the imperial army, and she, Galla Placidia, would be freed.

This was her great hope, and her constant request of God.

And when she was released, Flavius Constantius would try to make her his wife.

Heartbroken still over Athaulf's death, Galla would not agree.

CHAPTER XXXIV

Three months later . . .

Diocese of Viennensis, near the border with Hispania; Mensis Ianuarius, AD *416*

'What kind of name is Euplutius?' Vadomar asked, but quietly. He was outside Galla's large tent, on guard as usual, fur cloak keeping off the worst of the chill wind.

Dog chuckled. 'You could say the same of most Roman names. They probably say the same of ours – ever think of that?'

Vadomar scowled again. Shrugged. '"Dog" sounds strange too, I suppose.'

Grinning, Dog cupped a hand to his mouth and mimed his howl.

'Vadomar?' Galla's voice.

Unlacing the tent flap, Vadomar ducked inside. Golden light from large oil lamps bathed the spacious interior; carpets covered the floor. Waves of heat radiated from an iron brazier in the room's centre. A screen partially blocked sight of Galla's bed. She herself was deep in conversation with Elpidia, a common sight. For the thousandth time, Vadomar gave thanks for the nurse, whose companionship, advice and loyalty had helped her weather the storms of not just the last few years, but her whole life.

'Nobilissima Femina?'

Galla straightened. 'Euplutius will be talking to Wallia by this point.'

'I would say so, Nobilissima Femina.' Upon his arrival in the encampment not long before, the Roman emissary had been taken straight to Wallia's tent. Wulfila, who happened to be passing by, had heard his name and rank, and had come to Vadomar, who in turn had reported to Galla.

'Euplutius' visit means one thing. Flavius Constantius and my brother are open to talks.' Galla's face was alive with hope.

'This would be my thought also, Nobilissima Femina,' said Vadomar, who had been optimistic that this time something might come of the negotiations.

'Be wary,' said Elpidia. 'Many's the slip twixt cup and lip.'

She didn't have to say that Galla had been with the Visigoth host for more than five years. She didn't have to say that her situation now was no different to the day Alaric had first taken her prisoner.

Galla took no notice. 'God has answered my prayers!' To Vadomar, she said, 'Go to Wallia's tent. Bring wine, ham, anything you can think of that will cause his sentries to turn a blind eye if you loiter about. If you can eavesdrop, so much the better; if not, any information you can glean will be useful.'

'I will do what I can, Nobilissima Femina.'

Dog got seriously grumpy when Vadomar announced he was taking the three wineskins stashed away at the bottom of his kit. 'Do you know how much I paid for them?' he demanded.

'Aye, you tell us every time you bring out the stuff,' Vadomar replied. 'It's for Galla, remember? She will recompense you too, so shut your mouth.'

When told what Vadomar was up to, Wulfila took his place outside Galla's tent without complaint. Vadomar made his way along the muddy track leading to Wallia's tent. The camp's location was decent, close enough to the sea to be able to catch fish, but protected from the onshore winds by an area of woodland. There was a deep ditch around the large, irregular rectangle, its spoil forming an earthen rampart atop which a timber fence had been built. It was amusing, thought Vadomar, how the Visigoths had adopted something so Roman.

He soon came upon Euplutius' escort, fifty Alani cavalrymen, stamping their feet and huffing into their hands as they waited. No fires had been built for them; it didn't appear any wine or food had been offered either. Vadomar, who felt antipathy towards them himself, wasn't surprised. These were men who had helped to drive the Visigoths from Viennensis. None gave him a second glance, just another warrior in what they saw as an enemy encampment.

Wallia's sentries were more alert. The one in charge, an irritable character with a limp and an attitude, spied Vadomar fifteen paces out. 'If it isn't Galla Placidia's lapdog, and bearing gifts too.' A wink at his nearest companions. 'He wants something, lads.'

Vadomar held up the skins. 'Good stuff, this. From southern Italia, I am informed.'

'A solidus says he wants to hear what Eu-snootius has to say,' said the lead sentry. 'Any takers?'

'We all know why he's here,' said a short warrior. 'And we all want his wine. Just take it and let him eavesdrop.'

The lead sentry hesitated.

'I thought he was called Euplutius,' said Vadomar, feigning ignorance in order to flatter.

'He is, but his head is up his arse. Sneering at us, he was, from the first moment he arrived. Could have sworn I heard him say "fur-wearing savages" under his breath. Nose-in-the-air prick.' A leer. 'It seemed natural to call him Eu-snootius.'

The sentry's disgust, not to mention his description, was enough to ensure Vadomar's laugh was genuine. 'An apt name.' He proffered one of the wineskins. 'Have a drink.'

'Don't mind if I do.' The sentry took a long pull. 'That's damn good.' He handed it to the next man. By the time the skin came back, it was sagging and empty. Vadomar smiled – he reckoned this was worth the gamble – and handed over the second.

'You sure? I ain't said you can listen in yet.'

'I am glad to share it: you seem like good men.' Vadomar held up the third skin. 'This is the best vintage. Campanian, from the slopes of Vesuvius itself.'

Incredulously, 'Is it the wine they call the "tears of Christ"?'

'The same.'

'Give it over and you can stay as long as you like, my friend.' The sentry's hand was greedily outstretched.

'Enjoy it,' said Vadomar, moving closer to the tent leather, pricking his ears.

'The nub of the issue, it seems to me, is the amount of grain you require.' There was the slightest suggestion of condescension in the high, nasal voice.

This must be Euplutius, Vadomar decided.

A heartbeat later, a second voice, an interpreter, said in Visigoth, 'He thinks we want too much grain, lord.'

'He has the look of someone who likes little boys,' said Wallia. 'What do you think?'

A snort, which might have been the interpreter holding back a laugh, then Euplutius asked, 'What did the king say?'

Smooth as olive oil, the interpreter replied, 'He asked if you know how many mouths he has to feed.'

'Well done,' said Wallia. 'He's shaking his head. Tell him ninety thousand. And he wants us to go after the Vandali, Suebi and Alani. We can't campaign for months with no supplies.'

'Ninety thousand, men, women and children,' said the interpreter. 'All of whom need to be fed while the Visigoths hunt down Roma's enemies in Hispania.'

It sounded as if Wallia had already agreed to his warriors becoming foederati, Vadomar thought.

'I am to take it my offer of three hundred thousand measures of grain is insufficient,' said Euplutius. 'How much did your king have in mind?'

The interpreter did his work. Wallia's response was instant. 'Double that quantity.'

'King Wallia would require six hundred thousand measures of grain.'

A sharp intake of breath. 'This, as well as lands in Viennensis after the barbarians in Hispania have been dealt with?'

Again the interpreter translated. Wallia made immediate reply. One word.

'Yes.'

Vadomar pictured the two Visigoths and the Roman staring at each other in a struggle of wills.

Euplutius broke the silence. 'As you know, I have imperial authority to formulate the terms of a treaty. Give the nobilissima femina Galla Placidia into my custody before I leave for Arelate, and I can accept your conditions.'

Vadomar's heart skipped a beat. Here it was, after so long, Galla's first real chance of freedom.

'Is he willing to swear an oath, with Almighty God as his witness, that Honorius will honour the treaty?' demanded Wallia.

The interpreter relayed the question in Latin.

'I am.' Euplutius' reply was firm. 'May He strike me down if I lie.'

The interpreter explained.

'Let us shake hands, like men,' said Wallia.

The translation followed. There was movement within.

Vadomar did not need to hear more. Thanking the sentries, he took to his heels. Galla's world was about to change for the better. Even as he rejoiced, he remembered Flavius Constantius' desire to take her as his wife. It was not just the Visigoths, he thought bitterly; among her own people she was a game piece, to be moved to and fro across the board by those who had power over her. He would make no mention of Flavius Constantius, though. Let her enjoy the prospect of freedom, and a return to Italia and her own people.

After more than five years, she deserved it.

She wept when he told her, burst into tears like a little girl. Elpidia took her in her arms, hugged her, said she was right, God had answered her prayers.

'You're sure about what was said?' Galla's watery eyes locked on Vadomar's.

'Yes, Nobilissima Femina.'

A sob, more tears.

Vadomar didn't know where to put himself, and when Elpidia gave him a tiny nod, he gratefully retreated to where Dog and Wulfila stood outside.

'Is she taken unwell?' asked Wulfila.

'No. I think it's a combination of joy and relief.'

'Must have been strange for her, living with us barbarians for so long. The boot will soon be on the other foot,' said Dog.

Wulfila cocked his head. 'Eh?'

'We' – Dog indicated himself, Wulfila, Vadomar – 'shall be living among the Romans. The imperial court at Ravenna, I expect. Be a sight different to the army camps we're used to. The place will be full of Eu-snootiuses.'

'Aye, well, they will keep their thoughts to themselves around me,' said Wulfila, tugging on his sword hilt.

'We will have respect,' said Vadomar. 'After all, we shall be the nobilissima femina's bodyguard.'

They grinned at one another.

Events moved fast. Galla was informed about the treaty later in the day by Wallia himself. Euplutius, he reported, was ready to depart the following morning. Already prepared by Vadomar's news, Galla kept her tears in check, solemnly thanking the king for his 'hospitality'. She would be taking the treasures given her by Athaulf, she told him. Wallia offered no protest, or to her assertion that a thousand warriors from her dead husband's faction wished to stay with her as bodyguards. For all his warlike manner, he was a practical statesman.

Euplutius came to introduce himself to her not long after, and Vadomar listened in to the emissary's smug explanation that he had succeeded in persuading Wallia to free her. Galla offered grave thanks, and assured him her brother would hear of his efforts.

'We have Flavius Constantius to thank also, Nobilissima Femina,' said Euplutius. 'He has been unrelenting in his efforts to secure your release.'

'Even so. I will convey my gratitude to Flavius Constantius in Arelate.'

'He will be overjoyed to see you returned to safety, Nobilissima Femina.'

A few more pleasantries, an explanation of how long the journey would take, and Euplutius took his leave. He was still in sight when Galla spoke again, Vadomar able to hear.

'Overjoyed?' she cried. 'Flavius Constantius is not related to me. We have never met. He is overjoyed because he wants me as his wife!'

'Maybe he does, maybe he doesn't,' said Elpidia.

'Don't you remember his letter? What a plebeian he is.'

'Flavius Constantius' desire to marry you and Honorius agreeing to it are two different things. Worrying about it doesn't do you any good either. Just rejoice in your freedom for now. You are returning to Italia!'

A sigh. 'You are right. I must be thankful.'

It was good advice, thought Vadomar. It applied to him also. He was alive and healthy. He had Dog and Wulfila and the twins, and many other good comrades. He served Galla Placidia, whom he loved. There was no possibility of anything else between them, he had reconciled himself to that. It was enough to be her bodyguard, to dedicate his life to her. Lastly, he remembered Keturah. For her, he felt only obligation. Not love. Not a desire for family, or to spend the rest of their lives together.

'I cannot live like that.'

'What did you say?' asked Dog.

Startled, for he had spoken aloud without realising, Vadomar said, 'Nothing.'

Dog grunted.

He would speak to her that very night, Vadomar decided.

Upon his return, he found Keturah wrapped in her blankets, face pale, features drawn. She complained of pains in her belly. It was not something she'd eaten, she didn't think, because there was no diarrhoea, and she did not feel sick. It was probably her time-of-the-month cramps, she said, worse than usual. A night's sleep and she would be fine. Agreeing, Vadomar hoped it was so, or he faced the quandary of either telling her he no longer wished to be with her before abandoning her, ill, or taking her with him and doing the same in Arelate.

She was worse the next morning. A sheen of sweat covered her face. 'I am sorry. I know we have to leave today,' she whispered. 'I'll be fine in one of the wagons.'

'No,' said Vadomar.

'What do you mean?'

'Your best chance of recovery is to stay here.'

'Galla Placidia is leaving this morning. You have to be with her.' A pause. 'I do not matter.'

'Of course you do. Galla will not stop me from taking care of you, and' – Vadomar prevented himself, just, from saying 'I' – 'we can follow on later.'

A weak smile. 'You are good to me.'

Guilt flayed Vadomar, but he caressed her hand and went to fetch the lekeis. That done, he spoke to Galla. She gave her permission, as he'd known she would, and assured him there was no hurry. She had plenty of good men to protect her. Even if she had left for Italia when he reached Arelate, she said, it did not matter. 'I know you will find me. I can rely on you, always,' she said, making Vadomar's heart twinge. He said farewell to Wulfila, Dog and the twins, and refused to let them stay behind. He and Keturah would be on the road within a day or two, he declared, catching up before Arelate.

He fetched the lekeis next, who examined Keturah, probed her abdomen, asked if she could be with child. She said no, her bleed was due any day. The lekeis tutted, and pressed here and there on her belly again. When his fingers were an inch above the right hip-bone, Keturah groaned with pain. The lekeis nodded, as if it made sense, and, rummaging in his bag, gave Vadomar a foul-smelling brew for her to take.

'It will clean out her guts.'

'What is wrong with her?'

'A blockage, maybe. Sometimes the intestines can twist on themselves.'

'Will this work?' Vadomar held up the flask just given to him.

Quietly, 'Maybe. Maybe not.'

'And if it doesn't?'

An expressive up-down of the lekeis' shoulders. 'Pray to whichever god you worship.'

Keturah vomited up the medicine a short time after drinking it. The second draught was no better. Curled up knees to chest, the only position that afforded respite, she drifted in and out of sleep through the morning. Vadomar coaxed her to drink some water, which she held down, but she refused to take more of the medicine.

By late afternoon, she said the pain had lessened. Soon after, it had returned throughout her whole abdomen. It was severe, Keturah groaning and weeping. When the lekeis visited a second time, Vadomar insisted she had poppy juice, which he knew Roman army surgeons used. This seemed to ease her discomfort, and she fell into a deep slumber.

The second morning dawned bright and cold, Vadomar's breath clouding before him in the tent. He had lain beside Keturah all night, worried, regularly placing a dampened finger under her nostrils to see if she was breathing. As the sun rose, the tent's interior brightened. A good night's sleep would have helped, he decided. If she could take drink and maybe food today, the worst of her illness might be over. He sat up, looked down at her.

Her cheeks were red and flushed, skin hot to the touch.

'Keturah.' He gripped her shoulder.

Her eyeballs moved under her closed lids. She did not wake.

Vadomar felt the inside of her wrist with two fingers. It was hard to find, but there was a pulse. He didn't know what was normal for her, but the thready, rapid beat was not a good sign. Laying a dampened cloth on her forehead, telling himself she would soon turn a corner, he went for the lekeis again.

Good news was not forthcoming. The lekeis felt her brow. Checked her pulse and pulled down a lower eyelid. The last saw his lips tighten. 'Mark the colour.'

Vadomar peered. 'It's a darker red than normal.' He had seen it in men with battle injuries.

'She has blood poisoning,' said the lekeis.

Vadomar's heart sank. This had also been his thought. 'She won't last long then.'

A sad shake of the head.

He gave the lekeis two silver coins, and with Keturah still unconscious, squatted down on his haunches by the fire he had lit outside the tent and prayed for her. Even as he did, guilt nagged, because the urgency he'd always had when praying for Galla was absent. He cursed himself, and tried harder. Longer. In the end, darkness fallen, a chill creeping into his bones despite the fire, he stopped. The gods were fickle; in all likelihood, they were laughing at him.

Keturah did not wake again, and died during the night.

Waking beside her corpse, Vadomar shed genuine tears of grief. He wouldn't have admitted it to a soul, but there was liberation mixed with his sorrow. Ending his relationship with her would have broken her heart, and he no longer had to do that. Her suffering over, she was gone to a better place, the place Christians called heaven.

Nonetheless, he felt guilty the whole way to Arelate.

Some hours after being reunited with Dog, Wulfila and the twins, Vadomar's remorse had been replaced with excitement. He was back with his comrades, and Galla was nearby, safe and well. According to Dog, who had had it from Elpidia, her first meeting with Flavius Constantius had gone off without major upset. There had been no mention of marriage, for now at least. Their conversation had been about Honorius, and Ravenna, and the incredible welcome she would receive in the imperial court.

It was a good start, Vadomar decided.

CHAPTER XXXV

Arelate, Diocese of Viennensis; Mensis Ianuarius, AD *416*

Galla had been in the town for several days, and was still unused to no longer being a captive. In part, she said to an amused Elpidia, it was because her bodyguards remained the same. It helped that Arelate felt familiar too, but in reality, her release would not truly sink in until Italia, until Roma. She longed to return to the city she had called home, but suspected that Honorius – who would soon know, thanks to messengers, of her freedom – would order her to the imperial court at Ravenna.

The thought of being reunited with her half-brother did not fill her with joy. Flavius Constantius' interest in her meant the emperor would perhaps keep his lecherous thoughts to himself, but there was no guarantee. Again she grappled with the possibilities that might unfold in Ravenna.

The most obvious, and easiest, was to wed Flavius Constantius. The idea made Galla's skin crawl. There were so many reasons why. Her second option was to do the opposite. Under Roman law, women could not be forced into marriage. She would then be left single, and by implication, available. Honorius' unhealthy interest might be aroused to new heights by her unmarried state, but with Elpidia's help, she hoped her half-brother could be kept at bay. And, she thought, there had to be suitable noblemen at the imperial court.

She wondered too about becoming a nun. There was significant appeal to a chaste, religious life. Dedicated to God, hers would be a peaceful and serene existence, free from the constant attention of men. Barbarian invasions would not concern her. The machinations of the imperial court would be irrelevant, and the identity of the next emperor. She was fooling herself, she thought. She cared deeply about who came after Honorius. Long had she dreamed about a child of hers succeeding her half-brother, and if she entered a nunnery, it would never happen. It was possible to love and revere God, and also to want power and influence.

She was left with two choices: to marry Flavius Constantius, or to refuse to do so in the hope and expectation of finding a suitable husband at Ravenna. She said as much to Elpidia, who chuckled.

'What?' demanded Galla.

'You don't just want any husband. You want one with suitable pedigree. One who might be appointed augustus someday.' Elpidia gave her a questioning look.

Galla felt a little self-conscious hearing her innermost desire spoken out loud, but there was no denying Elpidia's words. 'Yes, that is true.'

'How many suitable men might there be in Ravenna? From what I've heard, the majority at court are kiss-arses, catamites and sycophants.'

Galla laughed. Elpidia wasn't wrong. It was a fantasy to think she would find a strong-charactered nobleman among her half-brother's hangers-on.

Elpidia was in full flow. 'Those who fawn over Honorius, and help him feed his chickens, aren't generals or military leaders. Yet those are the type of men the empire needs. Hispania and Viennensis have been pacified for now, and Africa, but things could change in the morning. The empire no longer controls Britannia either, and Aquitania remains in the fold thanks only to Wallia and the Visigoths. The situation is ever precarious.'

'You don't miss much,' said Galla, shaking her head. 'What a politician you would make.'

Elpidia hmphed. 'Flavius Constantius, well . . .'

Galla's reasons to reject the idea bubbled up. 'I have already been married. The Church would take a dim view if I were to do so again.'

'There are ways and means around that. A suitably sized donation, for example.'

'I have been a widow for less than six months.'

'You would not have to marry Flavius Constantius straight away.'

'I barely know him!'

'True.'

'Until Honorius saw fit to make him a patrician recently, he was nothing but a commoner.'

'So I have been told.'

'Which means he only wants my hand to help him climb the social ladder.'

'Quite likely.'

'He is twice my age!'

'At least.'

'He's ugly.'

'I agree.'

'His army forced Athaulf out of Viennensis.'

'It did.'

'Do you not remember how many people died as a result?'

'I do.'

'But for Flavius Constantius, Athaulf and I could have seized power from Honorius.'

'Indeed.'

'There must be another general.' Galla thought. 'Bonifatius?' This was an officer with old loyalties to her who had fought under Constantius' command.

'He is in Africa. If he left, another Heraclianus might seize control.'

Elpidia was right, thought Galla, and if the grain supply to Italia was compromised again, the empire would be greatly weakened. She tried another tack. 'I don't love Flavius Constantius.'

'That is no argument. Many wives and husbands do not love one another, but their marriages still function.' Softly, Elpidia said, 'You and Athaulf were fortunate.'

Galla fought back tears, her mind filled with images of her dead husband and Theodosius, her baby son. 'I do not want to marry Flavius Constantius,' she whispered.

'He is the pre-eminent general in Honorius' army. He secured your freedom, in the process turning the Visigoths from enemies to allies. Flavius Constantius is the man of the hour. Some might say he can do no wrong, that he is the most powerful man in the empire after Honorius. Marrying him makes sense.'

'No,' said Galla, feeling as if the ground were giving way beneath her.

'Imagine. Your firstborn son would probably become heir to the throne. It is easy to see how Honorius would then make Flavius Constantius an augustus.'

Galla started. Blinded by her disdain, she hadn't seen it. Only an augustus could become emperor. Only an augusta could become an empress. The ranks were equivalent to the emperor's. Elpidia was correct: there were few, if any, courtiers who would impress Honorius enough to be elevated so.

'And if he was appointed an augustus, it is probable Honorius would make me an augusta.'

Elpidia's smile was broad. 'Indeed.'

The image of Athaulf, exhausted, leading the Visigoths away from Viennensis and into Hispania entered Galla's mind. Flavius Constantius had been the architect of that disaster, just as he had prevented Athaulf from taking the throne from Honorius. Bitterness welled up inside her. The thought of marrying him, sharing a bed with him, coupling with him, was repugnant.

Elpidia opened her mouth.

'No,' said Galla, her chin firming. 'I will not do it.'

The two women stared at each other. They were not slave and owner. They were nurse and the woman she had raised from infancy. They were almost-mother and almost-daughter.

'Very well,' replied Elpidia, but her face said she thought Galla was making a mistake.

It was a rare occasion when Galla considered snapping, telling Elpidia to mind her mouth. She was a slave who obeyed her owner's command. She bit back those words now, because once uttered, they could never be taken back.

And so it was left.

Severe weather kept Galla and the smug Euplutius in Arelate for a number of months. At last, though, it was time to leave. Flavius Constantius, who had courteously avoided mention of marriage again, bade her farewell and said they would see each other again at the imperial court. Galla thanked him for his services and, practised at lying, said she looked forward to their next meeting. Little did he, Euplutius or Honorius know, but she intended to go back to Roma. Honorius was there at present, celebrating a triumph, but would soon be gone.

Some days into the journey, at a crucial crossroads, it became clear they were not travelling to Ravenna. Euplutius, smugness absent, nonplussed, could do nothing. His escort comprised a dozen men; Galla's warriors numbered a thousand. He had to be satisfied with sending a hastily penned letter to Honorius. Galla's return to Roma was thus bittersweet. Her half-brother's response would be swift, and ignoring him would only work for a time. To her joy, Fritigern was still alive, and living in her house, now full of cobwebs and dust. Aided by Darme and Elpidia, she threw herself into the task of restoring it to its former glory. Vadomar and a score of Visigoths provided labour and protection.

There was time to reconnect with her old friends, who had returned to Roma years prior. To watch chariot racing at the Circus Maximus. To worship in St Peter's basilica. Two blissful weeks passed before a letter arrived from Ravenna. Honorius bade his sister a loving welcome back to Italia, and directed she present herself at the imperial court. Euplutius, who must have received a strongly worded missive with the same instructions, came that day to argue his case. Against Elpidia's advice, in love with the fantasy she was living, Galla sent him away empty-handed. She did not reply to Honorius' letter either. Another came a month later. She ignored it, and the third.

A detachment of a hundred domestici arrived with the fourth letter, the wording of which was a clear command for Galla to travel to Ravenna without delay. In response to Honorius' show of force, Vadomar summoned the entire Visigoth contingent. A thousand warriors swarmed in from the surrounding streets, boxing in the domestici. Weapons were drawn, insults traded, before Galla herself came to calm the situation. Suddenly aware that matters could not continue in the same vein, she ordered Vadomar to remove his warriors. Sullen-faced, he obeyed, but came to speak with her the instant it was done.

'We are sworn to protect you, Nobilissima Femina! We—'

Galla's upraised hand silenced him. 'I will not have bloodshed between my men and Honorius'.'

'He has no right to force you to Ravenna, Nobilissima Femina!'

'He does,' Galla replied calmly. 'He is the emperor.'

And there it was, she thought, noting Elpidia's look of approval. She would have been happy to see Athaulf seize power, but that dream had died with her husband. While Honorius' reign continued, to remain in Roma meant giving up her chances of gaining real power, of marriage, of bearing a son who could become emperor. She was not prepared to do that. It was her lifelong ambition to sit on the throne, or to stand behind it. If there was *any* possibility of turning those desires into reality, she *had* to go to Ravenna.

There was more. There always was.

In the absence of a suitable alternative, marrying Flavius Constantius was her best option. Bear him a son, and true power would come within her grasp for the first time. She took a deep breath. The price was worth paying, she decided.

Vadomar was still waiting expectantly. His loyalty touched her heart. 'You will stay with me?'

'Until my dying day, Nobilissima Femina.'

'I am grateful.' Her eyes said more, so much more that could not be spoken aloud.

Vadomar seemed to understand. He saluted, and withdrew.

'Ravenna awaits,' said Elpidia.

Her nurse also understood the decision she had made, thought Galla, and supported it. The knowledge was comforting.

*

Leaving the great pine forest that had flanked the road for miles, Galla looked out of the carriage. A warm sea breeze moved her hair; it smelled clean and salty. Her heart beat faster. In the distance was the wall encircling Ravenna and its port of Classe to the south. Sunlight bounced off the sea beyond, a sheet of beaten bronze. The location was beautiful. Tranquil.

Yes, I could live here, she thought.

She entered the city through the Porta Aurea. On the other side of a canal, she stopped to give thanks at the still-in-construction cathedral. She was much affected by the stunning mosaic decorating the semicircular arch over the main altar. Prayers said, thanks given, she clambered back into the carriage with Elpidia. Vadomar signalled to the driver, and they rumbled on.

Assigned luxurious quarters in Honorius' palace, Galla bathed and prepared herself for the inevitable meeting with her half-brother. Her concerns, which she had put to the back of her mind, returned in force.

'What shall I do if he tries to . . .' She could not speak the repugnant words.

'He will not.' Bustling around the room, putting away clothes, Elpidia was the personification of calm. 'You will ensure never to be alone with him. Honorius may be depraved, but he is not an Elagabalus.' This was an emperor whose reputation of sexual depravity continued to be talked about two centuries later. He had had four wives, liked to be referred to as a lady, and had reputedly prostituted himself in Roma's taverns.

Elpidia was right, Galla decided. All would be well.

Early that evening, Vadomar and six warriors accompanied her and Elpidia to the palace's grand reception hall. At its double doors stood a dozen grandly turned-out candidati. They bowed to Galla, and one respectfully pointed out that her guards would have to remain outside. The demand wasn't unexpected, but a tremor passed down Galla's spine at the idea of entering the heart of Honorius' domain without protection. She would not back out, however. Not now. With a glance at Elpidia for reassurance, she told Vadomar to wait until her return. Unhappy, he made no protest.

The doors opened. A mincing major domus came out and bowed, then, turning back to face the direction whence he'd come, announced Galla's name in a loud, affected voice. She did not hesitate. Resolve steeled, she walked forward with measured pace, alone. Conscious of courtiers watching from both sides, she kept her gaze fixed on the seated figure at the end of the long, rectangular room.

Silence reigned supreme; she could have heard a needle drop.

Honorius had aged. He was still handsome despite his jowl, and the paunch bulging under his embroidered and bejewelled purple robes. There were new lines on his face, and flecks of grey in his wavy hair. Galla felt a tinge of sympathy. This was not a happy man, a contented emperor. It was no wonder. Childless, two wives buried, unable to trust those around him, his hold on power always uncertain, with enemies and usurpers forever threatening to overthrow him, he had been under threat his whole adult life.

She was ten paces from the emperor when he spoke.

'Sister.'

'Imperator.' She bowed.

'Welcome, Galla.' He indicated an ornate seat on the dais.

The atmosphere lightened as she obeyed. There were many sidelong glances in their direction, but the courtiers began talking among each other in quiet voices.

A genuine smile creased Honorius' mouth. 'It has been too long. How many years?'

'Nine, I think.'

A sigh. 'And you a captive of the Goths for much of that time.'

'I was,' said Galla, thinking: and you did nothing about it. But for Flavius Constantius, Wallia might still have me.

'It must have been a terrible experience. My heart is gladdened to see you back in the bosom of your people.'

Honeyed words, thought Galla, doubting they were genuine. She continued to play the game, though. 'I am also happy to have returned.'

A moue. 'Yet it took four letters and a detachment of soldiers to see you come to Ravenna.' His eyes were hard now.

'I am sorry.' She filled her words with remorse.

'So you should be! Have you an explanation for me?'

Ravenna had never been her home, Galla explained, voice soft, eyes downcast. She had never lived at the new imperial court. The old family house was in Roma. The Circus Maximus was there. She had thought of Honorius often, had intended to travel to Ravenna when the time was right. She hoped the last, an outright lie, was woven into the other truths well enough not to be exposed.

When she was finished, Honorius regarded her in silence, chin cupped in one hand.

Galla met his gaze calmly, but her heart was pounding.

'I do not believe you, sister. Actions speak louder than words. I doubt you would be here but for my last letter. But for my domestici.'

A silence fell between them. Stretched.

Galla's mouth had gone dry. Maybe she had misjudged her half-brother. Maybe she was to be stripped of her rank, perhaps even exiled. She began to pray silently. When she looked up a couple of moments later, Honorius' mouth had softened. Galla gave him a shaky smile.

'I am willing to forgive and forget.'

'You are most compassionate, Imperator.' Galla bent her neck, part real, part feigned gratitude. She could accept Ravenna as her gilded prison, because it was here that her marriage could be best engineered.

Here she could bear a son who would become emperor.

Here she could become an imperatrix.

CHAPTER XXXVI

Some months later . . .

Ravenna; last day of Mensis December, AD *416*

On guard outside Galla's quarters, Vadomar was disgruntled. He didn't like Flavius Constantius. The man was a decent general, it was true, but he was also an unattractive boor, a jumped-up commoner, and twice Galla Placidia's age.

'Still sulking?' asked Dog.

'I'm not sulking.'

'Looks like it from here.'

Vadomar stared at the wall opposite and made no reply.

'She could never have been yours.'

Vadomar was startled. 'Who?'

Dog jerked his head at the door between them. 'Her.'

'Elpidia is far too old for me.'

'Funny! You know who I mean.'

Vadomar thought about denying it, and realised that a close comrade like Dog would have had countless opportunities to notice his demeanour around Galla. 'Is it obvious?'

'To those who know you.'

'Wulfila and the twins?'

A nod.

'And the rest?'

A shrug. 'If they do, it won't have come from us.'

It was a small consolation, Vadomar decided. He rarely did duty with anyone else.

'Anyway, better get used to her marrying Flavius Constantius. Honorius is hell-bent it should happen.'

'Galla Placidia does not want to.' More than once he had overheard her saying exactly this to Elpidia.

'Think she can say no to the emperor for ever?'

'She can do what she wants,' Vadomar retorted. 'And we Visigoths will help her to do so!'

'I have ten solidi that say you're wrong.'

Vadomar wasn't going to accept the bet; he would lose.

After a moment, Dog continued, 'Once they are married, if you're seen giving Flavius Constantius shitty looks . . .'

The advice was sound, Vadomar thought, even if he did not like it. 'I hear you.'

'She wants to be empress, and this is the way to do it.'

'I cannot argue with that either.' Vadomar had long since recognised the unstoppable progress of Flavius Constantius' rise. Architect of the empire's treaty with Wallia and the Visigoths, most senior army commander, and recently named to serve as consul alongside Honorius in the coming year, he was unable to put a foot wrong. The ultimate prize, it seemed, was to be Galla's hand. Vadomar had known this might come to pass in the end, but it was hard to accept, and Dog had seen it. His friend was trying to help.

The door eased open, and they faced forward. It looked bad to be talking if Galla Placidia came out.

Elpidia emerged.

Vadomar gave her a friendly nod.

'The mistress wishes to see you.'

Vadomar affected not to notice Dog's wink, delivered over Elpidia's shoulder. He pushed on the door and, letting the old nurse go first, closed it behind him.

Galla was waiting. In a dark blue dress, pearls around her throat, she was, in Vadomar's mind, the vision of beauty. He bowed. 'I am here, Nobilissima Femina.'

'Approach.'

He halted six steps from her. Bowed again.

'Vadomar.'

He met her gaze. 'Yes, Nobilissima Femina?'

'The emperor wishes me to marry Flavius Constantius. You will be aware of this.'

'I . . . Yes, Nobilissima Femina.'

'Flavius Constantius is in agreement. I, on the other hand, have objected to my half-brother's proposal at every juncture.' A glance at Elpidia. 'This you probably know as well.'

'Yes, Nobilissima Femina.'

'My opinion has changed. I will marry him.'

'I understand, Nobilissima Femina,' said Vadomar, even though he did not.

'Tomorrow, the first of Ianuarius, my half-brother intends to give me formally to Flavius Constantius.' A pause, then, 'I will argue. I will protest in vigorous fashion.'

Consternation filled him. 'I do not understand, Nobilissima Femina.'

'After this long, I will not accept the betrothal meekly!'

Vadomar was even more confused.

'You and your comrades must not react when I do – even if I shout.'

'Very well, Nobilissima Femina.'

'Because I will give in after a time.' Galla smiled. 'My objections will be a ploy, nothing more.'

Comprehension blossomed. She didn't want her bodyguards mistakenly drawing weapons in her defence. 'As you wish, Nobilissima Femina.' He bowed. 'I am your servant.'

'You are far more.' A long, meaningful look.

Vadomar grinned. 'Nobilissima Femina.'

'You may go.'

He saluted and walked out, feeling as if he were ten feet tall.

Vadomar had not long left the room when Galla heard the heavy tramp of feet outside. It was mid afternoon; she knew who was approaching her quarters. 'Do I look presentable?' she asked.

Elpidia tucked a few stray hairs behind one of her mistress' ears, stood back with an appraising expression. 'You look like an augusta,' she said.

'Shh,' said Galla, but she was smiling.

Vadomar spoke a challenge, which was answered. He knocked and entered. 'The magister militum is here, Nobilissima Femina. He asks to visit you.'

'Send him in,' said Galla, making a minute adjustment to her neckline.

Flavius Constantius entered without his bodyguards. Dressed in a magnificent tunic with embroidered roundels at the shoulder and bottom edge, he bowed deeper than was necessary. 'Nobilissima Femina.'

'Call me Galla, please,' she said, baiting the hook.

He was pleased. 'Galla. Such a beautiful name.'

She inclined her head, and gestured to Elpidia, who poured wine.

Polite conversation followed, she enquiring how the situation was in Viennensis and Aquitania, and if his soldiers' morale was high after the summer's campaign. In turn, he asked if she enjoyed life at the imperial court, and how the chariot racing at Ravenna compared to Roma. The to-and-fro petered out soon enough, both parties aware that there was more to his visit than small talk.

Elpidia served again. Galla had drunk little, but Flavius Constantius' glass was empty. He supped deep, smacking his lips in appreciation. 'A fine wine.'

'I have my major domus to thank,' said Galla.

He raised his glass. 'To your major domus.'

She mimicked his gesture.

Silence fell.

Galla did not break it. Let him be the one to speak first, she thought.

Flavius Constantius coughed. 'Pleasant though this is, Galla, I did not come to praise your wine.'

'I see,' said Galla. 'Why *are* you here?'

A chuckle. 'Do not play games.'

'You wish to marry me.'

'I do.' A bold, covetous stare.

'No.'

He stared, not quite believing. 'No?'

'You heard.'

'Your half-brother the emperor wishes you to.'

'He cannot force me.'

'You would disobey Imperator Honorius?' cried Flavius Constantius. Red spots had appeared in his cheeks.

Be careful, thought Galla. Do not enrage him. 'Under Roman law, women cannot be made to marry against their will.'

'You did not answer my question!'

'Would you address me in so discourteous a manner if you were my husband?' Galla threw back. Women were traditionally subservient to men within a marriage, but her social position far outranked his.

An embarrassed clearing of the throat. 'Forgive me, Galla. I grew overexcited. I dearly wish for us to be husband and wife, you see.'

'It is only a year since I was widowed.'

'Tragic circumstances,' said Flavius Constantius. His humility was eye-blink brief. 'Life can be short for everyone. You are still young enough to have children. Why give up that chance?'

He had hit the nail on the head. Galla demurred, however, saying she continued to mourn Athaulf and Theodosius. The unbidden tears in her eyes were heaven-sent. She breathed into her grief, and more flowed. 'I am sorry,' she murmured.

Like most men, Flavius Constantius was disarmed by a crying woman. Bowing, apologising for taking up her time, he beat an undignified retreat.

Galla waited until the door shut behind him before smiling at Elpidia.

The next day, the beginning of the new year, dawned grey and overcast. Honorius had summoned everyone to the reception hall for midday. No reason was given. Rumours were rife. The slaves gossiped in the corridors and kitchens. The Visigoths were all talking about it. News had spread beyond the palace. Expectant crowds gathered outside its gates.

The most popular rumour was that the emperor would announce the marriage of his half-sister to Flavius Constantius, but there were numerous other stories. Honorius was going to make his favourite hen, Roma, a magistrate. He intended to sail to Constantinopolis in the spring to forge a new alliance with the boy emperor Theodosius II. A fresh invasion of Hispania was planned, to crush the Alani and Vandali who had so far escaped Wallia's attentions. There was even an outrageous suggestion that Honorius intended to wed Galla himself, regardless of the scandal and outrage it would cause.

The various speculations were relayed to Galla by an annoyed Elpidia, who'd heard them from Vadomar, who in turn had heard them himself or been informed by the Visigoths. Once Galla might have placed some store in the last rumour, but her encounters with Honorius since her arrival suggested the gossip about his impotence was true. He had shown no interest in her whatsoever; his eye did not wander over female slaves or courtiers either. It had made the months of her refusal to marry Flavius Constantius easier to bear.

Now she lingered at her dressing table, overflowing with open cosmetic boxes and implements. Elpidia combed and arranged her hair, the ivory pins skilfully hidden from view. Her eyebrows were next, Galla inspecting Elpidia's tweezer work with a silver mirror. An application of chalk followed; this rendered her complexion a pleasing pale white. A dab behind each of her ears with a perfume phial would give her a faint but attractive scent.

'Understated but beautiful will be the best look,' Elpidia opined.

Galla, holding a string of translucent pearls to her throat and gazing into her mirror, murmured in agreement.

Finally they were done.

'I am ready,' said Galla.

'You are, and have been for years. This is your time. Embrace it.'

They stared at one another, Elpidia proud, Galla musing over her life. How from her earliest years she was cared for by Stilicho and Serena. How she had expected to marry Eucherius, whom she had loved. How, after numerous false starts, the union had never eventuated. The years spent living alone in Roma, with no suitable husbands to be found. The falling-out with Stilicho and Serena. Alaric's sieges, and his eventual taking of the city. Her captivity, and after Alaric's passing, her first encounters with Athaulf. The wandering through Italia and Viennensis. Their love affair and marriage. Her pregnancy. The birth – and death – of Theodosius. Athaulf's brutal murder. Her humiliation during Sigeric's short reign. His death and Wallia's ascension. The treaty made with Flavius Constantius, and her release.

If the incredible story had been recounted to her, she might well have thought it a pack of lies, but it was not. Truly, she thought, God is with me. I might not have always realised, but He has been there every step of my journey. She gave fervent thanks; she also resolved, when empress, to erect churches in Ravenna worthy of His name.

Honorius grasped the nettle the instant Flavius Constantius had joined him and his half-sister on the dais. The new year, he declared, would begin with joyous news. Galla Placidia was to marry Magister Militum Flavius Constantius, with the emperor's full blessing.

'No!' Galla's cry carried the length of the reception hall. To her relief, there was no commotion beyond the doors. Vadomar was playing his part.

In the stunned silence that followed, Honorius' mouth worked. He could not believe his ears. For Galla to refuse in private was one thing. To do so in front of his entire court was quite another.

Purple-faced, Flavius Constantius was outraged, yet dared not react until the emperor did.

'I am Imperator. I command you to marry him,' Honorius grated.

'I will not.' Galla's chin jutted as the courtiers gasped.

'This is an outrage.' Flavius Constantius could no longer contain himself. 'Imperator Honorius is divinely appointed. You cannot refuse.'

Galla stared right back at him. 'That is precisely what I am doing.'

'Your damned Visigoths are behind this. I know it!' This was delivered in a shout.

'I make my own decisions,' said Galla.

Flavius Constantius blustered and threatened, filling the air with words.

Galla, only partially listening, watched her half-brother sidelong. He looked out of his depth, and she wondered if she had gone too far. He was unused to challenge, unused to having anyone stand up to him. You must have *some* spine, Honorius, she thought. Find it.

'Enough!'

The emperor's roar stopped Flavius Constantius in his tracks. Silenced the muttering courtiers. Had the nearest candidati reaching for their weapons. Honorius took Galla's left hand in his. Weighed down by his magnificent jewel-encrusted purple robes, he paced towards Flavius Constantius.

'What are you doing?' Galla cried, although she knew full well. She did not pull free from his grasp.

Solemn-faced, Honorius put her hand into Flavius Constantius' outstretched one. 'I name you man and wife,' he declared.

Another stunned silence, the length of a heartbeat, and then a mountainous wave of cheering and applause.

Honorius gave Galla a grave nod. She offered a tiny inclination of her head in return, her acceptance of his will. Flavius Constantius, meanwhile, smiled the smile of a man who has got what he wanted.

Little did he know, thought Galla, but she had also obtained what she wanted.

Amid the cheering, she imagined one word, repeated louder and louder.

'Imperatrix!'

God has willed it, she thought.

Her deepest desire *would* become reality.

EPILOGUE

Galla and Flavius Constantius were married later the same day, or a short time after. In late AD 417 or early AD 418, she gave birth to a healthy daughter, Justa Grata Honoria. The baby's first two names were after two of Galla's maternal aunts, her maternal grandmother and her half-uncle, the emperor Gratian. The third was in honour of her half-brother, who continued to rule without any children of his own.

In July, AD 419, Galla brought into the world a son, Flavius Placidus Valentinianus. His first name was the same as his father's, and had also been borne by his imperial cousin in the east, Theodosius II. Placidus was for his mother, naturally, while Valentinianus commemorated her maternal uncle and grandfather, both emperors.

Less than two years after his birth, in February of AD 421, Galla pressured Honorius to confer the name *nobilissimus puer*, 'most noble boy', on Valentinianus. The title did not make him heir to the throne, but it significantly advanced his claim. Around the same time, again possibly bullied by Galla, Honorius elevated Flavius Constantius to the rank of augustus, associating him with himself as emperor. Galla's husband was thenceforth known as Constantius III. Not long after, Galla was invested by her half-brother as an augusta, recognition she had sought for many years.

Her path through life was destined never to be simple, however. The government of the eastern empire refused to recognise the accession of Constantius III. It is probable Galla and Valentinianus' new titles were not accepted either. Matters grew more serious in September of the same year, when Constantius III contracted pleurisy and died. Once more Galla had to rely on the affections of her half-brother, feelings that had never flourished before. She was fortunate to have Elpidia (and the fictional Vadomar), her legal and business administrator, Leontius, as well as plenty of wealth, and the force of Visigoths from Wallia's encampment. Constantius' bodyguards remained with her also, strengthening her hand.

Over the next eighteen months, court intrigue and further problems in Hispania and Africa led to a falling-out between Galla and Honorius. Fighting erupted on the streets of Ravenna between her supporters and his domestici. Ultimately, the emperor had more power. In the spring of AD 423, Galla was exiled from Ravenna with her two young children, sailing with her household to an uncertain welcome in Constantinopolis.

Far from home, she walked a tightrope. Emperor Theodosius II and his wife, Eudocia, still childless, had no reason to support Valentinianus' claim to the western empire because he was a clear rival to the eastern throne. Some months later, on 27 August, AD 423, the world again changed unexpectedly. The thirty-seven-year-old Honorius succumbed to dropsy, an ancient term for oedema, swelling under the skin caused by heart failure. His death opened the door to Galla renewing her son's claim. Theodosius II, who wanted the western throne for himself, would not have agreed, but the proclamation of a usurper in Roma, a former court official of Honorius', Iohannes by name, gave him cause to reconsider Valentinianus' position.

It was a case of the devil you know. In early AD 424, Theodosius II recognised Galla as an augusta and Valentinianus as a nobilissimus puer. This elevation meant her son would become western emperor upon reaching manhood. Theodosius II also gave his blessing to the betrothal of his baby daughter Eudoxia to the almost five-year-old Valentinianus. Because the latter was so young, Theodosius II decreed that Galla would act as regent for him in the west.

To this end, he provided her with an army and a general. They were necessary because Iohannes was unprepared to step aside. (Interestingly, the usurper was an able ruler, possessing the qualities of mildness and intelligence.) At first, the struggle for power in Italia went Iohannes' way, but he was undone in the late spring of AD 425, when a local shepherd led Galla's forces through the marshes around Ravenna and into the heart of the city. Taken prisoner, Iohannes was conducted to Galla and Valentinianus at Aquileia. In the hippodrome there, his right hand was amputated – a traitor's punishment. He was then forced to sit on an ass and paraded around the arena while actors hired for the purpose beat and mocked him. After this brutal degradation, he was beheaded.

Soon after, the arrival of sixty thousand Hunni forced Galla to accept their commander, a former supporter of Iohannes named Aetius, as one of the western empire's most prominent generals. His appointment did not prevent the investment of Valentinianus III as emperor in Roma in October of the same year.

Through a combination of skill, intelligence, wiliness and ruthlessness, Galla Placidia succeeded in keeping her son on the throne until he reached adulthood. In the spring of AD 438, with Valentinianus III recently married to Eudoxia, who was already pregnant, she was able to release the reins of power. She may have thought all her trials, tribulations and sacrifices had been worthwhile.

AUTHOR'S NOTE

After five books set in the medieval and Napoleonic periods, I find myself in the ancient world once more. It's good to be back; the interlude has refreshed my passion for all things Roman. How and why did I choose the fifth century AD? Before explaining, a little insight into the ideas behind my novels.

As a reader, I grow bored of never-ending series about the same character(s). Fantasy, historical fiction, crime, it doesn't matter. I gave up on Kay Scarpetta, Patricia Cornwell's indomitable detective, after perhaps the fifth book, when her cop friend Marino comes around to eat her home-made pasta for the umpteenth time. I have never finished the Sharpe novels by another famous Cornwell – shock, horror!

From the outset, therefore, I made a conscious decision never to write a long series. Many readers love following the same character over and again, but that ain't for this author. The silver lining in the cloud for taking such a path means I can move around in history. What's not to love about Crassus' campaign into Parthia, Hannibal, Spartacus, the Varian Disaster, the invasion of Macedon and Greece, Richard the Lionheart, Napoleon and Russia, and the Vikings in Ireland? My flitting about once caused another author to pass the slightly cheesed-off comment that I get to cherry-pick all the best bits of Roman history. My reply was, well, if you decide to write a twenty-five-book series and I don't, them's the consequences.

This novel came about in part thanks to my brother, who gave me a biography of Galla Placidia a few years ago. I was very taken by her story from the start, but it wasn't until 2024 that I had the time to consider writing about her. Strong-willed, focused, resilient, she went through the most extraordinary changes in fortune, yet eventually reached the heights of imperial power. I hope I did her justice.

You might have finished this book wondering what happened to Galla Placidia after the events described. Sadly, there wasn't a happy-ever-after. Her son, Valentinian III, made a poor emperor. His unwise actions ultimately led to his assassination, which in turn precipitated, a mere quarter of a century later, the complete collapse of the western Roman empire. Fortunately, Galla Placidia did not live to see this.

Long-suffering fans have waited more than a decade for the Hannibal saga to be completed. After this novel, you will be pleased to know, I will take up that story again! I didn't finish the series way back when because books two and three didn't light up the world, and I was advised by my then publisher not to continue the series. A full-time author with two young children, the only breadwinner, I took their advice. Now, with a new publisher who is happy for me to return to old stamping grounds, I have come full circle. Hannibal book four, working title *A Land Aflame/The Burning Land*, will come out in the spring of 2026. (Yes, yes, I know one of Bernard Cornwell's Uhtred novels is called *The Burning Land*, but there are dozens of books called *The Road to Rome*, and that didn't stop me.)

There's more to the continuation of the Hannibal story. In January 2026, some months before the publication of the fourth book, *Cannae: The Longest Day* will be launched. A novel written in radio-play style, recounting the famous battle from a dozen points of view, it will be released in audio format only for twelve months. Please understand that this is an experiment by my publishers, Orion, and has never been done before. I am thrilled to be the authorial guinea pig. It is not being done to annoy readers who prefer books in the physical or digital form! *Cannae* will be released in hardback and digital in January 2027, ahead of Hannibal book five, the final volume in the series. I also have a secret project, a second book I hope to write in 2025 (to be published in 2026 or 2027). The most amazing story, it is set in a completely new time period. More than that I cannot say.

I spend a lot of time researching, but I am time-constrained: produce at least one novel a year, or my kids don't eat. I joke, but it's also true. That being said, I managed to consult and/or read many more texts than usual for *Rome*. The late Roman Empire, you see, was a very different beast to the Republic, and I didn't know that much about it.

For a good number of years, I managed to find academics who were willing to read my novels and save me from major foot-in-mouth moments, but I failed this time around, in the main because I didn't have the time to seek one out. I also think late-Roman scholars are relatively thin on the ground, in the UK at least. Any errors in the novel are therefore mine and mine alone. Please forgive them. To save reading the long list of texts below, the three main biographies of Galla Placidia I used were by Oost, Salisbury and Sivan, each excellent in its own way.

Some of the texts used during the writing of this book include: *Book of the Pontiffs of Ravenna* by Agnello, *Sidonius, Poems and Letters*, translated by Anderson, *Cassiodorus: Variae*, translated by Barnish, *Rome in Spectacular Cross-Section* by Biesty (a kids' book, but it's great!), *Roman Military Equipment* by Bishop and Coulston, *History of the Later Roman Empire from Theodosius I to Justinian* by Bury, *Dans la Rome des Césars* by Chaillet (extraordinary maps of Rome), *Unit Sizes in the Late Roman Army* by Coello, *The Rise and Decline of the Late Roman Field Army* by Cromwell, *Roman Clothing and Fashion* by Croom, *Childhood, Class and Kin in the Roman World* ed. Dixon, *The Late Roman Army* by Dixon, *Honorius: The Fight for the Roman West AD 395–423* by Doyle, *Warfare in Roman Europe AD 350–425* by Elton, *War, Women and Children in Ancient Rome* by Evans, *Scholae Palatinae: the Palace Guards of the Later Roman Empire* by Frank, *The Fall of the West: The Death of the Superpower* by Goldsworthy, *The Fall of the Roman Empire* by Grant, *Ravenna:*

Capital of Empire, Crucible of Europe by Herrin, *Ravenna: Its Role in Earlier Medieval Change* by Herrin and Nelson, *The Western Fathers* by Hoare, *Children in Late Ancient Christianity*, ed. Horn and Phenix, *Imperial Tragedy: From Constantine's Empire to the Destruction of Roman Italy AD 363–568* by Kulikowski, *The Sack of Rome in 410 AD: The Event, Its Context and Its Impact* by Lipps, Machado and von Rummel, *Late Roman Infantry AD 236–565* by MacDowall, *Soldier and Civilian in the Later Roman Empire* by MacMullen, *24 Hours in Ancient Rome* by Matyszak, *Child Emperor Rule in the Late Roman West, AD 367–455* by McEvoy, *Western Aristocracies and Imperial Court AD 364–425* by Matthews, *Chariot Racing in the Roman Empire* by Meijer, *Roman Heavy Cavalry (1)* by Negin and D'Amato, *A Companion to Medieval Arms and Armour*, ed. Nicolle, *Gallia Placida Augusta* by Oost, *Marriage, Divorce and Children in Ancient Rome* by Rawson, *Arguments with Silence: Writing the History of Roman Women* by Richlin, *Rome's Christian Empress: Galla Placidia Rules at the Twilight of the Empire* by Salisbury, *Galla Placidia* by Sivan, *The Late Roman Army* by Southern, *Cosmetics and Perfumes in the Roman World* by Stewart, *Roman Military Dress* by Sumner, *Roman Warriors: the Paintings of Graham Sumner* by Sumner and Elliott, *Military History of Late Rome 395–425* by Syvänne, *The Fall of Rome* by Ward-Perkins, *History of the Goths* by Wolfram.

Read all my traditionally published novels and wanting more? Seek out my crowdfunded digital novellas *The March* (a follow-on from *The Forgotten Legion*), *Eagle in the Wilderness*, *Eagles in the East* and *Io, Saturnalia!* (all three feature Centurion Tullus of the *Eagles of Rome* trilogy). There is also a stand-alone novella, *Centurion of the First*, set on Hadrian's Wall in second-century AD Britain. Don't own an e-reader? Simply download the free Kindle app from Amazon and read the stories on a phone, tablet or computer. If you don't read e-books, all but the last two are available in print and as an audiobook, *Sands of the Arena*.

I don't just write; I work as a historical guide too, leading tours in Italy and Germany. The first Italian tour ran in November 2024, and was a huge success. Interested? Look up Hidden History Travel (hiddenhistory.co.uk) and search for my name. Like travelling on two wheels? I also work as a historical bike guide. Check out Ride and Seek (rideandseek.com), which runs epic cycling trips that I am involved with. These tours include Hannibal, Caesar, Napoleon and Marco Polo.

I also raise money for the charities Combat Stress and Médecins Sans Frontières (MSF), also known as Doctors Without Borders. As well as fundraising by walking Hadrian's Wall in Roman armour (twice), in 2014 two friends and I marched from Capua to the Colosseum in Rome. The result, the 'Romani Walk', is on YouTube (link: tinyurl.com/h4n8h6g), narrated by Sir Ian McKellen – Gandalf!

I also fundraise for Park in the Past (parkinthepast.org.uk), a community-interest company that is building a Roman marching fort near Chester in north-west England. As I write, the partly constructed fort is open to the public. It's well worth a visit.

Thank you to my amazing editor, Sam Eades, and to the ever-enthusiastic Paul Stark in the audio department, who came up with the idea for a radio-play-style novel. I am grateful to the entire team at Orion too. You work so hard to make my books fly, and I appreciate it.

And now to you, my fantastic readers. I love your emails and comments/messages on social media. Keep them coming! I often give away signed books and goodies, as well as auctioning them for charity – stay tuned on these media. Sadly, historical fiction is a shrinking market (yes, it's still true in 2025). A short review or a rating of this book, left on Amazon, Goodreads, Google, iTunes, Kobo, Waterstones.com or any other platform would be a real help. Gratitude!

Thank you to my children, Ferdia and Pippa, whom I love greatly. How did you grow up so fast?!

Ways to get in touch:
Email: ben@benkane.net
Facebook: facebook.com/benkanebooks
Instagram: benkanewrites
Bluesky Social: bsky.app/profile/benkaneauthor.bsky.social

Twitter: @BenKaneAuthor
My website: benkane.net
Soundcloud (podcasts): soundcloud.com/user-803260618
YouTube (short documentary-style videos): tinyurl.com/y7chqhgo

CREDITS

Ben Kane and Orion Fiction would like to thank everyone at Orion who worked on the publication of *Rome* in the UK.

Editorial
Sam Eades

Copy editor
Jane Selley

Proofreader
Kate Shearman

Audio
Paul Stark
Louise Richardson

Contracts
Dan Herron
Ellie Bowker
Oliver Chacón

Design
Tomás Almeida

Editorial Management
Anshuman Yadav
Charlie Panayiotou
Jane Hughes
Bartley Shaw

Finance
Jasdip Nandra
Nick Gibson
Sue Baker

Marketing
Ellie Nightingale

Production
Katie Horrocks
Paul Hussey

Publicity
Sarah Lundy

Sales
Catherine Worsley
Esther Waters
Victoria Laws
Rachael Hum
Ellie Kyrke-Smith
Frances Doyle
Georgina Cutler

Operations
Group Sales Operations team

Rights
Rebecca Folland
Tara Hiatt
Ben Fowler
Alice Cottrell
Ruth Blakemore
Marie Henckel